GATES of FIRE

SECOND AMERICAN EDITION: REVISED

by ELWYN CHAMBERLAIN

NORTH ATLANTIC BOOKS
BERKELEY, CALIFORNIA

Gates of Fire (Revised American Edition)

Copyright © 1978, 1983 by Elwyn M. Chamberlain

ISBN 0-938190-20-2 (paperback)
ISBN 0-938190-21-0 (cloth)

Publisher's Address:
North Atlantic Books
2320 Blake Street
Berkeley, California 94704

Cover Design by Elwyn Chamberlain and Paula Morrison

Gates of Fire is sponsored by the Society for the Study of Native Arts and
Sciences, a nonprofit educational corporation whose goals are to develop an
ecological and crosscultural perspective linking various scientific, social, and
artistic fields; to nurture a holistic view of arts, sciences, humanities, and
healing; and to publish and distribute literature on the relationship of mind,
body, and nature.

Library of Congress Cataloguing in Publication Data

Chamberlain, Elwyn M
       Gates of Fire

       I. Title
PZ4.C4424Gat   [PS3553.H249]   813'.5'4   77-18319
ISBN 0-938190-20-2 (pbk.)

For SQUAW and CHICKSUR

It is not good for the Christian soul
To hustle the Aryan brown,
For the Christian riles and the heathen smiles
And it weareth the Christian down.
And the end of the fight is a tombstone white
With the name of the dear deceased
And the epitaph drear: "A fool lies here
Who tried to hustle the East.

—Rudyard Kipling

NEW DELHI (*Int. News*) A dejected Mr. and Mrs. James Weatherall today announced that they were leaving India apparently abandoning as hopeless their highly publicized and generously financed search for their daughter Laura. Addressing the modestly attended press conference at the New Delhi airport where the investment banker and his socialite wife were awaiting a flight back to New York, Mr. Weatherall conceded that the three-month quest to locate his only child had produced no information.

Joining the Weatheralls here was Richard Murray, famed American song writer and father of Jeffrey Murray, a long-time friend of Miss Weatherall. According to the parents the young Murray had traveled with Miss Weatherall to India some twenty months ago. Mr. Murray stated that he had not been in contact with his son for some time prior to the departure for India and has no idea as to his son's present whereabouts.

According to sources that have assisted in the search for the young American couple, a third member of their party was Robert Stanley. Mr Weatherall acknowledged that Mr. Stanley may have broken off from the trip at some point and returned to England or the United States. This report has not, however, been verified.

Mr. Stanley is a well-known American entrepreneur. Often cited as a contemporary example of rags to riches success, Mr. Stanley acted as a presidential emissary during both the Kennedy and Johnson administrations. Mr. Stanley returned to private life and moved to London some four years ago. He had the reputation of being an intensely private man. His activities in recent years were the subject of widespread speculation with a number of press reports leading to actions for libel. The suits were all settled out of court.

Before her departure for India Miss Weatherall had been a social presence in her own right. She was usually referred to by the social columns as the flaming redhaired beauty from Hobe sound and Park Avenue who acted as if she preferred Greenwich Village. The young Mr. Murray was the subject of some public attention for his activities surrounding the now famous Woodstock Music Festival.

I

LONDON. The afternoon sun filtered through the drawn curtains of the house on Tregunter Road and Laura felt sleepy, childlike, and not in the mood for sex. "In love with his own cock," she thought, and would have turned over except he was so expert, like a magnet inside her generating waves.

"Dial Jeff for waves," she thought.

The phone rang for a long time and. There was a knock at the door. It was the manservant.

"Yes?" said Jeff hoarsely.

"A call for you, sir. The gentleman calls himself Stan. Shall I say you're asleep?"

"Say I'm just..." Jeff paused. Something hung in the balance, he wished he knew what it was. "Say I'm just waking up, I'll call as soon as we..."

"What sir?"

"As soon as we do wake up."

"Shall I take the number, sir?"

Jeff smiled at Laura.

"No, uh... we have his number."

*   *   *

For Robert Stanley or Stan as he was known, life had become a complicated affair. By his own account he had been born cynical and doubting, a result of early poverty in the slums of New York. But at the age of five when it was found that he could read *The New York Times* from cover to cover his future was assured. In his twenties aided by scholarships he climbed to the top of the academic heap, discovered antibiotic formulae that netted him millions, and in his thirties became a U.S. presidental appointee, trusted with unprecedented decision-making powers. And now at forty, having discovered the joys of LSD, he'd become the kingpin in a far-flung underground enterprise to manufacture and distribute it. Robert

Stanley was handsome, bisexual, Napoleonically built, and uncouth.

As Jeff and Laura arrived at Stan's townhouse in Chelsea, an old Irish hag named Jenny emerged from the front door. She had the vigilance of a policewoman and never forgot a face. She liked Jeff.

"Come on in," she yelled cheerily. "Haven't seen the likes of you two since New York, now have I?" She gestured with an upright finger. "He's either on the phone or asleep. Go upstairs and find out for yourselves. Are ye hungry? I'll bring ye some breakfast after a spell. Come, let me take yer bags."

They climbed a circular stairway to a three-story drawing room where an extraordinary Aubusson carpet, vanloads of vintage furniture, and priceless paintings were thrown together as if in a junk shop. Over the fireplace one of Van Gogh's last paintings gave out insane vibrations. Stan himself was in bed on a balcony, phoning Washington. An inveterate caller, he would phone anywhere from anyplace at anytime. At the moment, it was obvious from his voice that he wanted something.

"Make yourselves comfortable if you can find room," he yelled down. "I'll be right with you ... just doing my morning round-the-world tour."

"Somehow he always manages to make one feel uncomfortable," Laura thought, "a very eccentric bird indeed." In spite of her suspicion that he might be dangerously crazy, she was attracted by his strange perceptiveness, a certain chicken-soup warmth, and high powers of concentration. His acting ability was tops: he could appear perfectly normal, in the most uncanny low key way. She had seen him do it. Pull himself together just as a scene seemed about to fall in.

"So you've come to see me. Don't tell me why, let me guess." His icy grin warmed to a smile. "I mean it's really good to see you both ... Mademoiselle Weatherall, and friend Jeff Murray."

"We had a message there was some business you wanted to discuss," replied Jeff, "that's why we came right over."

"Did I?" said Stan. "So many phone calls. What business? Oh yes."

"Another Woodstock, I suppose," said Jeff somewhat contemptuously.

Stan giggled. "Was it that bad? Didn't you make lots of money, lots and lots of money?"

"It's pretty heavy in the States just now," Laura put in, "that's why we left, acid as cheap as a subway ride, everyone's freaking out."

"Freaking out?" Stan responded. "Not at all ... everything's happening as it should ... increasing the speed of human evolution, making some people smarter, causing others to jump out windows ... whatever. But the human adaptation rate must speed up! Otherwise we'll be finished! Not much time left." He slapped his knee. "Some people are much smarter now than before. Many people in government, highest positions, are much smarter since acid."

He looked up smiling benignly. "Of course as I am a natural genius it is of no concern to me whether people are smarter, but it is nice to have a few more people around one can talk to...like you two for example. Of course, if people are really stupid by nature then there's not much one can do about that.

Narrowing his eyes, he stared at them. "I want to turn on India next," he said matter-of-factly.

"India?" They both looked incredulous.

"What on earth for?" Laura said.

"Biggest market yet," Jeff muttered knowingly.

"Not at all, my dear Jeff!" Stan said irritably. "India is the soul of the world. Of course you wouldn't know that! And it's falling apart. Too many fools at the top spouting too many textbook principles! They need new solutions! They need acid there to wake up. Think they've got a democracy, socialism. It's just a mess. The same colonial farce. Nobody likes it and they gotta come up with something new."

They all looked at each other. Jeff thought about the money the British had made introducing opium into China and tea into India, and doubted Stan's good intentions.

Stan droned on, pompously lifting one finger and gazing off into space. Jeff was the instrument he needed to carry out his plans. He'd be reliable because he was greedy. After Woodstock he was in deep! He was just the one. If anyone could find a way to make money off the Indians, Jeff Murray would. After all, it was a very big market.

"Do we understand each other?" Stan said to Jeff after breakfast.

Jeff's eyes flashed.

"I see we do." Stan paused. "Of course it might be dangerous! India is India. You don't know of course, but they will think we're making money and they'll be after us for it."

"You don't plan to make money?" asked Jeff condescendingly. "I suppose you're turning into a philanthropist then."

"It won't be a giveaway but at their exchange rate we'll be lucky to break even."

"How many trips do we take in?"

"One million for starters."

Jeff whistled under his breath.

Laura was sure Stan had flipped.

"Now you know," Stan sighed.

*   *   *

Jenny could be heard letting someone in downstairs.

"Who's that?" Stan yelled.

13

Up the stairs padded a young man with straight black hair halfway to his waist, wearing white buckskin leggings, his hands and arms adorned with numerous silver and turquoise rings.

"A panther," thought Laura.

"Ah, Carlos," said Stan, obviously pleased with the interruption. "Have you met Jeff?"

Jeff nodded before Carlos could answer.

"And this is Laura Weatherall."

Carlos nodded wisely at Laura. He was Stan's number one boy, pimp, bodyguard and social secretary. Handsome, part Indian, part Spanish, it was rumored in London that he was an Inca of ancient lineage. With men he acted seductive, to women he seemed strongly sensual. An androgynous quality about him made him desirable to both sexes and although he always seemed relaxed his reflexes were those of a cobra. Money turned him on and it was a well known fact that for bank notes of the proper denomination Carlos would dance your tune.

"Be a good fellow and pour us all a drink," said Stan.

Carlos poured double doses of gin with plenty of ice and not much tonic. The afternoon wore on, thick with cross purposes and preparations. Stan was maddeningly disorganized, but finally bags were loaded and they all bundled into a long Mercedes and slipped noiselessly out of London through the evening traffic.

Hours later the highway gave way to a bumpy country road and they found themselves on an avenue of ancient oaks. Moonlight streamed through the branches, casting intricate designs on the snow. Suddenly a large fortress-like structure loomed up.

"My country seat," said Stan, laughing and rousing the others.

A young man appeared with a flashlight and they entered a large hall filled with echoes where roaring fires burned in two fireplaces. The walls were covered with swords, daggers, and other battle paraphernalia. Ancient suits of armor stood guard like iron ghosts.

"Alex," said Stan to the young man. "This is Laura Weatherall and Jeff Murray. They've agreed to help us out. Carlos, you know, of course."

"Welcome," Alex said, peering at them from behind his horn-rimmed spectacles.

Laura liked him immediately.

"Are you hungry?" Alex asked. "We have..."

"We are hungry, my dear boy," interrupted Stan. "But Jenny has brought along a roast duck dinner for us. Alex is a vegetarian," Stan explained.

"I think I'd like to try the vegetables, if you don't mind," said Laura.

"Of course, my dear, have vegetables, it will mean more duck for us.

Ducks aren't very big you know. You'll have duck won't you, Jeff?''

"Sure," said Jeff exchanging glances with Laura.

"Then come along," Stan said.

Followed by Carlos and Jeff Stan bounded through large double doors into a drawing room beyond, while Laura followed Alex to the servants' quarters where he was living.

"Welcome again," he said setting out plates on a pantry table. Steady blue eyes smiled from an intelligent face. He had a long pedigree in the acid world, extending back to his Harvard undergraduate days.

"I'm hooked on trying to find out what really happened when I first took acid," he said, between mouthfuls of bean sprouts. "Research is very expensive, you know. I couldn't afford all the equipment myself. Stan's been very generous."

"Are you the Alex who came up with different variations like..." Laura rattled off a few of the familiar names. Alex nodded.

"Then I've heard about you."

"Really," he said, wondering how much she'd heard.

It was Laura's first vegetarian meal and she found although she didn't mind it she certainly wouldn't want to make it a habit. After dinner Alex got out a strange-looking stringed instrument and Laura remembered that friends had told her he'd been to India.

"I've heard you have a teacher in India," she said, as he tuned the instrument.

"How did you come to know that?" he asked, gazing beyond her.

"Can't remember. Heard it somewhere. Is your teacher one of those orange-robed swamis?" Laura had had enough of swamis.

"Not a swami," replied Alex emphatically "and no orange robes, nothing. Naked. He lives in jungles, likes tigers."

Tigers interested her. "Stan has asked Jeff and me to go to India. Could you put me in touch with your teacher if I go?"

"I can give you a number where you might get news of his whereabouts. I never know exactly where he is. That's his picture over there," he said, pointing to a small photo on the mantelpiece.

Laura got up to look. Something about the face she saw shocked her deeply. Was it the face of a saint, or a swindler? The eyes stared out at her. They seemed alive. Or was it some sort of ghost? She felt unnerved.

"Don't worry, he won't bite," said Alex.

"He looks like a heavy," Laura replied, returning to the table. "Thanks for the dinner. I'm dead just now, perhaps I should go and find out where I'm to sleep before they all get too high out there."

Alex lit the way with his flashlight. There were few electric lights and in the dark, the rooms full of covered-over furniture looked ominous and unpleasant. When they finally reached the great hall again, they heard music behind the double doors. Above it Stan was talking and laughing.

"Never stops, does he?" Laura remarked. "Does he still take speed?"

"Doesn't need it," Alex smiled. "Money's his drug. I'll leave you here then. Stan knows where you're to sleep. Good night."

"Good night and thanks."

Through the doors Laura saw three girls sprawled out on fur rugs smoking joints. Carlos and Jeff were slouched in chairs. Stan was talking.

"Have some coke?" he asked, producing a piece of paper with a line of white crystals.

Laura took some to show she wasn't ruffled by the situation. She wondered if the girls were kept in some special castle tower and whether any more were hidden away in its ninety-odd rooms.

"Where do I sleep," she asked Stan.

"You're not going to leave us now, are you?" Stan grinned. "We're just beginning...How were your vegetables?"

"Delicious. And how are your ducks?"

"Ready to eat," he whispered in her ear, glancing at the girls, "like to try some?"

Laura felt like smacking him. Instead she made herself yawn.

"Carlos will show you to your room then.... Carlos!" Stan sighed. "And take some candles with you, I don't believe we got around to connecting the lights up there."

*   *   *

They climbed the staircase off the great hall and after losing their way several times came to a door that Carlos unlocked. Inside the room smelled of tuberoses and reminded Laura of her mother's place at Hobe Sound.

"Wherever did the tuberoses come from?" she smiled.

"There's a greenhouse here," he said, "I thought you might enjoy them."

Carlos lit candles and an apartment of several rooms materialized. The walls were covered with tapestries and needlepoint.

"Very grand," Laura observed.

"Not a bad place to spend time in." Carlos shrugged.

Laura forgot the bad vibes downstairs; felt like locking the door and sleeping for a week in the huge medieval bed with its scarlet damask curtains. Carlos lit a fire, and stood watching her eyes until she had to look away.

"Is there anything you think you need?" he asked as though she had forgotten something. "Or want?" he added softly.

What?" She turned to survey the room.

"This," he said, spinning her around, drawing her close.

16

"I'm sorry." She pulled away. "I think I'd better get some sleep."

*   *   *

The next afternoon feeling rested, Laura sat in the wide bay window and gazed out at the winter landscape. From rows of oaks along the drive the last golden leaves blew away over the snow like confetti. Beyond lay cut fields and stands of chestnut and sycamore. In a pond at the far end of a promenade the last ducks and wild geese were calling.

A soft knock sounded at the door. It was Carlos carrying a tray with some soup, toast, and a pot of tea.

"I was thinking you might be hungry," he said smiling as he arranged the dishes on the table. "Sit here and eat."

She observed him while she ate. There was something attractive about him, yet dangerous. The muscles in his broad back tensed as he leaned over to fan the coals until the new wood caught.

"Where are you going now?" she asked as he stood up facing her.

"To lock up. Stan and Jeff, they had to go back to London, something Stan is forgetting. They will return tomorrow. What will you do now?" He stared at her.

"Oh read I suppose, something like that." She returned his stare until he looked away.

"You will need more firewood. I'll come again around nine." He picked up the tray and went to the door. "See you later," he said evenly.

*   *   *

Had she fallen asleep reading? She'd been in the middle of a strangely vivid dream in which a tiny white-haired old man who looked like Santa Claus was dancing naked. What a strange dream. Now Carlos dropping an armful of logs by the fireplace had jarred her out of it. He sat down on the edge of the sofa and smiled at her.

"You were dreaming."

"Was I? I don't usually dream." She shut her eyes. It was so real. She opened her eyes and looked at him. "It was more real than you are right now."

"Want some Afghani smoke?" he asked.

She nodded.

"Hard to get these days," he said, lit a small pipe and handed it to her. "A friend laid a kilo on me."

"He must like you very much."

"He wanted something."

"Were you able to help him?"

17

"Yes." Carlos looked at her. "It pleases me to satisfy people's desires; though most don't know what they want, or are afraid to tell. Too much of repression in this world . . . you know. Better to be happy, yes?" He smiled his prostitute smile. "You tell me what you want," he said, "or don't you know."

Gazing thoughtfully at him, she knew she had only to make a move and they would spend a long night, high, inside the warm dark curtained bed.

"Shall I go now?" he asked.

She was unable to answer.

He stood up, leaning over her. "I dig you. Go to sleep now. I'll come back later."

* * *

For a long time she stared into the fire, her mind a blank. On the edge of sleep and falling off, she was suddenly jolted by the perception that something was moving in the fire. Staring in frightened disbelief she pinched herself hard. Yes, there was something in the fire. An apparition, a tiny man, The little man from her dream. Now he was there before her dancing again. She bit her lip. He was not naked now, but wore cloth around his stomach. "It's this hash," she thought. But the room was there, solid and real before her, and she was awake. She got up and drew near the fire until she could see the hands of the little old man were cupped in front of his mouth. He appeared to be yelling but she couldn't hear him. With a poker she stirred the hot coals hoping that he'd disappear, that she was hallucinating, but he merely jumped from one place to another. She wanted to run out the door, to yell for Carlos. Then the tiny figure beckoned her closer. Trembling, she knelt by the fire. "I can't hear you, please talk louder," she whispered.

As if a broken speaker system had come booming on, suddenly she heard him, loud and clear.

"Lock the door," he said. "Do you hear me? Lock the door."

Stunned, she didn't move.

"Listen to me, Laura Weatherall! Lock that door!"

Being called by name terrified her. She got up and locked the door but returning, found him gone. She knelt and poked the coals again. She'd thought he was going to tell her something important. Why else lock the door? Then she caught herself. Lock the door. What about Carlos?

For a long time, unnerved, she stared into the fire. Finally, she got up, showered, and fell into bed exhausted, leaving the door locked. In her dreams he came again dancing and shouting words she couldn't understand. All she remembered when she woke the next morning was that he had said she needn't worry, that he would see her again at the end. At the

18

end of what, she thought.

The dreams disturbed her so much that she got up and without dressing went to the kitchen where Alex was having breakfast.

"I think I might be going crazy," she laughed nervously over coffee. "Or perhaps it's your acid. Does it spread?"

Alex listened to her story, methodically munching his toast.

"It's the burning bush," he explained. "What seems inside is outside and what seems outside is inside. Sometimes you reach a peaceful state of mind where the two come together. Then they disappear into each other and you get in touch with things you don't understand. Space is just a function of time, and time is a function of space. Both are illusions. Don't disbelieve what you saw."

"You mean it was real?"

"What is real?"

"Wasn't I . . . projecting?"

"What is that?" said Alex. "I mean what do you think it is?"

"Isn't projecting when you go mad and start seeing things?"

He smiled. "Just believe in what you saw, keep your visions to yourself, and see where they lead you." He paused and looked at her intently. "And if you do go to India call Indra in New Delhi at 67896."

*   *   *

Four days later at Heathrow outside London it was freezing and even the brandy they'd drunk as the limo sped them toward the airport hadn't helped. Laura hoped the flight would be on time. She hated these departures where everyone stood around making up things to say.

"And so a new adventure begins," observed Stan pompously when the flight was finally announced. "Call me from Delhi as soon as you get to the hotel. I'll be nervous about getting all that stuff through customs. Remember, if they say anything, give them money right away. Right?" He looked hard at Jeff. "Don't be shy about it, just shell it out. After all, they worship it there."

On the plane, half the people were asleep. The through passengers from New York looked gray and exhausted. A fresh platoon of doe-eyed hostesses in saris gently tucked in the new arrivals. The soft Indian music sounded out of place in the plastic interior of the 747, poetically referred to over the loudspeaker as the Emperor Shah Jehan. Finally they were airborne. "Escape," Laura thought, doubting that it was really possible, as Britain and Europe disappeared in a gray-and-white swirl outside the window.

*   *   *

19

But as they emerged from the plane twenty hours later in New Delhi, down the open ramp and onto the soil of India, Laura sensed that something was different. Was it the air? She'd escaped and she could smell it. The metallic odor of Europe was gone and there was an earthy smell which excited her. Wood smoke hung in the air. Lights burned dimly through humid mist. It was warm!

As planned they went through customs separately so that the tablets of LSD, all in bottles marked with the labels of known firms, would be overlooked more easily.

"You are bringing in so many tablets?" The customs clerk looked at her with implacable dark eyes, as he unzipped the first of her bags. "Do you plan to sell them?"

"They are vitamins. I am bringing them in for friends."

He stared at her thoughtfully.

"You are coming here as a tourist?" He held her passport in front of his face so that he could look over it. He'd seen many like her: skinny white witches who dropped from the sky, profaning the holy Earth of India with their flimsy see-through dresses, their bare legs, and their suitcases full of medicines and cosmetics. To him they represented a new kind of being, one that fed on magic pills and made love in public places. How thin she was! He thought of his plump wife and his eight plump children. He wanted to keep them plump. Leafing through her passport, he noted that she traveled a lot. Travel was expensive. Then he saw the fur slung over her arm.

"I'm afraid we will have to charge you for these, Madam. The customs' duty is 90% of value. What is the value?"

Laura put on her blandest smile. "Will this cover it?" she asked, palming a hundred-dollar bill over the edge of the counter.

He took the bill from her hand with a glance over his shoulder and pocketed it. After all, it represented almost a quarter of his annual wage—who would not forgive him? Without further word he stamped her entry papers and unsmiling passed her through.

Outside the terminal in the dawn, turbaned coolies were everywhere. Like sparrows a gang of them descended on the exotic Western couple, pushing through them towards a broken down taxi.

"Change money, Sahib, change money?" they shouted crowding around Jeff. "Good rate. I geev you good rate, you change money with me?"

"Did you get through without paying?" asked Jeff, helping Laura into the taxi.

"I had to pay a hundred dollars."

"It was your fur," he said, "But so what? We're here and at least it's warm."

The cab, which seemed to be held together with coat hangers, started with a lurch. Soon it was careening wildly through the early morning traffic of suburban Delhi, maneuvering between potholes and people and other vehicles that crossed the way. The driver blew his horn at everything from oxcarts and herds of goats to the long black cars of the politicians. The eyes of India stared in through the car windows. Laura stared back, seeing everywhere disorder bordering on chaos. The dinginess, the tattered and frayed look of everything came as a shock after the bright plastic facade of the West. "You could go crazy here and no one would ever know it," she thought. "You could die and no one would care."

The hotel, however, was like a luxury hotel anywhere in the world: concrete, steel, glass, doormen, thick carpets, giftshops, palms, and fat guests. Yet there was a difference too. The soft obliging manner of the staff. A hint that clock time meant very little here and that orders when given might be carried out or entirely forgotten.

The sun was just rising and the ruined tombs, the forts and battlements of the Moguls floated in the mist against the pink sky.

"Good set for a mystery movie," Jeff thought out loud.

"I feel like I'm in an elevator going down," Laura whispered. "It's so quiet."

Jeff doled out tips to barefoot boys who were bringing the luggage into the room. "It's supposed to be Lotus Land," he said, "the land of forgetfulness. Let's get some sleep."

But sleep did not come easily for Laura that morning. She closed her eyes wondering to herself about the chance events which had brought her to this unlikely spot halfway around the world. Her thoughts went back to Woodstock where this trip had all begun.

*   *   *

The rain had come down in buckets all night long drenching the festival crowd. Rip Van Winkle, his white beard flying, a twinkle in his eyes, sported over the hills roaring with laughter at the goings on. But no one looked for him that night or cared. The heavens collided while the fabled *rishi* danced, his footsteps resounding merrily from hill to kyll.

Below it was a different matter. Inside the structures and bubbles, the buses and the tents, the air was heavy with incense; the scent of group lust drifted out into the New York monsoon. Laura knelt, naked, open to receive him, her body flushed, her dark red hair loose to her waist. Jeff entered her, his green eyes intent, lips distended, muscles taut. Once they had locked together there was no movement, only tension mounting between them, inner contractions. Did they know of the Kama Sutra, the pleasure palaces of Moguls, their fabled pastimes at Fatephur Sikri? Not quite. But somehow the spirit of Asia had come alive here on Rips's old stomping ground, atavistic, out of control, bent on transforming the future through these sons and daughters of a New Age.

In the morning Laura and Jeff rode out on his Arabian mare to survey the scene. He was elated by the success of the strategy. Largest acid drop and distribution ever undertaken finished twenty-four hours before the advertised event was to start. The scam was a success: that it had turned into something not quite expected was hardly of concern to him. Let the gates be thrown open. All come in free.

She held his waist lightly as they trotted through the melee of people and mud. It was unreal: Laura Weatherall, 610 Park Avenue and Hobe Sound, was not exactly prepared for the scene.

At the staging area Jeff had a fight with one of his partners over the tangled cables and equipment, touchy performers, road managers, the vibrations of greed. She watched him as he gave orders and was obeyed, shucked out bread and was salaamed. It was all a game, like the Monopoly they used to play as children after school, left alone in apartments while their mothers, who were friends, had their hair done at Bendel's, and their fathers got drunk at "21."

They rode beyond to the lakes, where the sun pierced the clouds to glitter on choppy waves, split the veils of mist rising from oaks and willows, bathing hundreds of naked bodies with magic light.

She thought she might be in love with him. He had opened her—with acid, with his sex. But who was he really, this Jeff, with the rich songwriter for a father, the boy she'd known since childhood. They'd never gone further than going to the movies on Saturday night and when Laura went to college she'd almost lost track of him. They remet by accident: through a mutual hash connection. She sensed a new Jeff. When he was near a switch turned on inside her and they seemed to touch essences. Even so, she wondered whether she was confusing soul with meat? She didn't even know why she had come to Woodstock, a spur of the moment thing. She wanted to forget about thinking. She wanted to let herself feel free, whatever that meant. Above all she wanted freedom from Laura Weatherall and all she was supposed to be.

Heliocopters had landed in the late afternoon delivering superstars, newsreel photographers, others of the hip elite. The mud dried. Portable radios announced that an entire nation was focused on five hundred thousand people getting it on in the Catskills. Some said it was the beginning, others thought it might be the end. Red Rudy and some of the older hippies gathered on the hill with binoculars like Civil War generals. Whatever it was, it was an event not soon to be forgotten.

After the sun set the dwarfs peddled their wares: "Hashish, cocaine, LSD," "mescaline, mescaline," "smoke, smoke, smoke." Peeping behind bushes and lounging in trees, selling or giving to the hundreds of Snow Whites and Princes. Entranced, some lay down in the leaves for hours, even days. Some inched over the ground, seeing the microcosm. Some were on bad trips. Everyone was helpful and above all cool.

Next day there was a giant hangover. Laura and Jeff threw blankets over their bubble, hung up a DO NOT DISTURB sign, and crawled under their furs. A day later came the famous garbage mess: The press and the U.S. government began looking for Jeff. But he and Laura escaped to 610 Park Avenue; it was late summer and her mother was in Newport, her father drunk on a boat in the Mediterranean. They were safe at 610 Park under the very noses of their pursuers.

When they appeared at a party after Labor Day they found themselves superstars in an underground besieged. Having pulled off the Woodstock scam, Jeff was an overnight celebrity. People wanted interviews and photographs. Fat sons of gangsters called with new and bigger festivals dancing like sugar plums in their pea brains. Everyone's hair was getting longer and it became impossible to filter out friends from foes. They moved to a Fifth Avenue penthouse where security was tight.

Months passed and the Chicago trials began. Superstars of riot and rock commenced to watch each other nervously, wondering what was going to happen next. They'd landed on top of a mountain but the dogs, Mitchell and Nixon were barking and out for blood. Charlie Manson manifested as a pop witch, Weathermen and women united. Altamont exploded. The manic energy of the sixties was a collapsing helter skelter. And the mountain became a volcano.

One night as they lay reading in bed Jeff turned to her.

"The scene is going bad," he said.

"We could split to London, it can't be worse."

"Forget America?" he asked.

"I doubt we can ever forget it, maybe it'll forget us."

"I wonder how long we'll be gone?"

Jeff shrugged. "A day, a year.... Maybe we'll never come back."

II

"Mr. A. K. SUNDARAM downstairs in the lobby to see you, sir," a voice crackled through the phone.

Laura was half asleep. "Would you repeat that," she said, trying to remember where she was.

"Mr. A. K. Sundaram here to see you, sir."

"Jeff," she whispered. "Jeff! Wake up!" She kicked at him with her foot. "Someone called Sunderyumyum is coming. Wake up!"

Minutes later an Indian counterpart of Stan appeared at the door: handsome and athletic, dressed casually but expensively. "I am Sundaram," he said. "Welcome to India."

"Jeff Murray and this is my wife, Laura."

The two men shook hands. Laura wondered whether Mr. Sundaram was hip. His face was an expressionless mask behind an Adolf Hitler moustache. Coffee came in behind him with a waiter.

"We've just arrived," Laura said in her best Farmington teatime manner. "You'll have to forgive us if we're not quite awake—jet lag and all that. Will you have some coffee with us, Mr. Sundaram?"

"Please call me Sundar," he said, easing himself into a chair. "I received a cable from Stan to call on you. How is he?"

"He's fine. We just left him in London."

Sundaram's round, passive face examined them. "I haven't seen him since our Harvard days. We were close friends then but India is so far away, so many things have changed. Do you suppose he'll ever come here?"

"He's thinking of it," Laura said. "How do you like your coffee, Mr. Sundaram?"

"With cream and sugar," he replied. "And please—call me Sundar." He ventured a smile.

After the first few sips, Sundaram brightened and became effusive. "I am very glad my old friend Stan sent you to me," he said. "It is good to see attractive foreigners here in Delhi. We see so many Germans and English, even Russians nowadays. They are so big and fat. They give us inferiority complexes.''

"I'm afraid most Americans are even bigger and fatter," Laura said.

"But you—" Sundaram gestured grandly, "—you are not only thin but beautiful too. Ah, both are beautiful," he added laughing.

"Beauty is only skin deep," Laura said.

"Ah, but skin is what we are," replied Sundaram, "is it not so, Mr. Murray?" He slurped his coffee noisily, put down his cup and rose. "I will not disturb you any longer, you must rest now. But you will come to me this evening, yes? I have a house near by. There's a party and I will take you. It will be a good chance for you to meet some of the 'in crowd.' And from tomorrow, please feel free to make my place your home. I am a bachelor." His eyes twinkled. "You can even move in if you like, if you get bored with this." He pointed around the room. "Friends of mine own it, very boring hotel." He laughed explosively.

"How will we find you?" Jeff asked.

"I will come and fetch you. Or if I am unable, my driver will come. You must relax and let things happen, you are in India now. Don't think, enjoy." Sundaram's eyes glittered. And now I must go, I'm late. May I take my leave, Madam?" He bowed formally to Laura.

"Tonight at seven-thirty," he said, holding onto Jeff's hand as they walked to the door. "It is a great pleasure for me to have you both here. Get some rest, we'll meet again this evening."

*   *   *

"I bet you didn't dream you'd be holding hands with gentlemen the first day in India," Laura giggled.

"And with eye makeup!"

"Oh, they all wear that," Laura said. "But what do you think the 'in crowd' is?"

*   *   *

They spent the late morning unpacking. Nothing looked right.

"We have to have some new clothes, don't you think? Otherwise we'll look like hippies and scare people."

Jeff agreed. "It's still the fifties here."

"Of which century?"

"We should be able to find some things in the hotel shops," he said, not wanting to move.

Laura nodded. "First we'll have lunch downstairs and see what people are wearing. When smuggling it's best to be invisible."

That evening they stood together in front of a large mirror. Laura began to giggle. "You look like a cricket star," she said. Jeff had bought a pale doublebreasted mouse colored suit which fit snugly over his athletic body. Underneath he wore a white turtleneck pullover and on his head a dark red turban which the shopkeeper had insisted he buy.

"You will look very handsome in thees," the shopkeeper had said. "It will make your green eyes look like zee emeralds. Then you will have more success with thee vimen, heh? You don't like? Yes, it is right?"

Laura found it impossible to get used to a sari so she had bought pale blue chiffon pants and a matching blouse embroidered heavily in all the necessary places with sequins and small glittering stones.

"How do I look?" she asked.

"You'll probably be raped before the evening is over," Jeff said. "In fact, it might happen right now." He pulled her toward himself, watching in the mirror. "But serously, these Indian men will go crazy you know. Shouldn't you wear something more than that?"

"I have my silk shawl," Laura said. She twirled a flowered fabric in the air and then wound it about her. "In public I can look just as wrapped up as they do." Opening her jewelry case she put on some of the most impressive items. "But they won't see me, they'll only see this," she laughed, holding up a bracelet of matched rubies and diamonds. "Isn't dreadful? Belonged to my old Aunt Ethel in Palm Beach. They're supposed to be impressed with glitter here, I've heard, even pray to it. It may open some door—eez not right, Meester Jeff?"

The phone jangled. "Good evening," Sundaram's voice screeched. "Are you ready?"

"Be right down," Jeff said.

There was sputtering on the other end. "You are not ready?"

"No, no. We'll be right down," Jeff yelled into the phone.

When they reached the lobby they spotted him pacing nervously in a tight-fitting mod evening costume. He failed to recognize them at first, but then noticed Laura.

"How very clever you are, Madam," he exclaimed, eyeing the rubies. "Extraordinary, most extraordinary," turning to Jeff. "And you, sir, you look just like a Pathan."

"Is that all right?" asked Jeff good-naturedly. "It was the shopkeeper's idea." He pointed to the turban.

"The Pathans are our most accomplished enemies. But we love them nevertheless because they are so beautiful. They are an ancient race of thieves who like to think of themselves as Moslem—really they are just thieves. They all come large like you, six feet or more, sometimes seven. And many are green-eyed, like you, and very dangerous." He tittered, rolling his eyes.

There was a pause during which they all looked at each other like

26

strangers in an elevator.

"So," Sundaram finally said. "Shall we go? It's not far away."

A series of costumed doormen guided them out of the never-never land hotel to where Sundar's sleek grey limousine was waiting. The driver saluted and opened the door. Jeff was impressed. Obviously Stan's friend was important.

A few minutes later they were driving past guarded gates into a luxurious compound somewhere near the center of Delhi. Hidden by lush gardens was a sprawling stucco and cement villa. It had round windows and rounded corners and made Laura think of Santa Monica. The scents of jasmine and gardenia mingled in the soft night air. From somewhere inside came a loud imitation of the Rolling Stones.

Sundar introduced them to their host, Dorje, a Tibetan aristocrat's son who escaped from Lhasa with a fortune in gold six months before the Chinese invasion. He was very fat. Laura thought he looked like a gangster. It was impossible to guess his age. His huge face sat on his body like a moon on the horizon. He led them through several rooms full of people engaged in animated conversation.

"It's a cocktail party," Jeff whispered.

They both laughed. "Then we'll have to play cocktail party," Laura murmured.

There were numerous well-dressed young people chattering in a mixture of Hindi and English. "It's the fifties all right," Laura thought.

"It's like Rock Hudson and Doris Day with sincerity," Jeff whispered.

A number of young couples were talking about their "kids." Laura wondered where they picked up this sort of thing and what all the mod clothes from London had to do with talking about the kids. She spoke to Sundar of it.

"My dear, in India all foreign imports are just fashion," he explained. "They are shuffled, re-shuffled, jumbled in the most preposterous combinations, because in the end we know that they are just passing fads.

Laura wondered about the India outside the compound. She had already seen enough to understand that India was a great sea in which one could easily be drowned. And these people, with their fake sincerity and their talk about the "kids," were they not also nervous about drowning?

Groups of voluptuous girls from the Bombay film scene twittered like finches around handsome young army officers, who strutted about catching glimpses of themselves in mirrors. A number of Westerners were scattered through the crowd.

"I give this party once a year," said the moonfaced Dorje in a high voice with an Oxford accent. "It absolves me of most of my social debts—really it's nothing. In fact," he turned aside to them, eyeing

27

Laura's rubies, "in fact, it's a drag." He winked at Jeff.

Jeff wondered how turned-on Dorje might be. Laura noticed a familiar tired face nodding to her from across the room. It was Charles Hooker, her brother's old friend.

"Laura Weatherall, of all people," he said, ambling up gimlet in hand and sounding like the Yale Club. "You're the lahst person I expected to see in India, absolutely the lahst. Are you alone?"

"I'm the lahst person who ever expected to be here," she replied. "I'm with Jeff, remember Jeff? He thinks he might want to make films here."

"Yes, the film scene here is very exciting. It seems that absolutely everyone is coming to film in India. I may build a studio in Delhi. I wanted to return to the West for a little while but they—" He snickered, gesturing toward the room full of people. "They won't let me leave."

Laura, thinking of the Hooker steel fortune, could guess why.

"Where's Jeff?" said Hooker.

"Over there, talking to that...er...girl."

"You mean the great Sharma." He nodded. "Of course, but where is Jeff? I don't see him."

"In the turban," Laura said.

"But you can't mean it? It isn't—?" He gaped. "But it is. The suit and that turban." Hooker burst out laughing. "You know, I'd been trying to decide whether he was an Army man or a cricket star. I might even be able to use him in my next film."

"He's very good at acting," Laura said wryly.

"Woodstock wasn't too bad for starters," said Hooker. "But how on earth did you get to this party?"

"A friend of a friend from London," Laura said. "Calls himself Sundar—you know him?"

"But, of course, my dear, doesn't everyone? He brought you here? You're very lucky. He's a Cabinet Minister, practically in her arms."

"In whose arms?" asked Laura.

"Why, Mrs. Ghandi's of course," replied Hooker.

Laura couldn't imagine the neurotic-looking A. K. Sundaram being in anyone's arms.

"Would you like to meet a few people?" Hooker asked. "I'm sure you'll find them most amusing."

Beneath the chiffon and sequins Laura's sleek body moved freely sending out tantalizing waves of freedom. Many of the women present would have destroyed her instantly had they the power. The men on the other hand would have eaten her alive. She found she rather liked causing a sensation after wearing blue jeans for so long.

Hooker introduced her to three young Sikhs standing together near the bar sipping drinks. They watched her with large serious eyes, their swarthy faces set off by pale pastel turbans, and Laura wondered what they would look like with their long black hair hanging free. She was also aware of the difference between their probably lascivious thoughts and the formality of their outward behavior: the stiff gestures, the handsome masks.

As they stood playing this wordless game, Laura's attention was caught by a movement on the periphery of her vision and turning involuntarily she saw a man whose body seemed to be shining through the clothes he wore. Later it was hard for her to describe that first impression even to herself. As she looked, he too turned, and their eyes met across the crowded room. Might he be Alex's teacher, the man in the photograph she wondered? Excusing herself from her admirers and trying to look casual, she made her way hurriedly among the guests for a better look if just to be sure she had really seen him. Entering another room she found him again standing in a dark corner talking with an old woman. Sundaram was not in sight but the fat Tibetan host was. She took Dorje aside.

"Who is that man talking to the older lady?"

"Ah, you mean Indra," replied Dorje. "He is talking to my aunt. She has known him for years. She is so fascinated by him that I am afraid she may someday give him all her gold. Then she would have to come and live with me." He tittered.

"But who is he?"

"Ah, he is Indraji. He was a great athlete and major in the paratroopers under the British years ago—Rajput, I believe. He is very mysterious even to those who know him well—disappears for long periods of time."

"I'd like to meet him if you would introduce me," Laura said.

"But of course."

After they had been introduced, Dorje left and Indra continued talking to the old lady in Tibetan. Laura waited patiently, trying to connect this tall man in the Saville Row suit with the photo Alex had shown her.

After some moments he turned aside from his conversation. "Don't be put off by these clothes," he said to her. "It is I, the same one as in the photograph." He smiled. "Just now I must talk to this old woman who does not understand English. Please go out onto the terrace and wait. I will come presently."

On the terrace the air was filled with the scent of roses, roses in urns, roses in the garden, climbing roses on the house. He finally came out.

"How could you know I've seen your picture?" Laura asked immediately. "Has Alex written you, or—" She thought somehow she'd made a mistake.

"How do I know—" he said, cutting her off with a wave of his hand. "Do not go into it too deeply...not too deeply. But how did *you* know—that is the question which is interesting." He laughed and turned to face her. "Are you all right?" he asked, matter-of-factly like a physician.

The question made her uncomfortable. Why should this perfect stranger ask her if she were all right? It made her wonder if she was really "all right," something she'd not thought about for quite a while.

"I'm still a bit travel weary, I suppose," she said. "I've only been here twenty-four hours, not long enough to really see India yet."

"You are seeing it now," he said, staring at her.

"Now?"

"Yes." He was still gazing at her intently.

"What brings you to a party like this?" she asked to change the subject. "I was told you stayed naked in the jungle. I didn't recognize you in these clothes with a turban."

"But of course you did," he said. "How else did we meet?" He waved one large hand in a graceful arc toward the house. "Roses," he muttered under his breath.

"What?" asked Laura, bewildered.

"Nothing, nothing but...roses. I like them, I grew up with them once, I like sitting in rooms heaped with rose blossoms." He sighed. "But nowadays I try to remain invisible as much as possible. Life has become dangerous and cheap here in India. I risked coming to this party thinking you might show up."

"But how could you have known I would be here? Are you a friend of Sundar's? We didn't know we'd be coming here until this morning—"

"I came three days ago to Delhi," he said. "To be at this party. The old lady invited me and said there would be someone I should meet at a party being given by her nephew."

"Me?"

"Yes, she described you in detail three days ago, how you would look and what you'd be wearing."

Laura's heart jumped.

"Then when Dorje brought you over she said to me in Tibetan 'that's the one' meaning you."

"I don't believe it," Laura said without thinking.

"I know you don't. Nevertheless, it is true. And if our meeting had not taken place in this manner by chance as you call it, you can be sure I would not be talking to you at this moment."

"If I'd phoned the number Alex gave me..."

"It's an inoperative number." He looked at her; burst out laughing at her perplexity.

"How old are you," she said, deliberately interrupting his laughter.

He laughed even more. "Don't be frightened, don't try to break my waves," he said calmly. "I'm sixty."

Laura was amazed, he looked thirty.

"Look," he said, taking hold of her shoulders. "We must not be seen here by too many of these people. Delhi is full of gossips, I prefer remaining invisible. Can you remember numbers?"

She nodded.

"Can you remember—" He gave her a number. "Can you remember it until tomorrow?"

She nodded again.

"Then tomorrow morning at exactly 11 A.M. please call that number and we will arrange to meet somewhere quietly. What is the number again?"

She repeated the number. He dropped his hands. "I must go now," he said perfunctorily.

Before she could say goodbye he'd disappeared into the thick shrubbery of the garden and Laura turned to see Sundaram standing in the double doors leading to the terrace.

"I see you have been talking with Indraji," he said.

"Yes, do you know him?"

"He was a classmate of my father's at Simla. They were on the wrestling team together." Noting her surprised look, Sundaram chuckled. "You will find, my dear, that nothing in India is what it seems—this is not a standardized place like the West. He's a most unusual fellow. Did you like him?"

"I don't know," Laura replied. "Something about him seems unreal, as though he's not quite alive."

"Or more than alive."

"Is he really sixty?"

"Yes, he's really sixty, perhaps more." Sundaram smiled. "Will you see him again?"

"I think so. He's the teacher of a friend of mine."

She told Sundar about Alex, the picture he'd shown her, about the old Tibetan lady, Dorje's aunt, and the "coincidence" of their meeting.

"You must not tell these things to anyone else," he said earnestly. "People will think you're crazy. It might be dangerous for him as well as you."

"Should I not see him again?"

"By all means, by all means, see him again if you like—but be careful and be quiet about it." He shook his head. "He's rather extraordinary—disappeared completely from '47 on, reappearing only three years ago. He has my father completely 'freaked' as you would say."

"Why?"

"Because twenty-five years later my father is an old man, but Indraji looks exactly the same as he did when they last saw each other, at a dinner for Mountbatten just before Independence!" Sundaram laughed. "There

31

are many stories about him, he's a tough character," he added. "I should be extremely careful if I were you—most women go nuts over him." He glanced inside. "Would you like to meet the Prime Minister's yoga master? He is talking with your husband."

Sundaram introduced her as Mrs. Murray to a black-bearded man in white robes. He nodded and continued to talk to Jeff, who was arranging to take Yoga instruction from him. Laura knew Jeff meant to use the contacts from this party to get his acid distribution started. Bored, she stood aside, still shaken by her meeting with Indra. Suddenly, she felt almost as if she were tripping, felt tingling sensations and for a brief moment everything turned red. Noticing the three young Sikhs to whom Hooker had introduced her were still at the bar, she decided a drink would steady her.

"Gin and tonic, please," she said to the bartender, who was busy and didn't respond.

The youngest of the trio came to her rescue with an imperious shout and the drink immediately appeared. "Won't you join us?" he said, displaying a dazzling set of white teeth. "Right over here, come!"

His macho attitude annoyed her somewhat. "Sure, why not?" she replied, trying to mirror his toughness. After a second gin and tonic she felt better. Still why had this Indra disturbed her so? Something familiar but unrecognizable had peered through a crack inside her. She resented it, yet was unable to mend the crack. Immobilized psychically, she felt like a chicken with a circle drawn about it, unable to move.

"I am Harpal," her new acquaintance was saying. "And these are my brothers, Harjith and Kuljit."

Six obsidian eyes projected waves toward her, but she didn't mind. Sex put her on solid ground. While he talked Harpal's eyes undressed her. She played the game and could see that it excited him, kept talking about nothing, laughing at him with her eyes. He asked her for a drink at his flat, and cracked his knuckles in anticipation.

"Really," she said, catching sight of Sundaram, "I've just arrived from Europe and I'm still dreadfully tired. I think I have to go to the hotel just now. Rest. We'll meet again, no doubt."

"No doubt," Harpal said serously, holding her hand. "No doubt."

She left the bar then and found Sundaram.

"I have to go to sleep," she said, "jet lag, I guess."

He looked surprised. "So early? Wait until the crowd has thinned. The scene will become more interesting."

"I'm exhausted. Sorry to be such a bore, Sundar." She took his hand. "Do you think you could send me to the hotel in your car?"

"But of course."

"Jeff must stay if he likes," she said. "He recovers from flying faster than I do."

"Of course."

"Please tell him I'm leaving, yes? And thanks for a very interesting first evening in India."

Sundar led her to his car. "Your friend Hooker is having a few people for dinner tomorrow. I will probably see you there."

"I hope so." She smiled her best ladylike smile. "Good night."

"Good night."

*   *   *

A. K. Sundaram watched his car disappear down the drive and returned to the party. The remaining guests were gathered in the library listening to Mick Jagger tapes. His contemporaries in the diplomatic corps had left and there were no foreigners except Jeff and the longhaired son of a high ranking American diplomat. The boy, who was the bane of his father's existence, offered Sundaram a smoke.

"Ganja?" he asked.

The boy nodded. Sundaram refused politely. Two young Army officers were smoking with their girlfriends and several sons and daughters of Delhi's rich merchants were dancing frantically.

Dorje was standing with his back to Sundar. "Now that we're alone," he announced conspiratorially, "would any of you be interested in dropping some acid?" he held out a handful of orange colored tablets.

Sundar flinched. He knew that Dorje had the reputation for being outrageous and could afford it, but he wished the Tibetan had waited until he, A. K. Sundaram, Cabinet Minister, had left. It seemed like a plot. To his horror Dorje turned toward him.

"Well, who will try first?" Just to prove it was like eating candy, Dorje popped three tablets into his own mouth. Sundar took one which he pretended to swallow but didn't. He would send it for analysis the next day.

"So acid has arrived in Delhi," said the longhaired American boy laconically, pocketing two for later.

"Here—open your mouth," Dorje said, making a show of popping one onto Jeff's tongue.

"That's a surprise," said Jeff coolly so that everyone would hear.

Skepticism filled Sundar's alert mind and he wondered just what was going on. Jeff, unaware of the suspicious Indian nature and what it could lead to, was elated that Dorje had been so cooperative. "The beginning," he thought and settled back in his chair.

*   *   *

Alone in a big double bed, Laura awoke unable to recall where she was, sat up for a moment, looked out at the sunrise and dove under the sheets for more sleep.

Then the phone was jangling. An Indian phone, impossible to hear on it. She hesitated but the ringing persisted. Finally she picked up the receiver and slid it into bed with her.

"I say Laura, it's Charles—yes Charles Hooker. Hi!" he yelled. "Are you there—are you awake?"

"What time is it?" she answered with a hoarse yell.

"It's ten-thirty."

She came awake suddenly. Her call to Indra was to be made at eleven. Trying desperately to remember the number he'd given her she let Hooker go on.

"I wanted to ask you and Jeff for dinner. I'm having just a small—"

What was the number he had given her?

"Small dinner party this evening." The phone crackled. "Are you there?"

"Yes, yes. I can't say for Jeff... No, he isn't here just now. No, exploring Delhi I suppose. Yes, yes, I'll come with Sundaram then, he's already... yes, okay dahling... lovely, byeeeee."

She fumbled blindly to get the receiver back on the hook. What was that number. She jumped out of bed and rummaged in a suitcase for her traveling clock, called for the time, and put the clock beside the phone. "Don't write it down," he had said, so she had kept it in her mind, repeating it until—until the gin and tonic. She flopped back on the pillow, closed her eyes, concentrated, and finally recalled it.

The room boy came in with coffee, pretended to clean and cast furtive glances at her. He was young and handsome and spoke good English. He seemed to be waiting for something to happen. "Like Carlos," Laura thought. She could feel waves of frustration coming from him. Were all the men here uptight?" Was Indra uptight?

At exactly eleven she lifted the receiver and asked the operator for the number. The phone rang and rang. Her heart fell, she was certain she'd remembered it wrong. Then his deep voice was on the other end.

"Can you remember an address?" he said. "And come as soon as you are ready?"

She had her pencil. The phone was crackling again. She cursed it under her breath.

"Don't worry, you'll remember it." He repeated the address. "Don't write it down," he added.

"But I already have."

"Then look at it for a few seconds and tear it up. I'll be waiting here for you."

34

There was a click at the other end.

Would she go immediately? What was tearing up the address he had given her supposed to be about? "Play the game," she said aloud, tearing up the slip of paper. Would she hurry? No. She would take a long bubble bath.

Afterwards she would take great care dressing and putting on make-up, go down to the coffee shop, have a Bloody Mary, scrambled eggs, and coffee and it would be mid-afternoon when she arrived. Remembering Sundar's warning she decided she must be careful to avoid giving this Indra the idea that her interest was anything more than casual.

*   *   *

So it was that at exactly three p.m. she arrived by taxi at the address he had given her. A half-open rusted gate was the only break in a high crumbling wall that stretched for a full block. Several "Shops" made of tin and wood scraps grew on it like barnacles, beggars and a few lepers lounging against them. A skinny old man wearing a turban and a pair of ragged shorts darted out of the gate to open the taxi door. Venturing a kind but toothless smile from his stubble of white beard, after a verbal battle in Hindi with the driver, he beckoned Laura to follow him. Inside the gate was a jungle of vines, ancient mango trees, and palms whose untrimmed brown fronds rustled in the dry January wind. Hidden in this tangle of vegetation were the remains of a vast mansion dating from colonial times. Decaying pillars and fallen beams marked the long veranda where once, Laura supposed, handsome regimental officers and their ladies had sipped tea. The old man led her down a long hall past silent dusty rooms smelling of mold and rotted wood, full of Victorian furniture and large engravings, photographs of swarthy faces, faded color reproductions of gods and goddesses. At last they came to a small terrace that opened onto a patch of well-kept garden, planted with flowers and vegetables and bordered with roses. There was a well and a small fountain splashing into a white marble pool.

Indra was lying naked on a charpoy. A cherubic young boy was rubbing his legs. In one corner an ancient fan rattled. Laura sat not daring to speak, as he turned on his stomach so that the boy could oil and knead his back. Pretending at first not even to notice her arrival he finally propped his head up on his arms and smiled. There followed another long silence during which he continued to smile, studying her with his dark eyes while the boy massaged his feet and hands.

"Is this your house?" she asked finally.

"They say it belongs to me." He signed and turned over to sit up. His body glowed like a young athlete's. "It's an inheritance. After a long fami-

35

ly feud during which the man who called me his son was poisoned by another who called me brother, it came into my hands.'' He shook his head as if to shake memory from his mind. ''A long story, filled with episodes of infidelity and deceit.''

''Now what will you do with it?'' she asked sympathetically, familiar herself with property and family feuds.

''Not sure,'' he said. ''Thinking of setting fire to it, thinking of climbing on top—on the roof—and having this boy set fire to the whole thing.''

He placed his hand affectionately on the boy's head and spoke to him softly in Hindi. The boy, who was squatting at Indra's feet, grinned. ''You see, he would do it, he would really do it. A very grand fire it would make too, would it not? Light up all Delhi, ha! These houses are prisons. Always remember: it is better to live in a shack, a shack won't dictate your life.... Better yet, live naked out of doors and be free.''

His nakedness and wild talk were so bizarre—was he putting her on, she wondered. Yet there was an element of dead seriousness about him too.

''But it must be very valuable,'' she said, trying to keep some thread of conversation going, ''here in the center of Delhi.''

''Delhi!'' he laughed. ''You can't imagine what Delhi was really like. Now it's Kiev or Detroit, not Delhi. Money is no problem for me. I can do very well without it. The problem is that if I sell it some greedy beggar on horseback will make a bigger prison here, a skyscraping hotel where he and his fat friends and their fat spoiled quarrelsome children and even fatter wives will live with pants, shoes, and miniskirts. Let them.'' He gestured gracefully. ''They are all going to the dogs. The best people are all gone, killed in '47, dispossessed, gone crazy; only the garbage is left. They have no teaching because they hate teachers—they are without proper gurus. They think they know everything and that life is—'' He paused, arching an eyebrow at her, ''Just a bowl of cherries. All they want is money for jam.'' He grinned, showing his teeth and gazed at her a long time, scratching one leg and trying to see into her.

She found it hard to look at him directly. She was nervous and not accustomed to having philosophical conversations with naked men. His body glistened smooth and sleek in the failing light. Far away a faint roar signaled the mounting confusion of Delhi's rush hour—the ''cowdust hour'' with its pungent odor of thousands of fires kindled in preparation for the evening meal.

After some time the old man brought out an oil lamp and the boy fetched tea and a concoction of what appeared to be dumplings floating in cream.

''Do you always flavor your sweets with bhang?'' asked Laura, recognizing the dish cooked with cannabis, cardamom, cinnamon, and nutmeg.

"You have a dangerously perceptive taste, Laura Weatherall," Indra said.

"I've had some experience."

"In this weather, in Delhi, a small amount of bhang is sometimes taken in the food," he said, ignoring her challenge but interested in her show of strength. "It is good for the health at this season. We grind the spices together into the batter of the dumplings which we call pakoras. Bhang and opium and many other poisons are used in small amounts by us to regulate the system. If you are neurotic or have too many attachments to body or property, and if therefore you are filled with frustrations, then you should not use drugs, even as medicine."

"Do you mean me, or one?"

"You," he said, staring up at her. "You have had too many drugs."

She looked skeptical.

"Yes, yes. I know you do not believe me—you do not understand too well. These drugs are all poisonous, toxic. All poisons are initiators into different states of being with the world. Each has its special path, its ritual and rite. The power that comes can kill you if you do not understand the procedure that must be followed. It is too complex. You have to have a teacher with you. There are many things we don't tell—"

"Unless?"

"Unless the student passes certain tests."

"And I would probably flunk," said Laura.

"No one has given you the opportunity," he replied listlessly, closing his eyes.

"How come you came to Delhi anyway," he said, his accent imitating American slang, sounding like a police sergeant.

"My husband is a . . ."

"Be careful what you say, don't incriminate yourself."

"Quite right," Laura said. "He is *not* my husband."

Indra grinned.

"We're here together to make a film."

It was no use. He just grinned at her. She felt extremely uncomfortable but she couldn't tell him the truth—at least not now.

"Why are you grinning?" she asked finally.

"That's a riddle for you to unravel Laura Weatherall," he said. "You *can* unravel it—all of it. That's why you are here.

For the first time their meeting seemed serious to her.

"You spoke about some power coming," she said. "What power?"

"Ah, you Americans, you are always so interested in power. Don't you have some story in the West called the Sorcerer's Apprentice?"

"Yes."

"Well then," he said, laughing, "there is only one power, *the* Power." He made a careless gesture with both hands, accidental yet beautiful. "It comes automatically as a result of practicing the ancient teachings—if you know the methods. If you use the power in this world, however, it will finish you. It is meant to be used only in getting people out."

"Are you a sorcerer then?"

"Sorcery is the application of power in this world. Your Western scientists are sorcerers. Mathematics is their secret language. They have stolen it from the gods. But they are neither kindly nor pure and so the power they have is about to destroy them and their system."

"You're not answering my question," said Laura.

"The only reason for using power is to bring people to their senses so they will want to go across," replied Indra.

"Go across—what does that mean?"

"That's a Buddhist expression." He sighed and leaned back on one arm, smiling at her as though she were a new toy. "Hogwash, all this talk is useless, it only drives one crazy. Ask me no questions and I'll tell you no lies."

The old fan rattled on. As Laura watched Indra she had the peculiar impression that he was not really there, that if she rose to touch him there would be nothing.

"The world is a bridge," he whispered, almost to himself. "Pass over it but do not build on it. He who hopes for an hour may hope for eternity. The world is but an hour. Spend it in devotion. The rest is unseen."

"What is that?"

"Oh, just an inscription on a gate." His voice drifted off. Then he asked, suddenly, "Will you come with me to the Himalayas tomorrow?"

"Tomorrow? With you?"

He nodded. "Tomorrow or the day after."

Laura panicked. "Actually I'm late now, for an appointment," she replied, hearing her voice echoing somewhere.

He smiled.

She felt immobilized and disconnected, and when finally she was able to get up, lurched toward him as if propelled by some other force.

But his hand came up in a gesture that signaled both a blessing and a halt. "You will call me tomorrow?" he said.

She stood still, fiddling with the fringe of her shawl feeling like a child again. The sensation was so strong she could even smell her mother's perfume in the air.

"I'll call you tomorrow. By then I'll know about going with you."

"Of course," he said.

The servant had a taxi waiting. She gave Hooker's address and the driver wheeled off into the night through the dimly lit streets. Outside the car window a gray and uncomfortable India slipped past and she knew instinctively that Indra wanted to throw her into it. "I'd never make it," she sighed aloud.

They were passing through wide boulevards of a suburban development—expensive but absurd whims rendered into concrete and tile. The car slowed, then stopped outside the gate of a house set deep within an oasis-like compound. She paid the driver and walked in. "Poor Charles," she thought, looking around her, "he can't seem to get out of Beverly Hills."

She was greeted by Sharma of the night before, who as it turned out was Hooker's girlfriend.

"Sorry I'm late," Laura said, "I got lost shopping."

After Indra, Sharma was relaxing. Laura admired her magnificent breasts, naked beneath a wisp of sari.

"Never late," said Sharma, laughing melodiously. "Come, your Jeff is here. He's waiting over there for you." She gestured and then disappeared into another room.

*   *   *

"Sorry I didn't make it back last night," Jeff said. "Business."

"I can imagine."

"It was good for us," he protested. "Ten people turned on. No freakouts, all good trips. Everyone wants more."

"Did *you* give the acid out?"

"No, Dorje—beautiful cat. He was the host, after all."

"I thought you might have been fucking all night."

Jeff grinned. "The important thing is the contacts I managed to make. The sooner we get rid of the stuff the sooner we'll be *out* of here!"

"You don't like India?"

"Not much, people are too uptight here."

"Maybe it's you that's uptight," said Laura. "How about the girls?"

"Like rabbits. They want you to be a rabbit too," he noted the angry look that crossed Laura's face. "Don't be a jealous wife, you're free too, you know."

"Free to do what? This looks like a man's world to me. They think I'm a whore, I can tell."

"That's because at home they're all ruled by their wives," Jeff said. "Wives mean something here. They're trained to make homes men want to come back to, know how to take care of them."

"Don't be romantic," Laura said. "These chicks aren't exactly what I'd call homemakers."

But she was angry. First Indra had intimated she was impure, now Jeff was down-tripping her. Men were all the same.

Jeff turned and wandered off to another part of the house. Watching him go, Laura felt depressed, frightened. Indra had touched something deep in her; the cellars of her mind, pried open a little.

Looking through the crowd she saw Harpal, again.

He watched her, his face impassive as a Greek Statue handsome under a magenta turban pinned with a large blue stone.

"Good evening," he said. "Do you want a drink?"

Something inside her wanted to act recklessly, aggressively, whatever the consequences. "I want *you,*" she said with a calm smile, making her eyes travel down his body and up again.

He was thrown off guard and looked away before taking up her challenge.

She knew he considered her behavior insubordinate, but enjoyed upsetting him. He stood very still, his legs apart, at ease in the military fashion. Only his left leg moved slightly, rhythmically from the knee.

"You have missed eating," he said.

"I'm not hungry."

"Then will you have a dance before we leave?"

They danced in a dark corner. To her surprise he moved well.

"Where did you learn to dance?" she whispered in his ear.

"On South Randolph Street in Chicago," he answered. "I was supposed to be going to the University of Chicago but I spent most of my time on South Randolph learning to boogie. They liked my turban, you know." He paused.

"And now?"

"Now I'm a landowner. Our father called me back. We all have to live on our land now, otherwise under the new laws we might lose it."

Her body felt warm and soft. He never went to the Indian prostitutes. Getting it free in America had killed all that for him. He wondered whether she could sense the extent of his sexual frustration, how long it had been since he had a Western woman. But his instinct wanted mindless submission. Fascinated by her open sensuality, he nevertheless disliked a woman who talked back.

"Now we can go," he said, catching her hand and pulling her outside onto the terrace. The evening had turned cool, almost cold. As they walked down the drive he motioned to a jeep parked just beyond the gate.

"Sorry about my car," he said, helping her up. "We have many roads where only jeeps work. We are a poor country you know. We have to use the same vehicles for everything."

A few minutes later they pulled up at a modern apartment hotel.

"One of Indra's prisons," Laura thought.

Everyone at the door saluted Harpal and an elevator carried them to a small mirrored alcove of white marble, beyond which lay polished wood floors, thick carpets and a wall of windows overlooking the city. The room was crowded with treasures: campaign chests, carved screens, trophies, animal skins. There were hallways on either side leading to other rooms. Outside rose a waning saffron moon.

Harpal excused himself to make sure no one else was in. Neither of his brothers had lived abroad. They would never understand that she was not a prostitute.

His mind balked at the idea of trying to explain them to her. Explain the customs and demands of his caste? Could she imagine how the total lack of privacy had infected all of them? His brothers were primitives, echoes of another time, another life. Himself, he was split in two: half West, half East.

"Take their science but keep your customs," his father had preached. How naive, how idealistic, an impossible combination that was going to kill them all. Now they wore uncomfortable pants and owned hotels they disliked living in. Day by day their lives seemed more confused and useless. They were going toward destruction, to be lost forever in a sea called "modern."

"We're alone," he said facing her in the darkened room, silhouetted against the long glass wall. Embracing her he slipped off her blouse. She began unbuttoning his shirt.

He felt her cool hand on his chest and his muscles rippled involuntarily as she moved close to him. South Chicago flashed across his mind. As she fumbled with his belt, he thought he would explode. He picked her up, carried her to a smaller room and lowered her gently onto a low sofa. Standing over her he removed his clothes until only his loin cloth, the last remnant of the old ways, remained. Gently he lifted her head against his erection. She could feel it against her cheek, solid and throbbing as she gazed into his dark eyes and removed the cloth.

He felt like a burning fuse. Pushing her back on the sofa he tore at her clothes and eased himself down between the softness of her thighs.

Free of the turban, his hair swung over her, a mass of silky black curls. Coming up in a crouch beside her, he brushed it back with a defiant sweep of his hand.

"Now you see the Harpal of Hindustan," he whispered hoarsely and standing up, brought her with him, lifting her into the air.

She straddled his waist and slowly slid down onto him. Hot blood throbbed inside her. Thrusting her tongue inside his mouth she locked her arms around his strong neck. Still inside her, he lowered himself to the floor until he was sitting cross-legged and he had her, slowly, and deeply, on the floor of the room, holding back his orgasm, letting it come on and shutting it off.

The muscles of her vagina opened and closed on him.

"I'm going to fill you with good Sikh sperm—a flood, he whispered.

"My American cunt will digest you," she said coolly.

"You digest *me?*" he hissed. Pulling back he slapped her hard across the cheek. His teeth showed between taut lips.

"You digest me, the son of sons of sons of warriors?" He laughed crazily and lowering his mouth on hers, fastened his eyes unblinkingly upon her. The pain on her face pleased him.

His violence excited her.

"You wanted to know how it is to be fucked by one of us, didn't you?" he whispered into her mouth. "To take a little taste? Digest?" he said, panting. "You may eat, but you will never digest."

Then suddenly he tensed and was listening, like an animal in danger. Laura turned to follow his gaze. Two figures stood in the dark loosening their belts. Fear gripped her. But Harpal held her still, continuing to fuck her.

Expecting him to attack the intruders her fear turned to rage as she recognized his older brothers, Harjith and Kuljit.

Squatting near her Harjith took her hand in his and drew it under his loincloth. Harpal exploded inside her and she cried out for more of him, but he withdrew and stood up trembling. Harjith pulled her between his legs guiding himself into her mouth. By force she was sucking him, her head held firmly between his strong hands. Then there were two other hands stroking her thighs and Kuljit was inside her like an animal. She felt herself tense and wished she had some cocaine. It was rape but she had to go through with it if she wanted to come out in one piece. Yelling something in Punjabi, a primitive high pitched yell which sent needles through her, Karjith came in her mouth. She gagged and must have passed out because when she came to she was alone with Kuljit, the eldest. He smelled of sandalwood. He had turned her on her back and covered her with a fur. He squatted beside her, a naked giant stoking her forehead and speaking in broken English, his handsome face serious if not kindly behind a flowing black beard flecked with gray.

"I am oldest brother," he whispered, taking her in his arms as though she were a small toy. "Harpal my babou, I teach him everything. Now you meet the teacher."

He manipulated her body skillfully like a sculptor playing with clay, each time entering her slowly, pressing her thighs and buttocks into new shapes.

The pressure inside her increased. Her nails dug into his back. She started to scream but he filled her mouth with his tongue. She opened her eyes to see his inches away, wide open, watching. Then she exploded and wave after wave of pleasure ran through her until she lay senseless floating on a lake where beautiful white water lilies nodded heavily in the sun. She could hear the slap slap slap of the water on the sides of a boat as she lay snuggled between her father's legs.

When she finally opened her eyes again, Harpal was standing over her, staring down at her gravely, a blue silk lunghi around his waist. She couldn't speak but extended her arm, catching his leg just above the calf, drawing him closer. He sat down beside her on the floor.

"Now you know how bad we are," he said sadly, looking away. "But you must forgive them, it is our custom and you must forgive me as I must observe that custom."

"Always?" Laura asked.

"Usually only with prostitutes," he replied.

She kept her fury hidden and drawing his face down kissed his eyes. He stretched out beside her and as she moved over him kissing his neck, sucking and biting his nipples, he became excited again. She wasn't a prostitute but maybe she was worse. A witch perhaps. Her head went down kissing his thighs, caressing his penis like a sacred object. Then abruptly she raked her long nails across the small of his back, drawing blood.

"Bitch!" he yelled struggling to pin her down. But she got free, and jumping on top of him, sank her nails into the tender flesh just under his armpits. Crying out, he twisted away. Blood trickled down his sides. He became enraged. Before she could get up he had his knee on her back and had pinned her face down. The sperm of his brothers was in her vagina and he decided to bugger her. He had never before buggered a woman, only young boys—kept as prostitutes, trained for the purpose. He liked it. His grandfather's boys were famous, a few even dressed as girls. The boys were tight and he, Harpal, was big. The victim usually squirmed and cried out, but always succumbed. Now he watched her sphincter muscle expand and contract as it swallowed him up like a mouth. Lying on top of her he massaged her clitoris until she began to arch up involuntarily. Panting with rage and lust she cried out and he could feel her orgasm. Then trembling he exploded inside her over and over again.

For a long while they lay silent and motionless together. Finally Laura got up and brought a hot towel to bathe him but he was asleep. She felt tired but triumphant. She'd outlasted them all. She showered, and when she came back he'd awakened. His eyes were slits.

"I'm sorry," he gestured weakly.

"Turn over and I'll do your back." She pushed at him gently. The nail marks had stopped bleeding, but the muscles of his back were tense. She kneaded and stroked his back, applying pressure to a special place that Jeff

43

had shown her low on the spine. Soon he was asleep.

Quickly she examined her clothes. The snaps on her pants were ripped off. She put them on and tied a turban cloth around her waist to hold them up. Her blouse was a mess, but she decided it wouldn't be noticed beneath her shawl, which was still intact.

"Good enough to get to the hotel," she thought and with her hand on the elevator door, paused. What else? She wanted to teach them a lesson. But what was the lesson? She'd been treated like a prostitute: weren't prostitutes always paid?

Bending over Harpal's sleeping form she carefully removed a large diamond ring from his index finger, another with sapphires and diamonds and from a third finger an enormous pigeon's blood ruby set in gold.

"Gentlemen never wear jewelry," she could hear her mother saying.

When Laura arrived at the hotel the entrance was deserted, except for Jeff who happened to be waiting for a taxi with two girls.

"I'm taking them home," he said quietly. "Be back in a few minutes. Don't go to sleep, we have to make plans."

In the room she threw off her clothes and ran for the tub. When Jeff returned she was still in it and he noticed the bruises where Harpal had hit her.

"I went off with a Sikh," she answered cooly. "I wanted a taste. Turned out he had two brothers and it's their custom to share."

"You took on all three?" Jeff stared at her in disbelief.

"And you were right, they did treat me like a prostitute," Laura laughed. She hoped her confession was upsetting him.

"So I tried to think of myself that way and didn't put up a fight. Anyhow, I'm alive and that's something. They were all over six feet, very rough, very expert. You don't really know a country 'til you've fucked with the people, do you? Enlightening . . . but corny too."

"Corny?" Jeff's eyebrows went up.

"Can't explain . . . There was no contact—I was just an object. I'm sure *you* understand that. Like rabbits."

"But don't prostitutes get paid?" he said coolly.

She splashed him. "Hand me my bag," she said.

He held it out to her.

"My hands are all wet, open it and see what you find."

He brought out a gold box.

"Open it."

"They *gave* you these?" he asked, withdrawing the rings.

"They treated me like a prostitute so I behaved like one."

"But you can't do this, Laura," he said, as if she were a naughty child. "Do you have any idea how much this thing alone is worth?" He held up the gold box.

"That's not the point, it's the idea that's important."

He sighed. "This box, it's solid gold. Must be worth a hundred thousand. They'll be coming around here mad when they wake up."

"No they won't." Laura smiled, shampooing her hair. "They're afraid I might tell the wrong people. That," she pointed to the gold box, "will keep them from telling anyone. It would cause too much embarrassment."

"But they'll be after it on the sly," Jeff worried.

"Maybe, but I'll be gone by then. I've decided to go away with Alex's teacher."

Jeff gaped at her.

"You certainly don't need me here. We've more or less established our identity, now it's just a waste of time for me."

"How long will you be gone?" he asked uncertainly.

"No idea. Can't you do without me?

Jeff feared his own weaknesses if left alone. How could he ever explain that? Although he hadn't been treating her well he was deeply attached to her.

"I have a certain amount of work here," he said. "I want to get rid of as many trips as I can. It's starting out well. But I'd like to leave as soon as possible. Bombay by the middle of April."

"That's three months," she said. "I won't be gone *that* long."

"But this is India, Laura."

"What is that supposed to mean?"

"I mean you can't say just like that how long you'll be or how long I'll be. Can't you see nothing works, there's no communication system. Once you leave you can't really say you'll ever be back."

"Nonsense," she retorted.

"Don't you feel it in the air?"

"No, I don't. Just because you have to yell on the telephones doesn't mean they don't work. And there are trains and the mails. Don't worry. I don't plan to disappear. I'll be back long before you think."

"It's important for you to come to Bombay."

"Then I'll meet you there," she replied irritably. She found it ironic that he should treat her so casually but resist her going on a trip by herself.

"I think we should leave this place in a few hours," he said, "I don't want those three guys storming in here. Too much at stake."

"I'll stay up and pack then," Laura agreed. "Where will we go?"

"To Sundar's. He's invited us and it's what Stan said to do in case of any emergency. Have you made arrangements to leave with this *gooroo?*"

"You don't have to say it like that," she said, irritated. "You'd better phone Sundaram."

*   *   *

45

"He wasn't even pissed at being dragged out of bed," Jeff reported after he'd called. "Said he more or less expected it."

"What did you tell him?"

"Nothing. Just that we were fed up with this place. That we'd be round before breakfast."

"Does he suspect you're dealing acid?"

"No. He took some himself the other night at Dorje's, though. Probably thinks Dorje has it."

"Anyway you'd better keep the suitcases locked at his house." She paused. "I think I'll call him now."

"Who?"

"Indra. Alex's Teacher."

"Can't you do that at Sundaram's? We should get packed and ..."

"It's almost 4:30, he'll be up. Maybe if I call this early we'll be able to leave today."

She picked up the phone and asked for the number before Jeff could protest. There was an immediate answer on the other end.

"Hello, No, I'm not asleep. Yes, we can leave anytime ... what is this Sundaram's address?"

She gave him the number which he repeated.

"Then I'll be there for you at eleven. If you have warm clothes bring them. Otherwise you can get what you need where we're going."

He hung up abruptly, leaving her holding the receiver. "Certainly don't waste talk in this country, do they?" she said.

"No," said Jeff, "Things happen fast. A guy brought 200,000 trips from me this evening. The whole transaction took ten minutes."

"You've got that much money on you?" she gasped.

"Not quite. He gave me a check on a Swiss account. It has to go to Stan first, when it clears he'll get the stuff."

Laura was relieved. "Really, you know, these people are all heavies. You must promise to be careful."

*   *   *

A. K. Sundaram's face remained expressionless as Laura described her evening. That she took some loot amused him immensely.

"My South Indian soul revels in such mischief with Sikhs," he chuckled. "It will drive him absolutely crazy when he finds the jewels gone. You'd best return them though or his brothers will make things rough for him."

"Poor Harpal," she said. "But couldn't he have sent them away?"

"Certain clans from Punjab are very incestuous, especially theirs. They enjoy doing things together you might say—communal life, you

46

know.'' He laughed. "Shall I return the trinkets for you?'' he added after a pause, looking straight at her. "You certainly don't want them?''

"Firing from the hip,'' she thought.

"No, I don't want them, of course,'' she said aloud. "Just wanted to stop them from gloating or gossiping. I may look it but I'm not a Methodist missionary.''

"My dear,'' Sundar retorted, "all you foreigners are missionaries. Everyone who comes here from abroad thinks they are on a mission of one sort or other. After all, India is supposed to be underdeveloped.'' He guffawed, staring directly at Jeff. "But I think I will let Harpal spend the day trying to locate you and at five this afternoon I will send word that his trinkets are in my possession. When he comes and receives the good verbal lashing he deserves he'll have been sufficiently reprimanded. These people have their private mafias, you know. India has always been ruled by family gangs....'' Sundar thought a minute. "I will demand a commission, and I'll donate one ring to a good cause—in your name. To leprosy, maybe. At least you'll know your efforts weren't entirely in vain.''

He paused and took Laura's hand.

"My dear girl,'' he said, "India is an odd place. You might be in a dangerous situation four months from now, who knows? Maybe hanging from some Himalayan cliff. And there, out of nowhere, would be Harpal to save you.''

She gave him the box with the rings in it. He held it, clicking his tongue.

"So they are putting their money in gold nowadays? Very interesting. I doubt they have paid any tax on it. If they leave things like this lying about what do they have locked up? They'll be most upset that I have seen it.''

"That's what I thought,'' Jeff said.

"I'll call them later this morning,'' Sundar said. "No point in prolonging the agony. They might kill each other.

III

AT EXACTLY 11:00 A.M. a servant announced that Indra was waiting in a car outside.

"Will you come and say hello to him?" asked Laura.

"This is not America, my dear," replied Sundar. "We aren't what you call folksy here. We're not even really one nation. Just a collection of fiercely independent clans, and although we respect each other's rights we aren't gregarious. He's a very shy man. Useless conversation between us would embarrass him."

"Be careful," Jeff said, taking her in his arms. "Got your backpack?"

"Yes, everything. See you in Bombay. Do you know where you'll be staying?"

"Ambassador, I guess." He glanced at Sundaram who was smiling broadly.

"Yes," said Sundaram, laughing. "By all means, the Ambassador. It belongs to your friend Harpal. You see, Laura? One Himalayan cliff, coming up in Bombay!"

*   *   *

"Are you all right?" said Indra quietly from the deep padding of the limousine.

"There it was again," thought Laura, "that frustrating question..."

"Yes, of course," she replied, slipping into the opposite corner of the seat as the car moved out into traffic.

"This is for your sake." He gestured at the car. "I usually travel by bus or train, but I thought you might be tired after last night. In the car you'll be able to rest. Here, lie down on the seat and I'll sit here." He pulled down one of the jump seats.

She lay down thinking what a weird scene it was to be riding in a limousine with a half-naked yogi whose hair, now untied, hung to his waist. "What makes you think I'm tired?"

"Didn't you have a rather strenuous evening?" he asked patiently.

"I was up quite late," replied Laura brushing a strand of hair out of her face. "I suppose I look tired."

"The loot you took," he said pointedly. "What has happened to that?"

"How could you know about that?" gasped Laura.

"I was watching."

"Watching? From where?"

"From here." Indra pointed to his brow.

"You were watching me from here." She repeated the gesture.

"I watched some of it. I hope you were persuaded to return the loot. Those boys can be tough. It would be dangerous for your friend Jeff."

"You're telling me you watched me last night, saw everything?" she stared wide-eyed at the limousine's padded ceiling. She wanted to scream.

"What is all that to me?" he answered calmly. "I am out of this world. This humdrum morality, it is all custom...all relative. Balance is always restored one way or another." He laughed softly. "One man may like to eat roast pig, another drinks all night, another prays all day, another has intercourse all night. For every act there is a reaction." He turned his palm up, then down. "Each action is echoed back and balanced out by opposites. It is the law of **this** world." He gestured outside the car. "When you get partly out of it, you'll know. That's why I can go and see whom I like whenever I like."

"Do you know Harpal?" Laura asked.

"You mean the Harpal you were with last night?" he replied. "Yes, many times over, he is one of our mass-produced products. But my dear Laura Weatherall, you are testing me," Indra said sternly.

"Yes, I was," she admitted, truly shaken. Like others, she'd found the idea of clairvoyance groovy or far out. Confronted with its real implications however, her systems signaled *Danger.* She curled up on the seat feeling cold. "Should I feel guilty?" she asked.

"Do you feel guilty?"

"That's the problem. The Laura Weatherall part of me feels guilty, but there's another part that feels free, unblemished, never feels guilty at all, only joy...pleasure. Is that wrong?"

"Are these joys and pleasure feelings beyond fear?" he asked, leaning forward, athletic-looking, intense. "For if they aren't, isn't it true they're not free?"

Laura couldn't answer.

"Is it unafraid, this deeper part of you that feels only joy and pleasure? Has it embraced the fearful? When pleasure is over will this deeper part still feel a joy that is able to resist the outer one, the Laura Weatherall one?"

"Onion skins inside onion skins," Indra whispered, gesturing a forefinger. "You are getting at this knowledge through sex, which is one way, but not the best way. Liberation through the world of desire can catch you in the skin trap. Yes? Trapped in this." He pinched his smooth flesh. "I suppose it is important to go through it if there is no other way."

He sighed, and leaning back, gazed out the window at the disasterous poverty of the Delhi suburbs. "A hole is a hole," he said with a sidelong glance at her, "and what fills it, fills it. And the pleasure liberates you for a little while, but there are other ways, even more pleasurable," he said emphatically, "once you learn them."

*   *   *

Indra sat, watching the landscape slide by, a landscape so altered, it bore little resemblance to anything he'd once known. He let her sleep and finally as dusk overtook them, unpacked some food from a compartment under the jump seat. "Why go on with this?" he thought, looking at her. But it had happened that way. It was not his action.

The smell of coffee woke her.

"I've been asleep a long time," Laura whispered, lifting herself on one elbow.

"Sleep is good," he said gently, handing her coffee.

It tasted of spices and pepper and real cream.

She glanced out the window but saw only her reflection. "How long have we been driving?" she asked.

"It's almost midnight now. Just before dawn we'll arrive at the outskirts of a village where they know me under a different form. There will be a place to stay. You'll change into clothes I've brought for you. The village lies at the beginning of the foothills, in jungle land called the Terai. From there we'll walk to another place."

Finishing her coffee she drifted off again and dreamed of her father—whom she'd never been permitted to disturb from his endless financial transactions. He was alone in a vast office waving an American flag shouting orders to people outside who looked in at him through the windows. Then she saw her unbalanced mother, her face a disaster from years of martinis and sweet desserts. She was trying to drive her Rolls somewhere, eating a chocolate ice cream cone that dripped into her lap. Laura woke giggling. In her infrequent dreams she'd never seen her parents looking so real.

Soon the car stopped. The first pink glow of dawn illuminated a lush landscape. She slipped into the rust colored skirt and blouse which Indra handed her. There were also a pair of rubber sandals and a faded red wool shawl. When she'd finished dressing Indra braided her hair and tucked some roadside flowers into it. Handing her a small cloth bag, also red, into

50

which her essentials had been put, he said a few words to the driver. The car made a fast U-turn and disappeared.

It had been years since Laura had walked anywhere in the country. The rising sun shot rays of light through the jungle ozone and pungent wood smoke hung in layers. Soon roosters were crowing, peacocks screamed, and the sound of water rushing through steams and irrigation canals to the plains beyond, soothed her nerves. Flowers of every description bloomed in the hedgerows and the fields were high with wheat, mustard and marijuana.

They came to several roadside shops—haphazardly patched together with discarded boards; covered with tin roofs. Inside, where open fires were already glowing, boys prepared food while old men in white dhotis and turbans, some wrapped around their ears to ward off the morning chill, sat stoically sucking hookas and sipping tea from brass cups.

At the outer limits of the village, numerous people were squatting at the edges of neat green fields performing their morning ablutions, each seemingly oblivious of the others.

"Them that shits together stays together," observed Indra with a Texas drawl.

"Where did you learn to talk like *that?*" asked Laura, startled.

"American soldiers. I knew some long ago in Burma."

Past the fields they came to mango groves surrounded by crumbling walls. There were houses too, most of them mud, with thatched roofs. Upon seeing Indra, several passersby clasped their hands. "Salaam, Babaji," said an old man in a long black frock coat, bowing his shaved head. A boy ran up to them and after touching Indra's bare feet, turned shyly and ran back toward the center of the village. There were no motors. The only conveyances were slow creaking ox carts, pony-drawn tongas carrying children to school, and bicycles that shared the road with donkeys, pigs, water buffaloes, cows, and stray horses.

Soon many villagers were coming to meet them. "Nameste, Maharaji," and "Salaam, Baba" mixed as both Hindus and Moslems paid their respects. Some were smiling, others deeply serious, touched Indra's feet and fell flat on the ground in front of him. A number of children trailed behind them. "Vat iss your name? Vat is your native place?" they yipped at Laura.

Indra said something in Hindi and they stopped.

"I told them you are French," he said under his breath. "They are taught those two ridiculous sentences in their classrooms nowadays and want to practice their 'English' on you. They don't study French."

A leper caught sight of them and came shuffling along, his stubby oozing hands outstretched. "Maharaj," he wailed, "Maharaj."

Indra threw him a coin which landed in the dust. Smiling, the man picked it up between his toes.

"His too is the smile of the Divine One," Indra said, "note it well. The smile of destruction."

The village was a jumble of decaying provincial administrative buildings from the days of the British Raj, and other haphazardly erected dwellings in various states of disrepair.

"What happened here?" asked Laura sensing some disaster.

"Many things," Indra said, "from time out of mind. Much blood has been spilled here. The last calamity was an epidemic of cholera about fifty years ago, brought about by the magic of some fakir who had been mistreated by the inhabitants. After a year most of them were dead." He winked.

They came to a small hut of mud and stone in a grove of old mangoes, surrounded by a low stone wall. Behind it a grassy pasture, clipped like a lawn by grazing cows, sloped gently down to a small river where villagers were beating wet clothes on rocks. Herons and kites wheeled in the air, glittering against the sun.

Stooping to enter the low opening of the hut, Indra beckoned Laura to follow. Inside in a pit filled with white ash, a fire smoldered.

"Sit here to my left and slightly behind. Cover your head with the shawl; the more motionless you can sit, the higher you'll score in their estimation." He smiled, indicating the villagers who were gathering outside.

"Women will come to wash my feet. There will be singing and worship and one of them will feed me. They will also set out a plate for you. You *must* eat all of it even if you don't like it. After some time, we'll be left alone. Then in the evening there will be a repeat performance. There's a small room behind this where later you may sleep."

He grinned and his dark eyes twinkled. "Eat, rest, and be merry," he whispered, "for tomorrow I begin to kill you."

Although startled Laura had no time to consider the meaning of what he'd said. A woman had entered, her steel gray hair pulled back tightly above refined features, carrying a large brass bowl filled with pungent water which she placed in front of Indra. Kneeling she gently lifted his leg and put his right foot in the water.

"And how would you like to go," he said in English, glancing at Laura while the woman bathed him. "By fire or by water?"

"What?"

"You must answer," he said. "How would you prefer to go?"

"To go where?" she said flatly.

"Out of your body, to go out of your body."

"You mean when you kill me?"

The woman was now washing his left foot.

52

"Yes."

"But I don't want to go anywhere," she whispered, "I'm very happy right here."

There was a pause as the woman wiped Indra's feet gently with a fresh towel. Then she lifted up the bowl of dirty water and gazing directly into Indra's eyes began to drink it.

Laura winced.

"Are you all right?" he said aside to her placing his hand on the woman's head. "Are you still happy where you are?"

The woman began to back out. Laura felt slightly ill.

"Here you will see many strange things you may not understand. Do not, as they say, 'freak out.' If you drank that water you would probably get typhoid. But if you believe me, nothing can harm you, remember, *nothing.*"

"That woman has faith by birth," she said, thinking that she would never have enough faith to drink bath water.

He nodded.

"I would have to learn mine," she thought, and doubted it was possible.

A young man came in with a small hand organ, some tobacco and hashish which he presented to Indra. Then he prostrated himself. Indra warmed his hands over the fire, seemingly indifferent to the supine figure.

"You can't 'learn' faith," he continued, staring into the fire. "It comes either by circumstance of birth, or through certain experiences, usually at times of great danger to you. According to the ancient teaching, you must be born on this soil, Aryavata." He thumped his fingers on the mud floor. "Otherwise, you must die here and be reborn. I know it sounds parochial, but I can't help that." Smiling gently, he laughed and placed his left hand on the head of the prostrate young man who rose and backed away meekly, his hands pressed together.

"He's been extremely unfaithful and mischievous. That's why he had to wait," Indra hissed.

Laura found him unnerving. This man who moved in so many worlds—who was he really? Was he joking or serious?

A group of women of assorted ages had come crawling into the small space holding the ends of their saris frimly between their teeth, forming a half-veil to indicate modesty. Their leader presented a large brass pot filled with tea which Indra placed on the glowing coals. He had prepared a small chillum of tobacco and hashish, and was drawing deeply from it. Finishing, he poured tea into brass cups which he passed to the women and Laura. The women held their cups and began singing softly. One woman beat a drum. Finally Indra coughed, took up the hand organ and began tuning it. The women droned on and finally Indra began to accompany them, lifting their off-key voices to the proper level, taking up their song and drowning them out.

Laura sat up. Who could have imagined he would sound like this. More a force than a voice. A bridge across life manifesting courage. It made her want to faint, to wail and dance. Turning he gazed at her and as the music faded, only his eyes were there, floating in the smoke.

After receiving an ash mark from his thumb between their eyebrows and prostrating themselves one by one, the women left.

Outside in the shade of the mangoes it was already midday. Only a few people still lingered and though waves of heat and light filtered through the leafy cover, inside the hut it was dark and cool.

A woman entered with food, spooning quantities of a gruel-like substance onto two large brass plates heaped with rice. From another pot she added big round pieces of unleavened bread. After pouring water over Laura's hands and giving her a towel with which to dry them, the woman presented her with one of the plates. Repeating this procedure with Indra she then seated herself in front of him and began to feed him.

"Poor people's food," grunted Indra, "standard fare here."

With a singleminded relentlessness, the woman stuffed food into Indra's mouth.

"Healthiest food you'll ever eat," he said, swallowing, "and remember you *must* clean your plate. But not too soon or she will give you more." He raised an eyebrow. "See my plight. I must eat until she thinks I'm full—it's part of the ritual."

The flies had found the food and hovered in swarms. There were so many it was difficult for Laura to get the bread from the plate to her mouth without swallowing a few accidentally.

"Don't think about it," Indra said. "Eat the plate if necessary. Remember, they're *giving* it and they are poor people." He opened his dark eyes wide. "For them it is a great sacrifice."

She looked weakly at her plate, still half full, crawling with flies.

"You must learn how to stock up like a camel. Some days we may not get food."

Finally Laura forced the last morsel down and water was quickly brought for her to wash a second time. She found a certain irony in washing when it was obvious the flies didn't wash.

"Rest now," Indra said, motioning to the small room in the rear. "It's the hot time of day. I'll lie down out here."

The meal seemed to have formed an insoluble lump in her stomach and she was thankful to be able to stretch out on the straw mat. There was a low window about a foot square through which she could see the river through a haze of shimmering heat. Here and there groups of people dozed beneath the ancient trees.

"Out of time," Laura thought, closing her eyes. "Paradise never seems to choose those who inhabit it."

The sharp cries of birds roused her and Indra, his face hovering in the doorway, handed in a cup of steaming tea.

"It's cooler now," he said. "Time to go for a bath. Bring your towel and that large cloth."

When she emerged from the door of the hut he was there waiting. A crowd of about fifty people had gathered, all sitting silently. Laura noticed a number of naked men who appeared to be yogis.

"They have come to test me," Indra said. "Most of them are sorcerers. I will deal with them later. First the bath."

At the river's edge children were bathing hedonistic blue-black water buffaloes, who lounged in the water chewing their cuds. Young farmers, male and female, bathed their sinuous bodies in the crystal clear water. Nearby the grinding stones of a mill clattered cheerfully. The air was filled with the scent of cannabis and jasmine. Golden fields of mustard and emerald cane sloped away into the late afternoon haze toward the Ganges.

Indra took Laura by the hand and led her far out into the shallow river. Jumping from rock to rock and wading through small pools, they reached an area surrounded by bullrushes and papyrus. There he showed her how to gargle, to blow water out through her nose yogi fashion and how to bathe under a cloth.

"It's extremely important one never be seen while bathing," he said. "Don't ask why."

Then he hurried away through the rushes to have his own bath. When he returned she was floating on her back, listening to the water bubble about her. He showed her how to put a cloth around herself and to dress inside it.

They returned in the failing light. Smoke from the evening fires hung in the still cool air like veils. At the hut the waiting crowd of devotees and curious villagers had doubled. Their faces glowed the color of burnished copper in the light of a large fire, which had been built in a pit outside the door. Laura ducked into the hut to dry her hair over the inside fire and watched, hidden, as outside Indra, naked, dried his hair in front of an audience, squeezing out the four-foot long strands and snapping them—whiplike—until they dried.

A young woman darted from the crowd and offered him scarlet hibiscus blossoms. Indra sat down cross-legged in front of the fire facing the crowd. Smoke undulated about him. Without turning he flung back his left arm, and snapped his thumb and forefinger as a sign for Laura to come out.

Laura, her head covered with the red shawl emerged from the door, seating herself behind him to the left. Around them were piled fruits, sweets, and other food offerings. A very dignified old man wearing a Gandhi cap sat to their immediate right, waving incense.

Indra picked up a three-foot long silver pincer resembling a sword, called a chimtah, with which he stirred the fire. One large and three small iron rings were attached to the grasping end. When he brought it crashing down on the burning logs the clang of metal and flying sparks sent ecstatic fervor rippling through the crowd.

Withdrawing a quantity of white ash from the fire he applied it to his body, patting and dusting for almost five minutes. Again he plunged the chimtah into the fire. This time he withdrew a small black coal which he ground into powder and applied with his thumb to his forehead. Muttering incantations he applied the same mark to Laura and the old gentleman on his right. Then with a substance from a small round box he applied three red spots in a triangular pattern around the black.

The crowd was silent except for a strange man in his late thirties who kept looking at Laura, talking what seemed like nonsense. His athletic body was partly covered with rags, on which hundreds of buttons, bangles, and trinkets were sewn, tied, or pinned. He could have been a freak, a court jester, or the village idiot. His head bobbed up and down quickly, like a water bird, and from his shaved head weird predatory eyes glittered. Laura felt unnerved.

"Moslem sorcerer," Indra whispered, "rascal, he needs punishment." He paused. "Would you like to see him dance?"

Sitting very erect, arms held stiff, Indra stared at the fire, muttering under his breath. It was then, for the first time, Laura saw that he was becoming invisible. That she could actually see through him. What remained took the form of an old disheveled sphinx. Many in the crowd covered their faces in fright.

The strange man toward whom Indra now focused made faces, obscene gestures and shouted in a mixture of Urdu, Hindi and Bengali.

Out of the almost invisible form beside her he spoke.

"Within five minutes that man will begin to dance. Watch."

A few moments later the man began gesticulating wildly yelling at the other yogis and sadhus, who sat silently watching. Then rising slowly, he screamed and pointed to the place where the transformed Indra sat. When he had got up altogether he began to dance like a marionette as if his limbs were being manipulated. As he danced he removed his clothes humming nervously and suddenly burst into a high-pitched song. "Like a prostitute from Lahore or Dacca," Indra whispered. Someone in the crowd began to accompany the singing with weird sounds from a hand organ. Whirling and wriggling in the flickering firelight, the spellbound man fell in a frenzy and rolled in the dust, clutching his stomach with both hands as though he'd been shot. The dust stuck to his sweaty body and turned to mud as he jerked spasmodically like a dying animal. Resuming his ordinary shape, Indra stood up, and with his foot nudged the body gently until it sprawled full length on its belly.

Laura was holding her breath, the scene strange beyond anything she'd ever imagined.

"I have just managed to—as you would say—exorcise this animal," Indra said dryly. "Are you all right? I've removed a demon from him and frightened it away. Really, the Christians got the demon business all wrong. Demons are just disembodied souls that manage to squeeze into new bodies. Sometimes they are better than the one already there. This one will be a different person when he wakes up, but not for long. He's a very bad case—quite mad from having two people inside him. Of course he'll want to follow us now, but I'm too lazy." Indra wavered. "And I'll not allow it," he said finally, "he's just another fourth class sadhu. He'd never be able to get the real thing so where is the point to it."

Many of the yogis who had been waiting to test Indra now prostrated themselves before him, touching his feet, leaving presents and offerings. A young Moslem fakir poured sparkling gems from a chamois bag.

"Now I've frightened them," Indra murmured, blessing each with a smudge of ash on the forehead. "Please observe. If I'd used words to describe the problem of the man, given a lecture on insanity or schizo-phrenia—they'd have argued with me or wouldn't have understood. Instead, I've used my shakti.* A yogi gets more of this shakti than others through his practice. They are scared stiff now. Ridiculous, yes?" He patted the head of a very old woman who nuzzled his right foot, waiting for his blessing. "You can't cure insanity by words. What you have seen is the only way."

Indra put a smudge of ash on the woman's forehead and then fell silent. A stream of devotees, many of whom had walked long distances, now came forward respectfully, whispering a word or two as they prostrated themselves before him. Whole families approached. Children were pushed to the ground by nervous parents. On each Indra would place his hand, muttering softly but not looking. He remained aloof: serene and implacable.

After the people had gone they sat in a silence, broken only by the crackling of the fire and the cries of night herons hunting in the river. Indra smiled, muttered something in Hindi to the old man in the Gandhi hat, who was preparing a chillum, withdrew from the fire a small glowing coal which he placed on top of the pipe and after inhaling deeply, took up his stringed instrument and sang.

His voice floated over the rhythm of the strings—an otherworldly

*shakti: spiritual energy—force

sound, running past stops, crying out at men and gods alike. Dredging up memories, opening doors, bouncing off her inner self, his music made Laura feel like weeping.

A waning moon hung in the sky over the mangoe trees and a warm wind had come up from the plains. The fire was low. The old man with the Gandhi hat had fallen asleep.

"Are you all right, Laura Weatherall?" Indra paused smiling. He looked as fresh as when the evening began.

She nodded.

"Then you'd better get some sleep, tomorrow we move on. There will be horses for us at three-thirty in the morning. We must escape this place before the sun rises and people can follow us."

IV

MISTS WERE RISING. The night sounds of the jungle were giving way to the chattering of monkeys, and whistling mynah birds. Laura could just make out that they had come to a river wash strewn with twisted driftwood, thorn trees, and massive boulders. Beyond, the foothills of the Himalayas rose like a wall against the first light of morning. It was cold and the horses' breath steamed white in the darkness.

Indra dismounted. "I'll make some bread and tea and then we'll rest," he said, helping her down off the horse. "Come gather some wood with me, it will get your circulation going."

He lit the first small pile of twigs while Laura gathered more. Soon the pungent aroma of spicy tea filled the air and he was kneading wheat flour in a round brass bowl.

Taking the ball of dough gently between his palms, he rolled it gently, pressing it and slapping it until it became a pie-shaped disk about nine inches in diameter.

"Roti wallah,* har har," he grinned holding out the disk of dough. "You have seen them, no? The men who sell these rotis on the streets?" Into the fire went the dough, which puffed up into a balloon that he turned until it was golden brown. "Catch," he said, tossing the bread into her hands.

She caught the balloon but it was too hot to hold.

"Put it in your lap to cool," he directed, handing her a brass cup filled with tea. "Watch out, that's hot too."

She waited while he prepared his bread, returning some to the flames as a sacrifice along with a few drops of tea.

They ate in silence. He wolfed his food hungrily.

"Don't you ever have indigestion?" she asked.

"Too full of poisons," he said, chewing. "Best not to think too much about food. As I told you before, eat the plate if necessary."

"Could you eat that?" She pointed to the brass plate.

---

*Roti wallah: one who makes and sells unleavened bread called rotis.

"If you ground it up with a file I would happily eat it," he replied laughing. "But it's copper underneath. I'd be out of my senses for a week or so. You'd have to take care of me."

*   *   *

Stretching out on his shawl, he sighed and rolled over on his stomach gazing at her. "Alone at last eh? Laura Weatherall. It's not right. I must think of another name for you." He smiled, resting his head on his hands. "Don't let me sleep too long. We have twelve hours to go before we reach the top of those hills. There's a temple there where we'll rest a day or so before going on."

He was soon fast asleep and something about his smile and the way he had pronounced her name gave Laura the impression that she had at last taken on some sort of reality for him, had passed some sort of test. "What a strange being," she thought, observing him. She knew she was deeply attracted to him. He looked like a hero resting after battle, a young Ulysses. The thought that he was sixty only increased her feeling. He said that he was out of this world, but why then was he so sensual, so full of energy and vitality? She wished he would touch her, hold her. She would have made love to him in a moment, and wondered whether it was entirely out of the question. Yet she was also afraid he might know her feelings for him, for she feared his power, and the deep mystery that surrounded him. Spreading out a blanket near by she lay down, and fell into a fitful sleep filled with frustrating unfinished dreams.

Less than an hour later she was awakened by a sharp blow on her leg, and opened her eyes to see an enormous monkey the size of a small man, standing only a few feet away, about to throw a rock at her. Frantically she tugged at Indra's hand. He woke with a start and was instantly on his feet, chimtah in hand, running after the animal, who seemed to be the leader of a large band that had surrounded them. "Ahoo," Indra yelled. "Ahoo, Ahoo," chasing them for some distance, jumping from rock to rock, like one of them.

"Ah," he said, when he returned, covered with sweat, "it's getting warm. I slept too long. It's just as well they woke us. Can you see that white spot up there?" He pointed to the hills. "That's our first stop. We must reach it by sundown. It's a safe place, out of the jungle. Now let's bathe in the river, it's about a hundred yards from here. The horses can drink, and we'll be on our way."

"And from now on I'll call you Uma." He helped her pack up the utensils. "That's your new name. I saw it in my sleep. I can't stand that Laura business."

"Uma?" she asked. "What does it mean?"

"It's the name of a fearful goddess." He laughed. "That will give you something to live up to."

*   *   *

After a week of walking and sleeping in small temples, they arrived at a sizeable town perched on a saddle of rock. Beyond, loomed the mountains: icy, remote, unreal. It was bitter cold and the streets were crowded with dirty near-naked coolies, huddled around open fires. In the bazaar old men sat smoking hookahs of opium and eating majoun, while they spun out raw wool or knitted it into sweaters.

A thin young man dressed in Western-style wool pants and a cable-stitched sweater appeared suddenly. Smiling at Indra with deep affection, he took the reins of the horses and led them through a maze of alleys that stank of open sewers and rancid street shop mustard oil. Finally passing through an archway they entered a compound where they dismounted. Frightened half-naked servants scurried out shivering, and disappeared with the luggage.

"Like the keep of a medieval castle," Laura thought as they followed the young man up a stone stairway.

"Where are we, and what's happening?" Laura whispered.

"Don't ask questions," Indra chided. "It spoils the drama."

"I will go now and tell my father you have come. He will be so happy to see you," said the young man in English, touching Indra's feet.

"Will he indeed?" Indra muttered to himself.

A servant conducted them to a small room in a tower of the enormous fortress-like house where a charcoal fire burned in an elaborate brass box and carpets and tapestries hung on the stone walls to keep out the dampness. They sat down, warming their hands and soon the wife of the household arrived and prostrated herself before Indra. Taking no notice of Laura she proceeded to wash Indra's bare feet with steaming water and afterward to anoint them with oil. Laura wondered whether she would drink the foot bath as the other woman had done, and when she didn't, Laura caught Indra winking at her across the fire.

After this, the room began to fill up. The old men of the family hobbled in first, grunting as they flopped onto the floor to prostrate before Indra. Then the younger men arrived, and last came a stream of women and girls. Tea and a tray of sweets were brought in. One of the old men began to sing softly, facing Indra and gesturing dramatically.

"He's the elder brother of the head man of this house," Indra whispered in English. "Spent his whole life running away to sit with sadhus and yogis, but he never had the guts to stay, give up this high life."

When the singing was over and after Indra passed the sweets to

61

everyone, they were taken downstairs through dark passageways into a large three-story room magnificently paneled with slabs of carved oak. On one side, the paneling had been opened to reveal a large curtained bed like a stage. They sat down in front of it and another ornate brazier filled with hot coals was brought in and placed before Indra.

After a short time a jaundiced hand appeared from inside the curtains and a gaunt man in his pajamas struggled out, groaning and fell on his knees where he remained for some time until Indra blessed him.

"After so long a time, now only you come to me," the sick man wailed. "I have been waiting a long time for you, Maharaji." He fixed his watery eyes on Indra. "Look at me! Nothing is left—even my eyes are losing sight. I am becoming a skeleton."

"This is Miss Weatherall—'Uma,'" Indra grunted.

The man took no notice. "Why have you taken so long to come?" he repeated, declaiming so the entire household might hear. "Why?" He thrust his bony hands toward Indra in supplication.

"Because you are an infidel, " roared Indra and the man fell back as though struck dumb.

"A faithless hypocrite, piling up money, drinking on the sly. You have cancer of the liver—I warned you not to drink but you continue because you don't believe me," Indra narrowed his eyes and showed a toothy demonic grin.

"But I watch you," he went on, "I can watch you from anywhere, anytime I please—and I have seen all the mean things you do."

The man shielded his face with a skinny arm.

"Boozing slyly, there in your bed, bossing all the poor women of your household, emasculating your sons with you sarcasm . . . They are all tired of you, you miser. Even your old mother over there in the corner has begun to despise you. Why should I do anything for you . . . devil! You are lucky to see me at all."

Prostrating himself again he clutched Indra's toes with trembling hands. "Please," he whispered hoarsely, "you must. You are a great saint—you must show kindness."

"Sometimes kindness means dispatching," Indra said, loosening the man's fingers. "You know dispatching, Mohan Singh? Now that you have reached the end you are frightened, eh? Get back into your bed, it is not good for you to get so excited. Your liver will get worse and I will be blamed."

Clutching at the side of the bed, the man lifted himself slowly and painfully through the curtains.

"It is easier for a camel to pass through the eye of a needle than for a rich man to enter into the Kingdom of Heaven," Indra said quietly. "I smell death in this house."

He stirred up the coals in the brass fire box while the youngest daughter placed a number of elaborate dishes of food before him.

"Don't eat too much," he cautioned Laura. "Don't ask why."

"I am fasting," he told the daughter in Hindi, "but this lady will have a little."

The girl looked disappointed but obediently took all the dishes away after Laura had taken as little as she could without seeming ungrateful.

The old mother, who had been watching from a corner, lurched across the room like a spider and knelt reverently before Indra. He kept her prostrate for some time before placing his hand on her head, bestowing the smudge of ash with his thumb.

"This animal is trying to outlive her son," he said to Laura under his breath. "They are all hypocrites. See all these photos?" He pointed to large framed portraits of chubby-looking men with shaved heads in orange robes and turbans. "They read all these false prophets and yet they call on me to come and heal them. All infidels, utterly lacking in faith. Let them sink, I say."

Laura was too tired to reply. She longed for sleep but she knew she was on exhibition and would probably have to sit as long as he sat with her knees flat on the floor and her back erect. She wondered whether a hot bath were a possibility.

Some time later the sick man's wife came in and after a few words with Indra in the local Pahari language, she motioned Laura to follow her.

"She'll show you to a room where you can bathe and rest until evening," Indra said. He smiled. "I will have to sit here. I'm not supposed to need any sleep because I'm considered immortal." He chuckled.

There was a knock on the door and a small boy appeared with a tray of tea and sweets. Her body ached all over. For a few moments she had no idea where she was. She had been with Jeff in a dream, they'd become separated and she was vainly looking for him. Then she caught the musty smell of the room and the present rushed in. The boy leaned against the bed, staring at her as though she were an apparition from space.

"Vat iss your name?" he asked.

"Laura," she answered.

He held the teacup out to her. "Maharaji is waiting for you," he said in stilted English. "Drink!" Handing her the cup he ran out of the room.

By the time she'd bathed, dressed, and rejoined Indra, the large room was full of people, the bed curtains were open and the sick man lay dazed, propped up by pillows, his head wrapped in a white silk scarf. Indra sat on the floor gazing into the fire. On his left were the women of the household and some curious friends, on his right the men filled up the remaining floor space. A large group of students, friends of the sons of Mohan Singh, had found places at the rear.

Indra motioned Laura to take her place beside him. A group of musicians hired for the occasion were tuning their instruments. The wife of the dying man lit incense sticks, waved them in front of Indra and stuck them in one side of the brazier. Then she lit bits of camphor on the end of a large brass salver, and waved the lights in front of him, clockwise, while her daughters rang bells and passed the lights to her husband who struggled from his bed, muttering sacred syllables while he waved the lights at Indra, almost burning him. After that followed sons, daughters, and grandparents until the entire family had waved lights.

One of the musicians began an invocation that was half song and half declamation, accompanying himself on a shruti box. He was joined by a violin and then a harmonium and after a while the room was rocking with music and song. Women and girls clanked chimes together in fast time. Some of the students began impiously to clap their hands. Indra held his silver chimtah horizontally, bouncing it in his open palms so that it made a metallic clanking that sounded like chains. Some of the students shouted in rhythm with the music: "Jai Govinda, Jai Jai Jai Ram. Hari Krishna, Jai Govinda." All the gods were invoked.

When the song-story was finished, Indra picked up his three-stringed instrument and began to tune it. He tuned and tuned, waiting for the people to stop fidgeting. They dared not leave, yet they were rich and not accustomed to waiting for anything. Laura had noted before how he used the tuning of his instrument as a psychological weapon. When the impatience of the trapped audience had reached its peak he began his song, a salute to Kali, the goddess of destruction. The fidgeting stopped at once for Kali was dangerous; her name was rarely mentioned in the houses of the rich though she lurked everywhere beneath the surface of their lives: Ma Kali, the destroyer-defender, the Goddess of death, of battlefields, cemeteries, and burning places. Ma Kali with her bowl of blood and her necklace of human heads.

A hush fell over the room and servants peeked from corners. The students in their imported polyester pants and expensive sweaters folded their hands and stared into their laps. The middle-aged sons of the dying man looked nervously here and there while the older folk stared intently at Indra, entranced, hearing a voice out of the long gone past. They knew the song well, and the power of the dark voice that flowed from his lips and from his eternally young body. He had turned a salute to himself into a celebration of death.

Overcome with emotion, the old mother of the dying man began to sing in a high, faltering voice, "Jai Kali, Jai Kali, Kalabvenasane, Jai Kali."

The others looked at her disapprovingly but she went on and was joined by her brother, the old man who had sat with many sadhus and yogis.

Then Indra did something that jolted them all. With one hand strumming his instrument and without stopping his song, he reached out and tossed his chimtah to Mohan Singh.

Laura could feel a wave of energy go through the room.

The dying man caught the chimtah with his feeble yellow hands and began bouncing it up and down in time with Indra's music. A boy grabbed the tabla from one of the musicians and started beating it wildly. The other boys all straightened up and began swaying. The middle-aged sons left the room.

"Ah," thought Laura, "these are the dangerous ones. They want to see their father dead and are afraid Indra will revive him." She had a sudden feeling, here in this medieval house tucked in the foothills of the Himalayas, that everything she had been trained to think of as reliable and bright might be a giant mistake.

The excitement was mounting. Indra had closed his eyes and was projecting all his power into each phrase. She noticed that he had begun to make himself transparent again and wondered if they could see it.

Before them all the dying man appeared to have come alive: his weak body now sat erect, held up by some force awakening within him. He bounced and rattled Indra's chimtah in time with the music. Color seemed to be returning to his haggard yellow face.

One of the sons reappeared with servants bearing hot drinks and sweets. It was obvious he wanted to put a stop to a scene which to his mind was getting out of hand. But seeing Indra the servants squatted down with their trays, afraid to pass out the food in spite of the nervous prodding of their master's son.

Suddenly Mohan Singh jumped out of bed and began to dance. To the horror of his family his white dhoti unwound and fell to the floor. He went on, his emaciated body clothed only in a pair of undershorts, bouncing on his skinny yellow legs, and flailing his hands and arms in poses of the Goddess Kali.

The old women began to groan and the old men to clap their hands. The dancer threw his glasses into the crowded room.

The old mother crept into her alcove off the main room and began to worship her private idols, waving a tiny oil lamp in front of them.

The students thought it a big joke: the great banker Mohan Singh, bad tempered Scrooge, scrounge, and secret drinker, was freaking out in front of their faces.

They clapped together in unison, egging him on, shouting:

"Hoy, Hoy, Hoy, Hoy!"

It sounded to Laura like a Cossack drinking bout.

Indra sat absolutely withdrawn except for the tips of his fingers and his lips as he guided the pace of the music, coming in just before the end of each round, and speeding up the rhythm imperceptibly so the momentum increased.

Neighbors began to wander in, having heard the sounds they knew meant something more than the usual evening of music at Mohan Singh's.

His sons stood in the corners near the doorways, their arms folded on their chests and their dark moustached faces flushed with embarrassment at seeing their father in such a state. They welcomed the new arrivals loudly, trying to disrupt the scene. But it was useless. Indra was too powerful for them. The room was spellbound, Mohan Singh was bewitched. Sons and neighbors squatted with the servants, their eyes fixed on Indra.

The music reached a frenzied peak. Mohan Singh stood immobilized in front of Indra, shuddering, his tongue locked outside his open mouth. Everyone knew that the malignant spirit which had inhabited his body was ready to come out. Indra had enchanted the beast that lurked within. Now he would kill it.

Just then the old man collapsed in front of Indra. He seemed to shrink up like a deflated balloon and then lay motionless on the floor.

There was an audible gasp.

At the same moment Indra crouched on his haunches, began to beat the body of Mohan Singh with his chimtah.

One of the sons lunged toward Indra but his uncle who had sat with sadhus caught his pants leg and brought him crashing into the laps of two astonished women.

The wife of the sick man counted furiously on her rosary of rudraksha beads, her eyes fixed on Indra and on the body of her husband.

Then the body moved. The hands went out, reached for Indra's feet, held them.

For a long time the room was silent; no one moved and only the smoke from the fire box curled into the air above the crowd. Then the servants left, carrying their trays to the kitchen. The students backed out through the doors. Everyone else vanished into the recesses of the house. Only the brother of Mohan Singh and his old mother remained. Both prostrated to Indra, received his blessing, exchanged whispered conversation with him, and disappeared.

Alone now except for Laura, Indra remained crouched over Mohan Singh, gazing into space. After a long while, he lifted the man into bed and shut the curtains.

"Are you all right, Uma?"

She stretched her cramped legs and was about to speak when he put his finger to his mouth.

"We must go at once," he whispered. "Tomorrow that animal will find he has been healed. I will have his disease. I must be at a certain place by that time. If I am here I'll be trapped for weeks by all sorts of sick people wanting to be cured. If I can be alone where I won't be bothered, I

66

can heal myself in three days." He helped her up. "Go to your room at once and collect your belongings. I will arrange for the horses to be brought round and to have two boys accompany us part of the way. We must make haste. I'll meet you at the rear of the house in a few minutes. Lose no time!"

V

IT WAS PITCH DARK in the deserted streets as the horses, bridle bells tinkling, made their way through the ancient maze of the town toward its eastern gate. Two boys holding burning tapers ran beside them. At the old gate Indra tossed a few coins and dismissed them.

As the cobblestones gave way to sand and clay and the road broadened, Indra urged his horse into a canter, then to a full gallop. Sitting erect with his hair piled high on his head, naked except for a loin cloth and billowing cape, he sped through the night with Laura riding hard at his heels. Again a feeling of dreamlike unreality possessed her. She felt involved in some otherworldly drama in which the gods were participating. Was she still a witness or had she become one of the players? She wondered.

They were riding up a steep walled canyon. In the east the sky had lightened. Reaching the summit they turned a corner and saw the peaks of the Himalayas glowing pink in the darkness like gigantic lamps, reflecting the first rays of the sun. The sight was so awesome Laura reined in her horse and almost fell off.

Indra slowed to a walk and turned around.

"Are you all right?" he called. "There's a tea shop just ahead, we'll stop there and rest."

Unbelievably as they rounded the bend there was a small stone building which seemed to be growing out of the cliff. A young man in ragged clothes ran out, greeted Indra, and helped them to dismount.

Laura was shocked when she saw him in the light. He'd aged perceptibly and looked like an old woman. Seeing that she was disturbed, he wrapped a shawl about his face, which only added to the transformation.

"This is the ancient road to Mount Kailas, the holiest pilgrimage place in all of Asia." he said. "These tea shops are spaced along it for hundreds of miles. Once the road was thronged with travelers—but now that is all finished. Our destination is only about five miles from here. I will take a bath down there in that stream and perform my morning prayers. Then we will go on. You can take a bath if you like, but the water is very cold."

He disappeared toward the sound of rushing water. Laura stumbled down a rocky hill toward a water course in the opposite direction. There seemed to be water everywhere, bubbling out of the mountain. She could feel the cold as she approached and wondered if she could bear it, but without letting herself stop to think she took off all her clothes and jumped in. The water was so cold it took her breath away and climbing out she felt burned rather than chilled. Shaking, she wrapped herself in a cloth, gathered up her clothes, and stumbled blindly up the path to the tea shop.

The proprietor, modestly excusing himself, bade her dress in front of his kitchen fire. Tea was bubbling in a brass pot. Removing the cloth Laura squatted naked before the fire until she stopped shaking. All the aches and pains from the long night's ride had vanished with the shock of the cold water. Feeling revitalized, she dressed and went out.

Now the great mountains were shimmering with blinding white light. She sat on a stone wall that edged the terrace in front of the shop, watching clouds form at the bases of the peaks, and patches of sun light up the forest below the snow line.

Indra came up the hill covered with his shawl and went directly to the kitchen. After some time he came out, bringing tea and freshly made bread. He looked refreshed, but she could see that the whites of his eyes had yellowed.

"Yes," he said. "Old man Singh's disease is on me. But don't worry," he shrugged. "I only require three days alone and it will be gone."

An old man and two boys were sitting nearby slurping their tea stoically, their pinched faces framed by ragged woolen scarves wound tightly against the morning cold.

"Maybe they'd feel better if they took a bath," Laura commented.

"Don't judge," said Indra sternly. "You would never have survived what they've survived, the solitude and poverty, the bad food—always getting the last and worst of everything shipped up from the plains." With a shrug he got up and paid the proprietor.

Mounted again they left the main road to follow the stream. The path wound precipitously down the mountain. Barren hills gave way to thickets of scrub oak, then forests of towering pines, deodars, and ancient rhododendron trees with scarlet blossoms.

The stream, meeting others, had become a river. Delicate green fern and white orchids thrived on its misty banks. "This is the way everything was forty years ago," whispered Indra. "From the first hills to here it was paradise—before the human greed got let loose."

Far down in a lower valley rose the gray stone towers of a temple complex. Gigantic fir trees hovered over it, their ancient gnarled branches like arms protecting the walled compound. A small village perched on a knoll opposite the temple. The houses and roofs were of fitted stone. There were stone steps and terraces with covered balconies of intricately carved wood. The place seemed deserted.

"Where have all the people gone?" asked Laura.

"To the cities to make money. This is a most secret place of pilgrimage. The stones of these temples were dismantled hundreds of miles away across the plains and brought into the hills by oxcart over a thousand years ago."

"But why?"

"To escape Moslems. Long before the Moguls, other Moslems invaded India. They were fanatics."

Indra reined in his horse, looking from window to shuttered window. "This place is run by a gang of Brahmins now," he said quietly. "Keep close and do as I say. Long ago they were extremely rich, but then the treasures of the temple—rare diamonds and so on—got stolen. Many of the people left, and the real treasures of the place—its great secrets—were forgotten and are unknown to most of the degenerate animals who now run it. You will see them soon. Their principal wealth now is hashish. The finest in the world is grown and made here and given to the temple by the devotees. But the priests are thieves who sell the hashish to smugglers and then report to the police. The police pick up the smugglers, extract a handsome price for their release, and return the hashish to the priests to be resold to new victims. They also smuggle gems from China and Nepal.

"Nevertheless the place has thousands of years of holy vibrations. What you see now goes back only a thousand years. Before that there was a temple of copper and wood, sheltering only a single stone worshipped since the beginning of time. It's now in one of the temples buried under a statue of the goddess. I'll show you.

"What the place needs is a good epidemic to clear away all the human trash. Anyhow we'll do what we've come for, and they won't disturb us. They're afraid of me. I killed one of them once."

"You *what?*"

"It was an accident," he said, grinning.

Laura had the sensation that she was being pulled along by some kind of magnet. They dismounted and walked through empty streets. Even the shops and tea stalls were shut. Then as they neared the temple they heard music and singing.

"Kali puja," Indra said, "a three day celebration."

They stopped at a small door built into the high granite wall of the temple. "This is the only way in," he said. "Come, I see the proprietor of the tea shop across the way is on duty. He'll tend to our horses."

The man bowed deeply to Indra and they exchanged a few words before entering through the small door.

Inside under the ancient firs a solemn dance was in progress. Concentric circles of devotees and villagers were dancing around the principal shrine, moving clockwise and counter clockwise, alternately. There were seven circles in all: children in the first, old ladies in the second, and old men in the third. In the fourth and fifth were married householders, in the sixth priests and their families, and in the seventh sadhus.

Large torches burned at the four corners of the temple and at the entrance a gold statue of the many-limbed goddess glittered in the flickering light.

"Look," Indra said. "Do you see something green on the statue?"

Laura noticed a flashing object about the size of a turkey egg. "Yes, what is it?"

"It is a four hundred eighty carat emerald, mate to the Kohinoor diamond."

"But I thought they were broke?"

"Confiscated by the government. It was all they had left and they would have sold it."

The stone flashed like a traffic light. The dancers circled, singing in rounds to the slow, methodical beat of a drum. The priests were everywhere, young and nearly naked, wearing only scarlet loincloths, scarlet cloths over their shoulders, and peaked hats of scarlet silk.

"They do look like a gang of pirates," Laura commented.

"Come, we'll find our spot," said Indra, moving on.

Some distance away, through a maze of other temples and shrines, they came to a place constructed as resting places for pilgrims and mendicants. Here, they found a large-sized room with a fire pit cut into the stone floor, worn smooth with use. The arches facing the courtyard provided a degree of privacy. In minutes Indra had a blazing fire going in the pit and the man from the tea shop arrived with their bags.

"It's the last night but the dance is only beginning," observed Indra. "It will go on 'til sundown. Then they'll take the goddess inside and do sacrifice and worship her," he said. "Come, let's go to the river now and bathe." He led her to a place where two rushing rivers came together to form natural pools among the rocks. The late afternoon sun had dropped behind the hills and under the ancient trees it was dark and cold.

Laura dipped her hand into the water. It was icy but warmer than her morning bath. Indra disappeared downstream. She replaced her clothes with a cloth and jumped in.

Although she was an expert swimmer, she wasn't prepared for the force of the current and had to struggle immediately to prevent herself from being sucked under. Clutching desperately at the rocks, thinking she might drown she cursed Indra for not warning her and it was all she could do to drag herself out. Overcome by a fit of shaking she hurriedly put on her clothes and scrambling up the path collided with Indra. "Did you enjoy your bath?'' He smiled. ''Are you all right, Uma? Come, the fire waits for us.''

The drum beats had quickened. Inside the inner circle of dancers the goddess was being carried clockwise on a palanquin by four priests with shaven heads. Naked sadhus and mendicants rolled over and over on the stones in front of the procession.

''The dance will end soon,'' Indra said as they warmed themselves in front of their fire. ''Then I would like you to go into the temple with me. I want to show you something.''

Appearing pale and transparent, almost golden in the flickering light, he gazed at her a long time with narrowed eyes, looking through her for someone else. Finally he spoke again. ''The statue is now in a small structure at the center of the temple. The holy stone is under the statue. Each day it is uncovered, anointed with water, oil and flowers, and worshipped.''

He was whispering to her now even though they were alone.

''At my signal you will begin to say the following words over and over, either to yourself or aloud. You will say: 'Oh Mother, forgive me. At the heels of your precious feet I come. Oh Mother, forgive me.' And you are to meditate on just what it is you want to be forgiven.''

He looked at her, opening his eyes wide. ''Got it?'' he said in flat American.

''Do you agree to try?'' A faint smile curled across his mouth.

A flicker of hesitation passed through Laura's mind and she knew he'd seen it. ''Oh Mother, forgive me''—it sounded so absurd. Could she really trust this ancient youth? For the first time in her life she felt profoundly alone, yet wondering what the result of this ''initiation'' would be, she was repelled by her own deep skepticism.

''I'll do as you ask,'' she said softly. ''But will you stand by and not abandon me?'' She stared into his eyes, hoping to make some sort of compact.

''I'm a madman, Uma,'' he said, staring back. ''Some day you will know everything—how and why I left this world, how I come and go, and you will come to know of my other lives, as I have learned to know about them.'' He looked away from her and poked the fire to ease the tension.

''If at this moment I asked you to come with me, to leave this world forever—would you do it? It *is* possible.''

She got the point.

''Aah—you turn pale. You lack faith. You want me to stand by you but will you follow me?'' He poked at the fire again. ''But you will,'' he said confidently. ''You will. That's why we're here together. Come, we'll go inside now. It's time.''

Monolithic twin statues of naked gods, their penises erect, guarded the passageway to the inner sanctum. Carved from gigantic blocks of jet black stone they were polished smooth by centuries of touching and flowers were tucked in the crevices of the arms and at the genitals. Inside the sanctum it was warm and damp. Torches and lamps glowed. Priests resembling long-haired toughs performed rituals for groups of bare-chested devotees who crowded the small covered courtyard.

A number of people were walking around a stone structure at the center, where inside shut doors the goddess and the stone were being prepared for worship. An atavistic energy resonated from the structure itself.

A way cleared for them at once as Indra walked in, tall and gaunt, holding his chimtah like a riding crop so that its rings rattled loudly.

"Prisoner in chains," Laura thought. "Am I that prisoner?"

As they began to walk around the sanctum she had the distinct impression that a rope was tied to her navel. It felt like an umbilical cord fastened on a winch so strong she could lean back and be pulled along.

Many of the devotees gaped at the sight of Indra walking with a Western woman. On the third time around, they were directly behind the sanctum when she heard his voice.

"Now," he said turning to her abruptly. "Here. Prostrate yourself on these stones, let your hands touch the stones at the base of the shrine and repeat what I told you."

Placing a firm hand on her back he pushed her to the floor.

She heard herself repeating: "Oh Mother, forgive me. At the heels of your precious feet I come. Oh Mother, forgive me . . ."

Warm dampness oozed from the stones through her shawl. She heard the shuffling footsteps of devotees as they passed or stopped to watch her. "Oh Mother, forgive me, Oh Mother, forgive me." It was as if some other Laura were saying the words. She remembered she was to meditate and began enumerating her hangups; pride, faithlessness, skepticism, sensuality and everything else that haunted her. The outer world faded. She was alone in a warm dampness. "Oh Mother, forgive me. At the heels of your precious feet I come. Oh Mother . . ."

Suddenly, a curtain opened in the darkness behind her closed eyes and she saw a beautiful woman, about her own age, lying in the grass smiling at her.

"Mother," she gasped, realizing it was her own mother now. "Crazy mother before she was crazy." The picture was so real she felt filled with joy and began repeating the words directly to the vision telling it about her hangups, and asking for forgiveness. Each time she repeated the plea a ripple of energy shot from the base of her spine up through her body. She relaxed, let the ripple turn into a wave, and began again to repeat the words. A chorus of bell-like voices began to sound inside her and she

73

sensed that she was lying on a giant tuning fork which was resonating at a low vibration, awakening some ancient connection with the stones.

Suddenly a part of her resisted, "You are Laura Weatherall of 610 Park Avenue, New York City," it said in a masculine voice and she realized with dismay that she had heard this voice on other occasions, even with drugs. "You are Laura Weatherall of 610 Park Avenue," it repeated like a tape loop and then, "You lunatic, Laura Weatherall, prostrating my body on this filthy floor to a statue . . . to a stone . . . you are Laura Weatherall of New York City, you don't do things like this, nasty things like—"

Yet the image of her smiling young mother was still there and the waves were getting stronger. If Laura Weatherall was not in control who was? Were things out of control? Over and over she repeated "Oh Mother, forgive me . . ." and after each repetition, from the base of her spine the rippling spread out. Her body was a pond, a very still pond into which someone was throwing stones.

Then there was a hand, Indra's hand and she got up, dazed and was led around the sanctum to an intricately carved spout that jutted from the stones.

The ripples inside her had become big waves.

A small pool carved in the shape of a lotus caught the liquid from the spout. It looked like slop water. Filling his cupped hands, Indra lifted them and let the whitish water spill down over her hair and forehead. Then quickly another handful was thrown in her face, and a third.

"Now, drink it!" he ordered, holding a cupped hand to her lips. "The milk ocean of eternity," he said. "Drink!"

Something inside her screamed. The body she imagined she inhabited was becoming a sea, rocked by mountainous waves.

She felt his hand then leading her before the open doors of the sanctum, beyond which a golden statue glowed with light. The space was packed shoulder to shoulder with worshippers and lamps waved crimson and gold, flashing gem stones, and the matchless emerald flashed *Go.* Suddenly bells of every pitch and timbre began ringing together.

"Now again," whispered Indra, pushing Laura to the floor.

Something inside her frayed and snapped as she went down and from an infinitely distant point she felt Laura Weatherall and all her burdens leaving—through her eyes, through her mouth and ears, sucked out by a powerful force inside the sanctum that was absorbing Laura Weatherall into itself.

The great waves crested about her, but some newly awakened part of her remained a centered, motionless nucleus. Then everything went blue, streams of golden light radiated out, and the air filled with the sound of a woman's voice, very cultivated, very old, very hard, speaking broken English with an Asian lilt.

"What do you want? What do you want?" the voice repeated slowly. "Ask and it shall be granted . . . What is it you want?"

"I am tired of Laura Weatherall, can you take her back?" Laura replied. Although her eyes were wide open, she saw nothing but waves into infinity, ultramarine and gold in every direction.

"Is that what you ask, eh?" The voice echoed over the waves.

"Yes," replied Laura.

"If I take her, the price is very high." The voice hesitated. "If I take her, I take everything. Do you understand . . . the price is too high, eh?"

There was a long pause.

"Why don't you ask for something else?" it went on. "Ask for something else."

"I feel you are already taking her," whispered Laura, "please can't you finish the job?"

"If I take that burden, then finally I will have to take everything. Do you understand?"

Suddenly Laura Weatherall's resistance snapped and she opened and was emptying, physically, like an orgasm, yet not of her physical body.

*   *   *

After a long time she opened her eyes. The temple was empty except for a few priests who were staring at her. As she struggled up their looks enraged her and brought her down.

Indra leaned over to help. Something possessed her and she struck him with the back of her hand. He struck back instantly with a force that propelled her out of the sanctum, and she found herself in the temple courtyard running. Dark, cold fear was sweeping through her body. She had to escape. As she rounded the courtyard she saw one of the priests running after her. She ran faster but the priest was gaining on her and soon a long willow stick landed on her back. Rounding a corner she stopped short; three more priests were waiting for her, all with willow sticks.

"It's too unreal, none of this is really happening," she cried.

Rushing the three priests she grabbed for the sticks, caught one, broke it, and pushed past them. Remembering where the gate was she ran toward it but it was locked. She could hear the priests shouting to each other like bloodhounds and slipped between two shrines hoping to hide. Too clever to be fooled, however, they were soon upon her beating her sharply with the willow sticks.

The waves began again inside her, and breaking free, blinded by tears, she ran across the courtyard, stumbled, and fell headlong into a deep pool. The waves exploded, again and again she felt everything leaving her. "Stop. I will fulfill your request," the voice said. "I will take Laura

75

Weatherall from you. Do not bother to think about her anymore.''

Just then a hand appeared near her in the water. She grabbed it. It was Indra's. He lifted her out onto the warm stone pavement and carried her to their fire where she lay sobbing.

Bending over, his hair loosened, he whispered to her, his lips almost touching her cheek. "Repeat after me," he said and uttered a set of syllables over and over which she repeated after him.

Examining the places where the priests had beaten her he applied yellow liquid from an old bottle, covered her head with his shawl, and she fell into a deep sleep.

When she awoke the following morning she saw him lying stiffly in a blanket opposite her. The fire had almost gone out. His face looked thin and bright yellow. Examining her body she discovered her cuts and bruises had vanished.

"Are you all right?" he said, opening one eye like a parrot.

"Yes," she answered. "But *you* are not."

His eye blinked at her from under the blanket. "That is something I can handle." He smiled. "I'll go just outside the wall near the river. There is a small hut there, across the river, where I'll finish off this jaundice."

"That's what comes of healing these animals," he said after a pause. "I should stop it. Do you feel I abandoned you?"

"No, of course I don't."

"Do you feel I might abandon you?"

"No, I think I understand more now."

"Then that is good, we can proceed. You have surrendered to something very deep, very big. It is a first step. We'll remain here a week. I'll give orders for you not to be disturbed. There's a cell next to this one with a door. You'll move in there and someone will bring you lemon water twice a day. I'll see you at the bathing place at four in the morning and four in the evening."

"And then?"

"The remainder of the time close your eyes and repeat the syllables I have given you."

"All day long?"

"About fourteen hours each day if you can do it. You get the benefit—not I. It's up to you."

He got to his feet with difficulty. "Come," he said, "we can't begin another day without battling the whirlpools, can we?"

VI

A. K. SUNDARAM TAPPED delicately at a soft-boiled egg.

"My dear fellow, you must have some breakfast. You look tired. Here, at least try some of these South Indian rice cakes, they're called idlis."

Jeff stifled a yawn. "Seeing you all dressed up headed for an office so early in the morning makes me sleepy."

It had been over a month since Laura had left and, disliking Delhi, Jeff spent as much time in bed as possible. In fact he disliked India altogether and the later he got up, the less chance there was of coming in contact with it in the form of this enigmatic man in whose house he was a guest. Sundar's round body, expertly covered by Saville Row suits, his handsome face a mask, was passive and suppressed. Too Jeff, he was a neurotic turtle.

"I know it must be a shock to you, old man," continued Sundar, "but we do get up and go to offices—even in India. At least some of us do. We have a most alarming amount of paperwork. So many people, you know."

"You should let me teach you some American slang, Sundar," Jeff said. "You're so hip but you talk so square."

Sundar tittered. "It goes along with the early morning hours, I guess. But you don't realize, dear fellow, what a perfect disguise it is. And we must disguise ourselves here. We have so many castes, and tribes, not to mention religions. None of them get along. In order for me to be effective, I must sound neutral. The British were quite neutral so my way of speaking always suggests that."

Sundar marveled at the American opposite him, so relaxed, so urbane, so sloppy!

"In America you feel so free—you let it, as you say, 'all hang out.' For us this is impossible. We are governed by the idea of karma which predetermines our lives. And there are threats everywhere—no privacy, someone is always listening, watching, freedom is impossible unless you are very rich and also in the government. Even then," he glanced around quickly, "at any time one's most trusted servant may become a spy if he's

77

offered enough money.''

Sundar munched his toast. Did this foreigner take him for a fool? He—a South Indian Brahmin? Had he not known only three days after the party at Dorje's exactly what Jeff and Laura were up to? Of course, at first he'd suspected Dorje. But Dorje's safety, that of his entire family, as well as the gold they'd been allowed to bring in from Lhasa—was subject to pressure that he, A. K. Sundaram, had easily been able to exert in the right places. Foreigners had no idea how easily information was obtained in India. Yet what was happening in the West remained a mystery to him and he wondered about his old friend Stan.

"You haven't really seen anything of India yet, have you?'' said Sundar changing course. "I fear you've only met film folk and embassy couples—most boring.''

His lips were set in a superior smile that irritated Jeff.

"You want me to visit the Taj Mahal, I suppose?''

"No, no, that's not necessary.'' Sundar giggled.

They laughed together.

"There is a place I would like to take you, though. A woman I think you might be interested in meeting.''

Jeff shrugged.

"You don't like it here, I can see,'' said Sundar. "But you will. You will come with me and I will show you. You'll see how sensual we can be. We're so oppressed by our idea of 'duty' that when we let go it is something terrible! Don't forget, we worship pleasure. You vant to buy—hey, comm'on, buy, eat, vat you vant? I geef you.'' He stared at Jeff. "You will come then?''

"Who's the woman?'' Jeff asked.

"That is a surprise,'' replied Sundar. "She's an old friend of mine. And do you think you think you could bring some of your lysergic acid diethylamide with you?''

Jeff was caught off guard. "Sure, of course. How many?'' he blurted.

"Oh, say a hundred. Yes, a hundred will do very well for a start,'' Sundar answered, feeling triumphant.

"Only a hundred?'' Jeff smiled, regaining his cool. Are you sure that will be enough?''

Sundar fiddled with his napkin. Jeff had called his bluff.

"For the moment,'' Sundar murmured.

Jeff wondered how Sundar had found out he had acid, and how much else he knew.

Sundar was waiting for him to ask.

"What time?'' said Jeff matter-of-factly.

"What?''

"What time is this . . . encounter.''

78

"Ah, yes, tomorrow evening," replied Sundar, thinking that Jeff was very slippery indeed. "Tomorrow evening about eight, will that be suitable? We can have a drink here first."

"Anything you say, Boss." Jeff slouched in his chair. "I'll look forward to it."

* * *

The next evening Jeff found himself on the third-floor terrace of a modern house which would have been impressive in any country but in India was outrageous.

The house stood in a large compound of its own and there seemed to be no servants. Polished marble floors of the terrace gave way to teak inside, with thick white carpets covered with tiger and leopard skins. On the walls hung Bokhara rugs, Persian miniatures, and other expensive bric-a-brac.

"So this is A. K. Sundaram's hideout," Jeff thought, slumping into a pile of cushions on a low sofa. "Soft, so very soft." For the tough folks that used it he supposed.

Just then two tall young men with long hair appeared arm in arm with Sundar. "Jeff, I'd like you to meet Abhrim and Ismail."

Jeff nodded. Cruelty lurked around their artificially darkened eyes and their movements were the grown-up gestures of pampered children, self-indulgent and sensual. On the long fingers of their bony hands they wore numerous rings.

"Abhrim's grandfather was from Hyderabad," declared Sundar, "kept a diamond the size of a golf ball in his desk drawer wrapped in an old newspaper. And Ismail's great-uncle had his own railway train, given to him by Queen Victoria, and a fourteen inch...uh, as you say, cock—famous throughout India. He was awarded the title Son of the Empire by Victoria."

"Did she ride on it?"

"Who?"

"Queen Victoria."

"On what?"

"On the train."

"But Queen Victoria never came to India, my dear fellow," said Sundar, pretending not to get the joke. "You don't know much about our history."

Ismail took a pipe from a leather bag and held it out to Jeff. "You like some smoke?"

"Very interesting mixture," Jeff observed, lighting up.

"Then you know it?" Abhrim sounded surprised.

"No," Jeff said, coughing, "but I know it has jimson in it."

79

"What?"

"Jimson weed. Large white flower."

"Jimson we don't know," Ismail said. "It contains datura . . . a special variety."

"That's jimson."

"Yes, and other ingredients."

It was obvious to Jeff that drugs were nothing new here, they were all connoisseurs. He wondered if they had tried acid and whether Sundar would give some out.

Two young girls came sidling out onto the terrace towards them, their thighs and curving buttocks balanced beneath wasp waists by high protruding breasts. They wore flimsy saris glittering with sequined bead-work and tinkling ankle bracelets. Acknowledging the pressure of something new, Jeff's flesh told him he might enjoy himself even more than usual that night, and after he'd had one, that he could have them all.

Sundaram introduced them and Jeff stood up. One of the girls sat down with Ismail while Jeff and one called Ija remained standing.

"You have just come to India?" she said in a voice too mellow for her age.

"Yes."

"You must find it difficult adjusting?" Her large eyes blinked at him.

"Not too difficult."

"But they say the pace is so much slower in America, don't you find that."

It was the same boring conversation he'd had everywhere. He let his eyes travel between her lips and breasts.

"Let's sit down." He said, guiding her to a low divan. "Are you in films?"

"Oh no, we don't go in for films," she said seriously and broke into a smile. "My sister and I come from a family of courtesans dedicated to the god."

Jeff's mouth dropped open. "Perhaps I should attend your church."

She laughed. "Don't think about it too much; it is hard for you to understand, I know."

"Why?"

"Here, sometimes, religion and sex are combined. But tell me . . ." She reached up and brushed a strand of hair from his forehead. "Why are you Western men all wearing your hair so long?"

"Don't think about it too much . . . you know the story of Samson?"

She nodded. "Should I cut your hair tonight and make you my slave?"

Jeff's green eyes glittered. "You wouldn't want me to lose my strength, would you?" He focused again on her breasts.

Abhrim came over to them and tugging at Ija's arm, spoke sharply to her in Urdu.

She pried away his hand casually continuing her conversation with Jeff. "Abrhim is too old-fashioned," she said lightly. "His grandfather had over one hundred wives, so you can see it is somewhat hard for him to adjust to the ... new equality."

"In those days if we wanted something, we took it," declared the handsome Abrhim.

"Now you must ask," Ija said sighing, "you must learn the manners of our new society."

"I don't want them," Abhrim retorted.

"You are too much a man." She cast a furtive glance at Jeff. "You should have been born less handsome, Abhrim—your good looks are going to ruin you."

Melting under her words, he forgot about wanting to interrupt the conversation, and began lighting up a pipe.

"Opium, you join us?" Ija asked Jeff, motioning to Abhrim to sit beside them.

"Not just now," Jeff replied. Distracted by the arrival of an American girl followed by two men wearing turbans, he excused himself and wandered in their direction. The girl was frail but sensual, and had a freaky look that interested him. "You've been in India for a while?" he asked, introducing himself. "I'm Jeff."

"Five years," she said flatly.

"That's a long time."

"Depends on how you look at it. Long for a Texas girl like me, short for India. Believe me India's got plenty of time." She rolled her eyes.

"You like it here then?"

"Like it?" she echoed, as if that were beyond anything she had ever thought of. "It's not liking, it's love or hate," she looked at him hard and her expression changed. "I've tried to leave, got as far as Geneva once. Checked into a hotel there and said to myself, 'you're going to stay here and do something constructive.' Next day I went outside and saw the faces of all those bankers doing all those constructive things—even the men I'd thought handsome once, weren't handsome anymore. They seemed dead. I went to the airport and caught the first plane back.

"And—" said Jeff, glancing at her two companions.

"Where's your wife?" the girl asked, changing the subject. "I saw you at the party Charles Hooker gave."

"She's not my wife," replied Jeff, "and right now she's off with a yogi somewhere."

The girl sighed, "I had enough of that preaching stuff in Texas. My father was one, he used to sell Bibles, a strict religious type, you know? I couldn't even wear makeup—I mean in 1965! Now tell me what that has to

81

do with anything?'' She laughed. "I rocked Bombay for a few years but it's getting to be a drag now—everybody's getting so uptight.''

"How'd you 'rock' it?''

"Believe it or not, I came here to study yoga—and well, there's all sorts of yoga, you know?''

"And those are your... gooroos?'' Jeff indicated the two men.

She giggled. "Them? Oh no, they're my dates sort of, they're smugglers.''

"Your dates!''

"Funny isn't it?'' she laughed. "But they're just like Texas ranchers, I understand them. And they give me diamonds, bags full of 'em.'' Her eyes sparkled. "They're old friends from Bombay. I brought them here to meet Kamala. You've met her?''

"Not yet. She's the... she owns this place, I guess.

She helped me get started. Just as I was running out of bread I happened to meet her and she took me in. I learned a lot. Not sex—everyone knows that, but all the other things, especially how to get the loot from the customer.'' Her eyes were mocking him.

"Takes guts,'' replied Jeff, shaking his head.

"Not guts, just an empty stomach, and you have to learn to be detached.''

"I'll bet,'' said Jeff.

"Some of these guys are real freaky—hot climate you know. Ready to pop all the time.'' She looked around the room. "See how they keep twitching their toes and knees.'' She looked at Jeff. "Maybe you're ready too?''

"Maybe,'' he murmured.

Sundar sidled up to them. "Did you get some punch?'' he interrupted.

"What?'' asked the girl.

"Some punch,'' Jeff repeated, "no she hasn't had punch. Come, Miss Texas—my friend Sundaram will get you some. He's promised me a most unusual evening.''

She rested her hand lightly on his arm. "Be careful,'' she said, "this is a rough country. They're not simple here like us. They know things we haven't even thought of. You'll see—fifty-seven varieties of everything and more.''

They followed Sundar into a dimly lit room off the terrace. Low divans with cushions hugged the floor. One wall was a mural of a Mogul palace in which princes and concubines were depicted in erotic scenes and postures from the Kama Sutra.

Half a dozen young men sat around with girls provided by Kamala, one more beautiful than the other. In a corner a small orchestra was playing.

Hashish joints were passed. Someone dimmed the lights so that the candles in the bronze wall brackets seemed to burn more brightly.

"Is the punch strong enough?" Jeff asked Sundar.

"Quite," Sundar answered. "These are supposed to be some of the more advanced people in Delhi. I'm interested to see just how advanced they really are."

Jeff noticed one or two of the guests going through quiet changes as their perceptions began to change. Suddenly he realized that, like Stan, Sundar was probably a voyeur.

Just then a tall woman arrived and seeing Sundar came towards them.

"Ah," said Sundar to Jeff, "here is your guru." He stood up to greet her, his diplomatic mask crumbling, "Kamala, this is my friend Jeff," he said, and sat down in a daze.

Kamala was hardly a girl. Her dark kohl-rimmed eyes glittered. Her jet black hair piled high on her head was entwined with garlands of jasmine, revealing velvet soft skin at the nape of a truly regal neck. For the first time in his life Jeff felt humbled. Here was a real woman, primeval and infinitely devious.

Refusing the hashish he offered, Kamala drew Jeff's attention to a near- naked girl who had materialized in the center of the room. A hush fell over the guests and the only sound was the drone of the tampura. The girl's eyes were large and darted back and forth like a frightened bird.

A small jeweled triangle hung from a silver chain around her waist. Bells tinkled at her ankles and as she gestured with her hands her breasts stood out as if they might give milk at any moment.

"Ah—" groaned one of the men.

Suddenly a young man appeared, high hipped, wasp waisted, with broad shoulders like a figure from an Assyrian relief, his oiled body naked except for a silver codpiece shaped like an erection, from the tip of which, like a flood of sperm, a shower of gems sparkled on gold threads. Walking solemnly to the center of the room, he balanced a large flat basket on his head.

An uneasy murmur followed as the girl lifted the basket from her partner's head and placed it on the floor. Then the youth began a ritualistic dance crouching and side-stepping round her quivering body. Squatting in front of her he moved his hands slowly up her thighs as his torso swayed. Parting the jeweled covering between her legs, he began sucking and licking her hairless vagina, pumping his body so that the jewels on the tip of his silver phallus rattled.

The orchestra quickened the pace. Suddenly Abhrim stood up, his pants bulging, cheered wildly in Urdu, rushed toward the girl, and pushing her partner aside, thrust his tongue inside her. Trancelike, the girl swayed while Abhrim slobbered over her, emptying his pockets of thousand-rupee notes.

When Abhrim's ardor finally cooled the young girl unfastened a catch on the lid of the basket and at her command, announcing itself with a sudden loud hiss, an enormous black cobra reared its head.

Jeff watched the skin tighten around the corners of Kamala's eyes and forehead. "It is a very dangerous animal, this one," she muttered without averting her gaze. "This one is the king of cobras, rarely it ever gets tamed."

A few of the guests well into their trips went under the pillows, moaning. One of the smugglers threw wads of hundred-rupee notes onto the floor while the other pushed the girl from Texas down between his legs.

Smoking serenely on an opium pipe, Sundar looked on, his knees twitching.

The cobra hooded out, a hand's breath, hissing softly as the girl began to dance in front of it, moving slowly, contrapuntally against the rhythms of the musicians, until she and the serpent were locked in a simultaneous undulating wave of recognition.

Calming, the serpent reclined in a graceful sweeping S and wound itself about one of her legs, inching around her thigh, across her waist, and over her breasts.

Someone threw out thousand-rupee notes. "There's enough money on that floor to feed twenty families for twenty years," whispered Sundar, his eyes bulging like Mickey Mouse. Jeff couldn't tell whether he felt this was good or bad and wondered what Kamala's cut was as the "producer."

The music trembled and shrieked. The cobra wound its body several times about the girl's neck and began a slow descent between her breasts. She trembled, her legs apart, her body pumping as the serpent arching out in front of her, hissed and swayed like a pendulum, turned its forked tongue and lashing out nervously, stiffened itself and poked its head among the folds of her vagina. Whimpering and moaning ecstatically the girl collapsed on the floor in an orgasm of pleasure.

Appropriately the orchestra shifted to a slow raga. In the dim light, Jeff made out the girl from Texas being fucked by one of her smugglers in a dark corner.

The cobra's head glistened as it withdrew and slipped back into the large basket. Kamala's hand relaxed on Jeff's knee as she turned an expressionless gaze toward Sundar.

"You didn't think it was possible," she said. "Well, what do you say now?"

"Extraordinary," Sundar mumbled, rolling his eyes. He made a move to rise but couldn't. "I think I need some air ... it seems stuffy in here. Ah, shall we—can we make a move? Come ..." he motioned to Jeff.

To Sundar's horror, however, Jeff had begun removing his clothes.

Kamala leaned back. A faint smile was on her lips, as he removed his shirt and stepped coolly out of his trousers.

Acutely aware of the effect he was creating, Jeff knew that even without an erection, his equipment was larger than most of them had ever seen. He wanted to fuck, not watch some snake do it. A hand reached out and grabbed his leg, but he shook it off, went for the snake girl and gathering her up in his arms held her against his body and begin to fuck her slowly.

With a muted yell Ismail threw a wad of notes onto the floor. Jeff moved toward him, holding the girl, fucking her as he went, and with his free hand guided Ismail's erection into her open mouth. On played the musicians like mad machines, gaping open-mouthed as Jeff stretching his arms luxuriously, his legs apart, yielded to the mouths of the stoned girls who wanted him, and observed with satisfaction the jealous eyes of Sundar watching him.

Then suddenly he noticed Kamala had disappeared. "Save it for her," he thought, and dressing, left the room.

The terrace was floating in the tops of the palms. Kamala, her face a disinterested mask, handed him a frosted glass and though their eyes met, she seemed to be gazing through him.

"You didn't enjoy," she said.

"Not crazy about snakes," he shrugged, trying to match her indifference. But he was excited and his nerves were on edge.

"You have beautiful body," she said, "Perhaps you want something more?"

She had a way of putting him down with her eyes which he dug.

"In India we worship Goddess," she purred, gazing steadily at him. "In olden times each spring, the most beautiful youths were chosen to mate with her and after to be killed, like the drone bee who leaves its organ imbedded in the Queen. In late summer they were set free to wander naked, flowers in the hair, worshipped—free to have any woman, anything until the hour when their beautiful bodies were cut up and scattered over the fields." She smiled, sipping at her drink.

"Desire is irresistible my friend, a great secret, power is yours if you know how to arouse and satisfy the Goddess of Desire. She will give you everything."

*   *   *

Except for the sound of his breathing, it was very still. He was lying somewhere soft and trying to remember something terribly important when his eyes opened and he saw her face above him. With great effort he tried to focus. Was it Kamala's face, or was he hallucinating? Closing his eyes again, he tried to focus his memory but couldn't get past standing with Kamala on the terrace. It seemed days had passed.

When his eyes opened again she was lying there reclining on one arm gazing down at him. He tried to move but couldn't. He tried to think. Had she slipped him something? Fifty-seven varieties the girl from Texas had said. Be careful.

Now there were spaces between his perceptions, empty gaps during which his mind would slide away from him. But at least he could feel her warmth, and as he had first supposed, his body had not turned to stone.

Looking like the plump buttocks of an adolescent girl, her large breasts materialized beside him. "You need awakening," a voice was saying. Was it really Kamala's voice? It seemed to come from a great distance. "You need awakening," it echoed again, "you are asleep. You could do many wonderful things, but you're throwing it all away. What you need is fright."

Locating her face again he saw her lips moving and met the dark ageless eyes he'd found so hard to look at.

"You got no shakti, no love because you never had the real thing. You are vain, and stingy, and your Western women, they have no knowledge."

Now her hand was stroking his pectoral muscles, pinching his nipples between long finger nails. He watched his nipples stand up straight and saw small drops of blood. Blood! She was drawing blood! He gave the order for his arm to strike her forcefully but nothing happened; he felt nothing.

"You see, Mr. U.S.A., you can't do nothing." Her full lips opened and closed lazily above her breasts, "then—don't do anything, don't even think of doing . . . anything. I will teach you. I will teach you how to do nothing. Then you will have anything, everything you desire."

Her voice boomed in his ear like thunder. Was he going crazy? And they were not alone. Yet, he was sure he could make out a ghoulish looking dark-skinned man wearing a white cloth around his waist.

"That is my servant," she said, noting the terror in his gaze.

He forced his lips to move. "Why is he watching us?"

"He guards this body." She pointed to her breasts. "He is a eunuch, my slave. He serves me."

Jeff, his vision clearing, looked again, saw a large middle aged man; his lips red from chewing pan,* his black hair to his shoulders and long finger nails painted red.

"His testicles were removed when he was a child, poor thing—the parents needed more money." Her voice was flat. "An Arab friend of mine gave him to me when he grew tired of him. I've had him since twenty

*pan=betel nut

86

years. He is most reliable. Hassan," she said. "Come. Take Sahib to the other room and bathe him.

"You must have bath before coming to me," she whispered.

With what was left of his thinking apparatus Jeff reasoned that he was strung out on something. He didn't like the idea and tried moving his body again, but nothing happened. Not the punch, he thought, not the majoun, what then? Unless he was ill. He felt nauseated and wanted to piss, but it was impossible. Paranoia oozed through him. Can't trust any of these bastards he was yelling in a film that made no sense. And he had to piss.

Instead he was being carried in the bare arms of the ghoul, but where? Kamala wanted him castrated and this fiend, Hassan, was going to do it.

Now they were in an enormous bathroom. Why a bathroom? Ah yes to piss. There was a sunken tub. He watched himself being lowered into it by Hassan; felt neither the temperature of the water, nor the wetness. Couldn't move. At last he could piss though and he tried but nothing came. Did he really have to piss? His mind wandered again and came back. Hassan was kneeling by the edge of the tub, scrubbing him roughly with a wad of coconut husks, grunting.

Jeff left his body completely and began watching himself from somewhere near the ceiling. Dragging him onto a low cot covered with a sheet, the eunuch looked tense and excited. He shook a bottle of liquid and let it dribble out over Jeff's body.

Hassan's large black hands flew over the white flesh, slapping thighs, burrowing into muscles harder and harder until Jeff wanted to hit him, but he was not in his body. He watched as Hassan flipped him over and began to rub his back: now astride him working the muscles with his thumbs, down the buttocks, adroitly massaging the muscles near the anus.

Then he saw Hassan loosening the cloth around his own waist. "My ass," Jeff heard himself yelling hoarsely, "the bastard's going to fuck my ass," and watched him getting ready to do it, hard black cock, no balls, and saw Hassan ripping into his body.

Suddenly he was back in his body experiencing sharp terrible pain, if only he could control his muscles he would kill the bastard. If only, but the dark hands with the long red fingernails pinned his wrists down, and he felt the sullen heaviness of the eunuch riding him. Waves of nausea shook him. He thought he might be going to vomit or shit. Instead he pissed. Whatever it was, the drug was going out of him. As the warm piss flowed out under his stomach he knew he was coming back.

Hassan withdrew. Jeff found he could move his hand but knew it was still too weak to risk a fight. Pretending to be unconcious, he let himself be dragged again to the tub, doused with warm water, and dried. Then the eunuch picked him up and took him back to Kamala. She bent down gazing into his eyes, her voice was mocking, "So now, Hassan has given you

87

good bath and massage I think? Yes, no?''

He wanted to spit in her face, "Bastard," he whispered hoarsely pretending to be weaker than he was. "Where is that ball-less bastard?"

"No, no, no," she said, reprimanding him as though he were a child. "it was necessary for you." Her eyes narrowed. "It was my command. You Western fellows are too tight and you got too much pride, showing off, like tonight." Sliding her arms around his waist, she pressed herself against him. "Come here now, you beauty. Comm'on," she said.

"Get that son of a bitch out of here," he grunted gesturing to where Hassan was standing. "I'll kill him."

She cradled his head in her hands and the strength he had managed to recover went out through them.

"Now, now, now," she said, "do not try to shout. It is too frightening. It is not necessary for you to be so angry, you will exhaust yourself. It was me who did it through him." She glanced at Hassan. "We do not think of him as human. He is a loyal animal, something to be used, that is all. He is out of this sex business anyhow. Only my power controls him, he can do nothing by himself. Come!" She spoke to the eunuch in Urdu. "Kneel before this man here. Put your head at his feet and show him you aren't bad."

The servant did as he was told. Jeff winced.

"Ah, I forgot," she sighed, "you do not have slaves in America. Or you do not admit it. Here we are on good terms with them. Sometimes they are our best friends. For a few rupees in India you can buy anyone. Do you understand that Mr. USA?"

"What is this drug you've given me," Jeff managed to whisper.

"Ah ha!" she laughed softly, "the big drug dealer is asking Kamala what she has given him. You know? No, you don't. This is a tropical country my dear, there are plants that can cure you, plants that make you fall in love, plants that can kill you six months from now like a disease. I could even take you to a village of women in the Himalayas, where with certain herbs they can make a man s organ hard for weeks. The women enjoy, he dances their tune, then phtt, he dies. It is said they eat him then, I dunno.''

He was able to turn himself now so that he could see her as she lay beside him naked to the waist, a shawl of purple silk about her legs and thighs. He thought of a painting he'd seen in the Louvre. Her body was so free from imperfections it seemed unreal; her breasts large and full, the outcurve of her stomach matching the incurve of her hips, the high waist sloping to perfectly rounded buttocks, and the skin that shone as though lit from within, black silky hair, eyes like moonstones set with diamonds.

"You gave me such a drug?" he asked.

"Fool," she spat, "it is I, Kamala, I am the drug."

Hassan was summoned to massage her neck and shoulders.

"You too are beautiful," she sighed, as though reading his mind, "very beautiful male animal."

Stroking his thigh, her hand glided to his penis. Her voice was soft and lilting. "But you have the great defect, my darling, do you know what it is?"

Jeff stared at her.

"It is the pride. Pride is killing everything for you and will kill you too, in the end. Don't be so proud," she smiled, "most dangerous. You look in the mirror, you see a beautiful body." She held her hands above her head, stretching, "I know, I look too, I see mine. Is it not so? Yes? But always remember, it is not your body, it is a gift. What luck, eh? Think of this eunuch here," she rolled her eyes, "without balls or worse, think of the body of a leper," her eyes narrowed. "You have seen them, yes? So consider your body a gift and don't be so proud because also it is an illusion. Shall I tell you a secret?"

Jeff nodded.

"Nothing is beautiful," she whispered. "Nothing. You think I am crazy, but think. To the tiger or the monkey or the cockroach do we not look loathsome and hairless. The mountain is beautiful until you have to climb it. The thunderstorm is beautiful until the lightning strikes you." She arched up on her knees, "So where's the beauty? It is only our pride. Ha, it is so, you know it is."

The folds of her vagina glistened through the silky hair around them. He felt himself getting hard and wanted to bury his head between her legs but he dared not move, not yet.

"My name is Kamala, Kama, Desire, indestructible ... moving and creating worlds. As long as you're in this world my friend you must acknowledge it. If you do not ... if you misuse, then it will kill ..."

Obsessed now by her body, Jeff, wanting to take her, trembled, waiting for the right moment. The moon, sailing from behind a bank of clouds, shown in through the large windows. Motioning Hassan to a far corner of the room, Kamala lay down. Jeff felt her distended nipples rubbing against him and noticed that he'd broken out in a cold sweat.

She took his face in her hands and kissed him, deep long kisses, sucking and biting his lips.

"You want something," she whispered, "yes? Then you should take it."

Pushing his head gently across the smooth curve of her thighs, she guided his mouth toward the wet lips of her vagina which seemed to him like the moist opening of a great cave. Thrusting his tongue inside he looked up and could see her face like a second moon watching him.

Sitting up suddenly, she caught his hair, pulling him close to her. "You beautiful fool," she said softly, "I cannot buy you, but I will have you all the same, one way or another."

Falling back on the pillows she pushed his head between her legs again. "At least you are lucky," she whispered, wrapping herself around him. "I am a very clever woman. I know everything. Clever enough to take care of you well." She tugged at a shock of his hair forcing him to look at her again. "I will teach you . . . then you will do my work."

He could feel his strength returning. Whatever it was, for sure, was wearing off but he was in no hurry for revenge. For a long time he lay on his stomach between her legs, watching expressions of pleasure cross her face. Then slowly he inched up her thighs, licking and kissing her, sliding up to her breasts where he sucked at her nipples, biting them gently.

This aroused her. "Yes, yes, so you can move now," she murmured, "yes."

He knew the drug's effect was passing. He could feel his erection now and the pressure of the sperm in his swollen testicles. He let himself slide into her slowly, waited as she contracted groaning with satisfaction, then withdrew quickly and thrust himself in again hard and fast.

"You are so big," she groaned, "you must be more gentle."

Withdrawing again without pausing he drove himself into her, biting her breasts savagely. She cried out in pain and Hassan was there at once with his bamboo stick.

Jeff sprang up. Two well-timed karate blows had Hassan out cold on the floor. But Kamala had seized the stick and brought it down hard across Jeff's cheek. A second blow on his shoulder hit him.

"You must not be so violent with us, darling fellow, or something not nice will happen to you," hissed Kamala standing above him on the bed waving the stick. "Get down on your knees."

He knelt before her, buying time, praying for strength, his penis erect.

Quickly he grabbed at her knees, and throwing her off balance, got the stick away from her. She shrieked obscenities in Hindi, her dark eyes bulged with rage. He tore a strip of her shawl, stuffed part of it into her mouth and with another part tied her hands together.

Staggering into the bathroom, he washed the blood from his cheek and returned. "We'll see who's master," he whispered taking up the stick, bringing it down sharply on her buttocks until large welts appeared. "Now," he said breathlessly, "let's see how tight your ass is."

Straddling her, he parted her buttocks with both hands and spitting on the anus which lay exposed like some dark flower, slowly but firmly buried his organ inside her. "Baby, that's a tight ass," he breathed, pausing to watch her sphincter muscle twitch. She screamed, a deep cursing scream through the gag.

"Listen to me bitch," he said, his lips at her neck, his voice hoarse with the excitement of riding her rising body. "You and your Hassan, you feel that?" He withdrew completely and jammed. "You feel it?" he yelled

90

pulling her up by the hair until their eyes met. "Fucking bitch. You're getting your ass fucked all night long baby and if that eunuch wakes up...ugh, I'll kill him. You won't sit down for days." His hard thighs slapped against her buttocks and his mind spun out. He was a boy again in Hawaii riding the mare he'd received on his fourteenth birthday, riding naked on the beach. He'd had his first orgasm that way and hadn't forgotten the feeling of the warm animal beneath him, his hot sperm shooting out over her neck. Now it was Kamala. He let go inside her in spasms that left him trembling, his body convulsed in an orgasm that went on and on.

When he'd finished, bathed in sweat, he tightened her bonds. Then he inspected Hassan, who was coming to, bound and gagged him, dragged him into the bathroom and pissed on him.

As he showered and dressed he could hear vague noises below. End of the evening noises, the sudden cry of a girl, the crash of a glass, a curse. Music droning on.

The drug was still strong enough to keep him moving more slowly than he wished. Out on the terrace he stared silently at a sleeping Delhi, and slipped unseen down a stairway to the gate. First he'd have to go to Sundar's place to get his bag. Those with the acid, he'd been careful to stash in a locker at the airport. Out on the street he finally found a rickshaw driver and gave him Sundar's address

"You will wait there while I pick up bag. Then we go Palam airport, please."

"Double rate after midnight, double double rate sahib," croaked the driver.

"Sure," said Jeff, "but hurry. I've got a three-thirty plane for Bombay."

*   *   *

Because it was Sunday and because the evening at Kamala's had proved more strenuous than he expected A. K. Sundaram was having his breakfast in bed.

"Mr. Jeff sahib awake?" Sundar asked.

"Oh no sir, he is not here," replied a servant.

"He has gone out early?" said Sundar, sipping tea. "Did he say where he was going?"

"Sir, he has gone altogether. Last night, sir. About two in the morning, he came by motor rickshaw. I had to let him in the gate. Picked up his bag, sir, and left in the same vehicle."

"Probably moving to Kamala's," thought Sundar wistfully. "It will be more to his taste there. Get Kamala Dev on the phone at once," he ordered, "tell her I wish to speak with her."

The servant withdrew. Sundar flopped on a pillow. The evening had been most interesting. After Jeff was out of the way Ismail, Abrhim and the others had gone mad. Amusing to watch them as the acid took effect. The LSD was a most unusual drug, something one must look into seriously, might be prove useful in certain areas of investigation; persuasion. He wondered how much of the stuff Jeff had, whether Stan was involved.

The servant returned looking embarrassed.

"What the devil is the matter, James? Did you get her?"

"Yes sir, but..."

"But what?"

James was a devout Seventh Day Adventist. "Sir," he said, blushing, "she cursed me very bad."

"But why? What the devil for? Is she still on the phone?"

"No sir, she rang off, said you had..."

"Had what? Confound it, James, what is this all about?"

"Said you had better get the hell over there at once if you know what is good for you, sir."

"Oh she did, did she?" he said, pretending he would avenge both himself and James. "Have the driver bring the car round at once, I must find out what's bothering her. Perhaps she's drunk."

*   *   *

Arriving at Kamala's Sundar discovered the bruised and bandaged presence lying in state on her bed. Hassan was nervously applying balms and ointments to her injured parts. When she saw Sundar she rose on one arm.

"It is very dangerous for him, this thing that he has done," she yelled, hoarse with rage. "Why you give me that drug to give him in the drink, what was it anyhow?" She hissed like a wounded serpent. "It is you who have given it, Sundar—you, not I. It made a problem." She displayed the bruises on her buttocks. "Kamala does not need these drugs, she uses her shakti."

"I gave you the drug, my dear, because you asked for something, don't you remember? If you got so much shakti, why did you ask? Didn't you say you wanted to teach Mr. USA a lesson?"

"I had Hassan bugger him," she giggled.

"Well, that was certainly a mistake," deplored Sundar, observing her black and blue marks. "No wonder he..."

"No wonder nothing!" she shouted. "And make no mistake! The mistake was that your drug wasn't strong enough—he came out of it."

"Indeed," said Sundar.

"Listen to me, you son of a pig, do not tell Kamala what to do and

92

what not to do, understand? Director of Planning, ha! What planning? You little know-nothing, you—Peeping Tom! Because you went to school overseas you think you can play with me, bring scrum to my house. Be careful, Sundaram. Remember it was I, Kamala, who got you this planning job.''

"Yes, Guruji."

"Don't yes 'ji me," she yelled, throwing a banana at him.

"I mean it, I mean it," stammered Sundar, lunging toward the bed to touch her feet. She had to be appeased at any cost, he was afraid of her and she knew it.

"You don't mean it, but you will!" She smiled down at him. "That American scum, he is finished, do you understand my meaning?''

Sundar nodded.

"No one slaps Kamala around."

Somewhere beyond the thickly carpeted room a telephone sounded. A boy appeared with an extension. "There is a call for Mr. Sundaram," he said, "someone has come to the airport."

Sundar released Kamala's feet and took the phone.

"Yes," he said flatly, "who is it?''

"Sundaram, it's me Stan—Stanley from Harvard.''

Sundar's eyes bulged and rolled in their sockets.

"Ah, Stanley—so you have come to India!" Sundar put the phone to Kamala's ear.

"Yes. I'd like to see you for a few hours. I'm on my way to South India tomorrow."

"But of course, dear Stanley,' Sundar shouted, "my car will be there at once. At the Air India counter. My man will page you. Yes, yes, good-bye."

"Who is this Stanley," said Kamala suspiciously.

"An old school friend," Sundar said cheerfully, hoping Stan's arrival might take her mind off Jeff. "I'm afraid he's an American too."

"I don't trust these Americans," she grunted. "They're all blown up. They think they know everything."

"My friend isn't like that, really. He has held many secret positions in the American government—he may still. We must find out what he's up to." He decided against telling her that Jeff was a friend of Stan's.

"I can't see anyone until I'm healed."

"But none of your bruises need show, they aren't where . . ."

"How do you know whether they will show or not? It depends on who might be looking."

Even bruised and tired, she was so overwhelmingly beautiful that it was painful for Sundar to be with her alone for very long. It depressed him that he could never satisfy her. You had to overpower Kamala to satisfy her. "Jeff had overpowered her," he thought, "but I'm her slave." He laughed thinking how Hassan had buggered Jeff. "Well, I will take my leave then Guruji," he sighed, getting up. "I must receive my old friend Stan."

"You will bring him to me?"

"He says he's going south tomorrow."

"Then delay him," she said, "delay him for two days and I will see him. And meanwhile—" She fastened her eyes on Sundar. "Find out where that Jeff has gone. I want to know."

*   *   *

When his car bearing Stan from Palam pulled in, Sundar was waiting behind the shutters of the veranda. He wanted to watch his old friend unseen; first impressions he had learned were always the most accurate, especially if one did not have to react. Stan bounded out of the back seat like a cricket player coming onto the field. It was obvious he was in good health and, thought Sundar, how much he resembles one of us, his complexion, his brown eyes, thick black hair.

As planned, it was James who greeted the guest at the edge of the terrace, took his luggage, and asked him inside, and Sundar noted that Stan didn't sit but began pacing. "He's in a hurry," Sundar thought. "Maybe he's in trouble."

"Welcome to India, Stan," said Sundar, arm extended, walking briskly into the room.

"Land of mystery and intrigue," said Stan, hugging him.

"Well, you'll see that for yourself," replied Sundar, holding Stan at arm's length. "Your friends were in Delhi for a few weeks, I took them round to some parties and so on. In fact, Jeff was living here until he vanished yesterday."

"Perhaps he'll come back."

"And Miss Weatherall met a yogi. Last seen heading in the direction of the Himalayas."

"That, I knew about," said Stan. "A friend of mine is also a disciple of that yogi. We flew in together. He's just gone looking for them."

"What brings you to India?" Sundar asked, after they were installed in a cool room sipping ninboo pani.*

"Usual thing, I guess," replied Stan. "Sightseeing, you know, elephants, Maharajas, a leper or two." He shrugged, wondering how much Sundar knew about the acid, whether Jeff had turned him on. "And of course girls. I hear India's famous for them and I've reached the time of life when . . ."

"How many do you want?" asked Sundar.

*ninboo pani=lemon water

"I can have as many as I want?"

"As many as you can afford," replied Sundar blandly, "no one hates money here, it's good karma to have it. Eat. Live. Take. Enjoy."

"Sounds great, I'll have a dozen for starters."

Sundar shook his head.

"Too many?" asked Stan.

Sundar nodded.

"But what have I got to lose—only money?" sighed Stan.

"Your soul," said Sundar.

"Oh that. You really think I have one to lose?"

"Perhaps not. But your mind can sink into a kind of soullessness here."

"That's what they say," remarked Stan, "is it so?"

"In West you only have a segment—here we have it all, from animal to saint. And nobody will stop you from going in either direction."

"We've programmed out the dangerous extremes haven't we?" declared Stan.

"You've replaced them with unseen dangers of a higher order," Sundar replied. "But as long as there is physical danger man stays strong."

"I felt the people pushing at the airport," said Stan.

"Yes, it's physical. Hunger brings sanity."

"I suppose," observed Stan, slouching back in his chair. "Shall I tell you why I've really come to India?"

"The truth at last," replied Sundar. "I'll probably have to believe it."

"You may or may not . . . I have cancer."

"I don't believe it. You look so healthy. What you mean is, that doctors have said you have something they have named cancer."

"No, x-rays said it," replied Stan seriously.

"You've had all that?"

"Yes, biopsies."

"I see," sighed Sundar. "What type?"

"Lung."

"But you don't smoke?"

"I know," Stan laughed. "Ironic, isn't it?"

"But why come here of all places?" Sundar shrugged. "You want to die in India? They say it is auspicious."

"I came to see a saint of yours, Ananda Baba—the one who heals people. I'm supposed to fly south tomorrow, he's someplace outside Bangalore. Do you know him?"

"Quite well," Sundar replied thoughtfully. "I shall give you a letter of introduction, otherwise you might have to wait for some time."

"Will he be able to heal me?"

"That, my dear fellow, is between you and the Baba. He's a very holy man."

"Fine," said Stan, "now tell me more about the girls."

Sundar's eyebrows shot up.

"Well, I might as well get it as long as I can," Stan said. "How much did you say they were?"

"Oh, five thousand rupees—perhaps higher."

"I'd like three of the five-thousand variety for starters, they can be delivered this evening."

"I think it's better you rest first," said Sundar, determined now that Kamala as his agent should accompany Stan to Bangalore. "You've had a long trip."

"Now, Sundar..."

"Tut, tut, tut," Sundar replied. "You *must* rest, this is a tropical country. You are sick. I insist! At least for three days. Then you can go to Bangalore. In the meantime I shall wine and dine you and make arrangements to have three of the five-thousand variety waiting for you when you arrive in Bangalore."

"Land of mystery and intrigue," smiled Stan. "It's a deal."

"Meanwhile, there is someone here in Delhi I should like you to meet."

Stan looked hopeful.

"But only after three days rest in my house. Her name is Kamala. You might say she's the fifty-thousand rupee variety."

"Sundar, you're deeper than I'd imagined. Do you by chance have a sleeping pill?"

*   *   *

"America will abandon us to the Russians, you'll see. We love Americans, but they can't cope with the Hindu mind. Negativism, that's what they call it. A Mohammedan may marry a Catholic or a Jew, it's all the same God, but he may not marry a Hindu because they say we are idol worshippers. Christians feel that way too and its true. What they don't understand is that with us its a technique. Anything is an idol. Try ripping up your American flag and see what happens!"

Sundar had turned pedantic, the result of too much wine, too much chicken tandoori, and the nervousness he always felt in Kamala's presence.

Stan was staring at Kamala. Her body folded in yards of silk gauze against scarlet and pink cushions seemed to undulate before his very eyes. Sensing at once she was a priceless object in a display case he made a note not to become involved with her. It would mean slavery of the worst sort. On the other hand anything rare and precious could be bought.

"But do you not believe it is the soul that's at stake in today's world," Sundar droned on.

Kamala stretched languorously, displaying her breasts. "You mean it's for sale," she put in.

Stan was sure her nipples, projecting hypnotic waves, were aimed directly at him.

"Is your soul for sale?" he asked, shifting his gaze to her eyes.

"Before you can get to the soul you must conquer the body, is it not so?" She nodded slightly. "I hear you are going south almost immediately, what a pity. I would have enjoyed getting to know you better."

"Why not come with me?" Stan heard himself saying, somewhat to his own surprise, "As a friend of course, you can have your own suite of rooms. I understand there is racing at this time of year. You can go to the races while I visit my saint." As attractive and fascinating as he found her, he wanted for her to know that he had no intention of entering the lists as a potential conqueror. For that he was completely unqualified but he knew she was bound to attract interesting people.

"Your saint?" she asked.

"I am sick. I am looking for someone to cure me."

"You don't look sick."

"Lung cancer."

"I see," she whispered, glancing at Sundar. "Which saint?"

"Ananda Baba," replied Sundar.

"Him." said Kamala, obviously impressed. "Perhaps I shall come. I would like to see that saint myself."

"I think it would prove a most interesting experience for you," Sundar nodded. "You'll be seeing India through expert eyes," he said to Stan.

*   *   *

"You are Mister Stanley?" a voice said, as Stan and Kamala waited for their luggage at the Bangalore airport.

"I'm Stanley."

"I am Saladin," a husky young man said. "Mr. A. K. Sundaram has asked me to look after you and this lady. Do you have your baggage checks? Thank you, I will take care of everything. The car is just over there, you go sit down."

After the cold dry air of Delhi, the south, sweet and warm with the scent of jaccaranda and jasmine, felt better in Stan's lungs. The East End Hotel, an old Victorian structure set in acres of well kept gardens and clipped lawns, reminded Stan of a spa in Weisbaden or Saranac.

"I have arranged for you an audience tomorrow with His Holiness. Is it too soon?" asked Saladin, when they were alone in Stan's suite. "As the ashram is near Raichur, almost a day's drive from here, we must leave very early in the morning."

Stan nodded.

"And are you still wanting three beautiful girls tonight for party?" He asked.

Stan nodded.

"And your lady? She will also come?"

"No, no, no. We are only traveling together."

"Of course," replied Saladin. "Then I will take my leave and see you after dinner about 9 p.m."

Stan nodded.

Saladin did not leave the hotel at once, but slipped up a side stairway to Kamala's suite where he knocked softly. "Ah, Kamala, what good luck for me to see you again after so long." he said as she opened the door. His eyes sparkled. "It's been nearly two years."

"You remember me then?" she said, appraising him. "And look at you. You've developed . . . no longer a boy, eh?" She chuckled. She had seduced him out of boredom several years before in Bombay, but was surprised to see him in Bangalore.

"Then you remember?" he sighed.

"Of course. But how did you get here?"

"I'm managing some girls. We are here for the races."

"How's business?"

"Oh, it is excellent," he said enthusiastically. "The Russians are especially good customers."

"Russians?"

'Yes, there are many here selling tractors and they are very generous." He smiled. "The girls are getting fatter and healthier from all the vitamins and medicines I can give them now."

"And you have a date with the American for this evening?"

"Yes."

"To bring him three five-thousand rupee girls?"

"Sundar has told you then," he said, realizing at once that Kamala would be collecting part of his commission.

"Of course. Listen to me. This man is very rich. Just now, he is carrying over thirty thousand dollars in travelers checks and thousands of rupees in cash. You must put on a good show for him.

"You mean I must perform?"

"Most likely," Kamala said, "I don't think he is much interested in having them himself."

"Then . . ."

"Tell the girls the pay is a thousand rupees each, not a paisa more, understand? And make sure they don't understand English. When you deliver them, tell Mister Stan that you'll wait in the lobby until he's finished. I know his type. He will ask you to wait in the sitting room of his suite. When the girls are undressed, he'll want you to come in and do something with them. Watching, is his pleasure.'' Her eyes narrowed. ''Then you must say at once that the girls charge an extra thousand rupees each for being watched, and that it is up to him what he feels your performance is worth; but that usually you do not do these things with your own girls and you would want triple the same pay. He cannot give you less, so when it is over you will have thirty thousand rupees in your pocket.''

''Ah, correct,'' replied Saladin following her calculations.

''But don't be in a hurry,'' Kamala said. ''He'll want it to go on for some time, after all thirty thousand rupees is over three thousand dollars. Have you understood now?''

''Oh, yes,'' he said, ''it is a very good idea, you are too intelligent.''

''And when you get tired, make him have the big orgasm. And while he is lying in a weakened condition, whisper to him that he should rest up for the trip to His Holiness. That will send him to bed. And another thing—''

''What is that?''

''Bring the girls here to me before you take them to him. I will make sure they obey you. I have a potion . . .''

''Ah,'' he said, teasing her, ''will you give me some?'' He put his hand on her waist.

''You don't need potions,'' she laughed pushing him away.

''But how can I repay you for your good advice?''

''We'll see about that later. Now let me sleep. Oh, one thing more, you might get one fat girl just for variety.''

*   *   *

From the speakers on the mosques as the sun set over the city came the droning of the sheiks amplified, *Allah is God, there is but one God, Allah . . .*''

Tired but not sleepy, Kamala sat in a bay window of the old Victorian Hotel and gazed out over the race course with its border of jaccaranda trees. ''In Bangalore,'' she sighed to herself, ''there is still something of the old days left.''

A soft knocking sounded at the door. She opened it and there was Saladin dressed in expensive white flannel pants, a pale pink cashmere sweater, and imported Gucci slippers.

The girls trailed in after him, all Goan Christians of extraordinary beauty. Surely a dying man would be distracted by the sight of so much healthy tissue.

''Come here,'' she said to the girls cheerfully and pretending to re-arrange their hair, looked for lice.

''You don't imagine I would bring girls with bugs, do you?'' said

Saladin in English.

"Not intentionally, but one never knows," Kamala replied. "We don't want Mr. Stanley to get lice, do we?" She stepped back appraising them. "No VD, I hope? These Christian girls are so permissive, you know."

"Of course not," said Saladin, "but what does it matter if I'm the one who has to fuck them?" He pretended to look sorry for himself.

"You can't be sure. That's what I think may happen, but after watching you he may get excited enough to do it himself. He might even want to fuck you." She laughed.

"There is no price for *that,*" he protested, slapping his buttocks.

"There is a price for everything, Saladin," said Kamala dryly. "You just haven't thought of it yet, or you've never been hungry enough!"

Then she spoke to the girls in Hindi.

"You must do anything and everything Saladin says, understand? Whether you like it or not. It's a job just like any other and must be well done. Especially as you will be paid one thousand rupees each."

She took out her purse. "Now I'm going to give you each two hundred and when you've finished you'll get the balance."

One of the girls protested, demanding half-payment. "But my dear," said Kamala, glaring, "if you get half now, you won't work half so well, will you? Shall we replace you?"

The girl shook her head.

"Then do your work well and you'll get it all, perhaps even some bakshish, don't you trust me? It's all here." She displayed a wad of hundred-rupee notes.

The girl lowered her eyelids.

"Now, have some tea. It will give you a little lift." She poured out four cups. "One is for you," she said to Saladin in English. "A bit of my potion is in it. It'll make you last longer." She laughed. "Maybe even long enough so that there'll be something left for me."

Gazing ardently at Kamala, Saladin took the cup. Outside the sky was crimson and Kamala opened the large casement windows. "What a superb spring evening," she said languidly and turned chucking one of the girls under the chin. "It's time for you to go to work now. Have a good time." She shoved them out through the door like school children and lay down to relax.

But the American, Jeff, kept clouding her thoughts. "No one treats Kamala that way," she muttered, "no one!" And yet he had, and that intrigued her.

Reminding herself to phone Sundar about Jeff's whereabouts she drifted off to sleep.

*   *   *

A few hours later Kamala was awakened by a persistent knocking.

"It is I, Saladin, let me in."

She opened the door. The girls went directly to the bathroom.

A pokerfaced Saladin counted out thousand-rupee notes. Twenty thousand in all and handed them to Kamala.

"And for yourself?" she asked. "Did he give nothing for you?"

"Fifteen thousand," replied Saladin.

"Then I assume he had a good time?" Kamala asked dryly.

"Very good. Very good." replied Saladin.

The girls returned from the bathroom looking fresh and inscrutable. Kamala counted out eight hundred-rupee notes for each girl.

"Well," she said in Hindi, smiling. "Take them. They're yours."

Demanding a tip, the girls refused.

"Aha, aha," Kamala cried, feigning rage.

Kakshish, bakshish," wailed the girls in chorus. "We did good work. The customer was well-satisfied."

"Work," Kamala hissed, peeling off three more hundred-rupee notes. "You don't know the meaning of work." She knew that it was a formal ritual and that they would demand another round of hundred rupee notes. "That is all you are getting."

The girls stubbornly refused to take the money.

"Whores," she said, rolling her eyes melodramatically. "You agreed to one thousand. I have given as agreed, plus one hundred. Still you are not satisfied."

"But mistress," they all said together.

Kamala whipped out a second round of notes. "Now go, or Saladin will beat you. Saladin!"

The girls grabbed the money and giggling, beat a hasty retreat to the door with Saladin at their heels.

"May I return?" he whispered.

"As you like," said Kamala, sternly.

*   *   *

Twenty thousand less three thousand six hundred makes sixteen thousand four hundred." Saladin sat gingerly on a corner of the bed. "That is good."

"It's all right," Kamala signed. "But I've made three times the amount in half the time."

"Of course," said Saladin modestly, "but you are the great Kamala. We are only rabbits compared with you."

"And now you have learned a few tricks from me, eh?" She yawned uncurling on the bed to reveal her magnificent breasts. "You will escort us to His Holiness in the morning, I suppose?"

101

"That is Sundaram's order," Saladin replied.

Kamala gazed at him thoughtfully.

"May I stay," he said, "is it to late?"

"That depends."

"On what?"

"On what price you are willing to pay, my dear rabbit," she whispered carelessly, watching the effect of her words.

He stood up, his bronze face immobile in the soft light, he pulled the lining of his pockets out and laid his fifteen thousand rupee notes on the bed.

When she made no move he knelt on the floor beside her and stretching his arms out blindly, rested his hands on her warm thighs.

"Take off those ridiculous clothes," she said, pushing his hands away.

Removing his new pink sweater and shirt he stepped out of his pants.

"Have you had a bath since Mr. Stanley," she asked.

He nodded, not daring to meet her eyes.

"Then come, lie down here beside me," she commanded.

He lay down on his stomach, his lips on her breasts. Taking hold of his hair, she lifted up his head and with her free hand gathered the fifteen thousand rupee notes.

"Watch," she said and moving her hand over the candle of her bedside table, burned the notes one by one.

"Now," she hissed, letting go of his head, "let's see what you've learned in two years."

VII

AT FIRST THE fourteen-hour sessions, repeating the mantra* Indra had given her, seemed interminable to Laura. Her legs ached, her back felt broken, and her mind, relentlessly disobedient, wandered. After the third day however, most of her mental trips stopped, and by the sixth she was able to stay on track during the whole period. But what a track. And where was she going?

Each morning and evening Indra waved to her at the rapids. She was happy to see that his jaundice was clearing quickly, and though she only saw him from a distance, she began to feel a bond with him she had never before experienced with anyone.

On the last day of her meditations she heard the chorus of voices singing again and the waves she had seen before, appeared. Once, into this space came the three-quarter profile of a man looking at her out of one eye. She thought it must have been Indra but when he returned at the end of the week and told him, he only looked at her with his left eye and winked.

"Is that all?" he said.

She nodded.

"Good," he said, "and now I have a surprise for you."

She felt disappointed he wasn't going to talk further about her experiences, but a barefoot young man wearing a faded red cloth and an orange turban had just appeared.

"Alex," Laura gasped, "is it really you?" She wondered if anything had gone wrong with the acid distribution or with Jeff.

"Not too much converstation now," said Indra. "We have exactly twelve minutes to pack and eight minutes to reach the bus to Petoraghar before it leaves. Don't think, act."

*   *   *

*mantra=a set of syllables repeated during meditation, which seem act like keys in opening certain vibrational channels that connect inner and outer experience.

On the long dusty trip Indra spent the time talking with Alex in Hindi. Feeling somewhat indignant at being left out of the conversation, Laura dozed.

"Tell me why you've come," Indra asked.

"The man I work for has cancer, his name is Stanley," replied Alex.

"You mean some doctor has told him he has it."

"Yes, and he's gone to Ananda Baba hoping to get cured."

"Ananda Baba can easily cure your friend if he wishes," declared Indra. "But the cure will be expensive."

"Should I have brought him to you?"

Indra sighed, "Just as well you didn't. It's hard work, this curing business. Takes a lot out that has to be put back. I always lose a bit of hair when I do it. Let the Baba heal him if he will. So you have come to India to be with your friend?"

"And for other reasons," Alex said quietly. "Has Laura told you what she and her friend Jeff are up to?"

"No, not directly," said Indra. "But I put her to japping* a mantra for a week, and of course, the whole thing came out in my ear. Very interesting indeed. I have had this LSD, you know."

"No, I didn't know," said Alex. "When?"

"Oh, perhaps two years ago."

"From whom?"

"From a servant who worked for some Irishman from America who was living about thirty miles from here."

"Do you remember his name?"

"The Irishman's name? Was it Cleary or O'Leary . . . some such name. The servant's name was Prem Singh. Which do you mean?"

"You answered my question."

"It's a dangerous poison," Indra said. "Very good and very poisonous. You've had it?"

"I make it," confessed Alex.

"It's very interesting. I took it; nothing happened. Then I took a whole mouthful, about twelve tablets, still nothing happened. But the ordinary local poeple who got it went mad and still are. One boy became catatonic, others like saints. I should say it is equal to ten years of meditation. Imagine, ten years of meditation in ten hours. Should never be given except by an adept. Even then it isn't wise to open up the uninitiated to that extent."

"They put the Irishman in jail for doing it."

"That was foolish. Anyway, this stuff should not be passed out freely in India. You must remain uninvolved. When you leave me, leave India at once."

*japping = repetition of mantras

"But the distribution will happen anyway. Stan might agree to stop it if you saw him, but it's Jeff who has the stuff—and he's disappeared. No one knows where he is."

"But Jeff will get in touch with this one, won't he?" Indra glanced at Laura who had fallen asleep beside him.

"Maybe, maybe not."

"Well, we'll see," said Indra thoughtfully.

After sunset the bus stopped for the night in a small village and hoping to find a place to sleep, everyone tumbled out. Indra, with Alex, and Laura walked along the empty main street. It was cold and damp. Gigantic cedars and deodars towered over the line of closed shops.

At one of the small wooden doorways Indra stopped and knocked loudly with his chimtah. Bustling could be heard inside, the door opened a crack and an old man's startled expression changed to one of wide-eyed incredulity.

"Babaji," he cried and fell to the ground at Indra's feet.

"Shut up and let us in quickly," Indra said.

Scrambling up, the man let them into the warmth of a tiny blacksmith shop where a small fire glowed in an open forge.

"Shut the door before anyone sees," Indra commanded, "then prepare some tea. I once practiced here in another time," he said, turning to Laura.

"Practiced?" Laura looked surprised.

"My dear child, what do you expect?" said Indra patiently. "I'm a sanyasi, a yogi, siddha. I have all fourteen initiations and twenty-one past human lives that I know of. I play different roles in different places, sometimes at the same time. Let it suffice that once upon a time I played in a drama here which this man has not forgotten." Indra paused, watching to be sure their host was preparing the tea correctly.

"Let's have a chillum before tea and after that more chillum and more tea," he said gaily. "It will pass the time 'til daybreak, when we must leave, otherwise all hell might break loose here. We'll catch the bus on the road."

*   *   *

The next morning there was frost on the grass as they walked quickly out of town along the road and it was a relief to suddenly emerge from the damp forest over the crest of a ridge into bright sunlight. Scarlet rhododendron blazed against the blinding Himalayan snows that towered above them. Flutes echoed in the valleys below, where cows and goats grazed among bamboo groves. Soon they heard the grinding of the bus and minutes later they were squeezed inside like sardines.

"The yoga of the bus," Laura murmured to Alex. "How far now?"

"Far enough," said Indra, overhearing. "But don't ask silly questions, just repeat the syllables I have given you and time will fly by. It's because of you, after all, that we have to take these wrecks. I'd rather walk, it's shorter, but you two would not keep up. Some day perhaps you'll buy us a limousine." He winked at Alex. "Better yet, to be speeding through the Himalayas in your mother's Rolls Royce. We'd crash and that would be the end of us."

"You'd like that?" Laura asked.

"Some day I will tell you how much, my dear," he said, "and why I can't. Tried many times, but She won't let me."

"She?"

"Goddess—she keeps me here working for her. I'm tired of it. Will you go with me when I go?" He grinned at her.

The question frightened her.

"Ah, I know. You want to stay just a little bit longer. Thinking you might finally get the jam. Jam yesterday, jam tomorrow, I know."

After half a day's ride they reached a tea shop where they bought supplies and set off on foot. For three hours they climbed steadily to the top of a densely forested mountain. On one side a sheer cliff dropped down with a cave at its base. Around the other side was a large wooden temple with deer antlers and tattered bits of crimson cloth attached to its pagoda eaves.

"This is the home of Durga, one of mother Kali's emanations, the Temple of Tigers. Have you ever seen a Kumaon tiger? They're as big as water buffaloes, bigger sometimes. I must do certain things now to protect us while we are here." He bounded up the path. "Alex, you and Laura set up camp, I'll be back soon," he shouted.

Alex showed Laura how to make a twig broom and how to sweep the floor of the cave while he reconstructed a fire pit outside.

"Now for the wood," he said.

"The wood? Won't someone bring it?" Laura asked.

"Yes. Us!" replied Alex, laughing. He took an axe from his bedroll. "I'll cut and you carry, the experience might come in handy for you some day. Come on, you'll do all right."

"Enough," cried Alex, out of breath, when they had a sizable pile of logs on the terrace in front of the cave.

"I should hope so," panted Laura.

A chorus of locusts was singing in the high pines.

"Alex, you haven't yet hold me why you came to India," Laura declared. "Has something gone wrong?"

"Not exactly."

"Then what?"

"It's Stan—he thinks he has cancer. He's gone to a famous saint in the south."

"And you came with him?"

"Yes and Carlos," said Alex. "Carlos got off the plane in Bombay while Stan and I came on to Delhi."

Laura looked worried. "I don't like the sound of that! Carlos and Jeff don't get along at all. There might be trouble. Jeff's in Bombay then? That's where I'm to meet him later this month. But why didn't you bring Stan to Indra? He can heal, I've seen it."

"He wants to go to this other man, publicity, you know."

"But can he heal?" asked Laura.

"If he wants to, and for a price," replied Alex.

"Oh. Well, I don't exactly like Stan but I feel sorry for him."

Just then Indra appeared on the path. "Quite enough wood," he commented, "congratulations."

Laura sighed and made a face.

"This is what you need, dear child," Indra said, looking too young to be calling her a dear child, "hard work, seven years hard labor." He grinned and bared his teeth at her.

"I feel like Red Riding Hood," she said faintly.

"And I am the evil wolf," he cried, running back behind a tree where he peered out at them showing his teeth and howled menacingly.

"You won't forget him soon, I can tell you that," Alex chuckled.

"Is he human?" Laura whispered, "I mean sometimes he seems more than alive. Not dead exactly, but not alive either. I can't put it any other way, it's when he goes transparent and all that."

"So he's shown you that much, has he?" said Alex thoughtfully. "I don't have any answers—only some of them. Does he frighten you?"

"At first he did, yes. Very much. But now I'm used to things happening. I suppose there's a lot more?"

"Yes."

"I thought so."

*   *   *

"Someone is coming," breathed Indra, opening his eyes. They were seated in front of the fire, about to begin evening prayers. He reached for his conch,* put it to his lips, and as the last sound of it echoed through the forest, receding into the evening vastness, there came a reply.

"Halloo-o-o, Hallooooooo."

As a bird listens for a worm, Indra cocked his head.

"Halloooo," went the sound again.

"Jackals are rare here, this is the place of tigers," he said, "must be

*conch=a shell used as a horn by yogis

107

some other animal."

"Hallooo—is Maha*rodgee* there?"

"Ah," Indra started, "a human animal. I thought so. Who is there?" he called, "who dares disturb a sage meditating in the forest?"

Emerging from the darkness, crawling up the hill on all fours, came a big bony woman in a threadbare tweed suit and boy scout shoes. Over her arm hung a tattered alligator handbag. She crawled onto the terrace and started to get up.

"Are you the Maha*rodgee*?" she gasped.

With a wink at Alex, Indra jumped up and stood over her threateningly. "Get back down on your knees, woman," he shouted, rattling his chimtah at her. "Don't you know where you are? Remove your shoes at once."

Falling back on her knees the woman gazed up at him, smiling inanely.

Indra burst out laughing. "Woman," he said, "you are at the cave of a witch." He narrowed his eyes, then snapped his long hair in her face.

Her smile faded. "Then you aren't the same one," she whimpered. "You aren't the one who healed Mohan Singh Shah."

Indra glanced at Laura. "You see, what did I tell you."

"You *are* him then," the woman cried, falling at his feet.

Without a word Indra resumed his seat before the fire and began preparing a chillum, which he lit and passed to Laura. She smoked and then passed it to the woman as he directed.

"Oh no, no thank you," she said politely, holding up her hand. "I never smoke, really I don't." She turned her watery blue eyes to Indra.

"Smoke it," he said.

"But I . . ."

"Smoke it," he insisted.

"But I'm allergic to tobacco," she said, making a face.

"Alex," Indra commanded, "show her how to hold it and do it until she learns."

"But I don't—"

"What is your name?" Indra said.

"Elizabeth," she said meekly.

"You are the wife of a Methodist missionary?"

"No, Quaker."

"Nevertheless you are a Christian missionary's wife?"

"Yes."

"Do you know that I eat missionary ladies for breakfast?" he roared, crashing his chimtah against a burning log.

A shower of sparks flew out of the fire.

Laura was becoming frightened.

"Now you are coming here to me, a yogi, to do the work your Christian doctors cannot do. Either smoke or get out," he growled, and closing his eyes, froze in a posture of meditation, fists clenched on his knees.

Elizabeth cast a sheepish glance at Laura and Alex. Alex took the chillum from her hands and showed her how it was held. She fumbled with it, sucking on it and coughing, but soon managed to inhale several times without choking. Then Alex smoked and passed the pipe back to Indra.

He took it at once, finished it, refilled it immediately and passed it to Laura, who smoked and again passed it to Elizabeth.

Watching as she drew in on it, Indra laughed.

"Bola shakti durbar a ki," he shouted at her across the fire.

"Bola shakti dorabara a ki," she shouted back reflexively as if something locked up inside her had been suddenly released.

"Huh," he muttered, "I saw you coming this afternoon."

"But how could you. I..."

He shook his head as if ridding himself of a gnat, and turned to Alex. "She comes to me to do her work but doesn't believe I could see her coming. I will do your work, that might also surprise you," he said glaring at her.

"But I haven't told you what it is."

"Young woman, do you think if I can take away your tumor, I'll not know beforehand that you have it and are coming to me for that purpose? Really, this animal disgusts me," he said in Hindi.

Elizabeth burst into tears. "I'm so tired," she wailed, "may I go to sleep somewhere?"

"Wrap her in my blanket," Indra said to Alex. "Let her sleep at my feet." He rubbed his hands together. "Let's all 'sack-out' as they say. It's already too late to eat."

Laura and Alex bundled the large limp form of Elizabeth into a blanket.

"And more are coming, so get ready." Indra smiled wanly. "I see them...two first-class fools...It seems we cannot escape, even here...if one is kind they come and want to eat, if we are not they want to kill us."

*   *   *

The next morning before dawn Laura awoke to see Indra sitting in front of the fire staring at the coals. She lay under her blanket watching him through a small hole. He winced visibly as loud internal rumblings and farts issued from the lumpy heap where Elizabeth lay sleeping.

It was cold. Alex jumped up naked from his sleeping bag and ran toward the spring several hundred feet below. Knowing that she too was supposed to bathe in the icy water, Laura shuddered and burrowed into her blanket.

109

"Think what a hopeless wretch is lying there," Indra said as Alex dried himself before the fire. "But what to do? Who comes to this fire cannot be turned away unless he disobeys the rules."

Alex prepared the morning chillum and set a pot of tea to simmer on the coals. The aroma of cardamom attracted Laura and she sat up, holding her blanket around herself.

"Bonjour, Mademoiselle," said Indra, smiling his proud naked warrior smile, welcoming her to the battle of the new day. "Have chillum and tea before venturing down to bathe. It will protect you from the cold."

He sucked on the pipe. Sparks flew out and clouds of pungent smoke drifted from the corners of his mouth, giving him the appearance of a young dragon.

"To me it is all the same," he said. "Cold, hot, hot, cold. It doesn't seem to affect me. It is a boon passed on to me by my mother's guru—the one I sat with from the age of six . . . a great rishi, my first teacher."

When the chillum was finished, Indra poured tea, first into the fire and then into the cups set out by Laura. The sun, though not yet visible, had set the edges of the snowy peaks ablaze. Alex and Laura sipped their tea in silence. Indra took up his instrument and chanted to the sun as it rose.

The pale face of Elizabeth emerged from under the blanket. Fumbling for her purse, she extracted a tissue, blew her nose loudly, and tossed the wad of tissue into the fire.

Indra dropped his instrument and grabbing his chimtah extracted the tissue from the coals before it caught fire.

"Never do that again," he growled, throwing the tissue back into her lap. "It's against the rules."

Elizabeth made a face. "After all it's only a fire," she grumbled, smiling at him as if he were putting her on.

"Wipe that smile off your face," Indra commanded, "and remove those loathsome shoes at once."

Fumbling with the laces, Elizabeth grudgingly removed her shoes.

"Now give them to Alex," he said, "along with the stockings. They must be removed at least one furlong from this place."

"But, Maharodgee," the young woman objected.

Crash came the chimtah, inches from her hand. "How dare you!" he cried. "Give this bitch her shoes," he said to Alex. "Now, get out!"

Then he fixed her with his eyes. "But before you go, feel your left breast. You will find the tumor is gone."

Quickly Elizabeth turned away and reached up inside her sweater. The disbelief on her face turned to joy and she burst into tears, her large white bony hands over her eyes, the big clumsy body shaking involuntarily.

Indra jabbed the chimtah into the ground in front of him and leaned on it, staring at her disdainfully.

"You'd better bathe now," he said quietly to Laura. Laura jumped to her feet and ran down the hill in her blanket.

Alex appeared worried.

"Let that animal cry," Indra said, glancing at Elizabeth. "She needs it, she needs beating. Even now," he said after a pause, "she will lapse into forgetfulness and will say that the Surgeon General made a mistake and that really there was no tumor."

"How did you know about the Surgeon General?" wailed Elizabeth.

"She thinks I can heal her and not know the whole story," he said, laughing. "What a low type animal you are. And take a bath," he added. "Walk down that path about two hundred yards to the spring. You can't eat until you bathe—that's another rule."

"But my shoes..."

"You must learn to use the feet God gave you," he yelled, grinning.

*   *   *

They had just finished eating when far below in the forest they heard voices.

"As I warned you, more are coming," Indra grunted. "Two of them, first-class fools both. And we will have to feed them. I'm sick of it!"

A few minutes later, panting and out of breath, two men struggled onto the terrace. One wore a sloppy tweed suit and spoke with a Scottish accent while the other had adopted local dress and was wearing a kirta and dhoti. On seeing indra, they removed their shoes and bowed deeply.

"See you made it," puffed the one in the dhoti to Elizabeth.

"You are friends then?" asked Indra with deliberation.

"We met in the village," said the Scotsman. "She told us she was looking for you. We'd heard of you and since we were passing this way we decided to take the opportunity to meet you. I am Dr. Reginald D. Long, and this is my friend, Dr. Albert Loeb. We are in psychology."

Indra nodded politely. "Very interesting. But why come to see me?"

"You are somewhat of a legend in these parts," said Dr. Loeb in a sharp American accent. He had gray hair and a withered left hand.

"You want me to heal your hand?"

The man smiled. "Never thought of that."

"It's possible," said Indra. "Just takes some time."

The Scotsman cleared his throat. "We came mainly to hear your opinion of certain Western theories of psychology."

"You mean Jung, Freud, Pavlov and so on?" said Indra. "They are correct as far as they go, but that's not very far. I read their books long ago.... I think you want to be yogis or sorcerers, eh?" He laughed maliciously.

The two men looked at each other.

"In any case, this is not the hour for me to tell you anything. If you want to remain until after dark, then we may talk. Just now these dishes need cleaning. Take them to the spring and clean them with mud and ash. After that, I will have done what I have to do and will be glad to help you if I can."

Having spoken, Indra stood up and walked away toward the temple, leaving the two new arrivals staring into the fire.

"What does he mean?" Dr. Loeb asked Laura.

"He means you to go down to the spring and do the dishes if you want to stay." She disliked shrinks and was enjoying herself.

"We don't even know whether he's worth staying for. Why should we wash dishes for someone we hardly know?" said Dr. Long irritably. "It's ridiculous."

"Doesn't he realize we aren't fools, that he might even learn something from us?" said Albert Loeb. "It's possible we have valuable information too."

Glancing at Alex, he paused, "Say—don't I know you from somewhere? I mean, your face looks real familiar. Were you ever friendly with Tom? Of course, now it all comes back! Aha!" He glanced at his companion meaningfully. "He's the one I told you Tom was telling me about. of course, Tom thinks you've gone bonkers, you know." He smiled patronizingly at Alex. "I guess you realize that though." He continued. "Reginald, this is Alex, you might remember him—he was at Harvard about the same time you were."

"He's quite serious about the dishes," said Alex evenly, trying not to betray his feelings of disgust. "Otherwise, Laura and I . . ."

"I'll do them," said Elizabeth.

"You'll do nothing of the sort," said Alex. "If he'd meant for you to do them, you can be sure he'd have mentioned it."

"Well," said Dr. Loeb, getting to his feet, "I suppose if we're going to stay we'll have to do them. Shall we get on with it?" He turned to his friend.

"You mean you want to stay?" exploded Dr. Long.

"Don't you?"

"I'm not sure, if it means I have to do dishes. Really, Albert, I didn't come to the Himalayas to start doing the dishes of every yogi we run across. And you're the one who has all the questions—I should really leave and let you stay and do the dishes."

"I could have finished them during the time you two have been discussing it," said Elizabeth.

"It's not the work, it's the principle," said Loeb.

"After all, we're professionals. We usually don't sit around cleaning up after yogis, you know."

Alex went pale with rage. "It's time for me to rest," he said quietly, and disappeared up the path.

Laura put two more logs on the fire and curled up in her blanket.

"There's always a test," she said to the two psychologists. "But I can see you don't believe in buying unless you've read the label or there's a Good Housekeeping Seal of Approval. I can assure you it's impossible to do that here."

"But if none of the potions have labels, one might get poisoned," said the Scotsman, thinking himself clever.

"Yes, you might," answered Laura. She smiled. "Anything might happen to you."

*   *   *

When he returned, finding that the two men had indeed washed the dishes, Indra, deciding to reciprocate by preparing a banquet, spent the last hours of the afternoon with Laura, grinding herbs and spices.

By sunset the food was ready, and after Indra had performed puja,* Alex held the chillum out to him and lit it. Indra drew deeply and handed it to Laura.

"Sorry, but we're off the dope trip," said Dr. Loeb, his hand raised as Laura passed him the pipe.

"It is our rule," Indra said wearily. "One chillum after evening prayer. It is prasad of the Goddess, not what you call 'dope.' You cannot refuse it. After that we make music and then we eat."

"What's prasad?" Dr. Long asked suspiciously.

"It means gift. Ganja is one of the plants of the Gods. The sap of it is taken as an offering. It is given to the temple and returned as a gift—prasad. It must never be bought or sold. Your people have misused it."

"If you don't mind I'd rather eat," said Dr. Loeb, looking greedily at the food. "Be a shame to let all that get cold."

"There will be no eating until after the chillum. If you don't wish to smoke, then leave at once." Anger glittered in Indra's eyes.

"If that's his rule, Albert, then shouldn't we observe it?" asked Dr. Long.

"Unless you would care to leave?" said Indra hopefully. He began to tune his instrument. "I should warn you that this place is called The Mountain of Tigers and often they sleep around the temple just above here."

*puja=worshipping at an altar of certain idols and pictures with incense and offerings.

113

The two professors looked at each other.

Laura held out the chillum again to Dr. Loeb.

"Well I don't see much point in discussing important theoretical points after taking dope but..." He took the pipe, managed to swallow some smoke and then coughing, passed it to his colleague. "You see what it does, Reggie? Terrible stuff!"

"It is prasad," said Indra darkly. "It might even heal your hand, how do you know?"

Dr. Loeb glared at Indra. Elizabeth tittered, hastening to cover her grin. When the Scotsman had smoked and handed the pipe to her, she handled it like a veteran.

"I didn't know that wives of missionaries smoked," said Loeb facetiously.

"She's just showing off," Indra said.

Loeb rubbed his hands together briskly. "And now for some of that good food you've been preparing, eh, Baba?"

Ignoring him, Indra began to tune his instrument. While the two men started to fidget, Laura and Alex stared into the crackling fire.

Suddenly the silence was shattered by a throaty roar nearby.

"What's that supposed to be?" said Dr. Loeb loudly.

"Shhhh," whispered Dr. Long.

"Tiger," said Indra, continuing to tune his instrument. "If you will look to your extreme right, you will see the beast's eyes."

Everyone stared. Laura saw two burning orbs. They were so far apart it was difficult for her to imagine them belonging to the same creature. Then a sudden breeze brought a terrible stench that smelled like rotten meat.

Indra's face shone with a furious light. "Lovely, isn't it Doctors?" he said, baring his teeth. Then flinging aside his instrument, his hand clenched, he grabbed the chimtah, and rattling it yelled into the darkness: "Harr Harr. Hut Hut Hut."

There was a low growl followed by a crashing sound as the tiger retreated through the underbrush.

"If I'd been alone, I'd have sung to it and given it some supper," said Indra. "Female, most dangerous." Then he signaled Laura to serve out the food.

*   *   *

"Now," said Indra, preparing another chillum, "let's have an after dinner smoke."

"Oh, no," said Dr. Loeb firmly. "You said only before dinner."

"But this is an exception, Doctor. It isn't every day I receive visitors from the... uh, medical profession along with tigers. We must have more

114

chillums. I insist. Unless, of course, you and your friend would like to leave. It's much faster going down, shouldn't take over an hour to reach the bottom. I can loan you a flashlight.''

"Power tripping," muttered Dr. Loeb.

"Ah, you are beginning to understand."

The chillum went around. Laura sensed something brewing. Indra had the same bland expression when he had exorcised the Moslem sadhu.

"Now," he said softly to Dr. Long. "You were speaking of schizophrenia."

"Why, yes . . . what was it?" sputtered Long. "Ah, yes, we think there are two kinds of schizophrenia," he said, clearing his throat. "One which seems to be caused by the environment, and another which seems to be genetic. Maybe both are chemical in the end . . . ah, a chemical imbalance. I would be interested in knowing . . ."

"There is only one kind," said Indra, who had taken up his instrument and was strumming randomly, looking like a juvenile delinquent.

"Only one kind," said Loeb.

"Yes, only one kind . . . Another one jumps inside."

"What?" said Loeb sharply.

"Another personality—soul, it gets inside. There are hundreds of them everywhere." He waved his hands through the air. "All personalities without bodies . . . waiting to get new ones. When there is shock from the environment of a proper order and so on, sometimes they squeeze in. Then you have your schizophrenia. Chemical imbalance is just a sign that it is happening."

"Well, of course, that's an interesting folk theory," said Loeb patronizingly, "but it's not scientific. We're scientists!"

"What does that mean?" said Indra indifferently.

"What does it mean? It means we give credence only to events which can be measured and observed in a cause and effect relationship."

"I am giving you the cause," said Indra.

"But we have no instruments to measure the personality, or whatever it is that's disembodied or embodied. It's hypothetical."

Indra slapped his chest vigorously. "This is the instrument by which we measure."

Laura could see that while he was talking Indra was making himself transparent. She glanced at Alex who was also seeing it. She thought perhaps the Scotsman was seeing something too. Loeb, she was sure, saw nothing. She wondered how far Indra was going to go.

"Confound it, Baba," said Dr. Long, "there was something in that last chillum besides ganja."

"Mixture No. 77." muttered Indra.

"I am interested in these, uh, personalities floating around," said the

Scotsman, rubbing his eyes as if something had gone wrong. "There was a mathematician called Leibniz."

"He was quite correct, that Leibniz, as far as he could go given the world he lived in," said Indra. "These monads, unless they have become free, must follow their whims. Like a monad a soul is attracted toward its previous attachments in new bodies. It may even fragment itself altogether in some cases."

"What's your cure?" asked Loeb.

"We usually scare it out," said Indra. "It gets in through shock, so it must be shocked out."

"Like electric shock?"

"Unfortunately that doesn't work, it's too mechanical. Right theory; wrong practice."

Indra strummed softly on his instrument, fixing the Scotsman with his eyes as he grew increasingly transparent. Dr. Long now gaped open-mouthed at what he saw.

"But my dear Baba," continued Loeb, "we are scientists, we must have proof—" He turned to his colleague for confirmation. "Reggie, why are you staring like that?"

"Can't you see?" shouted Dr. Long. "He's not there! He's talking but he's almost not there!" He rubbed his eyes, a look of terror on his face.

Loeb's eyes went to Indra. Laura saw Indra flash out entirely.

"What's going on here?" yelled Loeb.

Indra's form reappeared. He was smiling vaguely and strumming his instrument. "You wanted some proof, Doctor, a demonstration perhaps." Then he flashed out again.

Dr. Long jumped to his feet, pointing to where Indra had been and from where the music now issued wilder and faster. Then he began to dance, laughing and struggling to remove his clothes.

Hearing the music, Elizabeth woke up and started to giggle.

"What's going on here," Loeb stammered, pale with fear. "Stop this nonsense at once!"

"Shut up," said Alex. "Don't interfere."

Stark naked, Dr. Long was now dancing around the fire, his eyes rolling in his head.

"But he's a married man, he has a wife and children," Loeb shouted, lunging forward. Grabbing at Long's leg, he was kicked back. "Reginald!" screamed Loeb, "sit down."

Over the sound of his instrument, Laura could hear Indra's laughter as he materialized before them.

"You've put some drug into that pipe," Loeb accused him.

"Oh," said Indra politely, "then why aren't you also dancing and the others?"

"But he's going to fall of the edge," Loeb moaned.

"Nothing is going to happen, Dr. Loeb," Indra muttered. "Your friend is what you call schizophrenic. You didn't know that, did you.... That's why he is so interested in it and has become such an authority. I am merely giving you a demonstration. The 'other' inside him has taken over. The one you call Reggie is in a state of shock. If this other can be coaxed or scared out, your friend will be, as you say, cured. Perhaps he'll write another best seller about it."

Suddenly there was a roar at the edge of the encampment. Everyone stared speechless as an enormous white tiger with faint black markings crept along the ground toward Dr. Long.

"Reggie, watch out!" screamed Loeb. But the now fearless Scotsman, arms flailing, skinny white body bouncing up and down in time to Indra's music, danced on.

"Ah ha, mira Baba. Ah...ho. Nameste, nameste durga," sang Indra, as Long danced and fluttered like a wounded butterfly before the huge cat.

Grabbing Elizabeth, Loeb dashed frantically into the mouth of the cave. Laura and Alex found themselves frozen in place, speechless.

"She's been attracted by this 'other' one's dancing," Indra shouted over his instrument. The beast's tail began to twitch, her ears went back.

"Ahhhagrrr," Indra roared and flinging down his instrument, knocked Long out of the way and brought down his chimtah on the beast's head. The tiger rose up on its hind legs, a full nine feet, and bounded into the night.

Sweaty and covered with dust, Dr. Long crawled on all fours towards Indra, leering, his tongue hanging from his mouth.

"We'll bathe him in warm water and wrap him well in blankets," declared Indra, "and we'll sleep in the cave tonight. Are you all right Laura Weatherall?" he asked smiling. "Remember, it is all illusion."

*   *   *

In America, Dr. Albert Loeb was a huge success. Considered extremely advanced in daring to combine the techniques of psychiatry with those of yoga, he'd been one of the first to introduce the rarer forms of yoga to the psychological elite of the West. He even had an ashram of sorts called The Institute, high in the mountains of New Mexico, where people paid seventy-five dollars an hour for his counsel, and with an inner circle of initiates he imagined he was exploring the mysteries of Raj Yoga.

But here in India, his face haggard, his beard coming out white in patches, he was beginning to fear for his own sanity. Crisis upon crisis had weakened him; concepts had been shattered, theories set to crumbling and now a naked yogi had somehow managed to throw his colleague into a trance.

117

"Raj Yoga," Indra said disdainfully the next day during one of Dr. Long's worst fits. "Nothing but a name, some methodism made up by all those Anandas to make money. If you really knew it, what they call the Raj Yoga, you would be able to lift the trance!" He laughed in Dr. Loeb's face.

Dr. Long, still naked, was alternating between periods of wild excitement and long periods of immobility. Dr. Loeb had tried to get through to his friend but Dr. Long had only stared at him. Now his freakout had progressed to the sexual level and he had spent most of the afternoon chasing Elizabeth from one spot to another, cornering her and masturbating wildly in front of her. Which sent Indra into gales of laughter.

"See what an old monkey is inside your friend," he said to Loeb, who stared grim-faced at the antics of his associate. "A lecherous old monkey. In a few days I will be able to talk to it, find out who it is. Interesting, no? Right now, however, it is so crazed from having been suppressed all these years by the other inhabitant—the one you call Reggie—that it is going mad from wanting. I must let it have its way for a while; if it is suppressed now there will be little chance that I can lure it out."

On the third day Dr. Loeb awoke to see Dr. Long on all fours eating dirt.

"He said that he was an expert on schizophrenia," observed Indra, who was already sitting before his fire. "Let him see what it is, from the inside—take the taste."

It was then that Dr. Loeb realized he must get away and return with Reginald's wife. As a scientist he found Indra's theory most interesting, but as Reginald's friend and colleague his sense of duty demanded he bring up reinforcements. What disturbed him most, however, was a voice inside him that he usually ignored, which was telling him he really didn't give a damn about Reggie, but was using him as an excuse to get away.

After the morning meal Loeb took Elizabeth aside. On the pretext of washing their clothes at the spring they would escape to the road, where Elizabeth assured him they could catch a bus. They would find Reginald's wife and return by taxi.

*   *   *

"So you are leaving to bring up reinforcements," said Indra, as the two hobbled off down the path toward the spring.

"Oh no, Maharodgee," squeaked Elizabeth, as if anything of the sort were furthest from her mind. "We're going to the spring to wash our clothes."

Indra brought his chimtah down hard on the fire like a sword. "You are lying," he yelled. "How quickly the cure is forgotten once the patient is

118

well. I had to spend two days on the mountain getting your lump off my body."

Then he raised the chimtah in a gesture of dismissal. "Go!" he shouted. "I can't stand the sight of either of you! Especially you!" He glared at Loeb. "Leave me alone, find some compassionate Swami in orange who will fleece your pocketbook while he fills you with theories to take to your following in America. Go! If you stayed I might trick you into going out into the forest with me—alone. You might have an accident and never return, ha!"

He turned to Alex. "Let those two animals be gone," he said. "I am tired of them."

*   *   *

On the third day after the departure of Elizabeth and Dr. Loeb, Indra came down from the temple. "They are coming back today," he declared. "Prepare for the worst. They may bring the police . . . yes, I think so."

Laura looked surprised.

"You don't believe me," he said, "but it happens. I raised a man from death once. His family called the police. I had to hide in a cave for seven days.

"You what?" exclaimed Laura.

"Forget it," Indra shrugged.

Reginald Long was awake again. He'd been sleeping alot but now he was talking and yelling, frothing at the mouth, and farting. Alex told Laura it was the poisons coming out.

"What will become of him?" she asked anxiously watching Long, naked except for the blanket Indra had thrown over him, rock catatonically.

Indra sighed, "If his wife shows up he might get worse. What can I do? These things take time. That Moslem sadhu you saw was simple. This animal is complex. His patients have driven him mad. Another soul came in through one of them—the sickness of the patient always rubs off on the doctor if he's any good."

The voices of Dr. Loeb and Elizabeth soon sounded below quarreling with a third voice, which was harsh and businesslike.

"The wife," whispered Indra. "Don't be surprised at what happens and don't interfere. That's an order. If things get out of hand just repeat your mantra and shift into neutral."

Minutes later the three stood breathless at the edge of the clearing.

"Well, we've come back," said Elizabeth.

Indra said nothing.

"This is Reginald's wife, Florence," said Dr. Loeb.

Florence was an attractive blonde with a good figure.

"I had an English nanny named Florence," murmured Indra, a faraway look in his eyes. "She was very nice."

"What was that?" said Dr. Loeb nervously.

"I said you must remove your shoes and stockings if you wish to remain in this vicinity."

Florence removed her shoes and stockings and sank to the earth where she sat quietly for some time, observing her husband huddled in his blanket.

A "heavy," Alex was thinking.

Elizabeth and Loeb continued their argument in whispers while Indra began filling a chillum. "Why don't you have them come up?" he said. "It makes no difference."

"Who come up?" asked Elizabeth.

"Why the two police officers you have brought with you, of course."

Florence turned her gaze from her husband to Indra. "Just *what* have you done to him?" she asked throatily.

Before Indra could answer Dr. Long got to his feet and babbling incoherently, threatened his wife.

"I don't think he likes your being here just now," said Indra. "Maybe you should leave and let him finish what he came for."

"How long would that be?" she said. "We have two children and commitments. Reginald is supposed to . . ."

"Could be three weeks . . . or three years," Indra said nonchalantly.

"Look here," she said, "you aren't my guru. I don't even know who you are and I'm not interested. I'm only interested in getting my husband off this mountain."

"Then call the police officers," Indra said. "Let them carry him down, unless you think Dr. Loeb can manage. Let them come and smoke a chillum and then carry him down. I don't think that animal is capable." He gestured to where Loeb was huddled sullenly with Elizabeth.

"Elizabeth, could you go down?" Florence asked. "I mean, you speak Hindi and all that . . ."

Elizabeth, thinking of the tigers, laughed nervously. "Florence, really—my legs just won't work anymore. It's almost dark and I just don't think I . . ."

"I'll go. Give me the flash," said Loeb.

Indra took the first draw on the chillum. "I doubt you'll have to go far," he said, letting the smoke come out with the words. "The officers will be closer than you think. They know the reputation of this mountain."

The pipe had barely gone around twice before Loeb reappeared, followed by two young policemen.

"Please remove your shoes and be seated," Indra said.

Dr. Loeb removed his shoes and sat down but the two officers remained standing.

"Remove your shoes and sit down," Indra commanded in Hindi. "This is a holy place."

One of the officers fell to his knees and began untying his heavy boots. The other caught him by the shoulder and pulled him up defiantly.

"Do you not intend to respect the sacred precincts of a sanyasi's fire?" Indra said, his voice like a cold wind.

What they answered or whether they answered at all no one could tell. Faster than anyone's eyes could register Indra sprang upon the two men and flung them to the ground. The officer who had tried to untie his shoe sprawled unconscious, between Elizabeth and Dr. Loeb who stared speechless, too frightened to move. The other lay doubled up and screaming. "It's time someone taught you some manners," Indra was yelling in Hindi, beating the man with his chimtah until bloodstains covered his shirt.

"Stop! Stop! You're going to kill him!" shouted Dr. Loeb.

"I may just do that!" Indra shouted back. "Shut up—it's not your affair."

"But it is my affair . . . it is everyone's aff—"

Loeb never finished. With one blow Indra sent him reeling down the hill.

Laura, trying to stifle the fear inside her, began repeating her mantra.

Florence was now standing over her husband, who, frothing at the mouth like a rabid dog, gestured obscenely at her.

"Reginald, get up right now," she said firmly. "Elizabeth, for God's sake, help me."

Shaking himself like a lion after a fight, Indra sat down again in front of the fire. The man he had beaten lay with his arms outstretched. Alex, his face pale, dragged the other, still unconscious officer nearer to Indra, who placed his hand upon him.

"Can we get him up?" Florence was saying to Elizabeth. "Reginald, GET UP!" she screamed. The two women struggled with Dr. Long who had gone limp. Just then Loeb reappeared, brushing himself off, his face livid. "Let's get the hell out of here," he urged. "This guy's crazy!"

"Stop," said Indra quietly, without looking at them. "You are all crazy. You'll get hurt going down the mountain at this hour. Lost or hurt."

"The tigers." Elizabeth blurted, her eyes watering.

"I know there are tigers," shouted Florence, "I don't care. If you think I'm going to spend a night here . . . why. He's the one who's crazy," she pointed at Indra. "Look what he's done to my poor Reggie. Where we come from you'd be locked up." She glared at Indra.

"Have it your way then," Indra said calmly, smiling at her. "But take this." He held out a tiny newspaper package.

"What is that?" she said disdainfully.

"If he should get worse, give him some of this on his tongue. It will bring him around."

"What is it?"

"Never mind, woman," said Indra impatiently, "do as I say!"

Unwillingly, Florence thrust the small package into her coat pocket.

"Alex," said Indra quietly, "see that they get to the teashop. You might sleep there yourself and return in the morning. Take my flashlight."

Sagging under the weight of Dr. Long, the three started cautiously down the mountain behind Alex.

"Jai Ho," called Indra after them, muttering something in Hindi. The officers at his feet were coming to. The one whom he had beaten whimpered with pain.

"Maharaj, forgive us," they stammered in Hindi. "It was all the fault of the foreigners."

"Pigs," Indra snapped. "It was not the foreigners who kept you from removing your shoes and showing due respect." With the chimtah he hit the ground near the men so that they cried out in fear.

Laura winced.

"Always remember," he said to her, "if you want to win any contest, you must put your opponent off balance. Go for the feet first."

"What will happen now?" she asked timidly. "Won't their superiors come—and arrest you?"

"They'd have to kill me first," he said.

"No! No!"

"Yes, yes. That is what I want to happen. I want to go. But I cannot myself cause it. That would be what you call suicide. It's against the rules." He gazed at her. "You see, I'm not afraid of death."

"I can see," murmured Laura.

"I am sanyasi," he went on leaning toward her, "when you become sanyasi, you die. Legally I am dead, under the direct protection of the government of India, and the ancient body of Indian law." He motioned to the two men. "These people have no jurisdiction over us, but nowadays they are getting fresh. The government wants to finish us off and also there are many false yogis and sanyasins disguised for their own ends." He paused and raked the coals of the fire.

"As a sanyasi I have no past, no future—but in fact, I have had many pasts and hopefully not too many futures. I will tell you of this life, a few acts in the play I am playing now, because it may make me more believable to you. It is important, you see, that you believe what I tell you because— although you don't know it—your soul has, shall I say, been placed in my hands. I myself didn't know it until Dorje's aunt told me. She is—or was —an oracle at Lhasa. It was she who summoned me. It is because of her that you are sitting here now."

Laura stared in confusion.

"I cannot say more, someday you'll understand it all, although maybe not in this life. Now I shall tell you something about my recent past going back to the beginning of this life, my twenty-second on this earth. The twenty-first life was four hundred and seventy-five years ago, and the first was about three thousand years before that. Someday perhaps I shall tell you of the others. But remember it is all a play—lila—illusion. Don't think it's so important."

The police officers had gone to sleep. As he spoke, Indra stroked the head of one of them.

"One purpose in disclosing to you these things is to show you that it is impossible for you to control your destiny in this world. There is a way of influencing it but it cannot be controlled.

"I was born into a princely family from the state of Patalia, my father was a Gurkha, a follower of Guru Goraknath. When Alexander the Great invaded India, my father's family had already recorded five or six hundred years of history. My mother, an extraordinary woman, was of the royal line of Nepal and her particular family had carefully preserved and handed down much of that ancient wisdom.

"At the time I was born, in 1910 to be precise, the British ascendancy in India was at its height. My father was much involved with them but my mother kept apart. We lived in a grand house, I suppose you would call it a palace, and had other homes in Delhi, in Shrinagar, and Simla. From birth I showed certain signs of clairvoyance and so on, which disturbed my father but delighted my mother.

"When I was six, against my father's wishes and only successful because I was the third of four sons, my mother brought me to these mountains to sit with an eminent siddha who was then one hundred and three years of age. With this old man I remained until I was twelve. He was able to tell my mother a great many things about my past lives and gave me the instruction proper to reawakening the talents of one who we say is 'twice born,' or in my case, many times born. For six years I saw almost no one. I wandered these hills with a cow, reporting to the guru only at certain times. I learned many things and all came easily, for of course I was really relearning them. My guru sent me to other yogis for special teachings as was the custom.

"There are two kinds of gurus, you see. If I can teach you something you don't know, well and good, I am your guru. But a real guru is more than that: he must have had a guru, who had a guru, who had a guru and so on. Why? Ah—that is the greatest of secrets and I shall tell you. Because the real teachings are not written, in fact they are not even spoken but are communicated in a certain manner beyond even speaking or writing.

"But I digress. In my twelfth year I was given the initiation which is supposed to determine whether the student will go into the world or will, then and there, become a sanyasi. It is a very difficult and strenuous ordeal and all the years from six to twelve have been a preparation for it. It is given in one and one place only in India and has been given there since before the time of Gautama Buddha.

"Well, after the initiation of course I wanted immediately to take sanyas and begin the twenty-five year period of austerities that is required. But my father suddenly stepped in. He was the sort of man you had to have an appointment to see, and I hadn't seen much of him. I was extraordinarily big for my age and strong. He wanted me to join the Army. What could my mother do? She couldn't go against him. So I was sent to Simla and educated there at the schools of the British Raj with other boys of noble birth, many of whom are, at this very moment, generals and so on in the armies of both India and Pakistan."

Laura noticed Indra had a faraway look in his eyes.

"I cannot say I disliked it. We had good times. I was an excellent athlete and won many awards, also I was a good scholar. It was all easy for me—except I knew it wouldn't last. During this period and in the summers and long holidays, my mother also had her way. My old guru left his body during my first year in school when I was thirteen; from then on I was taken by my mother to an even older guru, a woman, one hundred and thirteen she was when I was thirteen. Can you imagine? She lived not more than ten miles from where we are now sitting. I went to her for six years. She had connections in Tibet and sent me to Lhasa three times during those six years. Once, getting back, I missed three months of school. Later on I went for several years. It was this woman who drilled me in the methods my first guru had only hinted at, and correctly foresaw most of the events of my life. I was with her when she left her body in 1941 at the age of one hundred thirty.

"To go on: my father got wind of my mother's doings and after I finished prep school, determined that I should become modern and scientific, sent me to the British pre-med in Delhi. I found it very interesting indeed, especially as by that time I already could heal people by touch. It amused me to learn all the Western medical theories and I excelled in all of them and became an intern to the Surgeon General. During this period, from 1928 to 1936, I spent all my spare time with my third guru, a Moslem saint. It was he who taught me how to become invisible—as you have seen—and other things.

"Many people think there is some line between the fundamental practices of Moslems, Hindus, and Tibetans. That is all trash. There is only one wisdom. It is most ancient and he who knows it, knows it whether he is Moslem, Sikh, Pathan, Mongolian, Japanese, or whatever. It depends on the unbroken line of gurus.

124

"Then came World War II. I had graduated and was serving under the British Surgeon General. My father's regiment was Gurkha—very ferocious—and he had me put into the medical corps of the Royal British Army proper, not the Indian regiments. The Queen's Own Regiment it was called."

Pausing to throw blankets over the two policemen, Indra put fresh wood on the fire.

"One day an order came through for volunteers to report for paratroops," he continued. 'Ah ha,' I thought, 'at last my chance to get out of my body. Once and for all out of all this nonsense.' Of course, I had been well trained by my gurus in the proper way to go out when this happened. I thought it might be the answer.

"I kept the order in my hand, reported the next day, and went into training immediately, near Agra under General Wingate. We would go up in those noisy B-27s and our parachutes would be attached to a wire. You had to jump, pushing hard with your left foot. Then just as you got past the tail, the parachute would open and you would float down, ever so nicely."

Indra smiled to himself. "Once mine opened only partially and then gave out at eighteen hundred feet. 'At last,' I thought, 'I'm on my way out,' and immediately went into the proper dhyan.* But nothing happened. I hit the ground, sprang up, rolled over and over, and nothing happened. I was furious.

"One man under my command fell twenty-four thousand feet and lived. We found him in a village later, playing in the mud with the children. He'd 'crossed over' on the way down out of fear—he was already halfway out of his body when he hit. When he didn't go all the way, he stayed in it like a child. He was exactly like a baby. They wanted to institutionalize him, but I said no, let me have him. I had learned acupuncture in Tibet. I wanted to try it on him. As long as the needles were in he came back to himself, to his correct age, when I took the needles out he sent back to being a baby. Then I opened up his head and applied electrodes directly to the brain. Slowly, after several treatments, he recovered. Nice English boy he was. Never got beyond Eighth Standard, but after that he returned to England, went to college and is today an eminent professor of biology.

"All that knocking about made him smarter," Indra smiled. Glancing down at the policeman. "I forgot to treat his back. We must get his shirt off before the blood coagulates. Get some water and boil it and we'll wash and bandage him up."

The man attempted to move. Indra put his hand tenderly on his head and spoke in Hindi. The man groaned but remained still.

"Where was I?" asked Indra.

*dhyan=Hindi name for meditation.

125

"Paratroopers."

"Ah, yes. After that training we were to drop into Burma. I requested leave and took my men into some jungle land on one of my father's estates in the Terai.† I taught them JuJitsu, Karate and Lathi fighting‡ which I had learned from masters under my father's direction. Those English boys got a real taste of the jungle. Then we were flown to Burma and we jumped. Right into a swamp."

He laughed, looking at her, and then proceeded to dress the policeman's wounds.

"It was a vast swamp with massive trees—absolutely poisonous—septic. In the center of it was a low sort of mountain and in that mountain was a Japanese bunker. We were supposed to take it. It took me fifteen days to collect my men in that swamp. We lived mostly in trees, built tree houses and so on. We couldn't see where the openings of the bunker were as the mountain was covered with undergrowth. One morning I decided to make a dummy out of bamboo and cane and grass. It took me all day. We put a helmet on it and in the dark I carried it out to where they would see it. They knew we were there. When morning came—rat tat tat tat—they emptied round after round into it. Then every day we made a dummy and every morning they used up more and more of their ammunition.

"We had cut their supply line," he said clearing his throat, resting his hand on the dressed wound of the policeman. "Don't worry about these wounds," he said noticing Laura's concerned look. "They'll be gone by morning.

"After six weeks in that swamp, our rations were finished and the men started eating snakes and frogs and big turtles!" He laughed.

"Did you eat?" she asked.

"I tried some," he answered, looking embarrassed. "Horrible!

"Then came successive days during which no shots were fired and I decided to go in. I was a crack shot . . . give me a pistol and I'll shoot the ash off a cigarette at fifty paces. We'll try it sometime?" He raised his eyebrows. "Lovely—you'd enjoy it.

"So I told the men I would take red and green flares. Green flares

†Terai=The stretch of land between the Gangetic Plain and the beginning of the mountains, it is foothill land and very steamy jungle area about ten to twenty miles wide in a long strip at the base of the Himalayas.

‡Lathi fighting=Fighting with a stick, as they don't have guns in India. This training is given to all boys when they are very young and then later on if they specialize or go into the army or the police they get special training in Lathi fighting. The sticks are measured to the heighth of those using them.

meant come, red flares meant don't come, no flare meant I'm finished, don't come.'' He chuckled. ''I went in the night, got to one of the bunker holes and lay there looking in. It was easy for me, I'd spent half my life in jungles. There was a big five-gallon kerosene lamp. Sitting around it were emaciated-looking Japanese. Two others were sleeping and there were stinking unburied corpses near them. I went in and let the bayonet do its work. They were so starved they had no energy to resist. Then I let the green flare go and my English boys came fast. When they got there, they started hacking the dead bodies into pieces, then they hacked at the putri-fying corpses . . .'' He paused. ''It was a really strange sight,'' he said. ''I learned a lot of Western psychology during that war.''

''After capturing the bunker we got out fast. There was a walled village nearby and we stayed there for a time. The people gave us plenty of good cow's milk, wheat, rice, plenty of vegetables.

''But I knew the Japanese would be after us and so I had the villagers make an escape tunnel about twenty yards long through a hill on one side of the village. One night about a month later Japanese machine guns started blazing in the night. I told the men not to respond—it was a trick to see whether we were there. Minutes passed and when there was no sound from them at all, I knew they wouldn't come in until morning. I collected about fifty or so villagers and all their cattle and made them go through the escape passage. Then I sent my men through, set dynamite and blew the whole village sky high.

''The following morning we found ourselves surrounded. I told all my people to run, that I would cover their escape. I thought it might be my chance to get out again. They ran for it and got away. I got hit, but the bullet struck a black obsidian medal of Goddess Kali that my mother had given me. It was about three inches across and was swinging on my chest at the time. The bullet hit it and dropped into my lap—huh!

''I got captured. The Japanese knew of me. The officer saluted when he arrested me and they were very courteous and polite at the beginning. When I was handed over to their secret police for examination and questioning it was a different matter. They stuck needles under my finger-nails and electrodes on my genitals . . . My hair still stands up when I think about it. Somehow I went into dhyan and stopped the pain. They wanted Wingate's strategy for Burma, but I never talked. The English were my friends.

''The second night I escaped by killing three guards with a large kitchen knife. I beheaded them. I had to behead six more on the way out. Kali did it, I didn't—I hadn't the strength, and after that, I walked to Gauharti in Assan and did puja to Kamakshi Devi. Then I walked to Delhi, they decorated me and at last I went home.

''I had wanted to leave this world and become a monk at the age of twelve. After these experiences I came back and took up medical practice again but it was useless. My mother then produced written instruction from my second guru, the old woman. In them she foretold exactly what would happen to me. In 1940, a year before her death, she wrote down everything—including that the medal of Kali would save my life. She also gave detailed instructions for the twenty-four years of austerity I was now to perform.

"I said good-bye to my mother and father, my brothers and sisters. Little did I know they would be wiped out in the unrest of 1947 and that I was never to see them again except one brother who managed to hide himself when the local Moslems ransacked our family residence.

"It was a fine spring day, I remember it well. I had loaded all my worldly possessions—books, surgical equipment, everything—on two mules. Only my mother saw me off. My father thought I was mad. As an officer and a war hero, I had been offered a high rank, Lieutenant General, even a British passport.

"I took one servant and walked with the mules east to the Ganges below Hardwar. There I burned the books and chucked all my possessions into the river, stripped naked, and swam the Ganges. I then walked to Nepal where I spent twenty some years living naked following her instructions."

He laughed softly, gazing down at the sleeping policemen. "You think this low trash means anything to me? I should kill and bury them right here and now, but it is too good for them; besides She has commanded me not to take action. I cannot even get out myself unless She commands it."

"You frighten me," Laura said quietly after a long silence. "You're so final, so pure. It makes me feel so polluted." She shuddered.

"Only *it* feels polluted," he murmured dispassionately, grasping his own flesh with his large hands. "*It* feels polluted, not you. You cannot be polluted. You are pristine, uncreated, stainless, indestructable. Sometimes if this is realized strongly enough, you can manifest your former body after you've left it."

Laura looked incredulous.

"Want to prove it?" he whispered, staring at her. "Get some dynamite. Yes, dynamite. Tie it onto my head thus." He demonstrated. "Then put a long fuse and light it. Ah, you are wondering. No. Yes. Is he serious? Just do it and see. Just light the fuse, a long fuse and sit and watch. Boom! You will see an explosion. Then again you will see me. I will be here looking just the same, and speaking as I am now."

For a long time she sat looking at him helplessly, assailed by her own confusion.

"Try it," he said smiling. "Try it and see. All you need is some dynamite. It's easy to get. You won't know 'til you try."

VIII

"TRUST YOU GOT a good rest?" said Stan to Kamala as the rented car sped along a dusty road toward the ashram of Ananda Baba. "You look especially fresh and glowing."

"I feel marvelous," she purred, adjusting her silk sari. "And you also are looking well."

"It is the healthful air of the Deccan, Madam." Saladin flashed a dazzling smile from his seat next to the driver.

Scrutinizing the young man, Stan wondered what his connection with Sundar might be. "But really, there was no need for you to come," he said to Saladin, "I'm sure it must be a bore to you."

"On the contrary," said Saladin, "I too, am a devotee of His Holiness and take every opportunity to visit him. This is a great chance, especially with the high cost of car travel. I also promised Mr. Sundaram I would look after you. It would not be correct for me to let you go off alone."

"I'm sure things will go smoother with Saladin's assistance," said Kamala. "Most reliable."

Just then there was a small pistol-like explosion, the driver pulled the car to the side of the road, and soon reported a flat tire.

"Very sorry, sir." Saladin explained. "Would you care to get out while the driver is making repairs. I have brought coffee in a thermos."

Stan and Kamala got out, Saladin unrolled a straw mat, and they sat drinking coffee under one of the old trees lining the road.

"The last Maharaja's father planted these trees on every road in Mysore," he said proudly, "so that we could have shade and fruit."

"The food!" Kamala cried out suddenly, pointing to the car where a monkey had jumped through the window and was rummaging inside. Saladin yelled and it sped away, but not without the lunch basket. Perched above them in the tree, it began eating and dropping banana peels on them.

"No matter," Saladin shrugged. "There is a good eating place in the next town, Madam."

Kamala glared at him.

"Not too clean," he admitted sheepishly. "But very good food.

129

Delicious biryani.''

"I don't eat mutton," she said disdainfully. "And neither should you when you are going to see His Holiness."

A number of people had by this time gathered to give advice to the driver and gape at Stan and Kamala.

"They think you are cinema stars," Saladin laughed.

Continuing on after the tire was fixed, toward noon the road became crowded with oxcarts, cyclists, pedestrians, and animals.

"Must he sound the horn continuously?" Stan yelled covering his ears.

"Otherwise it is not possible to drive, sir," Saladin shouted over the din. "How would the people know when to get out of the way?"

Nervous over the flat and anxious to make up for lost time, the driver sped along oblivious to the potholes in the road, darting out from behind bullock carts piled high with sugar cane and narrowly missing the oncoming traffic. Inevitably, at the outskirts of the next town, he hit something that scraped ominously along the underside of the car.

Stan looked out the rear window. "Something's leaking," he warned.

"Stop at once," Saladin shouted in Urdu.

The sun was high in the sky and heat waves shimmered over a parched landscape dotted with mud huts and palms. A terrible stench arose from one side of the road, where the sewage of the town was carried off in open ditches to a bog alive with pigs, buffaloes, and diseased-looking children. Passersby appeared locked in the oblivion of their own separate worlds.

Kamala turned to Stan. "In India nowadays everything is breaking down," she sighed. "No matter how much money one has, one sometimes gets stuck."

The Quality Hotel and Restaurant to which they finally repaired was not exactly Stan's idea of a place to lunch. Skinny half-starved youngsters in dirty drawers and aprons served the food. A patina of filth crusted everything and flies descended in clouds. They were given a cement cubicle with a bathroom on the second floor of the noisy building. Extracting cloths from her bag and spreading them over the soiled mattresses of the beds, Kamala fluttered like a butterfly in a den of cockroaches.

"You see what we have come to?" She said finally, stretching out on one of the beds. "Before we never had these problems. A hotel was a hotel, clean and pleasant, none of these people existed. Now the government robs the rich to make all of us poor. These low people are procreating like insects, running about everywhere in these public buses, leaving their filth everywhere. As a woman I should be more charitable, but really, sometimes I think a gas chamber is the place for these Congress Party people—in fact, it is too good for them. If I were ruler, I would have them trampled upon by elephants for what they have done to India in only

130

twenty-five years." She smiled. "But India will survive, it always has."

Successfully bribing a local politician for the use of his car and driver, and after a lunch was brought which no one ate, Saladin insisted they continue on.

The car was air conditioned and Stan fell asleep. Some hours later, as they approached the ashram, Saladin awakened him.

"But I see nothing," said Kamala, parting the curtains, "it looks like a desert."

"You will see, you will see." grinned Saladin. "It's just ahead."

Rounding a corner a hidden valley came into view between rolling hills covered with palms and other lush tropical foliage. Green paddies alternated with large tanks of lotus and fields of pale yellow and deep orange marigolds, roses and jasmine. Nestled against a cliff were a series of terraced gardens and white buildings, some, Saladin explained, cut out of the rock itself. The car stopped at a huge blue tiled gate where a guard stood, holding a walkie-talkie. "What is the name?"

"Saladin. His Holiness is expecting us. I am bringing Mr. Stanley and Miss Kamala."

"Do they think we are going to assassinate him?" muttered Kamala irritably.

After they were cleared the guard opened the gate and they drove through groves of giant fan palms, and meadows where deer and llama grazed among peacocks and flamingos. Here and there long low structures were visible behind carefully tended shrubbery. A hospital, crematorium, and library were pointed out by Saladin.

Stan wondered grimly which he would visit first.

In the parking lot they were greeted by a young blue-eyed blonde in a long saffron robe.

"Step this way?" said the girl with a midwestern accent. She sounded like a receptionist at some large corporation. "We would like you to sign the register and there are a few forms to fill out. Your luggage will go to your quarters. Of course, you understand that men and women stay separately here." She smiled at Kamala.

"I am familiar with the procedures of ashrams," Kamala replied good-naturedly.

"I believe His Holiness has arranged a separate cottage for you," she replied cheerfully. "As for Mr. Stanley and Mr. Saladin, let me see." She thumbed through a small notebook. "You will have adjoining rooms at the hostel. It's very nice, you'll be very comfortable. But you're late—we expected you hours ago."

"We had a breakdown," Saladin explained.

"Sorry to hear that. Anyhow, run along now and don't take too long unpacking. Just take a bath and I'll pick you up in half an hour. You'll just have time to make His Holiness' evening appearance. Then I believe the program is that he would like to see Miss Kamala this evening and Mr. Stanley tomorrow morning at five-thirty." She caught Saladin's eye. "And of course Mr. Saladin too. Okay?" she said cheerily to Stan.

"Okay." Stan nodded.

*   *   *

The broad terrace overlooking the valley was filled with people. At one end rose the quarters of His Holiness, designed it was said by a famous French architect who'd been an early devotee. Here His Holiness lived with the chosen few of his inner circle. Here were pools reflecting marble porches, raised and sunken gardens containing rare blooms and everywhere the sound of splashing fountains filled the air.

"You have seen Fatephur Sikri?" Saladin asked Kamala as they stood waiting for Stan.

"Yes."

"Does it not remind you of this place?" his eyes glittered. "It is too wonderful. A real palace. Surely he must be a great saint to get the money to do these things? Yes? They say foreigners come every day, showering him with it."

They were joined by Stan and the prim American girl whose name turned out to be Jai Devi. "It's almost time," she said. "See, they've lit the fires."

On a terrace of polished white marble four fires had been lit at the four points of the compass. Seated before them naked yogis chanted and made offerings. In the center a fifth fire burned, made on a raised dias. There huge logs sent yellow and gold flames high in the sky. The atmosphere was charged with the rhythm of chanting voices. Among the select group permitted on the highest terrace, many were on their knees or flat on their stomachs, hands outstretched toward a single doorway in a massive marble wall. For it was through this door that His Holiness was soon to appear.

Just as the sun touched the horizon, an attendant blew a series of high-pitched blasts on a silver trumpet, an expectant hush fell over the crowd, and His Holiness, a large figure cloaked in scarlet silk, his frizzed hair falling to his waist, appeared. Elevated wooden sandals kept his feet off the ground. His face was inscrutable, his form androgynous. All eyes were upon him as he glided across the polished marble, holding his right palm outward in the gesture of blessing.

"See the milk coming from his hand?" Saladin whispered. A trickle of white liquid seemed to be spouting out of the palm. "Try to catch some and drink it, but be careful—here he comes."

As His Holiness approached, Stan's mind flashed to San Francisco and the drag joints on Turk Street. He dove under the dripping hand, skidded and landed on his stomach. Saladin and Kamala knelt with outstretched hands. His Holiness passed by, but then, stopping as if in recognition of some unseen vibration, retraced his steps.

"Rise, daughter," he ordered Kamala in Hindi, extracting from his mouth an enormous gold locket and chain which he dropped in her open hands.

Saladin gasped.

Moving on past the select group to the edge of the terrace, he blessed the masses below. Then retiring to the central fire he flung off his cloak and seated himself, naked except for a scarlet loincloth, upon a slab of basalt.

Various groups of devotees now vied for the honor of singing to him. Strange wind instruments pierced the night air as drums beat out the message of the Divine Spirit. A famous film star, accompanied by her own musicians, swayed and chirped in the frenetic style of Hindi Talkies.

Stan was thinking that someone could make a fortune booking this show at the Paris Opera, or how about the Coliseum in Rome.

After the music, two devotees, an Indian man and a Western girl knelt in front of His Holiness and presenting him with fruits and flowers as bells rang and conches blared, lit a series of camphor lamps which they waved in His Holiness' face.

"This is the puja," whispered Jai Devi, who had come up behind Stan. "It is the greatest honor to be allowed to do puja to His Holiness."

Stan wondered if His Holiness cured him whether he'd have to stay here the rest of his life waving lights. He decided he could think of worse places, but what would he do for sex? Everything seemed so pure—at least on the surface. Did he want to be pure? When it came right down to it, perhaps he dug his own hang-ups.

There followed a ceremony at which those of the inner circle were allowed to kneel or prostrate before His Holiness receiving on their foreheads marks of holy ash from his sacred fire. To the hundreds on the lower terrace subordinate ashramites distributed ash in small packets, like sugar, printed with a colored photo of His Holiness and the words *"Ananda Baba Loves You"* embossed in gold.

When His Holiness finished the blessings, he was helped into his scarlet cloak, the silver trumpet sounded again, and he floated back through the small door.

Jai Devi sidled up to Kamala. "If you are ready, you can follow me and go in," she said, sounding like an airline hostess. "His Holiness is expecting you to dine with him."

"I shall have to return to my cottage first," said Kamala. "I have something for Baba and I would like to change." She smiled a haughty smile. "Is that all right?"

"Yes, of course, I will accompany you," said Jai Devi.

"But what will Mr. Stanely and Mr. Saladin do?" asked Kamala.

"We have three canteens: one for invited guests like yourselves, one for devotees on pilgrimage, and one for the general sightseeing public."

"I think I'll just go to my room," yawned Stan, "if I'm to get up before dawn. But this place is so big. How do I get there?"

"I will show you the way, Mr. Stanley," said the ubiquitous Saladin, flashing his teeth. "I too am tired. But not too tired to eat. We'll have something at the canteen before you retire."

*   *   *

While Kamala bathed, oiled herself, combed her hair and dressed, Jai Devi paced the drawing room of the small cottage. Kamala had thought of asking the American girl to help her dress but suspected, even though she looked it, that Jai Devi might not be of the servant class.

In fact, Jai Devi was the daughter of a millionaire from Des Moines, Iowa who'd been healed by Ananda Baba, decided he was God, and paid for much of the magnificent architecture of Baba's Ashram.

"We should really be moving along now you know," called Jai Devi, as Kamala put on the finishing touches of her eye make-up.

Jai Devi wore no make-up but then, as Kamala sensed, they were on different paths. At last, swathed in a scarlet sari embroidered with emeralds and topazes, her bare feet sparkling with gold toe rings and bangles of diamonds and rubies on her wrists, her neck, her ears and even her nose, Kamala emerged from her sitting room. It was obvious from the gasp that followed that Jai Devi was taken aback by her appearance and an amused Kamala followed her through the gardens to the private entrance of Baba's quarters. "We disciples must stick to our rigorous routine. I only see Him when my parents come," Jai Devi smiled robot-like. Then looking irritated, she pointed to a white clad young Indian standing nearby, "He will conduct you to Baba, I will see you later."

Beyond the gate they came to a courtyard where a baby elephant, swaying happily from side to side, munched at a pile of tender palm shoots. Entering a narrow passageway the young man conducted Kamala up a flight of stairs to a rooftop terrace overlooking the valley.

Ananda Baba was reclining on bright orange silk cushions. A young boy was dutifully kneading the muscles of his outstretched legs. Nearby sat an extremely handsome middle-aged man, his eyes closed in meditation. Torches burned. Puffs of amber cloud hung limpid in the evening sky. Kamala prostrated herself, careful to reveal the sumptuous curves of her buttocks as she went down. Slowly inching her hands forward, she placed

134

an offering under the Baba's right knee. His strong hand came down on her forehead leaving the ash mark and signaling her to rise.

"It was so hot today," he said gazing lazily at her, "we thought it would be best to dine outside..."

A servant waved a large peacock fan. The Baba was appraising her. "Very nice," he said after a pause. "Nice of you to come to see us at last... we've been expecting you for a long time now, do sit down."

"He has the power to melt you," thought Kamala, lowering herself into the lotus position. "You are too kind, Baba," she replied.

"It is a most auspicious moment," he said thoughtfully. "The meeting of two souls like ours."

"We have many friends in common," she observed.

"Yes, and may I present Major General Chatterji, retired. We call him Baji for short." He indicated the man on his left, who opened his eyes and bowed from the waist.

"Will you smoke with us?" asked the Baba, withdrawing a small ivory chillum from a bag. Kamala nodded.

The chillum was lit by an attendant, who brought a glowing coal from an ornate firebox. Ananda Baba drew deep draughts of the smoke and passed the pipe to the handsome bare-chested Baji, decked out in a white dhoti of sheerest cotton and an overdose of gold jewelry.

"Of course you know, Baji," declared Ananda Baba, "that next to our illustrious Prime Minister this lady is perhaps the most famous woman in India? At least the most desired."

The pipe was passed to Kamala and the Baba noted with interest her skill in handling it. "You have sat with yogis before I see," he remarked.

"Often," she replied, "at Kamaksha, Nepal, Varanasi—so many places."

"We have to be so careful these days with this," he nodded at the pipe as he took it from her hand. "These Westerners have gone crazy, spoiled everything. We do not smoke with them. We only smoke with our friends."

The General, who was reported to be one of India's great lovers and, if not one of its most illustrious generals, certainly its richest, undressed Kamala with his eyes.

"How fortunate, General, that our stars have crossed here on this beautiful night," sighed Kamala. "I came here quite by accident, a friend—"

"You mean by design," interrupted the Baba, and launched into a discourse geared to impress the rather humdrum mind of the General that there was a divine plan decipherable only by the Baba. "That is the meaning of Karma," he said, and motioned to a servant who brought an oblong drum called a dholac and placed it on the General's lap.

"Baji is an excellent drummer, most rhythmic." The Baba bent toward Kamala. "Sometimes I sit for hours just listening to my Baji play." He arched his eyebrows.

With an air of satisfaction, the General, hitting the drum several times, upended it, tightened the skin, and began to play and sing softly.

Ananda Baba, his dark skin glowing with a violet aura that set off his white glittering eyes, collapsed back on his pillows. The General had been switched onto automatic. Now he could relax and drink in the voluptuous creature before him—the very essence of desire. He would enjoy her, that was certain. Did she know the secret tricks of yogis? Perhaps he could even steal some of her energy. Ah, what delight... but also what a formidable partner.

"Alas, tonight our meeting must be brief, my dear," he said, staring at Kamala intently, after the plates of fruit and glasses of almond milk had been cleared away. "I believe I am to see your friend early tomorrow morning."

"Really, he is Sundar's friend; I came along to see you."

"Sundar? Ah yes, but of course."

"Sundar could not leave Delhi," said Kamala. "Nevertheless, he sends you his pranams. Mr. Stanley is a school chum of Sundar's. Some Western doctors have told him he has lung cancer."

"I have so many of these," said the Baba, turning lazily onto his stomach so that the boy could rub his back. "It has become a problem for me. What I have to find out first is whether a man or a woman is willing to change, to bend—something like that, otherwise they can't be healed. I must find out what they are attached to and pry it loose, take it from them, the disease usually comes along, too. But with these Americans, it is usually money they are attached to. Very touchy about it."

"God only knows, Baba," said the General, obviously sensitive on the subject, "we all need money."

"I have no money," sighed the Baba wearily. "What I get goes out, gets spent. I hardly eat. All this show is the maya* of my devotees. I am prepared to leave it tomorrow. Money must be kept moving, that way there is always more. But then who would know that better than this divine lady, eh, General?"

Baji nodded, trying to think of a way to get Kamala alone. He'd heard tales of her and longed to find out if they were really true, even at the risk of getting involved. That she could be dangerous excited him no end.

"You have a room in the hostel?" he asked politely.

"No, Baji, she has a cottage," the Baba answered, blocking the General's move.

*maya=illusory show

"I am tired now," said Kamala, bending to touch the Baba's feet, "so much of travelling, you know, may I retire?"

"By all means, my dear, I will see you to your cottage," said the excited General.

"Sit down, Baji," said the Baba, as if speaking to a dog. "She is not a child, after all, she will find her way. Good night, beautiful lady." He held out his hand for her to kiss. "And how do you like the slave I have given you?"

"Slave?" asked Kamala.

"Jai Devi." He smiled. "Do you not think it is wonderful that we have rich American slaves these days? Very interesting phenomenon, I think."

*   *   *

The following morning Stan woke up to the sound of amplified music echoing through the valley. "If you call it music," he thought, listening to a strident woman's voice singing the same phrase over and over again like a broken record. Deciding he was having a bad dream he buried his face in his pillow.

Then he heard Saladin's voice and came out from under the covers. In a pair of shorts, his hair tousled, looking very handsome, Saladin held out a cup of tea.

"What's the awful racket?" Stan asked.

"Oh, that, that is the thousand names of the Goddess sung by Hindus at sunrise," said Saladin, disappearing into the shower. Stan followed him. "Your turn," said Saladin, "better you should hurry. Baba will not appreciate we are late, it is already four-thirty. And watch out, the water is too cold."

"What, no hot water?" yowled Stan.

"Not here." Laughed Saladin, and pushed Stan in. "His Holiness does not approve of it."

Thoroughly chilled, Stan emerged, wrapped in a towel, to find Saladin holding a piece of cotton yardage. "A dhoti," he explained, "you must learn to wear it. His Holiness doesn't like pants."

Reaching under Stan's arms and around his waist, Saladin showed him how to fold and tie the dhoti. "There," he said, "now you look like one of our Brahmins."

"Now what?" said Stan. "Do I wear a shirt or..."

"You will wear only a shawl. I have brought one for you." He produced a magenta colored cashmere shawl. "Let me see ... Yes, you are ready now. Do you have an offering for His Holiness?"

"Yes, I have." Stan rummaged in his bag and found an IBM pocket calulator. "Don't you think he could use this?"

137

"That!" said Saladin unimpressed. "What is it?"

"An electronic calculator—addition, subtraction, and so on."

"How much it costs?"

"About four hundred dollars." Stan replied.

"Come come," declared Saladin, "that is hardly enough. You must give him something to calculate with."

"You mean money?"

"Yes, yes, you must," said Saladin. "Give, that you may receive."

"How much would you say would be correct?"

"At least ten thousand," replied Saladin unblinking.

"Dollars or Rupees," snapped Stan.

"Dollars, of course," replied Saladin brightly.

"I see," Stan said, "isn't that a bit high?"

"Do as you like," Saladin replied, feigning disgust. "You get what you pay for."

Saladin's behavior made Stan very nervous: "Yes, of course, let me see," and rummaging in his bag withdrew some travelers checks. "How do I make them out?"

Saladin wondered whether His Holiness would appreciate what he, Saladin, a Moslem, was doing for him, "Just sign them and leave them blank...then slip them under his knee when you greet him."

Sign them and leave them blank, thought Stan, struggling with his dhoti. "I have the feeling it's going to fall off," he laughed self conciously.

"Don't worry. Come, it's almost five-thirty."

The cool shadows of the clear Indian morning soothed Stan's fraying nerves. Peacocks screamed and mynah birds whistled in the thickets as they neared the entrance to Baba's compound. Once inside they passed through a dense grove of yellow bamboo beneath which bloomed hybrid hibiscuses, in dazzling color combinations. Reaching a lawn that sloped to a small lake they saw Ananda Baba playing with his baby elephant.

Saladin approached and fell flat on his stomach. Gracefully the Baba, naked except for a large crimson hibiscus artfully tucked into his frizzed hair, bent down and touched Saladin's forehead.

Was he expected to go down in the dirt too? Stan wondered. Glancing at the elephant, he thought of elephant shit and that he had just had a bath. "Never mind," he said to himself, "just do it."

Down he went, fumbling with the travelers checks which he managed to shove under one of Baba's enormous toes. It seemed an eternity that he lay there, waiting for that press of the thumb on his forehead. The wide legs of the Baba stood over him. Then the trunk of the baby elephant, swaying back and forth, touched Stan's forehead lightly with its pink tip.

"I am teaching him to put the ash on the foreheads," the Baba chuckled. "What do you think, Mr. Stanley?"

Stan stood up. The Baba squatted in the grass countrystyle, knees bent up, legs spread wide. Although he was fat, his body was solid.

"Sit down Mr. Stanley, and you Saladin."

"I should go see to Miss Kamala's needs, sir," Saladin said.

But the Baba motioned for him to sit, a great honor for Saladin.

"Just watch the trunk swaying and swinging, Mr. Stanley," he said. "Is it not beautiful . . . like a great pendulum? Tell me, can I do something for you?" He smiled.

"I have the feeling you could do anything you wanted," Stan replied.

"And what would you say if I told you I could not, Mr. Stanley?"

"I wouldn't believe you," Stan said.

"Ah, you would be quite right, but would you go away if I told you to?" The Baba fastened his now frighteningly dead eyes on Stan.

"Yes . . . I would go away," said Stan mesmerized.

"And stay away?"

"Yes."

Slowly the Baba extended his arms. Before Stan's eyes milk or something that looked like milk began to bubble up out of the centers of his palms and drip down.

"Incredible!" whispered Stan.

Saladin moaned and falling flat again on the ground, crawled on his belly to receive the milk.

His neck distended, Ananda Baba now opened his mouth disgorging a large black stone.

"This is impossible," Stan cried, as the stone, a smooth black cylinder over six inches long slid out onto the grass.

"Take it, Mr. Stanley," said the Baba's voice hoarsely, "it's yours."

Stan picked up the slippery stone.

Saladin's jaw dropped. People said this Baba produced lingam stones out of his mouth, but he had not believed them. Now here was the proof. They were extremely valuable too, worth far more than ten thousand dollars. Mr. Stanley has made money on this one, alright.

"Will you have time to spend with me?" the Baba asked Stan softly.

"Yes." Stan's reply was serious.

For a long time the Baba seemed to look through him as if making a decision. "Very well then, you may leave now. I will see you tomorrow sometime."

Saladin stepped forward and knelt. The baby elephant dipped its trunk delicately into a brass container filled with red powder and touched Saladin's forehead. Stan followed, clutching the stone and hoping his dhoti would stay on.

When they reached the gate through which they had entered, both men were still unnerved.

"Fantastic," Stan was saying under his breath, "really fantastic. Someone should book that act . . . to see that stone coming out."

"What?" said Saladin.

"Incredible to see this coming out," Stan said, fumbling in his shawl for the stone. "But where it is?"

"What?" Saladin cried.

"The stone—it's not here."

"You . . . you didn't lose it?"

"Why no . . . no . . . I—don't know, I—I must have left it on the grass. Maybe the elephant took it. . . . I'll go back and have a look."

Saladin was disgusted. What a commission he could have got if Mr. Stanley had decided to sell it.

Stan returned panting.

"It's gone—the stone, the elephant, the Baba, nothing!"

"Ha!" thought Saladin, "the Baba is playing tricks.

In the park, now bustling with devotees, they met Jai Devi.

"I'll be seeing you in about twenty minutes. I'm supposed to start some breathing exercises with you, Mr. Stanley. We'll be doing them for about two weeks," she said smiling. "And Mr. Saladin, please arrange to have a massage table from the dispensary. Mr. Stanley is to have massage, with hot and cold baths. You will assist."

Saladin nodded, eyeing her. Could he seduce this blonde beauty and how long would it take? At least she might be able to have sweaters and other luxury import items sent to him if it worked out.

"I will have everything ready," he assured her.

*   *   *

Kamala, too, had been awakened at an early hour—by Jai Devi who brought bed tea and gave her a few pompous tips on breathing and exercise. "She imagines she can teach me breathing," thought Kamala later. "She should live my life—then she would know something about breathing!"

But in a way the girl had amused her. Kamala had sipped her tea and tried to act good-natured, even though it was certainly not her habit to see any but servants before lunch. How she missed her servant Hassan. Would she be allowed to send for him? she wondered.

When Jai Devi left, she had decided to shower. Now as she dried herself dreamily in front of a mirror, there was a knock on the door.

"It is General Chatterji—Baji. May I come in for a moment?"

Kamala put down the towel and threw on a filmy sari.

"I'm dressing, General," she called, letting her breasts and one thigh appear around the door.

"I have a message from Baba," said the General, coming in. "He would like to see you as soon as . . ." He stared at her body open-mouthed.

"Oh, yes?" said Kamala, fidgeting with her sari. "Then I had better put on some clothes, hadn't I? Please sit down."

Retreating into the dressing room, she made sure the General could watch her in a mirror as she combed out her hair, slipped into her sari and drew it tightly across her buttocks. She even bent over and pretended to examine her toe rings so that he could have a really good look.

Emerging minutes later the essence of purity in a white sari, white cashmere shawl and white hibiscus in her hair, she stood demurely at the door. "Shall we go then, General?" she cooed.

Kamala could feel him wanting to grab her. But then she thought how much more interesting the Baba would be; that solid flesh, the throbbing energy, those pectoral muscles nearly as big as her breasts. And she had heard of his gigantic penis, almost like a stallion, with which he could do many unusual things. It would be better not to seduce this General unless the Baba willed it—better to direct her energy toward His Holiness.

The General conducted her through the park to His Holiness' private quarters, where she found him seated in the shady corner of an open veranda, cheerful with songbirds and the faint sound of splashing water. A boy in dark red with a pink plume in his turban held a purple silk umbrella over the Baba, while another fanned and a third massaged whatever part of the Baba's flesh was available to him from moment to moment.

"And so, you had a peaceful night?" he asked, as she prostrated before him.

"Thanks to you, Maharaj," she murmured, prostrating before him.

"And Jai Devi?"

"She brought me tea and demonstrated some . . . exercises she thought I might need." Kamala smiled faintly.

"It is important to give these people duties to make them feel they are doing something constructive—they think there is something to learn." He laughed uproariously.

The General was just seating himself. "You may leave now, Baji," the Baba added, still laughing. "I must speak with Miss Kamala alone for a while."

A disgruntled Baji left the room.

"All must serve, even Generals. That is the price of living with me," sighed the Baba, rolling onto one side. "And who is this dreadful American," he said, suddenly getting to the point.

"He was a classmate of A. K. Sundaram's abroad," Kamala answered, "and once a U.S. presidential appointee. He is very bright. A self-made millionaire from some pharmaceutical enterprises he owns. We believe he is the head of a group that has a new secret drug and that his

141

associates are distributing it in India. He may not even have cancer—we do not know.''

"What is the drug?''

"It makes you very suggestive, produces visions, hallucinations—they say it is used for brainwashing. His associate gave some to Sundar and Sundar has given some to me for you to try.'' She handed him a small envelope.

"Such tiny pills, and so many.'' He looked at her. "You have taken this?'' Kamala shook her head. "Then we shall take them together, you and I alone.... Let us see what trick this foreigner brings, yes?''

She nodded.

"Ah, and now this Mr. Stanley wants me to save him so he can continue to enjoy his millions.'' The Baba narrowed his eyes. "And I suspect he's a pederast too—highly oversexed.''

"Not quite,'' said Kamala smiling. "He enjoys both sexes.''

"A Moslem then,'' the Baba snorted. "He's just given me ten thousand dollars.'' He withdrew the checks from a bag and thrust them in Kamala's direction. "Shall I keep them, or would you like them?''

She played for higher stakes.

"No, no, dear Baba ... I couldn't take them. If I did I would probably throw them into a fire.''

"That would be wasteful,'' he said, smiling gently. "Someone will take the burden of them before the day is over, you will see. Not all are as wise as you, dear lady. But the question is—should I demand more from him?''

"Perhaps you could let time decide that,'' Kamala suggested. "Keep him here for a while and see whether he really has cancer.''

"That is exactly what I had planned,'' answered the Baba. "I will test him. But he seems to be constantly breaking wind and must be full of poisons. I have instructed that your Saladin will give him a purge, along with hot and cold baths and vigorous massage. Then he will have to go to the kitchen. He needs kitchen work, although nothing near the food. He can scrub floors, clean the burned pots, and so on.''

"But will he?''

"We will see how frightened he is of dying and if he is indeed a dying man we will find out! Meanwhile, Saladin must make his life as interesting as possible during the evenings.''

"He handed her a small packet. "This is the medicine for the purge. Have Saladin put half in a glass of tea today and give the other half in twenty-four hours.''

Sitting with one knee up Kamala had slowly let her sari part in such a way that only the Baba could see she wore nothing beneath it.

"Can you stay here with me for some weeks?'' he inquired, looking between her open legs.

"I have no other plans at the moment," she answered.

He gazed at her. "Good," he said, "then return to me this evening after the public audience. Meanwhile, be sure to deliver the small package for the purge to Saladin. I will see Mr. Stanley after a week. By then, I hope he will have stopped smelling so much."

*   *   *

Loud cries of protest echoed through the hostel corridor as Kamala arrived at Stan's room. Several young boys were bringing buckets of hot water. She entered behind them to find Stan laid out on a table, Jai Devi, pounding her fists into his flesh.

"She is strong, eh?" Kamala whispered to Saladin, signaling him to step into the next room with her. "I have just come from the Baba," she whispered. "He gave me this packet—it's for a purge. You are to give him half in some tea now, and the other half in twenty-four hours. Mr. Stanley will be very sick for one week, but the Baba asks you to see that he has an interesting time." Saladin looked puzzled. "Those are the instructions," she whispered, "now I must go."

As Saladin prepared tea on a hot plate, Stan pelted Jai Devi with verbal abuse.

"Come on, baby," he yelled, "ah...oh, let's fuck...ah, oh, no no...Love to eat that healthy American pussy. Ah, no...no, don't...too hot...water...ouch!"

Actually, Stan was having a terrific time. Jai Devi's massage made him want to yell. Yet as the hot bath alternated with the cold and he pretended to go crazy, he wondered whether he might not really go mad. There was a lot of real craziness inside him. Insanity, now cancer, he shuddered, "if he had any sense he'd have admitted himself to Sloan-Kettering."

Saladin came back into the room.

"You can have a rest now," he said to Jai Devi. "Sahib," he said to Stan, helping him sit up, "have some tea, special ginger tea from His Holiness."

Stan sat up and gulped down the tea.

"You rest now," ordered Saladin, "Jai Devi and I will just go into the next room for a while. Then there will be more exercises and baths."

"What a terrible man he is," Jai Devi whispered furiously to Saladin once they were alone in the next room. "Just terrible...Did you hear the dreadful things he was saying to me? And did you see that his *thing* was sticking up?" She glanced at Saladin and sat down stiffly.

"The things I go through for His Holiness." She sighed. "I suppose it's good for me, but..." She nodded toward the closed door with her big eyes. "He's a sex maniac, that's what he is."

"It is quite true, Miss Devi," said Saladin softly, sitting down

143

opposite her on the bed. "But it's a problem for all men."

"What's a problem?"

"The penis, the man's penis. It is the abode of the Devil, that is what we say . . . is it not true?" He fastened his eyes on her.

She nodded timidly.

"Yes. Yes, I can prove it. Take me for example," he whispered confidentially. "I have done everything to chase the Devil out of my penis. Prayers, diet, exercises, even cold baths. But still he is in there. It is a hard burden for us men to bear, this muscle of the Devil. It is a strange muscle you know, not like any other."

"Oh?"

"See," said Saladin, "I will show you." He stood up and whipped out his large brown penis.

Jai Devi jerked back in fright.

"Don't be afraid," he said smiling. "I hate it. It was getting me in so much trouble, I'll tell you. . . . But no more." He struck his penis briskly. "Now I am controlling it with yoga."

She looked up at him nervously.

"See," he went on, digging in his pants and extracting his testicles, "the muscle that controls it all is down here." He lifted his testicles up and pointed to a spot just behind them. "Here," he said, taking her limp hand, "put your finger there . . . don't be afraid . . . yes, there, yes." He twitched a muscle. "Can you feel it? It's hot there. Yes?" He withdrew her hand. "You felt it? That *is* the home of the Devil; when he begins to twitch it is hard to stop him, I'll tell you."

"Mr. Saladin," warned Jai Devi, "I think it's getting bigger."

"When it gets big, that means the Devil is taking over," replied Saladin, moving closer to where she was sitting. "I will do some yogic breathing and muscle exercises and it will go down." He sucked in his stomach muscles and pretending to do complicated breath control, let his erection come on.

"It's getting so big," she whispered hypnotically, "I've never seen one like that before."

"Then you have seen others before this?"

"My brothers, mostly." She laughed nervously. "I mean, well, Mr. Saladin—it's too embarrassing, I . . ." Her face was beet-red.

"Take it," Saladin said.

"What?" She almost fell off the chair.

"Take it. Take hold of it with your hand. You will feel how hot it gets. I am letting the Devil come out, the yoga didn't work. Sometimes it happens that way. So I will let him come out just for your sake, so you can see what happens."

Saladin closed his sphincter muscle, causing his erection to stand up straight. "Terrible, isn't it?" he said, looking down at himself and then at

Jai Devi. "Take hold of him, feel how hot he is."

Jai Devi locked her hard hand around Saladin's penis.

"Not so hard, he will get worse if you hold him too tight. Now, hold up the testicles and look underneath." Saladin knew that by now Stan must be watching through the keyhole. He had positioned himself so that anyone looking through it would have a good view. After all, had not His Holiness commanded him to make Stan's stay interesting?

"Don't you see it? Can't you feel it?" he said, contracting his sphincter muscle.

"Yes," Jai Devi said frantically, "it's jumping like everything. Oh, Mr. Saladin, I think you'd better put it away. It scares me."

"Put it back then, if you like. Just take him and stuff him back in my pants."

She took hold of his penis and tried stuffing it back into his pants but each time she had it in it would pop out.

"I'm afraid it has become so large, Mr. Saladin, it just won't go in." She giggled apprehensively.

"Then," Saladin turned around, "there is a knife in my back pocket, take it out and hand it to me."

He opened it and returned it to her. "Now cut him off."

"What?" cried Jai Devi.

"Cut him off!"

"But Mr. Saladin!" she wailed.

"There is no other way, Miss Devi, can't you see? I have tried everything. I have come to the end of the rope. Still the Devil, he is there inside!"

"But I can't!" Jai Devi pleaded. "It's living!" She burst into tears. "How can I cut a living thing?"

"But it's destroying my life, Miss Devi. The Devil is in it. You *must*!"

Jai Devi reached out hesitantly.

"That's it, hold it in one hand then ... here." He took her left hand and placed it on his stone-hard erection. "Now with your other, whack it off."

Jai Devi began sobbing again. "But Mr. Saladin, I can't—oh, please don't make me."

"Then suck," said Saladin abruptly.

"What?"

"Suck him," he repeated, guiding the tip into her open mouth before she could speak. "The only way to get him out is to suck him out."

On the other side of the door there was suddenly a deafening crash.

Jai Devi jumped up, wiping her mouth with her hand. Saladin, taking his time, replaced his penis and zipped up his pants. Then he yanked open the door.

"Oh, ah," groaned Stan, who lay in a heap on the floor. "Ah ... ugh."

145

"Just what are you up to?" Saladin demanded.

"I think I'm going to be sick," Stan said.

"Mr. Stanley, please go back and lie down like a good boy," said Jai Devi firmly. "You need more rest, you'll feel better after—"

A loud flatulent sound pierced the air. Suddenly the room reeked.

"Mr. Stanley!" said Jai Devi, scandalized. "*What* is happening?"

"I don't know!" screamed Stan. "Can't you see I'm sick?"

"I think he's going to be sick," said Saladin. "Let me handle him, Miss Devi."

"But really, I—"

A fart exploded again and Stan began to vomit. Saladin pushed Jai Devi to the door.

"Poor Mr. Stanley." She looked back over her shoulder. "Should I inform His Holiness?"

"Yes, you may do that," said Saladin, shoving her outside. "Go and tell him what is happening if you like." He took her hand and rubbed it on his crotch. "The Devil will wait for you."

"Oh, goddamn," wailed Stan from inside.

"I will go then," said Jai Devi breathlessly, "and report back."

"Be certain you do that."

"Saladin!" Stan looked up through bloodshot eyes, "Goddamn, I feel so...ugh...ah...oh, God. Saladin, what's happening? My God, what...please get me to the bathroom, I think I'm going to die!"

*   *   *

When the evening had turned into night and she was certain he would be alone, a carefully bathed and scented Kamala threw on a sari and unobserved made her way across the park to the quarters of the Baba. She found him sitting by himself in the dark.

"I have dismissed the others," he said. "Come, we will go inside." Taking her by the hand he led her into a dark windowless room, painted red.

In the center a fire smoldered in a pit, the smoke curling up through a hole in the ceiling. On one side, oil lamps flickered in front of an ancient statue of a yogi sitting in meditation, his lingam erect.

The Baba eased himself onto some cushions near the fire.

Kamala stood in front of him and for a long time he gazed at her through half-closed eyes. "Such beauty should not remain covered," he said at last. "I think you must remove your sari, eh?"

Kamala's sari fell from her breasts and unwound itself about her naked body.

"Now come here." He lay back on the cushions, extending his left

146

leg. "Let us see how good you are."

She knelt before him and massaged his foot, marveling at its enormous size.

"I have the chemical the American gave you," he said, producing a silver box full of the small orange tablets. "They even got the color right, how many do you think we should take?"

"They say one is enough," she murmured, moving her hand up his large calf muscle. "But perhaps two would be better just to be sure."

"Then here," he said, "put out your tongue, let us see what this Western magic is all about. Ah, that is good. Now I shall take." Popping two pills into his mouth, he stared at her full breasts bouncing between her arms, as she massaged him. "If it works," he grunted, "I will show you maithuna tonight . . . you know maithuna?"*

"I know of it, but have not practiced it, Maharaj," Kamala breathed.

"You do not know until you have practiced," he said. "It is dangerous to raise the shakti and should be performed with many offerings and mantras. We will do the full ritual another time. I will have you perform it with the General later perhaps, eh? It would be a great help to me in . . . uh . . . keeping him on the path. He is very much in his body. Do you know pranayour?†

She nodded.

"Perhaps then you know the bhands, the locks, eh? And the Shiva mantra?"

She nodded again.

"Very good," he chuckled, extending his right leg for her to work on. "You must repeat the Shiva mantra mentally, continuously closing the locks on the inhale of the prana, and on the exhale, slowly opening them. When the exhale is complete, close out all the locks and inhale, holding your breath for fifteen seconds. Do you understand?"

"It is not quite clear," Kamala said.

"Like this." He squatted, sucked in his huge diaphragm and then breathing in and out, expanded and contracted his stomach muscles, holding his breath and locking his chin to his chest. "The sphincter you cannot see but it is opening and closing along with the stomach and neck."

He let himself fall back on to the cushions. "When the time is right," he said, "and the shakti comes, I will show you." He thought about telling her how the orgasm was to be regulated but decided against it.

She massaged his broad shoulders, pressing them with her thumbs.

"Ah, that is very nice," he said softly. "You have the good touch. The boy doesn't have that touch."

*maithuna = a form of yoga in which sexual union is performed
†pranayour = breathing exercises

As she reached under his arms from behind, letting her body rub against his back as she massaged his large pectoral muscles, he seemed to puff up.

"You are Kama Devi," he groaned, "you are desire." Letting himself go limp against her body, he reached behind her with one arm and as he lay back, caught her hair and pulled her head down on his smooth chest.

Kamala felt a tingling sensation inside her, a loose, careless dreaminess she'd never experienced. "You have been looking at it," said the Baba, glancing down at his loin cloth.

"I have heard many tales about Baba's lingam," she murmured, "and what he can do with it."

"Fetch my lota‡," he said, his eyes glittering. "I have something to show you. Fill it with water from that brass bucket and bring it here."

Kamala brought the lota and squatted in front of him.

"You desire to be a first class yogini now, I think," he said. "You can give up whoring. You want more interesting experiences? If you stay with me you will learn."

"Remove the longote," he commanded, seating himself in full lotus. Pulling away the scarlet loincloth, she stared at the jet black penis of the Baba. Her lips parted.

"You will enjoy," he said, inserting his penis into the open mouth of the lota, "now watch it drink up the water." He began expanding and contracting his stomach muscles in a fast rhythmic motion, as though an electric motor had suddenly been switched on.

"I have heard of this but have never seen it done," she murmured, her eyes riveted on the swelling organ.

When the lota was empty he took up a damaru* and shook it, and kneeling in front of the Shiva statue, anointed it with flowers and sandalwood paste, offered incense, waved lamps, and finally prostrated himself.

Arranging Kamala opposite him in the lotus position, he tucked flowers into the crevices of her body, marked her forehead with ash and sandalwood paste and putting his hand under his penis let the water out. "Holy water," he said sprinkling her with it. "Got great shakti now, drink!" He held up his hands and let the water trickle into her open mouth and down her breasts.

Kamala groaned. The Baba's glistening skin had turned transparent so that she could see the bones and blood vessels inside pumping fluid through his body.

"It is beginning to work, that American magic. Is it not good?" He

‡lota=a brass vessel in which yogis carry water
*damaru=a two-sided yogi's drum shaped like an hour-glass

waved a lamp in front of her eyes.

Kamala felt a rush as though she were taking off in a plane. Through lavender and blue clouds she saw the Baba replicate himself, many-headed and thousand-armed, through a prism of waving lights.

"Now you must do puja." His voice reverberated inside her. He lay on the floor beside the fire with his legs apart, rattling the drum in his upraised fist.

Kamala dusted his body including the erect lingam with ash from the fire, until he looked like a pale gray statue. Then she lit incense, waved the lamps, and finally, after decorating the lingam with flowers, let coconut water trickle over it and down his testicles.

The Baba began to see Kamala glowing pink and filled with juices. "You are Kama Dev," he said, shaking his drum wildly in the air. "Come, you have finished the puja, now lower your body onto the lingam. You are the Goddess Kama, let your yoni embrace the living lingam. Take it all inside you, oh Goddess!"

Hovering over him, a phantom form, she slowly lowered herself.

"Ah, ah, grhrr," he roared, then rose to a crosslegged sitting position.

Wrapping her legs about his waist, her arms around his neck, Kamala stared into his wide-open eyes. "Ah grhrr...," he purred. "Now begin the breathing and the locking."

As he watched her concentrate on her breathing, her face shattered into a thousand mirrors, eyes closed, lips parted, groaning and chanting the Shiva mantra.

"You mine," he said into her open lips, "think only of my lingam, the Shiva lingam inside you... you Kama... you shakti."

Kamala felt as though she were falling through space. Taking her buttocks in his enormous hands he moved her up and down until her body tingled.

"You must anoint my lingam now, oh daughter of the Gods, anoint and worship. Together we shall rule as Raja and Rani. We shall rule India, America, the world!" He took her head in his hands roughly, forcing her to stare into his eyes. Her orgasm mounted and discharged in spasms, flowing hot around his organ.

The moment he had been waiting for had arrived. Holding her in the vise of his strong arms, with slow pumping movements, he directed all his concentration to sucking up her seminal fluid, as he had drunk the water in the lota.

"See me," he said, "here between the eyes, oh daughter of Bharata. Let yourself flow into me. Let your thighs and womb open... open and flow into me."

She could feel a sucking motion deep inside her as she let go over and over again. Before her eyes his form expanded to gigantic proportions. She

149

felt like a doll in the lap of a god.

Leaning down as though from a great height he began to suck her breasts. The softness of his large lips brought her to the verge of collapse. Frozen in space and time, she watched as he held up his hands and made the milky liquid spurt from them.

"Drink, spouse of Shiva," he moaned, "drink the elixir of immortality. You are mine," he growled again, "take it," he cried out hoarsely, his throat contracting in spasms as a long black stone came up.

*   *   *

For seven days and nights Stan purged. Bouts in the bathroom alternated with hot baths and rubs from Jai Devi, which he had hoped would develop into something more. But when the rubbing was over he felt too weak and exhausted to do anything but go to bed. Jai Devi was spending her spare time with Saladin, and although Stan resented it, he was so fascinated by the clever seduction of the uptight Iowa blonde that he forgot to be angry.

Finally on the seventh day he felt better.

"Mr. Stanley, you really look like a new man today," declared Saladin after a week, slapping him on the back. "I have good news for you. His Holiness wishes to see you. You must bathe and put on fresh clothes."

*   *   *

Of course, the Baba was sitting in his favorite corner under an umbrella, being fanned and massaged.

"You are feeling better now, Mr. Stanley, is it not so, eh?" he muttered as Stan went down on his belly to touch the large bare feet.

"I've been very sick," murmured Stan.

"I know. It is I who ordered it, Mr. Stanley. It was important to clean you out first, eh . . . inside? That is always the first step before we clean out the disease." He chuckled, then surveyed Stan through fluttering eyelids. "Your poison is coming out now, I can see that."

"You mean you *made* me sick?" said Stan astonished.

"But of course, nothing happens here that Baba doesn't control. You know how important control can be sometimes, eh?"

There was a long pause during which each waited for the other to speak.

"It is very beautiful here," Stan said finally. Watching the young boy rub the Baba's flesh was making him nervous.

"Ah yes, but it is so expensive to keep it all going, Mr. Stanley, so expensive."

150

"He's asking for more money," Stan thought and let the moment pass.

The Baba rolled on his side. "Now it is time, Mr. Stanley, for you to begin taking exercise—first some light work, then we will see. Of course, you will attend daily bhajan in the morning and evening on the first terrace. The other times you will spend helping out in the kitchen. You will meet some very nice devotees there, they tell me they really need some help. You don't mind helping, do you, Mr. Stanley?"

He threw Stan a long seductive smile, then raised his hand in blessing, his eyes closed. "You may go now, I shall see you this evening."

"So it's the kitchen," Stan grumbled to Saladin.

"But it is the rule of all the ashrams, Mr. Stanley. If you don't pay you must work. I hear there are several bank presidents also working in the kitchen these days. You will have good company."

"It's not that I mind working," complained Stan, "but I came to get cured of a bad disease. Time is running out for me—why should I waste my time working in the kitchen of some ashram?"

"But then why not make a donation?" said Saladin cheerfully.

"You must be joking," said Stan. "I just gave him ten thousand dollars!"

"But Mr. Stanley, the Baba knows that is nothing for a man of your wealth."

"How would the Baba know my financial status? Even I don't."

"Ah, the Baba sees everything, Mr. Stanley. If you will give him a big donation, then of course he will cure you. I tell you, you must give more money, then only will he heal you."

"And I tell you that I will give more after I am healed," Stan sputtered.

"But don't you have to pay a doctor whether he cures you or not?"

Stan felt angry. One didn't pay till the goods were delivered. It wasn't his habit. He remembered too well the cold dingy Bronx apartment where he'd grown up. And even though he was rich now, he hated parting company with money. "And what if I give more, and then he delays my cure. It could go on and on! Ten thousand," He cracked his knuckles. "I shouldn't have started, so now I have to give double the amount."

Still looking morose he followed Saladin to the kitchen where he was introduced to a Mr. Dutt. Mr. Dutt was a short stocky man with beady, slightly crossed eyes. Stan disliked him on sight.

"It is a very good thing for us that His Holiness has sent you, I can tell you that," said Mr. Dutt. "Without enough help we are becoming rushed. You will be washing up the pots, Mr. Stanley. We do them here." He led Stan to a long low depression on the cement floor at one end of the kitchen. There was a pipe with flowing water and a large bowl containing wood ash and coconut husks.

151

"Do I kneel or what?" said Stan contemptuously.

"You squat, Mr. Stanley." Dutt demonstrated how to wash the heavy brass utensils.

"But I've never squatted in my life," said Stan, gazing down at Dutt. "I'm afraid it'll be impossible for me to stay in that position for any length of time. If you can fix something up so that I can stand, it would be better."

"But the water is on the floor, you see, sir. It cannot be changed."

"Why not pay another twenty thousand," Stan thought to himself miserably. But the squalor of the Bronx was too close. "Then I guess I'll just have to learn to squat." He smiled at Mr. Dutt. "When do I start?"

*   *   *

As the days passed and the skin of his hands cracked and filled with grit; and his knees began to ache, and as the loathsome pots and pans arriving from the dining room piled up in endless greasy stacks, Stan began to feel there were forces operating beyond his control. He'd always won his battles because they'd been waged with reasonable men, but the rules here were all upside down, unseen, psychic. He felt repelled, yet fascinated.

Returning to his quarters in the evenings, exhausted from the scullery work, Stan would lie listening through the paper-thin wall to Saladin making out. And after he had finished, Saladin would come plodding in scratching his crotch suggestively, relating the lewd event in detail.

Stan tried to remain indifferent but the whole business was wearing him down. His breathing had become more difficult and he noticed that occasionally when he coughed there was blood. He was becoming a victim. They were out to make him a slave, and could care less whether he got well or not.

Unfortunately, he was certain the Baba could heal him. Sadistic and self-centered though he was, he was a man of great power. That was the rub. But were there any assurances he would do it, even if a million dollars were put before him? No. Why not just pay the money? Wouldn't it just be easier to give in and enjoy himself? Give twenty thousand to the Baba or even more, put Saladin on salary as a pimp, rent a cottage, have boys to rub him and luscious prostitutes to sleep with him whenever he liked. What was it in his character that had always prevented him from becoming involved. He had always been outside looking in. Here it was no different. The play was the same, only the cast had changed. "I'm getting in too deep," he said aloud, after a sleepless night. "It's time to get out."

The next day Stan was on the phone to Carlos whom he'd located in Bombay. "Very good . . . you've seen Jeff? I'll check in at the same hotel.

Make arrangements and meet my plane, I'll call you from Bangalore. No, I don't know when. I have to get out of this place first . . . No, I can't just leave, you don't understand . . . just follow directions! Right. And send the cable in care of Ananda Baba so he will see it—yes, and you'd better make it express, it must seem as though I'm being called away on urgent business. Good-bye.''

Mopping his brow he put down the receiver. The fact was the Baba's power frightened him and he didn't want to set off the bad vibrations which might be directed toward him if it looked like he was leaving of his own free will.

*   *   *

Later that evening as he was washing the last of the pots, a boy delivered a whispered message to Mr. Dutt.

"You are called by Baba," Dutt said breathlessly. "Go at once, I will finish your work."

The boy escorted him to His Holiness, and after touching the Baba's feet Stan sat down opposite Kamala, whom he'd not seen for some time. She lay curled up like a cat, looking more beautiful than ever.

"You have received a cable from Bombay," she said with a searching look, handing him a sealed envelope.

Opening it and after a suitable pause he handed the cable to the Baba.

"It seems that business requires that I leave this wonderful spot. Presumably I will be away only for a week or ten days."

Kamala was certain that the cable had been arranged.

"But we will miss you, Mr. Stanley," the Baba said, after glancing at the cable. "I hope you will return soon. Do you think you should travel when you are sick?"

"I won't be gone for more than a couple of weeks," Stan said, "it's most urgent—a money matter."

"Of course, Mr. Stanley," said the Baba, who didn't believe a word but admired a good game, especially when a man so close to death was playing it. "When will you leave?"

"First thing tomorrow, I expect. Saladin can drive me to Bangalore where I'll catch a plane. Will you come," Stan asked Kamala, "or will you wait here for me?"

Kamala gazed at him, trying to show him that she knew it was all a joke. "Naturally, darling Mr. Stanley," she answered finally. "I will wait here. I am so absorbed with His Holiness. He is teaching me so many things . . . and Bombay is hot this time of year. But you must hurry back."

"By all means," Stan said and touched the Baba's feet. "See you all in two weeks."

*   *   *

"Of course he is lying," the Baba grumbled after Stan had left.

"Naturally," said Kamala.

"Let him go then. His disease is too advanced for me to cure anyhow without making myself sick for months." The Baba's eyes narrowed. "But we must have more of this acid substance. It saves so much time. See how it has brought the General under our control? He got scared to death." The Baba chuckled. "It will be most useful for me. So many of the rich devotees need this kind of scaring. They will see me as a god. Then they will surrender and give more money." He wiped his nose. "They never take time to do the meditations required, and this will overcome that problem." He shot a glance at Kamala. "Shall I send you to Bombay with this man Stanley? I give you leave to go."

"Let us wait a few days," said Kamala. "I will go when the time is right. I hear they have a great quantity of the drug. They won't get rid of it all at once. I also have something to settle with one of Mr. Stanley's associates." Thinking of Jeff, she smiled a thin contemptuous smile. "Do you know of a man called Wasu in Bombay?"

"The big smuggler?"

Kamala nodded.

"He has been here. A very bad man. He has given us millions of rupees from time to time because he is afraid of us and thinks we are lucky."

"I know him too. He will do anything I ask," said Kamala. "I shall phone him and ask him to watch Mr. Stanley. At the proper time he will tell me when to come to Bombay."

The Baba nodded his understanding. "Come here," he said.

She knelt before him.

He took her head in his hands and pulled her gently into his lap. "If you are successful in this undertaking," he whispered, bending over her, "I will place India at your feet."

*   *   *

Back in the hostel Stan noticed there were no lights in Saladin's room although the connecting door was open. As soon as he turned on his light and began packing, Saladin appeared in his shorts, rubbing his eyes. "You are late," he said, stretching seductively.

"I had to say goodbye to His Holiness."

Saladin woke up at once. "You are leaving?"

"Only for two weeks." He handed Saladin the cable.

"I see," said Saladin slowly. "Business calls you away. You are a

154

dying man yet still you do the business, yes?''

''I'm not dead yet,'' Stan shot back. ''Will you drive me to Bangalore in the morning or shall I engage someone else?''

''I will drive if it is your desire,'' said Saladin, smiling.

''Yes, it's my desire,'' said Stan, absorbed in his packing, ''and I'll want to start before sunrise.'' He looked up. ''Could you have them prepare the bill now so that we won't have a long delay in the morning when no one's awake.''

From the tone of his voice Saladin was sure Stan was terminating their relationship. ''If he thinks he is going to leave without giving something to me,'' said Saladin to himself, ''he'll get a surprise.''

The problem of what to do obsessed him through the night. ''He will wait till the last to pay me off,'' Saladin kept thinking. ''At the airport in Bangalore where I cannot protest, he will give me some trifling amount.''

He knew that Stan still had ten thousand in travelers checks. He also knew if he took them and Stan complained, he could bribe himself out of it. Stan was a foreigner, and if the circumstances were compromising enough, he'd cough up.

The next day in a wild section of jungle that stretched along the road for miles between two remote villages Saladin pretended the engine had stalled. Jumping out, he quickly lifted the hood, disconnected a wire, and asked Stan to start the car.

Suspecting that Saladin might have pulled a wire, Stan examined the engine thoroughly himself. But Saladin was clever and the wire he had detached was buried in a tangle of old connections that would have misled even the best of mechanics. Just as he was losing all hope of making the plane, a cloud of dust behind them signaled the almost magical appearance of another car. It drew up beside them and the driver leaned out the window.

''My car has broken down,'' cried Saladin in English. ''This gentleman must get to Bangalore. Can you help us?''

''I am just now returning to there empty, you are welcome to ride.''

''But what about your car,'' Stan said, as Saladin began transferring the luggage from one car to the other.

''I will lock it and come back with a mechanic tomorrow.''

''But I can send a mechanic from the next town. There's no need for you to make the trip. If this man will take me, you must wait here and look to the safety of your car.''

''How shrewd he is,'' thought Saladin. ''But it is my duty, Sahib,'' he whispered, ''this man might be no good. It is best I come along.''

Relieved to find that the back and side windows were curtained, even if the car wasn't air-conditioned, and congratulating himself on his good luck, Stan eased himself down in the seat and was just dozing off when

Saladin began stroking his leg suggestively.

Stan froze. He was tired of this young hustler and wanted no more to do with him, especially in a car.

But Saladin unbuttoned his pants and rubbed his penis against Stan's leg.

"No," whispered Stan, blinking up at the driver, "put it away, he'll see."

"Take it," Saladin urged. "He won't see."

After that everything happened so fast it was only after he boarded the plane that Stan managed to piece things together. Saladin had pushed him onto the floor. The car had stopped and the driver, forcing his arms behind his back, had dragged him out. Stan bit Saladin's leg but got kicked in the stomach and passed out.

The next thing he knew the driver was holding a long knife barely two inches from his throat.

"You sign the checks to me, eh?" said Saladin, waving nine thousand dollar travelers checks in front of his face.

Stan squirmed and looked away.

"No, no, Mr. Stan," Saladin said coolly, "do not try to get loose. You will get your throat cut."

"You cut my throat and you're in trouble," said Stan, his voice trembling. "Sundaram . . ."

"A. K. Sundaram will do nothing. I am only asking for nine thousand, Mr. Stan, only nine thousand. If I cut your throat I will get ten. It is so easy to forge your name, it is nothing to dispose of your body here. Anyhow you are a dying man and a foreigner. No one is going to be interested in you. There would be no investigation. A. K. Sundaram would do everything to hush it up, especially if he got a cut. Really, no one would miss you, Mr. Stan. You better sign the checks. I am letting you off easy because I like you." He grinned.

There was an ominous silence while Stan tried to penetrate the barrier of Saladin's face. Rage churned in his stomach as the ludicrous nature of the trap into which he'd fallen became clear, but an inner voice warned him if he wasn't careful his stinginess was going to get him killed.

"How should I make them out," he said finally.

"Saladin Travels Ltd.," was the proud reply.

By the time he'd finished signing, something inside Stan had snapped. He felt used up, broken, too broken even to resist as they bound him hand and foot.

"Don't worry, you will be untied at the airport, Mr. Stanley," grunted Saladin. "But I'll have the knife at your back. So do not be foolish enough to yell out. And do not try to report these checks lost or stolen. I am an Arab, not an Indian. We have connections—even in New York. Most unpleasant things would happen to you."

"Before we start out," he smiled condescendingly, "would you not enjoy sucking off my friend? Abdul come here. Show Sahib what you've got."

Unzipping his pants, the driver stood in the half-open door, his arms resting on the top of the car.

"See, nice one, huh Mr. Stan, yes?"

Raising Stan's head he pushed it toward the erect penis.

"Suck, pig," he said, holding the knife at Stan's throat. With a groan the driver discharged into Stan's mouth, returned to the front seat and started the car.

"Now, me," Saladin ordered, pulling Stan between his legs. "We have two hours till the airport. Do a good job, Mr. Stan, I bet you never get good Moslem cock like this again."

Saladin had not freed him until they'd stopped beside the passenger entrance. Then, just as the car was surrounded by coolies eager to carry the baggage, Saladin had cut the ropes and dragged him out, pretending to help him.

"You'd better hurry, Mr. Stanley," he shouted in a loud voice, saluting and smiling at people he knew. "Remember when you return in two weeks, just phone ahead and I'll be here to meet you."

It was over so fast there had been no time for Stan to protest. "Besides," he thought miserably, looking out the plane window, "how could I have explained it to anyone?" His only thought now was which would come first, madness or death.

IX

THE EARLY MORNING flight from Delhi had arrived in Bombay toward noon and Jeff had taken a taxi straight to the Taj Mahal Hotel. Exhaustion overpowered him, but he couldn't sleep.

Fucked in the ass by a eunuch. He pounded the bed with his fist.

The glimpses of himself he was beginning to catch were too much to handle. He felt filthy. Got up, showered, washed his backside carefully and cursed Kamala.

"Drugs!" he thought disgustedly and felt like chucking the two suitcases of acid into the bay outside the hotel window. But the bread. What about that? Why was it always him who had to be thinking about the money end of things?

After a couple of days locked in his hotel room he became paranoid. Laura had always been able to cheer him up, but without her he was helpless. Even the room boy who brought food and fresh towels seemed to be spying on him.

Growing nervous about the acid he decided to check it outside the hotel. Reserving five hundred tabs to give away as sales promotion, he found an old, reliable English storage company in the phone book, took the bags there, and stashed them in a locker. It was his first time out in three days and his first time ever on the streets of Bombay. Yelling, grimacing, nameless brown faces—acres and acres of them—stretched out their hands to him for money, watched him, wanted to be him.

No matter how much enlightenment there might be here in India, it was a dangerous place. He was a foreigner. No matter how many friends he might make here, in the end they would let him down. He was sure of that.

Returning to his room he spent the next three weeks locked up, reading magazines and long Russian novels he purchased in the hotel bookshop. The Russia of Tolstoy was like the India he'd seen. Each evening as the sun set pink and gold across the bay, he would put up the shades and watch the parade of peddlers, whores, male prostitutes, money changers, and tourists in front of the hotel. Was this the road to Mandalay? The water that lapped at the gateway to India was full of garbage. No doubt the flying fishes were long dead.

Then one Sunday evening after he'd read all the books he cared to deal with, and tallied up his weaknesses for the hundredth time, he ventured down to the bar. Before he'd had time to order a drink a familiar voice called to him from across the room. It was the girl from Texas, and Carlos!

"Hello there, partner," said the girl.

"Hear you met Angel in Delhi," Carlos said. "Why don't you sit down. I'd like you to meet my old friend Wasu and his friend..."

"Hadji," the man said, introducing himself, "my name is Hadji."

Jeff sank into a chair.

"I have been looking everywhere for you, my friend," said Carlos. "Stan's here."

"Here in Bombay?"

"Not yet, but he will be, he's got cancer."

"What?"

"Absolutely. In the lung. He's dying." Carlos gestured dramatically. "Only one, two months left."

"Where is he?" said Jeff, thinking of the money Carlos would probably get.

"With some holy man," Carlos sighed, smiling faintly, "thinks he can cure him. I've told him he should go to New York, but he won't listen. You just missed him in Delhi. We arrived the day after you left. He's been with the holy man for three weeks now, his name is...ah yes, Ananda Baba."

"Ananda Baba can cure him," said Wasu, a big broad-shouldered man in a tan silk suit.

"If he spends enough money," said Carlos. "Otherwise, he'll let him die."

Wasu laughed. "That is also a possibility."

Jeff didn't like Wasu's looks. He had the bearing of a thug, his face was sullen, and although probably not over forty he had the eyes of one who'd seen too much.

The other man, Hadji, had the handsome face of a Greek warrior. His hair was hidden by traditional Arab headgear and he wore a white robe of softest wool.

"Arabian Nights," Jeff was thinking as he finished his drink and stood up to leave. The last person in the world he felt like spending time with was Carlos.

Wasu, his face haughty, motioned Jeff down. "Sit, my friend," he said, bringing a large heavy hand down on the table. "You have only just arrived—why are you jumping up so soon? I heard so much about you from my Angel and from...my friend Carlos. I want to get to know you." He leaned forward. "I have tried the pills you brought." He rolled his eyes

159

seductively. "Very good. I will buy a great quantity, yes? Do you have some?"

Jeff eased back into his chair. "Now?"

"Yes."

"I don't carry them around."

Wasu turned to Carlos. "And you...?" he asked, as if talking to a servant.

"You want more now?" asked Carlos. "They shouldn't be taken with liquor."

"I did not ask how," said Wasu coldly.

Fishing a small envelope out of his pocket, Carlos passed it to Wasu who took five tablets, dropped them in his drink and gave five more to Angel.

Jeff winced.

"Whatsa matter?" Wasu said. "Is good stuff, no taste at all." He mixed his drink with a spoon.

"Drink it," he ordered the girl from Texas. "You need it!" He waited while she drained her glass.

"Tonight you will come with me," he said to Jeff, bringing his big hands firmly onto the table. "I will show you something you never seen before." Emptying his glass, he signaled the waiter. "First I take you all to dinner. When stomach is empty, nothing goes right." He eased his heavy body out of the banquette. "My car is outside."

At the hotel entrance, a large gray Mercedes pulled up and two hefty bodyguards wearing dark glasses jumped out. After saluting Wasu and helping the passengers inside, they jumped in the front seat. Jeff noticed pistols strapped under their arms.

Wasu said something in Marathi to the driver and the car sped noiselessly through downtown Bombay. Turning south and then east they continued past the old city until they reached a sprawling shantytown where a room could cost a poor man half his month's salary if he was lucky enough to find one.

"We going to the airport for dinner, or what?" asked Angel looking bored.

"It is Sunday," said Wasu. "Always I go to my mother's to eat on Sunday. I don't take no one. Tonight I take all of you." He gestured expansively. "She always got too much food anyway."

They turned off the main road onto an unpaved dirt street paralleling an open sewage conduit. The terrible stench oozed in through the closed windows of the car. Angel covered her nose with her shawl as crowds of wide-eyed bystanders scattered before the driver's persistent horn.

"It is not good, eh?" said Wasu, a look of disgust and rage crossing his heavy face. "Breathe deep and it will not give the bad smell. After some

160

time you get used to it. My mother lives here alone. We are all grown up here, my father is died here. She won't move."

The car stopped and the two guards jumped out to fend off a crowd of admirers, mostly teenagers.

"Come, we get out here," ordered Wasu, reeling out of the car.

"Wasu, Wasu, Jai Wasu, Jai Jai!" Children in rags, old people, thin young men in tight pants, some smiling, others overcome with awe, all shouted in chorus: "Wasu, Wasu!"

Outside the stench was worse and Jeff took a deep breath. On a treeless wasteland between the highway and a distant power plant, hovels clung to the dusty earth. Coal smoke spewed into the evening air. The only water he could see trickled in the drains and open sewers that connected the huts. There was shit everywhere. Pigs and chickens were busy recycling the human shit into animal shit. Flies covered everything.

"It is the cauldron of Maria Ma*," muttered Wasu. "Who survives the disease here is real Indian!"

The bodyguards muscled a path for them to the entrance of a low tin-roofed mud hut. Inside a handsome tough-looking woman nodded to them and hugged Wasu.

"My mother she speaks no English—sorry, she never had no time to learn. I got seven brothers, eight sisters, all living." Wasu chattered with her in Marathi as he lowered himself onto a straw mat. "I was wanting that she should move to a good flat somewhere in one of those buildings I am owning, or hotel. It is no use." He gestured hopelessly. "She won't, maybe it is good, eh? People who know me see that my mother does not move. They are not so jealous then. They imagine I have no money to get her fine place? I tell them the car belongs to Congress Party, ha!"

Wasu's mother moved about noiseless and deft, squatting on the floor, rolling out chappatis for a daughter who cooked them on a wood fire. A large pot of meat swimming in fat boiled on a portable kerosene burner. The smell of sewage blended with cooking meat made Jeff sick. He wondered how this Wasu could make it with five thousand mics of acid in his system. Angel sat grimly in one corner as the meat was served in chunks on large mounds of white rice.

Wasu ate with his hand, slapping meat and rice into wads which he gulped down, smacking his lips in appreciation. The mud walls were covered with photographs, many of Wasu. He noticed Jeff looking at them.

"That is my father," he said, his mouth full of food. "After 1947 he made Corporal in the Army. When Wasu is born, he is sweeper, peon. We are low caste. Pretty good for us, eh?" he said, patting his chest

*Maria Ma=an aspect of Kali—goddess governing the disease cholera

161

arrogantly. "The Congress Party they raised us up. My father was one of six brothers, only him lived to have children. My mother, she came from Jaipur—all her family died. Now I got seven brothers and eight sisters, all living—all got good jobs making plenty money." He gulped down more food. "Eat, eat," he shouted to Carlos who was pushing food around on his plate. "You think you are some Brahmin, eh? If I don't know you are Mexicano, I think you act like bloody Brahmin." Wasu belched, then glanced at Hadji and slapped him on the back. "At least you are eating, eh? Moslems eat meat. We are low caste. All the low caste and Moslems they eat meat in Bombay—we have no quarrel."

"Your father was a very handsome man," said Jeff, glancing up at one of the photos.

"He's died last year," said Wasu, frowning. "But he's died a happy man, to see his son Wasu rich like Raj. Congress Party people give him fine funeral. He was a good worker for them, organizing so many people. Now they are after me, me Wasu." He sighed and touched Jeff's hand. "Can you imagine that they have raised me up and now they are attacking me? Yes, it is true. They want to finish me—ME, Wasu, they want to finish me off!"

"Last year police come and took me to the Government of India court. I'm having to get lawyers. The judge he say, 'Wasu, what you got to say for yourself? We got the goods on you, you big smuggler, selling the gold, the drug, the women. We know it, we got spies all over. We know all the rackets you have."

He wolfed down more food. "But I tell him, I tell the judge—Brahmin he was—'Listen to me, I am Wasu. I am low caste and black. You go ahead, you put Wasu in prison. The day I am going through the prison gate fifty thousand people will lose their jobs. Ha, yes it is so! Can you find fifty thousand people jobs? Can Congress Party find so many jobs? Not all can be doctor, engineer or judge,' I say to him. 'Bombay people they like gold, they like numbers and fucking. That's where the jobs are here.' " Wasu closed his eyes, his face expressionless. " 'The biggest customer for the gold is Government of India,' I say to him."

"What happened?" asked Carlos, who had managed to finish his food.

"He fined me three hundred rupees plus the cost and let me go free from the court. What could they do? It is true. Wasu does not lie. He has seen the world too much to lie. And I had something on that judge too, I will show tonight. Tonight I will take you to see where Brahmin judges like to go.

"This Congress Party is no good now, all crooks: socialism from books, big foreign cars to ride in. We peoples are not socialists, we are all capitalists. Let them come, these socialists, these communists. Let them bring the Russians, the Chinese, what do we care?" He laughed loudly.

162

"We go on forever, yes, it is true, Mr. Jeff. See the mud outside, smell the stink. We can survive it. We are on the bottom—they cannot move us.

"See the Indian man, he loves money more than anything. He loves women, boys, jewels, gold, and babies. You give any man three hundred rupees, he will buy some trash, some cheap stuff in the big market. Then he will bring his cloth out of the city and start selling on roadside. Next time you see him, he is in some small shop he has builded over himself. Next year you will see bigger shop, then cement will come and he will build hotel. Finally he own whole street, driving in Ambassador car. That's the way it goes." Wasu sighed. "Now Congress Party says pay taxes, put money in bank. Bank is just trap to keep track of the money so they can steal it later. I know them, my father all his life he work for them." He rolled his eyes.

Jeff managed to clean his plate by holding his breath and swallowing the greasy food in big gulps. This pleased Wasu who ordered his mother to fill up the plate a second time over Jeff's protests.

"Eat! Eat! Eat!" he yelled, "You peoples are too skinny." He glanced at Angel. "Her, I try to fatten up," he said. "She not gain any weight. Who wants to fuck skinny woman, eh, Hadji?"

He leered at the young Arab, then turned to Jeff.

"Hadji is prince, Dubai prince." He slapped Hadji on the back. Hadji flinched. "He is only baby, only twenty-nine years, but he got four wives and twenty-three babies, all fat. I have seen." Wasu nodded. "Eh Hadji, when you invite Wasu to Dubai again, eh? Some first-class women they got there. I ought to know, those sheiks they buy plenty of them from me." He winked at Jeff and licked his lips.

As soon as he had finished, Wasu got up and went outside with a jar of water. With loud gargling sounds he snorted water through his nostrils and spit out into the crowd as if they didn't exist. Carlos followed suit. Hadji held the water jar for Jeff as he washed before the wide-eyed children and old people hanging around the door. Angel, who hadn't touched her food, remained seated in the corner lost in acid visions.

When they came back in Wasu sat down in front of the fire with his mother. They had a long animated conversation in Marathi which turned into an argument, the mother gesturing wildly at Wasu and yelling at him. Finally he reached into his tight pants and with his big hands threw out wads of hundred-rupee notes onto her lap. Casting furtive glances at the visitors, she straightened the notes out. When she had them in a neat pile she locked them in a metal box, which she put in a large old-fashioned safe that was covered with a piece of flowered oilcloth.

"The bank," said Wasu, with a sardonic grin. He stood up and called in one of the bodyguards, who helped Angel to her feet. Her eyes were fixed.

They filed out. Wasu's mother stood at the door, her hands folded in front of her sari, her face expressionless.

In the car Wasu's big meaty hand came down heavily on Jeff's knee. "Now I take you to the 'theatre,' a place I own," he said, picking his teeth with his other hand.

Soon the sleek grey limousine was back in the teeming streets of Bombay central.

"This is prostitute section," Wasu was saying. "You have heard of Sukhalachi Street—the girls in the cages, yes?" He ordered the driver to slow down and opened the window. What appeared to be shops with small barred windows lined the street. Behind the bars girls were sitting.

"Not much different than Amsterdam," Carlos commented dryly. "There it's picture windows, here it's bars and more girls."

"Amsterdam?" Wasu asked.

"A city in Holland," said Jeff. "It has a quarter like this."

The car stopped on a side street in front of a nondescript cement building that resembled a small hotel or apartment house. The street was thronged with barefoot urchins, beggars, and cyclists. Wasu handed Jeff a roll of five-rupee notes.

"You please give to the beggars," he said, his eyes now bulging with visions.

One bodyguard opened the door and pulled Angel out while the other guard and Wasu bulldozed their way up some steps to the door of the building. Hadji and Carlos followed in their wake. When Jeff got out of the car, holding the five-rupee notes, what seemed like a hoard of grey ghosts of every age materialized out of nowhere, engulfing him, tearing at his clothes, grabbing at his arms, hands, and legs, clawing at him with leprous stumps of fingers and arms. Children scuttled under the legs of the old people trying to trip them and knock them down.

"Ah, sahib, paisa, paisa," they groaned, clutching at him.

"Give to the older ones," Wasu yelled from the top of the stairs. "The younger ones don't need."

In desperation, Jeff threw the money into the air. At least two hundred people reached like a cresting wave and fell into the filth of the street, old and young alike clawing at each other for the money.

Wasu roared like a bull, his eyes inflamed. "Now my friend, you have felt the touch of hunger, eh? I don't think you will forget it soon." He slapped Jeff on the back and pulled him up the stairs to the door.

"It's Wasu's joke," muttered Carlos as they entered the building. "He does it to everyone. There's a bathroom upstairs where you can wash off."

"You've been here before then?" Jeff whispered.

"I'm afraid so." Carlos sighed. "There is no place like it, you will see. Wasu invented it himself."

A big young man in a dark suit who looked like he might be one of Wasu's seven brothers saluted him.

"You are late," he said. "Everyone is waiting."

"Let them wait," said Wasu contemptuously, brushing the young man aside. "It makes more exciting for them."

He propelled Angel up a narrow stairway and down a long hall. The bodyguards stood by as he turned a key in one of the many doors that lined the hall and motioned them all through. They entered an air-conditioned, thickly carpeted dark room, a little larger than a motel room. Nondescript, overstuffed chairs and divans faced a series of wall-length windows. The windows opened into a brightly lit room, upholstered floor to ceiling with pink vinyl and lined with mirrors. Just in front of the mirrors was a network of heavy chrome bars. Jeff realized that what he was actually looking at was a mirrored room with a huge cage in it. There was a door at one end of the room that connected to the cage.

Wasu eased himself into one of the divans. Angel collapsed on the carpet beside him, holding onto one of his big legs with both arms. One of the guards came and removed Wasu's shoes and then stood against the wall with the other guard.

Hadji stretched out on a divan while Carlos and Jeff sat side by side on another. "Are there more rooms like this?" Jeff asked Carlos.

"Six." He leaned toward Jeff, talking fast and low. "Listen, this Wasu is the biggest smuggler in India, maybe in the world. He digs the acid, digs the freaky scenes, wants to buy maybe the whole lot. You have it with you?"

Jeff nodded.

"Good." Carlos relaxed.

"And these?" Jeff gestured at the windows they were looking through.

"One-way mirrors," whispered Carlos. "You will see, don't talk too much at first, he gets angry if . . ."

"Carlos," Wasu commanded. "Give this to your friend." He turned to Jeff. "Why are you sitting so far back? Come, move the chair here . . . I have some good kief for you, best hashish in Bombay . . . Come, we will smoke first. It's better." Wasu smiled, his broad nose flaring. "Angel, she tell me you are quite a stud."

Asian Muzak drifted in over a loudspeaker system.

The lights in the room brightened, bouncing off the pink vinyl and chrome. The doors at the end opened and a young girl was pushed into the cage by a fat attendant wearing a towel.

"Singapore girl," Wasu murmured. "Nice one, eh?"

The girl ambled to the center of the room, her big breasts covered with a see-through brassiere, her lithe hips and thighs rolling under black lace panties.

She stood before one of the mirrored windows brushing her hair back, and squeezing her breasts at the mirror.

Jeff thought she was very young to know so much. He was so intent on watching her he failed to notice that another girl, carrying a tray of drinks in small glasses, had entered the room they were in.

"Arak," bellowed Wasu, unbuttoning his shirt. "Goes good with the pills. Take. Drink."

"Made from palm juice," Carlos said to Jeff. "Like Aquavit."

When Jeff looked back at the mirrored room another figure had entered, a young, very muscular, male with an oversized neanderthal head. The attendant was locking the door of the cage.

Jeff sat bolt upright.

The ravaged face of the young idiot grinned in the mirrors, masturbating slowly as he watched the Singapore girl. One of Wasu's bodyguards cornered the girl who had brought the arak and fingering her idly, watched the cage over her shoulders.

Jeff looked at Carlos.

"Interesting scene, yes, crazies!" Carlos wagged his head.

Jeff felt sick.

Wasu took off his shirt. Beads of sweat stood out on an enormous stomach and breastlike pectoral muscles, firm as rocks. He was watching his bodyguard finger the waitress. He leaned over Angel and said something to her. She shook her head.

Wasu pushed her off his leg. "You do it," he said, knocking her with his knee. She stared at him. "I give you another chance, bitch!" he yelled, but she only stared. "Cunt," he said in Marathi. Motioning to the bodyguard. "She thinks she make Wasu angry." he mumbled. "She needs some good lesson." He whispered something to the guard. "Now she'll get it, you see."

The guard muscled Angel out of the room.

"Srini," Wasu yelled to the other guard, who made the serving girl kneel between Wasu's fat legs. With difficulty, Wasu unzipped his fly and pulled her face down on his penis.

"See, is good, no?" he said gesturing to the mirrored room.

The Singapore girl was backing away from the idiot. He followed her grinning, aware somehow that he was stronger and that it was only a matter of time until he got her. He lunged for her several times, grabbing at her panties, then stood swaying, flailing his penis at her. At first it was a game, but as his desire heightened, and the girl continued to evade him, the idiot became angry and went after her in earnest. Tired of running, she climbed the bars of the cage and kicked at him with her spike-heeled shoes. The sounds of the struggle were piped in over the Muzak.

Wasu lay back grunting as the serving girl sucked him.

166

"What the fuck?" Jeff said under his breath. "Who runs this place?"

"Wasu own it," muttered Wasu, "and he run it."

"He owns it," Carlos whispered. "But it is run by freaks—an international crowd, freaky psychologists who dig sex with crazies."

"Very humanitarian peoples," Wasu grunted, overhearing Carlos. "I give them plenty money for their crazy peoples."

"It's true," said Carlos. "They have these places—homes for crazies, morons you know—private, very high class. Very careful about things. All the doctors and nurses they dig making it with crazies or watching."

"Otherwise, who would look after them," said Wasu out of the corner of his mouth. "They have good program. Here in India, Turkey, some Western countries too, all are healthy. See the muscles." He pointed to the idiot in the cage, "Get plenty of work in gardens, plenty sex."

Wasu, tired of the girl between his legs, pushed her away. "I go take shower," he said, disappearing through a door at the end of the room.

In the cage the idiot had pulled the girl off the bars and was sitting on her fingering her vagina, opening it and looking into it.

"Do they put on these shows everywhere?" asked Jeff.

"No, no," whispered Carlos. "Wasu, he got to know them. They started doing it at their place. Then he is bringing them here. Very dangerous. Only special nights for high politicians, civil service officers. They don't know he owns it. He has something on them then. It's not always the crazies. Mostly he has beatings, sometimes animals, sometimes prison inmates, this is nothing..."

Another male, about thirty-five and raving, had been pushed through the door of the cage. The first one grunted ferociously at him and gestured for him to go away.

"You sell much of the acid?" said Carlos casually, ignoring the cage where the two wretches had started fighting over the girl.

"Half of it," said Jeff.

"You got the money for it?"

"The money is in Switzerland. Checks deposited to Stan's account. When they clear, the people will pick up their stuff."

"They trust you?"

"What else can they do?"

"What are you getting for it?"

"Twenty-five cents."

"You have it in your hotel?" Carlos asked, his eyes now following the fight. The second idiot had knocked the other out by pounding his head on the floor.

"Are you kidding?"

"Then where?"

"In a safe place, where it will stay until Stan comes or I hear from him." Jeff looked at Carlos, knowing he was nervous that Stan would die and he, Jeff, would have all that acid.

"What about cash deals?"

"Sure. But not in rupees, only dollars."

Wasu came in wrapped in a towel followed by a young boy. He sprawled out one of the divans while the boy massaged his back.

The second idiot lifted the girl into the air and threw her to the floor where he pounced on her and ripping away her brassiere, biting her breasts and squatting on her face, plunged his face between her legs. She screamed wildly and clawed at his back. He turned around and slapped her face until she kept quiet.

"Fuck her idiot, fuck!" Wasu yelled, propped up on one elbow. "He is so stupid he don't know how to fuck." Wasu snickered, turning to Jeff and Carlos. His huge body glistened with oil.

The young masseur stood waiting for Wasu to dismiss him. Instead, Wasu pushed the boy's head down between his legs.

You like to fuck this Hejjera?" he rasped at Hadji, who had withdrawn under his robes and headdress.

"No thanks," Hadji said. "He is too young for me, too tight."

"He'll stretch, you see." Wasu turned to Jeff. "Come, I like to watch you fuck him."

Jeff shook his head.

"He very talented boy," declared Wasu, "see, very clean, trained for it." He fingered the boy's anus. The boy raised his buttocks in the air.

Wasu beckoned to one of his bodyguards. The guard unbuttoned his fly, spat on his penis, and let it slip into the boy.

"We train them from six years," Wasu explained. "From six he is sitting on wooden pegs to keep it open—very good boy, very clean." He lifted the boy's head by his hair. The boy smiled inanely and started sucking Wasu again.

"Fuck!" shouted Wasu to the guard.

The guard had an orgasm.

"Now you," Wasu indicated Carlos. "Hey you, Brahmin Carlos, you come now, you fuck, he hot now, wants more."

Carlos hesitated.

"You fuck him!" Wasu yelled angrily, starting to get up. "Wasu like see Carlos fuck fat young boy."

Carlos dropped his pants and walked behind the boy.

"Let him watch in the room," Wasu instructed, taking the boy from his crotch and turning him round on his hands and knees facing the window.

But the participants in the scene had vanished, the room was empty. "Huh," grunted Wasu, slapping the young boy's buttocks. "Slap him,

Brahmin, he give you more action." Jeff glanced at Wasu who lay back, watching Carlos with the boy. Then he flinched.

Angel was being pushed through the door of the cage.

Wasu was talking to himself. "She think she say no to Wasu, ha? I am just dumb black bastard, eh? She will see... She got to learn some discipline."

A tall man with a scarred face, dark brown skin, and blue eyes entered the cage naked.

"Convict," Wasu said hoarsely to Jeff, "I get him out evenings sometimes. He very strong, like to rape women—eighteen times convictions Bombay courts. Can you imagine how hard up he gets in jail house!"

Jeff began to feel sick.

"I give him some of your pills tonight, see what he is going to do now."

When the convict saw Angel at the other end of the cage, she was clinging to the bars unable to move, fixed on her image repeated over and over again in the mirrors. He smiled faintly and licked his lips and beckoned to her across the room but she ignored him. Sidling up to her he slipped his hand under her dress. She tried to push him away but he grabbed her arm and held it, forcing her to stare into his eyes.

Suddenly she laughed hysterically. He slapped her across the mouth. She struck back at him, clawing and kicking, but he stood his ground, smiling ominously and letting her exhaust herself.

"Think what a chance for him, the black bastard," Wasu chuckled. "He never had no white woman before—he thinks she's something special." He called one of the bodyguards and whispered something in his ear.

Carlos had finished and lay stretched out on one of the divans watching the cage while the boy massaged his back.

Suddenly the convict caught Angel's clothes with both hands and ripped them from her body. She bolted away but he forced her into a corner and hovered over her, trying to kiss her. When she covered her face with her hands he moved down her body with his tongue until he reached her vagina. She closed her eyes, letting him go at her, swaying from side to side in the corner, hanging onto the cage.

Jeff had to leave and rose from his chair.

Wasu pushed him back gently. "You no like see white girl and black man, eh?" he laughed. "Listen," he whispered, letting his hand go up Jeff's leg. "I got something special for you later, you stick around. Angel tell me you got big one, eh?" He groped at Jeff's crotch. "Wasu, he like to see you fuck young girl—virgin... you fuck, eh?"

Jeff gave a start and Wasu turned his head.

A very large shorthaired black dog, almost the size of a Great Dane but heavier, had been let into the room. It wagged its tail excitedly, its penis glistening scarlet and poking out of the hairy foreskin. The convict turned. The dog bounded across the room and tried to climb on his back. He pushed it off but catching its collar brought it up to Angel's crotch where it sniffed and licked eagerly, while the convict stroked its penis with his free hand.

Suddenly he stood up letting go the dog and dragging Angel out into the center of the floor. The dog barked wildly. Straddling Angel, the convict caught hold of the dog and dragged it over her head, trying to force her to take the dog's organ in her mouth. She resisted, flailing her arms and legs, but he backhanded her across the mouth. Then, eyes bulging, his mouth open in a crazy grin, he lifted her legs up, entered her and forced the dog's penis into her mouth. The dog stood still panting and drooling as Angel sucked.

"It is interesting place, no?" said Wasu. He stroked Jeff's leg again.

Jeff sent an SOS to Hadji, the only other sane looking person in the room. "Who is in the other rooms?" said Hadji suddenly to Wasu.

"The other rooms?" Wasu jumped up, looking paranoid. "Who is in them," he said, lunging forward with a wild look in his eyes. Then he laughed and relaxed. "Customers are in the other rooms, of course. Ha, you think you fool me, eh? Customers, ministers, high officers, Brahmin judges. I stand in hallway sometime when they are leaving, they not know I own this place. After that they get scared to death of me. I got photos too, cameras hidden all over, got all that. They no touch Wasu. Watch, the dog going to fuck her now."

The convict had got Angel on her knees and was fucking her in the mouth while the dog mounted her at the rear, humping wildly.

"Sometimes the dog get stuck inside," laughed Wasu. "It is very funny. The dog he gets four times bigger. Once he get in, gets stuck. See what a good bitch she make."

The convict played with Angel's breasts as she bobbed up and down on him.

"I think she enjoy, eh?" boomed Wasu, going off into spasms of laughter.

Jeff got up and made for the door.

"Where you going?" Wasu lurched around and gave one of his bodyguards the high sign.

But Hadji stood up and came between the guard and Jeff. "Wait outside, please," he said to Jeff. "I too am leaving. I will just say something to Wasu."

Jeff waited in the corridor. A moment later Hadji strode through the door, his robes flowing, and took Jeff's hand. "Come," he said, tugging him past the fat guard who looked like Wasu. "This place stinks. I will take you home."

Outside, Hadji hailed a taxi. "Jump in," he said and stared straight ahead as the car careened out of the tangle of side streets into a wide boulevard paralleling the curve of the bay.

"I think you may be going in the opposite direction," Jeff said after a long silence.

"You are staying at the Taj, I know it, but I take you home with me." He smiled nervously. "It is no time for you to be alone in hotel room after such..." He turned to Jeff and shrugged. "I have not the words to say it. That Wasu is one very bad beast. He is so bad he doesn't even know it. He thinks he is a maharaja, but he is animal. He was raised up like an animal, he is an animal." He sighed. "India, it is too much. Too much poverty, too much of people, too much of sickness."

"Too much of nothing," muttered Jeff. "But your wives and children..." he said after a while, not particularly wanting to barge in on some family scene.

Hadji smiled. "They live in Dubai—you think I would let them come here?"

"How many wives do you really have?"

"Four."

"And children?"

"I have four wives and twenty-eight children—that Wasu he left out five. And I am twenty-nine years and I am happily married for seven years." He grinned, watching Jeff's face.

"That makes one a year for each wife for seven years."

Hadji flashed rows of perfect white teeth. "And what is your age?"

"Thirty," Jeff answered.

"Then we are brothers," Hadji said, extending his hand.

They followed an arterial drive on the shore of the seven bays, north of Bombay.

"Where are we going?" said Jeff quietly.

"Juhu," Hadji said. "It is a suburb of Bombay. It is like your Long Island."

"You have been to America?"

"Oh yes, several times. I don't like much." He smiled at Jeff. "No mystery. People too simple-minded.

"We will be there soon. At my house, you may have something to eat. I could not keep that man's food down. I vomit it up in bathroom... even I do not eat the beef and I am Moslem. Crazy, that Wasu. He is only business acquaintance, that is all. I despise him."

The car went through a gate in a long white wall covered with bougan-villea, bumped down a dirt road toward the beach, and came to a stop in front of a modern house. They got out and paid the driver. In the distance, Jeff could hear the roar of the surf. A bright moon sailed above palms that rattled in the wind.

171

Hadji went ahead, switching on lights. Pulling off his headdress he made for the bar at the end of a large room. He wore his hair short, like a curly helmet, and reminded Jeff of an Olympic swimmer from Munich he'd once known.

"Relax," Hadji said. "You like to have a drink? Comm'on."

"Quite a pad you have here," Jeff said.

"It belongs to the daughter of some Indian industrialist. She has gone to California to be free—to lead sane life. I rent it. I must come here for business. It is my Indian prison." He laughed, leaning over the bar. "What a terrible country, eh? Terrible and beautiful. From the animal to the saint—it has everything and every kind of persons. My heart breaks when I come here to see such suffering, to see what is happening to this country, day by day, rich or poor, all suffering . . ." He frowned. "And it is just beginning."

There was a noise in the kitchen beyond.

"Who is there," shouted Hadji sharply.

"It is I only, sir, Nazimudin."

"My servant has got up to see if there is anything . . . You needn't have gotten up," Hadji said to a young barefoot boy of fifteen or so who had come in rubbing his eyes.

"Nazimudin, this is Mr. Jeff. Nazimudin comes from my country. He keeps me from . . . 'freaking out'—is that correct?"

Jeff nodded.

"From freaking out here in India." Hadji smiled. "Then, as you are now up, Nazimudin, get us something to eat. Some chips, some lobster curry, something before going to sleep."

"Only two, sir," said the boy.

"Only two," said Hadji.

The boy disappeared. Hadji came from behind the bar, drink in hand. "Come," he said, putting his arm around Jeff's shoulder, "we smoke some good hashish now, eh? Then we have swim, then dinner, after that sleep."

They walked into a hall lined with photos. "See," said Hadji, pointing to the pictures, "These are my wifes."

Jeff saw four extraordinarily beautiful women.

"Plenty cool, as you say, no? And these are all my children, and here eldest son by first wife, my heir.

"But come." He tugged at Jeff. "Come in here, this room is for smoking." He took a mixture out of a box and filled a large hooka. "Nazimudin," he yelled.

"Sir?" the boy came running.

"Be a good boy, bring coals from kitchen for hooka."

The boy padded off and returned with a pan of live coals which he placed in the mouth of the hooka.

"Ah, that is good," said Hadji, dumping a large amount of the hashish mixture onto the coals. "Enough."

They smoked from separate flexible hoses. The sound of the hooka bubbled in the silence of the room.

Hadji gazed out at the sea, the whites of his eyes like gleaming moonstones in the half light. "The great Babur is said to have smoked hashish," he said. "Also Alexander—so why not us? The light in India has gone out. Day by day the spark is going. Even Moslem here is no good. My country is same. We are going to be finished. The oil, the gold, it is going to finish us. We believe in God but our greed will make us forget him. To know such things is not good. It makes me unhappy. Man should be happy, is it not so? Is it not right?" He smiled at Jeff.

Suddenly Jeff realized that he'd never felt warmth from another man, or never allowed himself to feel it or been aware it could exist.

"Come, let us swim," said Hadji. "Hooka is finished. There are towels just there. You can leave your clothes anywhere, come!"

He stepped into the shadows, threw off his robe, and emerged with a towel. Jeff followed him out onto the terrace.

"What's this?" Jeff examined a rather fresh scar about a foot long that ran from Hadji's shoulder blades to the small of his back.

"Oh, some guy, he almost got me. A sad combination of love and politics," he answered casually. "Politics is very stupid business."

The white surf rolled in on the beach beyond the pool.

"You dig surfin'?" Hadji asked.

Jeff nodded. "Got any boards, we could . . ."

"It is no good here, too shallow, too much garbage and jellyfish. These people they shit all over their beaches. When you come to Dubai we will go surfing, best you have ever seen—even as good as South Africa." Hadji threw his towel down. "Race you," he said, diving into the pool suddenly.

They emerged together at the far end. "Tie," gasped Hadji. He went down, tackling Jeff and dragging him underwater, bobbing like a porpoise. Then he was out of the pool, drying off and yelling for Nazimudin. "Here is djellabah for you. Come, let us eat. I am starved—stoned and starved. What a good thing," he said, shaking the water out of his hair. "What a good thing to wash off that creep Wasu."

Nazimudin had brought candles to a low table with cushions and stood by ready to serve the meal. As they ate, Jeff became aware of the large number of rings that Hadji wore.

Hadji saw him looking. "Jewels we think are very lucky. We like them." He laughed, eating his food quickly. "But I see you Western men you never wear—you don't wish to sparkle, eh?" He removed one. "Here," he said, tossing it casually to Jeff. "I give you this, then you will begin to sparkle. Wear it on left hand." Jeff caught the ring, a golden snake swallowing its tail, the head a large emerald. "It is just matching your eyes, man," Hadji said.

"It's too much," Jeff protested.

"If I give freely you cannot refuse. Please keep it. Really—I want you to have it."

Jeff smiled and covered a yawn.

"You are tired, I think. I don't blame you after that scene." Hadji got up from the table. "Another hooka?"

Jeff shook his head.

"No, quite right. We would be up all night, hashish after eating is not good."

Hadji led Jeff into a bedroom that looked like a safari tent. Cocking his head boyishly, he flopped onto the big bed, "Pretty cool, eh?"

"Come, you will sleep here with me, no?" he said. "It is better, yes?" He banged the bed again playfully. "Come, lie down here."

Jeff lay down.

"There is another bedroom," Hadji said, rolling to face him, "but it is not good to sleep alone. I never sleep alone in my whole life." He frowned. "I would not sleep. When I am alone, Nazimudin he sleeps at bottom of the bed." He looked at Jeff and was silent for a long time.

Jeff smiled. "Everything O.K.?" he asked.

"O.K." Hadji nodded. "I am just looking at you in the moonlight. I think you are very good-looking guy. I am enjoying the sight of you . . . what to do?" He winked. "Do you mind it?"

"Don't mind, I guess," Jeff replied, gazing at him seriously.

"I dig you . . . is it correct, eh?"

Jeff nodded. "Yes, it is correct."

Hadji took Jeff's hand, then moved closer and kissed his forehead.

"We believe men can love," he said softly. "You don't understand it, I know."

Jeff rested his hand on Hadji's waist, feeling the lithe body under the cotton djellabah. He had never really touched a man's body before like this and was surprised that he was allowing himself to do it. Letting his hand go up the fine long neck he pulled Hadji's head down onto his chest.

"I want to love," Jeff whispered, "but I don't know how."

"You worry too much about it," Hadji said, raising his head.

Without thinking, Jeff found himself kissing Hadji full on the mouth. After some time Hadji lifted his face.

"Love will come, man," he said. "It must. You need not worry so."

"I want more, can I have more?" said Jeff, burying his face in Hadji's hair. He felt the muscles of his own body relax as he stroked Hadji's neck and shoulders.

"We take djellabahs off," whispered Hadji. "Too hot for sleeping."

174

*   *   *

Three days later Hadji returned Jeff to the Taj. They drove in early from the clear air of Juhu to the sweltering muck of Bombay.

"See you later this evening, man," Hadji said as they arrived in front of the old Victorian hotel. "I got business to take care of, then I come by for you. We can have some food at a place I know. It's going to be my last night in Bombay for a while. Yes?"

As he lay dozing in the afternoon heat Jeff realized that something inside him was different. Even the room seemed to have changed. "Strange," he thought, after the years he'd spent making out with women, "how weird that it should be another guy."

But something else had happened with Hadji. Never before had he been able to get his mind off his own body, his own cock, to let go and stop watching himself. He'd used women like mirrors. But Hadji had made him forget himself, he hadn't worried about how he was scoring. He laughed. Was he going to turn gay in India? It was against all his instincts. Was he supposed to fight it or let himself go with it?

He thought of the stupidity of so many things he'd run after like the acid scene and money, the way he'd always treated Laura, the crazy scene at Kamala's. Kamala, he thought, disliking her even more than ever.

But Wasu had been the final downer, Wasu and his mirrored room. Look but don't touch. That had been a real eye-opener. The acid didn't liberate Wasu, it made him worse, merely amplified what was there from the beginning, beneath everything. Jeff didn't want to think about it. Everything seemed hopeless. He decided he wouldn't give out any more of the stuff and would talk to Stan as soon as possible, try to get him to give up the whole crazy idea. Turn on India—ugh! Certainly it was a real mistake to front acid to a man like Wasu. He shuddered thinking of all the Wasus in Europe and America who had got it.

The phone rang. It was Carlos.

"Where have you been, man?" he whined. "I been lookin' for you for three days, phoning . . . Wasu is ready to move, man, he really wants it. He'll take all we have."

"I'll wait to hear from Stan first," Jeff said. "I want to talk to him."

"Come on, man, it's business. You're supposed to be doing business, let's do it!"

"I'll wait," Jeff said.

"Stan is supposed to call me any day now," said Carlos angrily. "I'll have to say you won't give out anything, won't . . ."

"Tell him to call me. I'm always here till noon."

"Don't you truss me, Jeff? I don't think you truss me."

"I have my instructions," Jeff said. "Don't give to anyone till the money is in Switzerland. Doesn't Wasu trust you?"

175

"O.K., O.K.," said Carlos, "I'll come over and see you in a few days."

"Be sure to call first," Jeff said briskly. "I might be busy."

He put down the phone and buried himself in the pillows, thinking he could chuck all the acid in the bay outside the window. It would be easy. A bottle a night. Except Stan would be after him. He'd better wait. But where was Stan? And Laura? He suddenly felt responsible for her and began to worry. There was a knock on the door.

"It's Angel," said a faint voice.

Jeff got up and opened the door. She walked past him into the room, pale and sick looking, her hair tangled, reeking of brandy. She stood at a window fingering the curtain and gazing out at the street.

"What's happening," Jeff said. "You O.K.?"

"That bastard Wasu," she said, turning around, "he's always pulling things on me, always laying trips on me, spiking drinks and all that, getting me into situations like the other night..."

"Nobody's making you do anything you don't want to," Jeff said.

"Are you kidding?" she yelled. "You think I enjoyed it? You think I dig fucking with dogs and jailbirds while God knows who's watching? I was fighting for my life. I saw that convict bastard kill a girl in there a few months ago, strangled her and fucked her afterwards. With all those creeps laughing and watching."

"Why'd he throw you in there?" Jeff asked.

"Because he wanted me to go down on that girl who was serving the drinks, that's why, and I wouldn't. Me, I'll do most anything if I get high, but not that lesbian shit—I'm no freak, ugh!"

She lit a cigarette. Her hands were shaking.

"Then get out," Jeff said. "Just get on a plane and go back to Texas. You need bread, I'll give you bread, go!"

"Just like that, huh?" She smiled furiously. "I got bread—I could go myself. But it wouldn't be any better, shit. I know too much. He's got too much on me, he'd get me—besides I told you, I tried, I can't hack it."

"But Texas is Texas. It's a long way from India."

"You think so, huh?" She shook her head. "That's all you know, man. You'd be surprised to know he's very big at Vegas, got connections all over..."

"I'd be surprised," Jeff said.

"A lot of other places too." She seemed to drift off. Her eyes changed focus, as if she were looking at something far away.

"What is it?" asked Jeff.

"Nothing," she said. "I keep seeing things. Say, what is this acid shit anyhow? It sure ain't like anything else I ever had, I keep seein' things in corners."

"Like what?"

"Big snakes." She looked scared.

"You got the DTs," Jeff said.

"Naw," she said, "I know what that's like. This is different. I keep seeing real things in all the wrong places, ever since I got doused by your stuff in Delhi."

"Who told you it was my stuff?"

"Ismail. Say, that was a really far-out party, heh? That big snake and all." She edged onto the bed where Jeff was lying. "You really put those creeps uptight when you stripped down naked." She gazed at him, her eyes going in and out of focus.

"But you never fucked me yet," she murmured, putting her hand on his leg. "I wanta get fucked right," she declared, and began fumbling with his fly. "Come on, let's . . ."

"Cool it," Jeff said, "I'm beat. Been fuckin' three days solid since I left that place."

"I wanta get laid," she moaned. "I got to! I'm goin' crazy, I ain't been laid right."

"I thought that dog was doin' a pretty cool job on you."

"Fuck you, too."

She hunched up on the bed, staring wide-eyed at the corner of the room.

"What is it?" Jeff asked.

"Can't you see it? Can't you see there's a big fuckin' snake? Look!" she yelled. "You gotta save me, I'm going crazy." She started sobbing and edged her face onto Jeff's thigh. "I want some love. These people got no love in their hearts, only money and frustrations."

"Then get on the fuckin' plane and get outta here," Jeff said, getting up off the bed.

"Sorry." She stood up and brushed back her hair. "Guess you don't want me, huh?" Her face and mouth were twitching nervously. "Sorry I even bothered to come over here and see you. It won't happen again."

Jeff followed her to the door.

"Say," she laughed. "That acid? Maybe if I get enough I'll stop seeing all this. . . . Could you give me more?"

"I shouldn't, but I will," Jeff said, wanting only to get rid of her. "But promise not to bother me again for a while, O.K., and keep your Wasu away from me."

She nodded mechanically.

He got twenty tabs for her. "And don't take it like candy, you'll wind up in the hospital. Understand?"

*   *   *

About five the phone rang. It was Hadji.

177

"You are alone? I will come up."

Jeff had been half asleep, trying to forget Angel. Minutes later, just as he finished showering, Hadji was at the door.

"I am disturbing you, yes?"

"No," Jeff said. "You look very sharp."

"It's not often I wear a suit. Sometimes it is necessary to do business. But I do not like the pants, they are most confining. A useless invention of your Napoleon I believe." He mopped his forehead. "It is really hot. You are O.K.?"

"O.K.," Jeff smiled.

"I thought you might be uptight about..."

"Not uptight."

"That is good. Very good." Hadji smiled mischievously. "Let us get out of here then, it is too hot. I will take you to a fancy air-conditioned Moslem restaurant."

"Sounds good," Jeff said. "Let me get dressed." He put on the suit he had bought in Delhi and the dark red turban.

"What?" exclaimed Hadji. "It is not you? Ha! It is very good disguise. I like it. You look like one of those Northwest frontier fellows, Afghani."

Jeff let the turban unwind. "I wore it in Delhi," he said. "Fooled a few people too."

"It looks great on you, but not in a Moslem restaurant. You look too much like a green-eyed Sikh."

The restaurant had white tiled floors and a large courtyard full of trees and birds. Off long corridors were private dining rooms with swinging doors. The air-conditioning was by fan.

"I see I am mistaken about the air-conditioning," Hadji said, removing his jacket. "But anyhow, it's a good fan."

There was a low table and cushions on the floor. The waiter came and Hadji ordered in Urdu. The music of Islam drifted through the air.

Hadji smiled at Jeff and reached across the table.

"You come to Dubai," he said softly, taking Jeff's hand. "I am loving you very much. It is most strange for me, I never expect. I hope it is not too strange for you? In Dubai I have many houses, I will give you one."

"Why is it so strange for you?" asked Jeff.

"Because I have all these wifes, if I want I have boys, anything I want but—but I suddenly discover I am not feeling so close to them as I am to you."

"I think I'd probably see you once a week on Thursdays," Jeff grinned, "with all those wives and kids. What would I do?"

Hadji's eyes sparkled. "You would get married, of course. We Moslems, we can marry Christian or Jew, but we cannot marry Hindu. I find a good wife for you, rich. After the proper time you get another, perhaps a third. Then you can be very independent. You can help me in business, take care of business with the West. I do not like to go there. My father he is gone. I am eldest member of family; everything is on my head. My uncles they are no good, jealous. My brothers are double worse. There is no one I can trust. All are cheating me."

"Our wives would probably poison us."

"No, no, there are no problems there. Mine would rather see you than another wife. They would say to themselves: well, at least he's through with women, now we can rest easy."

Jeff laughed. "How do you know I wouldn't be unfaithful in the end?"

"Because we have love for each other, my brother. You may go to bed with whom you like, but love does not come and go. I know it. I know you know it too."

Jeff gazed at him.

"I have bad feeling about leaving you here," Hadji went on. "You are alone. Many peoples are jealous of you. It is most dangerous place for you." He nodded thoughtfully. "You don't know how dangerous. That Wasu, he can kill you anytime he likes, really. In a crowd . . . a knife . . . he has so many agents. Who would know, who will investigate? And who would tell me in Dubai, my brother—no one! I can tell you that."

The waiter came with steaming plates of biryani, pilaf, big round bread circles and tall cool glasses of beer.

"You come to Dubai," Hadji continued. "I will get a good Sheik—that is teacher. He will teach you Islam. Yes, you will become Moslem. Then you will come to your senses. You will have beautiful children."

"And boys to rub me?" Jeff smiled.

"Yes, why not?" laughed Hadji, clinking his beer glass with Jeff's. "You can have anything you want in this world but always you must use properly. Not to overdo, not to put down—not to debase? I think, yes—not to debase, not to misuse. It is not what we have, it is how we use, not what we do, but how we do—is it not so?"

Jeff nodded.

"We will have separate place somewhere for ourselves. I have very beautiful house at seaside. I never go there. In our world it is not unusual, two men. Nobody bothers. Anyhow, I am a ruler—no one tells me, I tell them."

"But you don't even know me," Jeff protested. "I'm really not . . . Really I've been pretty no-good up to now." He shook his head. "Yes, it's true, I'm afraid."

"Don't say I don't know you. Ha! I know all about you, don't be foolish. To know, that is from the touch, not from words."

"You'd get tired of me." Jeff laughed. "Have me poisoned."

"Now you are making fun," said Hadji. "Why do you make fun when I am wanting to be serious?"

"We'll grow old together then," Jeff said. "Two old lovers."

"Why not?" Hadji's expression was withdrawn. "If you go to bazaar in Arab country you will see plenty of old men sitting together. Many are lovers. Yes, it is true. And in Afghanistan, you will see they will even be knitting and crocheting each other socks.

"It is not the body we love. That goes. How can we love that only? You are disillusioned, that is why. Islam is calling you infidel. It means *without faith,* in-fidel. A man without faith or hope is infidel. You must have faith in your own immortal spirit."

"You must know it is very different from our way of thinking," said Jeff thoughtfully. "In the West men who love each other are thought to be ... well ..."

"Because they separate it from normal life. I know, that is all crazy. In West men are women's slave. Even though they are acting so mighty with the muscles and the bombs and such, really they are soft inside. Brought up all by women—women teachers, ha! No wonder you have no good army. No comradeship. If you had that you could win your Vietnams war. Your Western men cannot even defeat those little Communist bastards from Hanoi."

"Wait a minute," protested Jeff, "we haven't really tried."

"No, no," said Hadji. "You have tried like hell with your machines. But your men on their own, your men are too soft. Hand to hand you cannot win. But I could, any Moslem could. We do not allow our women to weaken us, only give us strength. We do not allow them to work outside. We treasure them in our house like dangerous dragon goddess. We make babies with them, we make love to them, and they are very strong for us. Not against us like women of your country ... not competing."

He took Jeff's hand again. "Listen, America is going to leave Vietnam. After that whole world is knowing how weak U.S. man is. The beginning of the end.

"Russian and Chinese will divide Asia, but Islam will survive. It is strongest religion in the world. We believe in God, why should we not fight for God? Your Christians, they do not believe. There is much trouble ahead. We will die happily for Islam if that is necessary.... Would you die for Christ? You come to Dubai, we will try forget this bloody world—you and I."

Jeff shrugged. "I have things I must finish here. Business, just like you. I would like to go—even tomorrow—with you. I'm tired of this place."

"Ah, now you are making sense."

"There is a man coming," Jeff said, trying to think of a good excuse.

180

"I must wait until he arrives in Bombay. He is the employer of Carlos."

"Then?" said Hadji.

"Then I will try to visit you. We can go on from there and see what happens." He smiled at Hadji warmly.

"Let us go back to your hotel then," suggested Hadji, breaking the silence. "I will say good-bye. My plane leaves early."

The night air was heavy with humidity and pollution as they got into Hadji's car and drove to the hotel. The streets were still crawling with beggars and hustlers, moving in slow motion past boarded-up shops, around and over clutches of the poor and starving who slept on sidewalks, against the buildings, and in gutters.

A few blocks from the Taj their way was blocked by a large crowd in front of a tall modern building.

"It is one of Wasu's hotels," Hadji said. "Probably he is giving out money. You stay in car, I will see."

Hadji jumped out and elbowed his way through the people. A few minutes later he returned, his face grim.

"It is that girl," he said.

"Angel?" Jeff cried opening the door.

"Stop!" Hadji exclaimed, grabbed Jeff and slammed the door. "You no go. She is dead. Jumped out window. It is not pretty."

Jeff bolted out of the car and pushed his way through the crowd.

Angel was spreadeagled on her back, her skull flattened. In falling, she had killed a leper, and a second leper whom she had also hit sat seriously injured beside her unable to get up. Flailing wildly with his oozing stubs, the man was demanding that someone in the hotel pay him the price of his broken leg.

"Falling from the sky she did not," he screamed in Marathi. "She is falling from hotel—hotel must pay!"

Jeff stared speechless, his hands clenched. No one was even looking at Angel.

The leper saw Jeff and directed a barrage of epithets at him. A police officer arrived and asked Jeff if he were a relation of the dead girl. He wanted to find someone to pay off the leper so that the crowd would go away.

Jeff shook his head silently and retreated to the car.

Hadji backed up to an intersection and screeched away towards the Taj.

When they reached the room Hadji exploded. "That Wasu has finished her off I know it. He was tired of her. Otherwise, you don't send dog to fuck her. After fucking by dog everyone knows it is over. Would you believe me if I tell you she really loved him?"

Jeff stood looking out at the bay, unable to meet Hadji's eyes.

"Yes, I know," he said, turning at last. "But I think it's my fault. She took too much LSD. First in Delhi, then here in Bombay. This afternoon

181

she was here raving, seeing things—wanted me to fuck her. I gave her more of the stuff to get rid of her.''

Hadji looked thoughtful. "You should have given her your sex, not the drug.''

"I kept thinking of that fucking dog and I couldn't.''

"You see?'' said Hadji, slumping into a chair wiping the sweat from his forehead; "but what is this LSD? I have not had.''

"You don't need it,'' Jeff snapped. "Maybe nobody needs it.''

"Jeff?'' said Hadji.

"Yes?''

"I implore you to come with me to Dubai tomorrow. This Angel, she is an omen. You must listen to me and do as I say. You must not stay here.''

"But I have certain responsibilities, especially now. I've decided to persuade the owner of the drug not to sell to Wasu and if possible, not to sell any more in India.''

"But cannot it be done in a letter? You are thinking you are too important. Do not think it. Just forget the whole business and disappear. Let them do what they will do. When I went into the crowd I knew I was going to see death. It is the angel of death. She is very close. You don't understand, you cannot see, but it is true, my brother.'' He stood close to Jeff, touching his shoulder lightly. "If I am leaving you here tonight, I am thinking I may never see you again.''

"Believe me,'' Jeff said, "I'll come as soon as I can. But I can't give the stuff to Carlos, not now.''

"Even if it would cost your life?''

"Don't worry about me, I can take care of myself. The man who owns it will come. I will persuade him and that will be the end of it. It's my duty,'' Jeff said, trying to appeal to Hadji in terms he would understand. "If I leave now, I'd just be running out on it, you understand?''

"And what will you do alone here, with those two wanting the drug from you?''

"I will sit here in the hotel. Not go out, give instructions not to let anybody . . .''

"Whew!'' Hadji shook his head violently. "You don't understand, man, in Bombay Wasu gives instructions.''

"That's a risk I'll just have to take.''

Hadji paced the room.

"I see your mind is made up then. What can I do?'' Here,'' he said, handing Jeff a package. "I am so mad at you I almost forgot presentation. It is Arab robe and headdress, like mine. See—soft, like Kashmir wool.''

He took Jeff's hands and held him at arms' length.

"If I may never see you again, is all right?'' he said, smiling. "I know we will meet again in next world. Surely it will be so.''

"Did you give me your address?"

"It is on that paper near the phone. You can phone easily from Bombay—very clear reception."

"I'll call you."

"Yes, of course," said Hadji from the doorway. He started to leave, then turned around. "My plane leaves at five-thirty. You *can* be on it. We can fly away together. I get you on board somehow if you are showing up. There is time still. Yes, you should listen."

X

THE RICKETY COUNTRY bus had taken them many miles through a jungle of dry scrub and thorn bushes big as trees.

"It's a 1028 Mercedes," Indra said. "Can you imagine how they are still keeping it together?"

Large areas of the side had been patched with odd bits of metal and in the front where fumes poured out past the driver, you could even see the road through holes in the floor.

Laura had no idea where they were. They had come out of the mountains by a different route, caught a night bus, and the next day were in Benares putting Alex on a flight to Delhi, where he would catch the London plane. Indra had even given him money. Laura wondered why he was so anxious for Alex to leave.

The landscape was a uniform dust color. Foliage on the trees was drying up or dead, and what green remained was covered. All day long the bus had stopped at pitiful dried-up villages, disgorging one full busload only to take on another. Except for three sadhus sitting up front, there were few through passengers. The upper caste sat in the first three rows, the middle caste in the center, and the lowest in back.

Indra insisted on sitting at the back, jammed between live chickens and cans of kerosene.

"When you are riding or walking with people, always try to stay behind them," he told Laura. "Your waves can be broken by anyone sitting or walking behind you—if they know how to do it."

Hour after hour the unchanging barren landscape slid by. Laura watched the people, absorbed with their relationships, admiring their grace, their forbearance, their courage. At each stop those leaving would have to battle to get out, while those entering would have to push each other through windows, pulling children, tattered luggage, and animals along with them. Fifteen minutes later the driver would return to collect tickets. Beggars and lepers, moaned, chanted, and cracked obscene jokes as they solicited funds.

Outside youths in shorts and tight pants shouted in at the passengers, poking large cucumber slices through the windows, warm soda pop, or trays of candy made of sugar, puffed rice, stones, and a peanut or two. Lower-caste women traveled in gangs, wearing cheap nose rings and new machine-made saris with gold borders that never tarnished. They were tough and quarrelsome. Upper-caste women wore homespun rags and sat immobile, staring fixedly into space like the idols they worshipped. Everywhere from loudspeakers and portable radios All India radio blared with frantic music from Hindi films.

"The luxuries, the pollutions, the mysteries of the plains," observed Indra.

Auk auk sounded the bus horn, like the cry of an aging goose, announcing departure. Skinny ravaged villagers, their joints swollen with hookworm anemia, waved to friends and relatives while swarms of flies fought over bits of dropped food.

Now the dust swirled up behind them and the country side was less populated. Women became sick and vomited out the window, splattering those in the rear. Though the sun was not more than an hour from setting, the wind that flapped the tattered canvas window curtains blew hot and dry.

They arrived at a terminal point. As the last of the passengers collected their belongings, Indra elbowed Laura awake and beckoned her to follow him.

"From here we must walk five miles," he said. "We'll reach our destination after dark."

"But where are we?" sighed Laura.

"We are here." He smiled. "Right here where you are standing and no where else. Don't ask foolish questions."

Darkness had come rapidly. Fires were burning in ramshackle tea shops where sweaty boys prepared bread and potato curry in large iron pots. An anxious commotion seemed to hang on the edge of the night.

They ducked into a hut where tired-looking travelers, laborers, and children in rags were seated at long tables. Outside Laura could hear the persistent beat of drums fading away, starting again and fading. "What's all the drumming about?" she asked curiously.

"Ah," said Indra, "this is the last stop on the way to the Gate. This village survives on transporting the dead and dying to the burning ground. You will see the bearers running on the path toward the fires at the other end. The drums accompany them."

Laura shuddered. "Is that were *we're* going?" she asked.

Indra nodded.

Tea came in brass cups, sweet milky tea and yellow balls of lentils stuck together with raw brown sugar. Flies crawled over everything.

"The eyes of the Goddess," said Indra waving them aside so that he could drink his tea. "They are her spies and her messengers. Billions of eyes watching and waiting."

Laura noticed the cook blowing his nose with his hands while he washed the utensils.

"Don't worry," Indra assured her. "You won't get sick as long as you are with me. It is impossible."

Laura marveled how calm Indra always looked. "An echo from another age," she thought, "come back to catch the final act of a five-thousand-year-old play: humanity at the brink." When she saw him like that, glowing with energy, it was like seeing a hero. But why did he still frighten her so when he radiated such strength? She found it impossible to frame the unthinkable.

"This may be the last food for some time," he was saying quietly. "We will have fresh water to be sure, and I have a sack of lemons and some brandy. I may have to get you drunk." He chuckled. "But don't worry, you're stronger than you think. You'll come through, don't worry."

Obviously it was going to be a test of some sort. She'd agreed to come, but as the time drew near she began to doubt herself. She knew he was trying to awaken something deep inside her, a lingering spark of faith, but she was fighting it, trying desperately to hang onto what remained of her old self. "What will I turn into if I really let go?" she kept thinking, and felt as if she'd been kicked in the stomach.

Outside the tea shop it was night. A runaway donkey careened down the street, mad. After it, followed by the relations of the deceased all jogging behind, came naked bearers supporting a corpse on a litter.

"We must hurry," Indra said, "otherwise it will be getting too late. There are too many wild pigs on this road, not to mention bandits."

A waning moon rose deep orange behind the thorn trees as they walked briskly along the broad foot path. The hot windy night was alive with mourners and mendicants passing in both directions. After a while a glow appeared on the horizon and moments after that, the smell. The smell of burning flesh. And the ludicrous thought crossed Laura's mind that it was like Burger King.

"Ah," cried Indra, "I see you can smell it. Like your American hamburger stands, no? You'll not forget it soon, I think."

How could she explain the associations crowding in on her? Would he understand "cook-outs" or barbecues?

He gestured ahead. "The largest burning place left in the world," he said. "Also the most remote. Do you recall I told you about an initiation at twelve that changed my life?"

She nodded.

"I am going to give you the same initiation. Don't be afraid, I am with you. I will always be with you. It is a risk, but one you must take. Remember, you are going to see a gate. It has nothing to do with endings. There are no endings, nor are there beginnings. All that is just maya— illusion.''

They were passing the first of many small temples, some hidden in the undergrowth, some grouped in open spaces. Their walls were constructed of human bones cemented with mud. Row upon row of gaping skulls fixed their blind gaze on the travelers.

"You must cover your head now and follow exactly as I say and do. We are nearing our destination. If you feel faint or sick, repeat the syllables I have given you.''

Here and there under ancient trees, the sacred fires of holy men burned brightly. Laura stared at a group of naked sadhus covered with dirt, their hair matted and filthy.

"These are Aghor sadhus,'' Indra explained. "The third class. It is one of the main divisions: they use filth and degradation whereas we go right to renunciation. Don't they remind you of Dr. Long? You see, there are many paths all leading to the same place.''

One of the Aghors beckoned them to sit down. "Let's join him for a smoke,'' Indra suggested. "These fellows are the watch dogs of this place. It is well for us to treat them with respect.''

Two naked men were squatting in front of the fire. Large rings with chains depended from the foreskins of their penises.

"Who are they?'' Laura asked.

"They are Nagas, simple-minded ones. They think by weighing down the penis they can kill desire. It is stupid. I tried it once. Delusion,'' Indra said, spitting on the ground. "He who eats dirt and filth becomes dirt and filth. He who chains his organ becomes chained to it.''

He paused, then accepted a small packet from one of the men. He noted its contents and took out his chillum. They were honoring him by an invitation to prepare the pipe, an act of homage paid to one of superior merit recognized on sight.

"In the end all must come here,'' he said seriously. "This place is itself a guru. Though very few know what to do here as they are without guru. But these men are not capable of higher paths just now. It is all the same. And it is better they come here while alive than as corpses. Yes,'' he said laughing at Laura's astonished face, "they will benefit greatly at the proper time.''

"See,'' he went on, glancing up as he prepared the chillum, "there is a dying one having himself brought here before time. He has good faith.'' Indra indicated an old man on a litter his bony arm outstretched, motioning the bearers to take him inside and place his body on a pyre.

"Jai Ho!'' Indra shouted at him.

187

The old man moved his head around trying to see Indra. "Jai Ho! Maharaj!" he shouted in a cracked voice.

"You are blessed," Indra yelled back at him in Hindi. "Go now and enter the Gate."

He went back to preparing the chillum, rolled bits of herbs together and murmured a mantra. Finishing, he took from his bag a small cloth which he dampened in water. Then holding the pipe with his arms outstretched he chanted loudly until it caught fire on its own. A ripple of admiration stirred the sadhus around him as he inhaled deeply and passed the pipe.

The next man had no cloth and had to pass it on. Suddenly all were rummaging in their belongings looking for pieces of cloth.

"They thought I would let them use my soffie," he said, chuckling. "See how low they are, they were even testing me on that! They hang around outside here smoking chillum and getting what they can. They are not to be given any secrets or instruction."

"Don't take too much of this," he added quietly, handing Laura the chillum. "It will dry you up too much for what you have to do. And it's early yet. Spread your cloth and sleep. We won't begin until later."

*   *   *

When she awoke his hand was on her forehead. It was warm and a certain electrical feeling roused her at once. The fire was out but the glowing embers shone on the sleeping sadhus, themselves like dying embers, their saffron and red robes crumpled into strange forms. Once Laura had wondered why the Indian people seemed able to sleep any time in any place. Now with the fatigue of the past months mounting inside her, she understood.

Paco pac pacoo wakoo pacpac pacoo. The call of a night bird echoed through the teak and mahogany trees which towered above them.

"Are you all right?" he said, guiding a warm cup of steaming liquid into her hands.

She smiled up at him. "A bit sleepy but all right I guess."

"It's lemon water," he said. "Drink! I will be giving it to you from time to time."

It tasted like hot lemonade. Laura wondered how long she was going to last.

"Don't plan," Indra said, aware of what she was thinking, "one moment into the future. Planning closes you up, spoils the play; you'll not be able to get the cues, or the clues." He smiled and stood up. "Now we must begin. Remember, I'll be with you, even though it may seem to you I have disappeared."

As they entered the cremation grounds, the jungle became sparse.

Smoke drifted and hung in the branches of the trees, bare of leaves in this hot dry season, Indian summer, when men go mad. Night breezes whipped fitfully at the pyres, blowing hot coals across the dusty paths that separated them. Here was the activity of death: the hustle and bustle of expectation at the entrance to a great city.

Laura felt as if one strand of a woven cord had snapped inside her. They paused as Indra, his brow furrowed with compassion, glanced down at the corpse of a young sadhu lying atop a carefully stacked pile of logs. Flowers covered his saffron dhoti, bright red hibiscus buds, jasmine, and marigolds tumbled down his naked chest.

Laura shuddered.

"Have no fear. This place is a gate. Every act is an act of the gods. We do nothing," murmured Indra.

"You are already dead," he said, gazing at her. "Or alive ... There is no difference."

The Dhooms—those in charge of burning bodies—darted in and out of the firelight, pouring ghee and oil onto the blazing pyres and poking the dying embers with large sticks to make sure the corpses were consumed. At one pyre an entire family huddled together in grief while on the ground beside them two small boys played marbles in the light of their burning relative. Few other mourners were left at that hour but there were many monks and sadhus meditating.

The smoke grew thicker and sweeter as Indra led her through more forest into an area so large its boundaries were lost behind distant hillocks. Here corpses of nameless ones burned by the hundreds—those unable to pay for a separate burning, those whom no one knew, the nameless beggar, the leper, the ciphers at the edge of life. Smoke drifted into the night, blue smoke that smelled like sirloin steak. The scene went beyond Laura's imagination. A hand jutting out from a pile of bodies caught fire and burnt to the bones like a flaming sign. Logs and stiff bodies tilted in every direction, some reduced to glowing coals, others only charred. A rigid corpse, the flesh burning away from the wide-eyed face to the skull, suddenly snapped into an upright position and exploded, sending bits of brain hissing into the flames.

"The mirror reclaims its image," Indra muttered.

Laura felt sick and reached out for him but he'd vanished. Wasn't he just there, hadn't she just now heard his voice? Looking for him she peered into the night through the flames and smoke. A feeling of total emptiness overcame her, deep and limitless, beyond shuddering or crying out. But wasn't it unnecessary, that feeling, was it not an illusion too? Something stirred inside her, and she knew whatever it was her connections to it were strengthening.

Then she felt his hand on hers. "Are you all right?"

"I don't know."

"There's more to it," he said. "Come!" And made a crude broom of twigs and swept until the hard dusty clay was smooth and free of debris. Then he scattered water to settle the dust and swept again. After repeating the process three times he gathered green leaves and spread these on the earth, and then on top spread the skins of a buffalo, a tiger and a deer, soft and worn thin with age. Over all he placed three pieces of colored cloth: blue, purple, and red on top.

The night wind sang balefully in the scrub thorn trees and drove low clouds across the moon. With ash trickling in a thin line from his closed fist, Indra carefully drew three large circles around the place he had prepared and divided them into eighteen segments, inscribing each with a sign.

"Do not be afraid," he said casually, "it's a most auspicious place. You know it otherwise you would not be here. Sit down now on this seat I have prepared for you. You may lie down if you have to. The only rule is that your back should remain straight whatever position you are in." He removed the red cloth he was wearing and sat down on it to her left, his head cocked slightly toward her but not looking at her.

For a long time they sat silent, then he said: "Please repeat this group of syllables with me and continue after I have stopped." He lowered his voice and began repeating a very long mantra. She repeated it with him. Slowly his voice died away, and she was saying it alone, her eyes closed, until it became automatic.

"Now open your eyes and focus on one spot in the fire," he whispered, "anywhere in the fire will do. Do not take your eyes from that spot and keep repeating the syllables. You should, in fact, be saying them even now while I am talking to you." He looked at her. "You are," he said. "Good."

Laura picked out a point in the fire and stared at it. After some time everything began to whirl around the point on which her eyes were fixed and disappeared into a void. She lost track of time. Turbulent at first, her mind quieted, and as she continued repeating the syllables she could feel their rhythm in her body, a vibration which rang through her like a very large bell.

Against this powerful sound she began to hear voices. The sound of a crowd in a large auditorium before a performance. The chorus of voices broke into song. It sounded like the singing of a chorus from a Mozart opera. As this singing picked up momentum she started to see something. The point at which she was staring in the fire of burning bodies began to expand and contract like the iris of some fiery eye. For what seemed like a very long time she stared while the singing became a great thunder in her head. But when she thought about it the bright opening became smaller and when she forgot to think, the iris opened wide.

Suddenly the voices became ringing bells, high-pitched electronic simulations. As though she'd been blinded, her eyes went blank with an intense white light, brighter than the sun on the snowy Himalayas. It was as if the eye had opened and she had gone through it. Pulsing with cellular light, the white turned to blue and she felt a tickling sensation up and down her spine.

When she regained self-awareness the blue screen hadn't faded or disappeared. She was aware of her surroundings. She could feel her body, warmed by the funeral pyre. She could feel that her eyes were wide open and that she was still repeating the syllables he had given her.

As if on cue, Indra's voice came from far away. "Now you will see the syllables you are repeating," he said.

On the blue screen that had replaced her sight, she saw the Sanskrit letters of the syllables in gold, pulsating like neon signs in some cosmic word processor.

"And now in the Roman," he said and a transliteration in gleaming Roman letters appeared.

She felt elated and excited. What she had seen exhilarated her and seemed unbelievably beautiful. "At last I'm 'seeing'" she thought.

"Good," his voice cut in, "you've got the hang of it, now. Very good. You will remain here for fourteen days. If you feel sleepy you may lie down. You may open or close your eyes, that will have no effect now. You will need less sleep as we go on. But be sure to keep repeating the syllables, and no matter what happens I will be here. I am always here."

After that it was as though she'd gone deaf. Syllables came and went on the blue field until all sense of time, place and being dissolved.

Then slowly, as if through blue mist, the corpse of a tall black man with enormous feet and a profile resembling an Egyptian priest appeared. Astride the corpse was a naked yogi seated in sidassan who resembled Indra. Was it he? She was uncertain. Veils of blue obscured the phantasm which shimmered before her. Her heart jumped and she knew she was becoming frightened.

Then his voice came out through the lips of the yogi and she thought she might pass out. An emission of energy in the form of a black cloud, like a swarm of bees, seemed to be coming towards her out of the fire, from the yogi. It made her ill. She felt like vomiting, was sure that when it reached her something very unpleasant would happen. Then she heard his voice again.

"Yes. It is possible to be in many places at the same time, as many as you want. Now listen, this is a very dangerous thing we are doing, most dangerous. One requires strong doses to go right. You have got on the wrong track—it was not meant to be. You are already very far along

191

although you do not know it. It is dangerous to be open and not have proper instruction. Now you will be instructed. Do not be frightened, be brave. There is *no thing* to be afraid of. You do not understand the precarious position you are in, do not understand that there is something to be won or lost. It is in this body.''

He slapped the corpse on which he sat.

"This body is like a battlefield and the stakes, dear child, are very high. You get this body after a long time. It's just a jumping-off point, energy changing into spirit, a launching pad—a great gift after many other tries, other embodiments. Would you care to see some of them?''

"See what?'' she asked.

"Would you like to see some of the other embodiments you have taken—to relive them?''

She nodded, too frightened to think.

"'I will show you some.''

At once the vision disappeared and was replaced by the form of a young woman. Laura started, it was her mother: she was young and beautiful, full of color and light.

"Now remember when you were five and she was laughing at your first attempts to maneuver your knife and fork.''

How beautiful she was, Laura thought as she watched. She could feel tears welling up inside her.

"I am taking you back slowly.'' His voice was muffled.

The image of her mother vanished and there was a hall, a space so vast that its boundaries were outside the range of her vision. She could hear voices echoing a language foreign to her. "How odd,'' she thought, but somehow it was very familiar too. Then she felt a hand stroking her head.

"This is the place where everything is,'' said Indra's voice, "everything past and everything future, it is at this level, like a reservoir. I am only opening your eye so that you can see it.''

"But what is this, where am I,'' she stammered, "I feel so small.''

"This is Russia. In Russia some five hundred years back you are embodied in a female dog, a very beautiful and sensitive Russian wolfhound. You are being stroked by your mistress, see, look up now. See how she is stroking you, see how much she loves you and how good she is to you. But she is very old and will soon die. See now, who is this . . .''

The scene changed and an ugly hulk of a man towered over her.

"Ah,'' said Indra's voice, "this is her servant. Your mistress is dead and this man has been left money by her to care for you, but see, he takes all the money and the food for himself. And now he is going to hit you—duck!''

She felt her body jerk away. Then the scene changed. She felt cold and overwhelmingly alone. Snow seemed to be falling all around her.

"Yes, it is clear now," said Indra. "You are going to leave that dog's body; rather than put up with the cruel keeper you have come to the grave of your mistress. See, there is her name on the stone in Russian, ah, and it is very cold, is it not? Your dog's body will soon freeze, here at the lady's grave." He chuckled softly. "For this act of faith you . . . uh, got promoted."

He laughed uproariously and her eyes went blank and again she saw him, seated on the corpse, laughing at her through the smoke.

"Aha, Uma—you are surprised, no? I am surprising you with my maya. But they are not mine, not anybody's. Always remember the world of bodies is maya.

"You like to see some more!" he shouted at her through the smoke and flames.

At once she felt strange and light and was in a different space. Suddenly the giant head of a snake filled her entire vision. She was terrified.

"I see," he said, "you were sitting on your eggs." He laughed. "Yes, yes, it is you, you are a bird. Many times you have laid eggs only to have them eaten by the serpent. You are old and weak now and will soon be killed by the kite who lives in the rocky cliffs above and has been watching you for years waiting to get you."

She felt herself screaming but heard nothing.

"Yes," his voice went on, "the fear of being eaten alive is very strong. It has happened so many times before."

The gleaming syllables appeared once more and she felt like a boat at sea in a great storm. The syllables were the rudder; she hoped they would prove strong enough.

"They are keys," he murmured, "and once the door is opened they are the rod and the staff. As I told you, this short path is a dangerous undertaking, but it is what the old Tibetan woman saw. It is your time for it. Your past actions have been spotless, your present birth is correct, the result of your accumulated acts. You need have no fear. But if by accident people who are unprepared by past experience are shown the things locked in the structure of their cells and genetic code, they will become mad."

She could hear the fires crackling now, consuming fresh corpses.

"Still, I know you do not beleve me," he signed. "You will think I have 'hypnotized' or 'mesmerized' you and that it is I who am pulling you into these states. That's why you still become frightened. You think it is *my* power but that is wrong.

"Though it is worshipped in many forms, it belongs to no one. You will know it . . . know that what is happening to you is correct."

Suddenly deep inside, she felt sleepy.

"Yes," his voice said. "Lie down and rest. There is plenty of time."

*   *   *

Slowly Laura became aware of warmth and the syllables going on and on inside her—a deep throbbing, like a heartbeat. The blue screen was gone, and she lay warm and secure wondering whether to open her eyes. When she did, and raised herself to a sitting position, the corpse and the yogi had vanished. It was day and the sun glared down through a white sky.

The Dhooms were stacking more corpses and wood on the huge pyre. At the edge of her vision she caught a glimpse of Indra's eyes floating in space, but when she turned to look they disappeared.

She sat erect and sipped a glass of freshly made lemon water that had been placed beside her.

"Remember when your eyes are open to focus on a point." His voice was broadcasting as if she were a radio set that had tuned itself in.

"Do not fail to keep repeating the syllables. Do not imagine that it is morning and you are waking up and it is all over. You are just beginning."

"Where are you," she asked, finding a point in the smoldering ashes before her.

"I am in the tree over your head," the voice said casually. Without thinking she turned and saw him squatting in the lower branch of a large mango tree which extended over her sitting place. His eyes were closed. She stood up and put out her hand toward his. He put down his hand until she could touch it. But there was nothing there, her hand closed on thin air.

She fell to the ground.

"Sit up," he said firmly, "you are not following directions. You are to stare at a spot. Remember. You are not advanced enough yet to let your attention wander here and there."

She nodded, resuming her position.

"Otherwise, it could be most dangerous for you," he added. "You see, we are doing these things so you may come to understand that there is more to things than you have been led to believe, than 'meets the eye' as you say." He laughed. "Don't ask how things work, do not try to discover the causes, that is the Pandora's box. What men call 'science' these days. Your Western peoples, have become too simple. They want only a certain range of wavelengths to be considered 'real.' They wish to exclude all others for which they have found no measuring instruments or no use. Your people will be gone through, destroyed, because they won't understand that existence is thicker and more complex than they have been led to believe." Suddenly he appeared in front of her. "Gone through," he repeated, and thrust his fist as if to beat his chest. But his arm went through his body as though it were made of jelly, and he laughed uproariously.

"In the West you suffer from the sin of pride. You think because your

194

science serves you, you are the creators of the world and its operators. You imagine you have constructed a world free from the unpredictable.

"The devils in the Christian religion—who are they but us sadhus and yogis. We are dark. We wear red. We carry the trident. Anger. Danger. Anger and danger to the weakhearted—those without faith or courage. The religion of the West was so frightened by chance, by fate, that it exterminated everything—everything it couldn't explain. Yogis carry tridents to kill you, the you who thinks he alone is the maker and shaper, the operator of this world—to kill the pride. Until you get killed, you can't get across."

"Where are you?" she asked after some time.

"Aha," he shouted, "I am everywhere! Just now I am sitting beside you but you will not see me. Reach out and touch me."

She felt his warm arm.

"But if you turn, which you must not, you won't see me." As if it were a great joke, he began to laugh until she laughed too.

"I must do these confusing things so that you will believe this ancient wisdom once and for all, otherwise, how could you be expected to believe? You cannot read what is unwritten, you cannot hear what is unspoken. Nothing of importance has been written or spoken.

"Whom you call your philosophers in the West, Aristotle and his school, they were afraid of wisdom, deathly afraid of it. Later they had crusades, killed dragons, burned witches, sent missionaries—even opened schools to stamp it out. All frightened hypocrites.

"Christ was a great Master, a great yogi. In India he is worshipped as Saint Issa. The Christian religion cannot be blamed on him. Your church councils made up a religion and being slaves and sons of slaves threw out the unseen truths which had been passed on through the higher castes. For these truths they substituted measurable appearances, in one stroke changed the rules of the game—they thought. But the unseen truths do not change. How can truth change? It goes on working whether people know it or not.

"And Christ did not die in Jerusalem. I can take you to his tomb at Shrinagar, in Kashmir, where thousands worship every year. Mostly Sufis."

"Are you Sufi?"

"I have studied with those calling themselves Sufis, but they are all branches. There is only one teaching. Its root is here, lost in antiquity. Moses and Manu knew, but did not record it. Gautama knew it but refused to teach it. A final teaching, shocking and shockingly simple—hard pill for people to swallow.

He sighed. "Once you know that teaching, once it has been shown to you, your life in this body can become too difficult, too painful. You long to get out. That is where the duty part comes in. It is not for us to assume the role of creator or destroyer.

"That is why I give you these keys to paradise," he smiled. "These signs and shows. It is my duty, and it is hard because things have gone too far toward the end."

The Dhooms started the fire with more fresh corpses. She shuddered.

"See what bad actions are etched on that face," he said, referring to the corpse of a middle-aged man which had just been thrown in front of her.

"And the woman beside him—would you believe me if I told you that hag's body was once beautiful, desired by thousands. I could show you her life if you like."

Laura held up her hand.

Indra laughed. "Too much, yes? And too boring. See how she lies there now and watch closely as the flames are kindled under that body which gave pleasure to so many. Watch it as it melts before you." He paused. The blue space was beginning to open up again. She felt relief that she might be getting away from the scene before her. She hoped that the body of the old whore would vanish but it didn't; on the contrary, it appeared even more vividly than before.

"Fire is a gate," he said. "There are other gates. Beyond them pleasure dissolves into the supreme pleasure."

The syllables of the mantra began, obscuring the scene. Some men in white dhotis had come, their Gandhi hats in hand, and were performing a ceremony over the old woman.

"They loved her so much they can't even give money for a separate burning," Indra chuckled from somewhere. "Her inner one is here now. It has become a ghost, what we call a Bhut or a Preat. It is so attached, even to that terrible old body, that it is hanging around."

"What can be done for her?" whispered Laura.

"Nothing. All the work must be done in this body. When the body goes it's too late to do that work, the fate of the inner one is sealed. It will go back into another body, perhaps even an animal, but for a long time the inner one will drift here and there according to its past actions. Eventually it will be attracted to like bodies and will go in, a letter looking for the proper envelope to be sent in, yes? Maya is endless, beginningless and endless. It just goes on and on until you are bored and ready to get out."

The Dhooms were pouring oil on the bodies, trying to get the whole pile burning again. As the fire caught she saw Indra again sitting in the flames.

"You can see me then," he said intimately. "Very good," he chuckled, "fire is my element. At least we know you haven't lost it, that you are getting better at it. The connection is getting stronger. You're becoming a better receiver."

"Why are you sitting on the corpses again?" she thought to herself.

"It doesn't matter where I sit," his voice replied. "I am having a conversation with the inner one of this woman. It is high time she came face to face with things. Don't be frightened, I am just trying to do her a good turn, trying to get her to really see her own body there, while it gets burned. She doesn't want to see it, she loves it so much and now it is going to be burnt. There is no chance of her changing anything now. It is high time she faced up to things and stopped wandering from body to body."

The flames mounted.

His fist came down on the stomach of the old corpse, and she saw a young women fighting with him.

"I think I see her now," Laura said.

"You may," he replied. "Her inner one is, as you say, freaking out. Most intense. That is why you see it. She can't stand me sitting on her body; still thinks it's her own body even when it's burning up right in front of her. She thinks she is powerful—it's a great laugh for me."

Laura watched as the form of the young woman flew out of the fire and landed in the dust a few yards away, curled like a fetus, breathing. Then it caught sight of her.

"If you get a female body," it screamed wide-eyed, "try to hang onto it, try to hang onto . . ."

The apparition vanished.

"Enough." It was Indra's voice again. "She won't try any more tricks. What a bother these strong-willed people become when they are directed toward their bodies. Know-it-alls who never know anything.

"But fire is fire." He laughed. "And always it is there for them, always burning."

Laura was frightened again, too frightened to think of running away. Weren't dead bodies supposed to be sacred? Or were they just garbage, just worm food?

"You are frightened because you have not really seen. Not yet. Not fully opened."

"Teach me to open then," Laura cried out.

"Believe only in me," came his voice, "believe only in me and you will see. I will vouchsafe to you the Divine Eye."

The blue screen opened again, shimmering, so wide she went into it and appeared to be sitting near the left big toe of a yogi of gigantic proportions. Many others were standing and sitting near her.

She felt her hair stand on end.

"I'm seeing!" she felt herself shouting.

A face floated far above, ageless and wise, decked with flowers. Smiling down at her he laughed, mouth open, his black eyes shining. The laugh was like the roar of the wind, and in his mouth she saw fire. Hands

197

came out of the sky and with fingers larger than bulldozers began to scoop up those around her and toss them into the laughing fiery furnace.

Then she was scooped up. There were others with her, some screaming, some praying. As the ground vanished, she hung on tight and her life flashed before her. She felt ashamed.

When she regained consciousness she was standing on a dark plain that reminded her of the Jersey meadows near Hoboken. Long rows of ugly concrete buildings stood against a dark brown sky. There were no trees and no other vegetation except mosses and fungi.

The earth was covered with small half-naked people, running in every direction. The tallest of them barely reached her knee.

They took no notice of her but were furiously intent on their own actions. Some copulated on the spot where they met. Males with erections caught females, threw them to the ground and fucked them. Others when they met began to fight. Those not fighting were eating. Those not eating were working, all at fast pace. There were hand-to-hand battles going on everywhere and dead bodies lay unattended.

She began repeating the mantra to cut off the terror inside her and looked around for Indra.

"Now you are seeing into the future of your cherished mankind," his voice suddenly boomed inside her. "Your beloved and cherished mankind to whom all of you are attached. In the desire world they turn deaf ears to Truth, see, this is the result.

"Is it not wonderful, is it not terrible? To see how the negative forces proliferate and spread like rampant weeds—mass communication, mass production. Jam today, jam tomorrow, jam all the time. And here it is, two thousand years later you see it all *really* hanging out." His voice roared with laughter.

One of the small male creatures had spotted her and ran toward her, its penis erect and red. It fastened itself on her leg, like a dog.

She kicked until the small creature rolled into the dust. Seeing her now for the first time others cringed.

"There are only a few large humans left," laughed Indra. "I have caused you to enter one of their bodies and you are seeing through its eyes."

"But how is it possible," she gasped.

"It is a great thing," he said. "You cannot understand yet. Space and time are just functions of instruments. Bodies are instruments. When you get out of them, you can look either way. You are nowhere. Really there is no 'where,' only 'that.' "

A hot wind began to blow, darkness covered everything and the syllables of the mantra flashed like lightning in the sky. Then it began to rain, a fine hot rain fell over everything as time compressed and she saw the earth was now covered with even smaller human forms about the size of rats. Many dead ones lay in the mud. Festering sores covered their hideous emaciated human bodies.

"Come," his voice said. "We will explore a bit."

Now they were flying low over the sodden earth, hovering here and there. On higher ground they discovered groups of small naked ones trying desperately to stay alive. Without tools they had built shelters of refuse and mud. There was nothing to eat but moss and fungi that grew in the drier places, and every morsel meant a life or death struggle.

In some of these colonies the bodies of the dead or dying were eaten by the survivors. Here, since everybody born might be a future meal, copulation and birth were a grim business. She guessed the average age of the creatures to be fourteen or fifteen but as they were so small it was hard to tell. Certainly no one was over twenty. Many were born dead and were eaten at once before they became diseased. Surviving children were forced outside the walls of the colonies where they fought children from other settlements with teeth and bare hands. Others dragged the dead back to be eaten. After the eating there were orgies among the survivors.

"Do they see me?" Laura asked.

"No," he said gravely, "you are no longer embodied because you have come to your senses, stopped desiring it."

"What?"

"Embodiment—when you cease to desire it, you get out."

The plain talk in the midst of the hideous apparition before her made it seem even more real and frightening. She noticed she could even feel the rain.

"But the rain seems real!"

"Like an amputee continues to feel the limb that has been cut off. So when one becomes at first disembodied, the inner one continues to experience certain basic sensations. *Real* is whatever we imagine it to be."

"Can't we leave this terrible place?" she asked, on the verge of tears. "Why do you have to keep lecturing me . . . in the middle of all this . . ."

"Because this is where we are and still part of you does not believe."

"Believe what?" she cried out.

"Believe in me. Understand, that the universe is moral! That it is not things, not bodies, not machines. Its form *is its content.* Not the action, but the *intent* of the action. I am the inflamed one!" he thundered, again assuming the shape of the gigantic yogi. "Time, the destroyer of the world, is in my left hand. All this you have seen, what you call future has happened many times before."

"But if I am seeing the future how can I be here?"

The smiling face towered over her. "I am showing it to the awakened one within you," he whispered. "The knower I have awakened in you

199

looks both ways, has no location. You are not your body, never have you been nor ever will you be in any body but for brief periods."

"Why am I so frightened then?" Laura asked.

"You think you are your body, this particular body you are now in. But it will end and you are afraid. Believe in me," his voice thundered, "I am beyond fear."

"You mean there's a soul that goes on?" Laura asked.

"Once you make one," he replied, "you have to manufacture your soul, it doesn't just happen. It's not given. It goes from one embodiment to another, strengthening itself until it doesn't require embodiment. It can't really be explained. The maker of the tool is changed by the way he uses his tool. Yet the tool cannot know its maker and every maker is a tool."

His form became transparent and dissolved into the blue field. Finding herself again in the comparatively safe territory of the burning ground, Laura felt relieved. The fires that crackled around her seemed almost friendly when she thought of where she'd been. She turned, expecting to see Indra beside her. Instead she heard his voice coming from the fire.

The smoke parted. He was standing naked on the burning logs, his hair unbound. "Look here between my eyes!" he yelled urgently, pointing to a spot on his forehead just at the hairline.

She obeyed at once. A dark spot appeared and as she stared began to grow and widen, engulfing his face, growing, threatening to swallow up everything. "Now jump!" he yelled again. "Stand up and jump! There isn't a moment to lose—jump toward the black hole!"

*   *   *

Early morning sun slanted through lingering smoke.

"Is it over?" she asked, not daring now to look either to left or right.

"Nothing is ever over, only different," his voice said quietly from her left.

A shudder, half sigh rippled through her body. "I feel quite weak," she said, "I have been here . . . ?"

"Twelve days," he said. "I cut it short by two days."

"May I see you now—please—in the form that is familiar to me . . . I mean if I turn and look at you? Will it be you?" She had difficulty saying it the way she wanted.

"I have shown you my true form," his voice said softly. "The form you speak of, the one you know as Indra by sight and touch, is only a manifestation. One of many. No amount of reading or praying nor doing of good works can bring you to my form. But yes, Indra is here. Turn, you can touch him if you like."

She turned and seeing him sitting next to her smiling, collapsed into his

200

lap and cried.

"I'm sorry," she said after some time, wiping her eyes on her skirt. "I can't help myself."

"You are confused," he said sternly, gazing down at her. "Your Western doubt is confusing you."

"It's very hard to shake off," she whispered.

"I know. They say you must die and be reborn on this soil to get rid of it. Do you believe that?"

She wasn't able to answer.

"We usually perform this initiation at twelve or fourteen years, rarely later. I have never given to any woman, although a woman gave it to me. When you have passed puberty they say it is too late. But you have seen," he said, shaking her shoulder gently until she looked at him.

"Yes, I saw."

"Then you will succeed. There is a time for everything. You may be late but yours will surely come."

*   *   *

The warm rain poured steadily on the metal roof of the northbound platform of the Benares Railway Station. They had taken their time returning to Benares, stopping at Bodgaya where he had shown her the holy ground of the Lord Buddha. Now they stood together, the tall half-naked yogi and the American girl, two among thousands who thronged the platform waiting for the train to Delhi.

His presence resounded through her and she felt like crying, but after what she'd learned, why should she? If it was all true, why feel sad?

"You are running away now," he said, standing close to her with his bare toes curled over the edge of the platform.

"I feel an attachment to you," she said simply.

"But it is of a different order."

"Part of me wants to leave, another part to stay."

"Part will stay. Only your body is leaving. It is running away from me. I have worn it down."

"I'm suffering from emotional indigestion," she said.

"*It's* suffering from the indigestion." He smiled, "Not you. Eat more and push the poisons out."

"You've taken me apart."

"And you wonder whether you can be put together again," he said, his eyes twinkling. "There's the rub."

"I'd like to bring Jeff to see you," she said to change the subject. "I'm going to Bombay to get him."

"I think you want to bring up reinforcements, like Doctor Albert

201

Loeb."

"Perhaps," she whispered, looking at the ground. "I hope I'm not like him."

"It is quite natural. It is difficult to change one's ways. See that young cow," he said, turning his eyes in the direction of a heifer further down the platform, who was stealing garlic from a hole in a large gunny sack. "Watch her. You are exactly like her and I am the coolie. Watch."

A coolie came and beat the cow with a small stick and she ambled along the platform, pretending to go away while watching the coolie out of the corner of her eye. As soon as she decided he wasn't looking, she returned to the sack and again began nibbling the garlic.

"The cow is naughty by nature." Laura smiled. "And hungry."

"And the coolie is not too harsh," he replied.

The train arrived and a confusion of pilgrims, beggars, holy men, animals, and coolies exploded around them.

"It's really a form of athletics," he said, watching a group of youths dive through the window of a third-class carriage. The platform turned to grease under the imprint of thousands of wet bare feet.

"You will remain here in Varanasai?" she asked.

"Don't know," he said shrugging, looking down at his feet. "Doesn't matter. I could be anywhere . . . don't make plans, you know. You can always reach me through the Delhi number. I let them know my whereabouts. Better yet, just call out with your mantra."

The third bell for the train's departure was sounding.

He pulled himself to attention and saluted, staring through her.

"Always at your service," he said softly. "Jai Ho!"

XI

THE SHORT FLIGHT had given Stan a chance to think about calming down. "I'll have a heart attack before I die of cancer," he kept thinking. But when he considered his trip to India had already cost him well over thirty thousand dollars he found it hard to remain cool. Ordinarily he didn't mind spending money. But when it came to losing it uselessly, he gagged. His otherwise poker-faced countenance would redden, his eyes narrow to bloodshot slits, as if trying to perceive the unseen powers lining up against him. Forces were gathering on every side. Since he'd worked washing pots at the ashram, he'd been having a recurrent dream: he was high in the branches of a large tree. There were persons he couldn't see at the bottom chopping at the trunk. It was inevitable the tree was going to fall and the unseen ones, whoever they were, were going to finish him off. Just as the tree fell he would always turn into a bird, but was never sure what happened after that because he always woke up.

When the cabin door of the Viscount opened at Santa Cruz airport in Bombay, the blast of hot humid air that rushed in sent him into a coughing fit. His face in his handkerchief, he bolted into the Inland Flight waiting room and was relieved to see Carlos. Carlos could see Stan was going through heavy changes.

"You have a car?" Stan rasped through his handkerchief, trying to spit out the bloody phlegm that kept coming up.

Carlos propelled him toward a waiting limousine. "Get in," he said, "I'll get your luggage. Give me your baggage stubs."

In the heavy evening traffic of Bombay Central the car moved slowly. "I'm very sick," Stan said quietly. "I hope you have a good place for me to stay."

"The best."

"I want you to find out who the Surgeon General of India is," Stan went on, "tonight. If he isn't in Bombay then have him recommend the best cancer specialist he knows. We can fly him here if necessary. I understand the Surgeon General is a cancer expert himself. Tell him about me and say I want a check-up." He glanced at Carlos. "Is it possible that

203

can be done this evening?'' He tried to smile.

"I'll try.''

"Not a bad looking place, Bombay,'' Stan murmured, peering out through the curtains of the limousine. "A little threadbare, eh?'' They pulled up at the entrance to the Taj Mahal Hotel and Carlos led Stan to the desk where he explained that Mr. Stanley was ill and asked that the registration forms be sent up the the rooms.

Once in their suite, Stan made for the bath. "Haven't had a tub bath since I last saw you,'' he groaned hoarsely. "This is going to be great. Can you call room service and have some tea sent up?''

Carlos braved the Indian phone system trying to track down the Surgeon General, then helped Stan into bed and sat rubbing his feet. "You look terrible,'' he said bluntly. "What happened to you anyway?''

Stan stared at the ceiling. How could he possibly tell Carlos what had happened to him, or anyone else for that matter?

"The cancer is growing inside me,'' he said matter-of-factly. "I'll probably choke to death in a few weeks.''

"But what was this Ananda Baba like? Many people here worship him as god?'' Carlos paced the room while Stan tried to tell him about Ananda Baba and the ashram, omitting anything of a personal nature.

Carlos knew there was more to it. "The woman Kamala sounds interesting. Will you go back in two weeks' time?'' he asked. "Maybe he will cure you yet.''

"Let's see what happens this week,'' Stan said vaguely. He had in fact thought of going back, but only because he wanted to revenge himself on Saladin. If he had only a few weeks left, he wanted to buy Saladin like a slave, no matter what the cost, to exhaust him in a final frenzy of money and sex, and then hire someone to kill him at the proper moment. The driver of the car should be exterminated too somehow. It was a fantasy he'd been working on for the last twelve hours.

Carlos noted Stan's tightly clenched fists, his flushed face and could feel the vibrations. "There's a lot he is not telling me,'' he thought. "He's lost some bread.''

"And where's Jeff?'' asked Stan.

"He is here, in the hotel,'' said Carlos, his face darkening.

"Call him up, will you? Tell him I've arrived.''

"You'll have to call him yourself,'' said Carlos dryly. "We're not speaking.''

Stan closed his eyes, trying not to lose his temper. "What is it now?''

"I have a big cash deal lined up. . . . He won't give me the stuff. Has it locked up in some storage company somewhere. Says he has to talk to you on anything other than straight deals through your bank in Switzerland. Iss really bugging me.''

"He's absolutely right," Stan said. "That's exactly what I told him."

"Juss when it means a big sale?"

"Especially on big sales. What would we do with all those dollars—if they were dollars and not counterfeit. How would we get them out of or into anywhere? I don't think you're thinking too well, my dear Carlos." Stan began to cough again. "Whether you're speaking to him or not," he said, "get Jeff on the phone and have him come here at once."

Carlos glanced at him.

"At once," Stan repeated.

Carlos picked up the phone and asked for Jeff's room. Stan heard Jeff pick up. "He's here," Carlos said. "Yes, he wants to see you immediately. Yes, immediately." There was a click at the other end.

Carlos hung up. "He's coming right up. He's on the seventh floor."

Stan had picked up a current issue of *Time* which he was pretending to read. "Now go into the other room and see what's happening with the Surgeon General. Have the hotel help you. Tell them it's an emergency."

When he saw Stan, Jeff tried to hide his surprise.

"Why don't you tell me I look like a dying man?" Stan said. "I can tell that's what you're thinking."

"Why did you come to this godforsaken country? You should be in New York Hospital, or Boston . . ."

"Because I prefer not to die in a hospital, and India's almost the only place you can do that. Doesn't seem too bad a country," he added, trying to keep things light. "How's the distribution going?"

"Half gone so far."

"The money is in the bank?"

"Yes, and the stuff has been delivered."

"Last time I saw you it wasn't finished," said Carlos. "You mean you finished it in the last week?"

"That's correct," Jeff said to Stan. "Can't he leave this room while I'm here? We really aren't getting along!"

"Well, you damn well better get along," Stan exploded. "At least respect the fact that I'm at death's door. Is that too much to ask?"

"I'd like to ask more," Jeff said.

"What? More what? What do you mean?" Stan sputtered.

"I'd like to have your permission to throw the other half into the bay."

Stan thought of the thirty thousand dollars he'd just parted with. "No, absolutely NO! You can't do this to me. What's got into you anyhow?"

"You must be out of your mind," said Carlos.

"You stay out of it," Jeff snarled. "I've seen enough to know it's useless here. They don't need it—it just makes them more fucked up."

"That's your private analysis," said Stan. "Have you taken a survey or something?"

"An American girl she jumped out the window a few days ago," said Carlos flatly. "Iss upsetting him."

"Well, people are doing that all over,' Stan said, "When they can't stand what they see, they jump or do all sorts of things."

"I have a sale for the other half," Carlos said.

"But it's cash. I told you it won't work," Stan reminded him. "What can we do with all those dollars in cash?"

"Stuff them in your jockey shorts and leave," said Carlos. "That would work."

"The man who wants it is a creep," said Jeff. "You want to cause a lot of suffering, then go ahead, sell to him. But it's a lot to have on your head." He eyed Stan.

"I don't care who distributes it. Their morality is of no concern to me. It's the cash thing. It's too dangerous. So easy for us to get ripped off." Stan nodded to Carlos. "It just won't do. Can't he give us a check in Switzerland?"

Carlos shook his head. "He doesn't operate that way—he doesn't keep records, only cash deals."

"Isn't there anyone else we can sell to here who can give us the money in Zurich?"

"There's a friend of mine in Goa," Jeff said. "An American named Grey."

"Where's Goa?"

"It's south of here, overnight by boat. It used to be a Portuguese colony, now it's a sort of hippy hangout on the ocean. Supposed to be a cool place. I've talked to him. We can front it to him and in six months it'll be all gone. Anyhow he's honest. We can even stay there while he sells it. Some nice houses right on the sea, very relaxing."

"I met a lady who admires you," said Stan. "Her name is Kamala, she traveled with me to Ananda Baba. Seemed to be quite interested in you. I think she would like to see you again."

Jeff wondered how much Kamala had told him. Not much he guessed. "Very far out, eh?" He winked at Stan who closed his eyes.

"I hear we missed you by only a day in Delhi. Too bad, you could have gone to the Baba's with us."

"You made it with her?"

"Yeah, once or twice," Stan lied. "What's that?" he added eyeing Jeff's ring, the one Hadji had given him.

Jeff held out his hand.

"You buy it?" asked Stan.

"A gift," Jeff said casually.

"Not bad," Carlos whistled, "real emerald."

"Who gave it to you?" Stan asked. "Kamala, I suppose?"

"Nope, an Arab I met who fell in love with me, wants me to go to Dubai and live with him."

"In the harem?" snickered Carlos.

"Why not?" Jeff smiled and took back the ring. "Might be interesting for a while. I'm fed up with this place."

"Trying to get a straight answer from you is like trying to pull a crocodile tooth," Stan complained.

The phone rang. It was Laura from the Santa Cruz airport..

"Interesting coincidence," said Stan, handing the phone to Jeff.

"Stay where you are," Jeff said. "We have a car. I'll be right out ... near Indian Airlines counter ... O.K. Right, about an hour, I suppose." He hung up.

"Did she know you were coming in today?" Jeff asked Stan.

"How could she know—I didn't tell her. She must be getting psychic out there in the jungle with Alex's guru." He lay back on the bed and started coughing again. "The driver is downstairs with the car. Carlos will show you. And when you've done that, Carlos, come back and get that Surgeon General." He turned to Jeff. "The Goa thing sounds good. We'll see what happens."

*   *   *

"Hello," Laura whispered huskily when Jeff surprised her in the crowded airport waiting room.

"You must be getting psychic," Jeff said, leading her through the crowd to the car. "Stan just got in a few hours ago. Is it true these yogis can see into the future? Maybe he taught you a few tricks, eh?"

"Of course," Laura said, getting into the car. "Why else would one go to a yogi?" She smiled at him, trying to look vague.

"I'm supposed to take you very seriously now, eh?" he said, closing the window against the stench of sewage. "How come you're not wearing robes?"

"Look Jeff," she said soberly, "I really had some heavy experiences."

Jeff could see that something about her had changed. He could see she'd lost a lot of the Laura Weatherall brittleness. They'd rarely been serious with each other.

"I suppose he wants your money," he said, turning toward her.

"Only to get rid of it, he doesn't need money."

"Does he understand trust funds—that they just keep producing income?"

"Of course, silly. I'd just have to keep disposing of it as it came in."

"Detachment, eh?" Jeff said.

"Mmmmm," Laura said, slouching further into the seat. "I'm a little freaked. He makes you feel so weak. He's so strong, so uncompromising. With him everything around you looks different, everything." She gestured out the window. "One is just putting in time here."

"How about love?"

"Mostly attachment, I'm afraid."

"I can see why you're freaking," he said. "Stan's freaked out too."

"Did his Baba cure him?" Laura asked.

"Not yet. I think he had to give up a lot of bread though. You know the look he gets when he's lost bread?"

Laura nodded. "That's good. He needs it. If he could let go of the bread, he could let go of the cancer." She changed the subject. "Indra would like to meet you. He sent Alex home, made him promise to give up the acid thing. He'd like to persuade you to give it up too."

"Then he should see Stan, not me."

"Why?"

"Because I'm tired of the whole trip and I'd like to get out but Stan's insisting, wants to get his money back, and if he dies you can bet Carlos will sell it to the first creep that comes down the street. He already has a first-class goon who wants what's left. I told Stan I'd like to throw it in the bay, but to him it's money. The closer he comes to dying the more uptight he is about bread. You'd think it would be different, but he's holding on tight to everything now."

He studied her. "You really do look different."

"Haven't seen a mirror for a long time," Laura murmured. "You've no idea what I've been through, what I've seen."

"Maybe you should be more careful."

"More careful?"

"These fellows know a lot about mind games—they're raised on them. They show you all these tricks. You ooh and aah inside and freaky things start happening to you. But mind tricks are tricks—it's a matter of concentration. After the mind games, after you've been zapped, then they try to sell you their religion. You know—life after death, life before death, eternal punishment, eternal happiness . . . And when they've got you feeling really guilty then the money pitch comes in."

"But not for themselves," Laura said.

"Of course not. It's always 'give it to my favorite charity.' It's not the bread, it's the power."

"That's true of teachers with big scenes around them, lots of charities and so on."

"Before you let your Indra burn your money," Jeff said, "give it to me. I'll be your charity case. You can live in a cave and I'll have a penthouse."

They both laughed.

"We'll ask Indra if that's a good idea—maybe he'll agree."

The car pulled in at the hotel. Jeff hustled Laura through the lobby and to the elevator.

"I'm too tired to think," she said as they came out on the seventh floor and Jeff showed her into the room next to his. "Bathroom," she sighed, turning on the water in the tub. "Would you believe I haven't had a hot bath since I last saw you?"

"I'm impressed," Jeff said, standing by as she opened her luggage. "Incidentally, your Sikh brothers are here."

"In this hotel? Harpal too?" She looked up.

Jeff nodded. "In fact I saw him just as I was leaving to pick you up and I'm afraid I told him you were due to arrive."

"Thanks a lot," Laura said, peeling off her clothes. "But I really don't want to see anyone tonight. It's too late for me, I'm used to going to bed at sunset."

"I'm afraid you'll have to see Stan," Jeff called as she made for the tub. "It's only eight-thirty, he's waiting to see you, really in a bad way. I think you might get him out of it."

*　　　　　*　　　　　*

Some time later Carlos opened the door of Stan's suite.

"We are very anxious to know everything that has been happening to you," he said stiffly.

"How is he?" Laura whispered.

Carlos shook his head.

"I think Alex's teacher could help him, the one I've been with. I saw him cure cancer with my own eyes..."

"Stan is just returned from one of these healers," muttered Carlos. "I think he has made Stan worse. He seems, er, so much rattled. Please go in, he is waiting for you."

Laura found Stan, his eyes closed, his face the color of old ivory. In his yellow silk pajamas, velvet robe and red slippers, he reminded Laura of a picture she'd once seen of a dead mandarin.

"For someone who's supposed to be at death's door," she said softly, "you look great."

Stan opened his eyes. "Death's door is supposed to be extremely narrow," he said weakly. "I'm not sure I'm going to be let in there."

"That's heaven," Laura said. "The only other one is plenty wide enough."

Stan grimaced. "What will happen, will happen, won't it?" Yet despite his fatalism he seemed to be asking for her help.

209

Laura sat down on the edge of the bed and began telling him about Indra. She knew if she sounded too enthusiastic he would stop listening. He had never been one to show emotion and she wondered now whether he simply had no emotions at all, or whether his immobile face masked deeper feelings. But as he told her about the scene at Ananda Baba's, how he had scrubbed the pots in the kitchen, about his purge, about the milk coming from the Baba's hands, she realized something had really shaken him up. As Indra would have said, he was on the brink looking over.

"You should really check Indra out," she said. "He told Alex that Anada Baba could heal you if he wanted to but that he's healed so many people he may have depleted his energy and might just string you along. Now he's building hospitals for advanced cases like you."

"To die in," Stan said. "Unless of course you give him enough bread. If you build him a hospital, chances are you won't have to go in it yourself." He grimaced. "And to have put me in the kitchen when I have so little time!"

She thought he might be going to cry. "Some doctors have told you you have little time," Laura said reassuringly. "How do you know? Cancer is a funny thing."

"I know, that's why I came to India."

"It's like inside each of us some other person is giving the orders," said Laura. "It can also give orders to kill the cancer, can't it?"

"Antibodies," Stan mumbled. "Listen Laura, I don't know whether I can take another ashram scene. I think time may be running out for me. I've got Carlos trying to locate the Surgeon General—he's supposed to be a cancer expert. After I see him I'll know. And we'll probably have to go to a place called Goa to get rid of the acid. Where is this Indra of yours?"

"I left him up north," Laura said, "but there's no telling where he is now, or where he will be. I have a number I can call in Delhi, they always know where he is, at least enough to track him down."

"A yogi with an answering service," Stan laughed. "How weird!"

"Not really," said Laura. "There's just an old servant whom he phones whenever he moves. I'll call him later after your plans are made. But why do you have to go to Goa? Can't you stay here and let them go?"

"No, because Jeff and Carlos are at each other's throats and I'm the referee. There's supposed to be someone there who can handle the deal properly, and American fellow named Grey. Carlos has a man here who wants to do a cash deal but Jeff says he's not to be trusted. In any case, cash won't work, it's too risky. I hope Carlos hasn't got us all in trouble letting this smuggler friend of his know we have the stuff. Once we get to Goa I hope things will get lighter. But you look beat. It's nearly eleven, you'd better get some rest, eh?"

"I just had my first hot bath in four months," Laura sighed, "feel pretty good."

"Ugh." Stan nodded sympathetically. "What a country."

*   *   *

Alone in her room after leaving Stan, Laura was having a hard time and sat looking out at Bombay harbor, trying to figure out why she felt so uneasy. The city, the hotel, the hot bath, seeing Carlos, Jeff, and Stan—all the old tapes she thought she'd erased were beginning to play again. She wished there were some sort of psychic demagnetizer that could erase them all at once and bit her lip, remembering that Indra had told her it would be hard. "Once you start getting out," he had said, "it becomes more and more painful to reenter until you've become completely neutral."

Do you want to spend the rest of your life living like a yogi? This was the question she couldn't answer and she felt guilt above her weakness. "It was the bath," she muttered to herself. "That did me in. I was all right until then."

She lay down and was dozing when the phone rang.

"Hello, I say, hello, Laura are you there?"

It was Harpal. "I know it's late," he said, "but may I come up just for a moment, on the way to my room? I'm just above you."

"It's almost midnight, I'm afraid I'm beat."

"Just for a moment. I really won't stay long."

His voice did her in.

"Then stop by. I'm just about to go to sleep, but I'll see you for a moment."

She had a pair of Jeff's old pajamas on. She thought of changing but decided against it. Changing was what she would have done four months ago. "Let him see me as I am, I won't go after him—at least that tape is gone."

When he knocked she opened the door and hid behind it.

"This is a stick-up," she said, coming up behind him after he had entered the room. "Give me all your jewels."

He spun around and caught her by the waist.

"Laura, Laura," he said. "Let me look at you." He held her at arms' length, smiling. "I was very angry at you," he said softly. "My brothers were ready to kill me."

"Don't think I wasn't angry at *you*," she said. "It served you all right. I should have thrown the things in the Jamuna River or something. It was Sundar who persuaded me to return them."

"But it's our custom."

"That's a line and you know it," she said, walking away.

Folding his hands in his lap like a naughty child, Harpal sat down on

211

the sofa looking sheepish. She loathed playing games with him, liked him but, knew if she was straight with him he'd take advantage of her. She had learned that much anyhow in four months.

"So," he said, slapping his knees, "Jeff told me you have been to see the Guru. That is very good."

"The Guru?" she asked.

"Your guru. All gurus are one Guru, it is all one teaching. Did you know that we Sikhs are known as the defenders of the gurus? We are the traditional defense against the invaders of India, we guard the Himalayas where the gurus sit. We are in the plains on our elephants, behind us is the army of naked sadhu warriors who are in the foothills, behind them are the gurus."

"You're telling me all these things, Harpal Singh, but you're looking at me like I'm a prostitute."

"I am not looking like. You are saying it. I am just enjoying you with my eyes." He grinned. "Even though you are covering your beautiful body with those disgusting men's pajamas. Your body has given me great pleasure. There is nothing wrong with pleasure. Some of our greatest sages have reincarnated themselves as prostitutes to teach men by giving them pleasure. If you don't experience love and pleasure, how can you ever get out of it. You will crave it forever in many lives. You have to go through it, not against it."

"But can't you get trapped in it?" asked Laura.

"Not if you don't want to. God is also in your body, you know. Guilt is just another form of selfish attachment."

"But I am saying something much simpler and you know it. The trouble with you Indian men is that you think every girl is a prostitute unless proved otherwise. That's the game you're playing."

"Ah, that is too deep," he said, sprawling on the sofa. "Woman, she is all woman. Man, he is half man, half woman. He's only got half as much as she has. He has to steal energy from her. That's why he wants to make sure he's got at least one woman somewhere, keeping his fire going. He wants to connect with her as much as possible to keep stealing her energy."

Harpal was not used to intelligent discussions with women, especially beautiful ones. Sometimes in Chicago he'd had such intellectual exchanges, but he found them exhausting. Some women would argue with you forever. He stood up and started pacing up and down in front of the windows, his hands jammed in his pockets.

"Food kills the urge," Laura said under her breath.

"What did you say?"

"I said food. I just remembered that I had forgotten to eat anything. Sit down, take off your shoes, I'll order something." She picked up the phone, dialed room service, and ordered a complete Punjabi dinner in Hindi. Harpal shot a glance at her, surprised to find that he had taken off his shoes. Grabbing the phone just as she was hanging up, he gave some additional instructions, and admonished the startled room service to be quick.

*   *   *

"You came for a moment on your way to your room. You stayed for dinner and now you're lighting your pipe." Laura smiled at him. "Remove your stockings please, and I'll massage your feet. Then you'll sleep better."

She squatted by the sofa and rubbed his bare feet. It was a sort of experiment for her. She was sure it was the last thing he ever expected her to do. When she had finished, he drew her up to his side.

"I see you have really learned something," he said. "To know enough to rub the foot in the evening, you a foreigner...that is very rare." He beamed at her. "But I see you are very tired, I shall go now, Madam."

"What did you call me?"

"It is what we are taught to call you in boarding schools here." He laughed. "I will see you again soon," he said, putting on his shoes. "I have a suite of rooms on the top floor—alone."

At the door he held her in his arms and kissed her neck. "Every moment away from you has been filled with remembering," he whispered. "I want to make love to you properly. I have thought about you now night and day for months. I am going to make up to you for that night, you'll see." Holding her head between his hands, he kissed her forehead, "I'll call you tomorrow in the morning, yes?"

She nodded.

*   *   *

Laura fell asleep on the sofa and dreamed about the little man she had seen in the fireplace in England. He seemed surprised to see her. He was wearing some torn rust-colored rags and was sitting in front of a hut, his long white hair and beard blowing in the wind. He waved and she could see him yelling at her and laughing. She felt herself floating over the ground toward him and just as she was close enough to hear him over the wind, was awakened by someone shaking her arm. It was Jeff.

She looked up at him. "I was having a lovely dream," she said. "How'd you get in?"

"We have adjoining rooms." He pointed. "I guess you didn't notice."

213

Lifting her up, he carried her to the bed, and collapsed beside her on the soft mattress. For a long while they lay without moving. Then she turned towards him, "I have to look at you to believe you're here," she said, brushing the hair out of his eyes.

"Strange, isn't it, how we're not together much anymore . . . we aren't, are we?"

His green eyes glowed. "That's because you're very good and I'm very bad," he said thoughtfully. "Now we're getting older, it's showing more." He got up, stepped out of his clothes, and kicked them into a corner of the room.

"All my life people have been attracted to this." He slapped his thighs, grabbed his crotch and slid between the sheets. "It's made everything easy. People are wonderful mirrors, when I smile, they smile. What I want, they want. It's like jerking off. And I keep wanting to repeat it 'cause it makes me feel so good." He turned to her. "Hopeless, yes?"

"And when it gets old," she said, stroking his body, "then what?"

"When that happens," Jeff said, "I'll be done for. I'm hooked on it."

"Are you making a confession?" she smiled.

He wondered what she would think about him and Hadji. "Confession," he murmured, "not even half a one . . . I think a lot these days and it scares me so I've been trying not to."

"Have you ever surrendered to anything?" she asked, staring into the dark.

"Almost. To a very beautiful lady, friend of Sundar's in Delhi." He shrugged. "Who turned out to be a fucking sadistic witch. I'm not going to make it, I know it. Think of all the acid I've taken, trying to get out of this." He slapped himself again. "It just got me locked in further, that's all."

"In is out," she said. "It's all the same, you know."

"Ugh," Jeff groaned, "now you've met a yogi, you think you've got the answer to everything. It's not like that, it's not that simple . . . just in and out."

"That's why you should see him," Laura said.

He yawned and rolled over. "O.K., O.K."

She pulled the sheet up around herself and lay awake beside him. For a moment in the darkness she saw the burning ground, the smoke drifting above the fires. Reaching over she brought his head close to hers.

"Listen Jeff," she whispered, "you're not alone, believe me. We're all going through it together and we're all connected."

"I know that," he said. "I really do, but it's all in my head. I don't feel it. Sometimes I wonder if I feel anything."

*   *   *

214

The next morning she awoke to find herself in his arms. He was asleep hanging onto her like a large child. It was good to feel him so close and for a while she lay with her eyes closed, pretending they were back in New York together. Safe New York. What irony.

The phone rang and when she reached to pick it up, his arms tightened around her.

"I thought you were asleep," she whispered.

"I am," he said.

"Shouldn't I answer it then?"

"No."

The ringing stopped and he guided her hand down between his legs. The ringing began again.

"Fuck," he said, rolling out of bed. "Might as well answer it."

"Yes," Laura smiled into the phone. "Oh, Harpal, yes, good morning."

"I was hoping you would have lunch with me," his voice yelled out of the receiver.

"I was asleep," she whispered.

"Lunch," he said, "lunch!"

"Yes, yes," she yelled back, "what time?"

"About one, I'll pick you up."

She replaced the receiver. "Now I've done it," she said to herself.

Jeff came into the room toweling himself. "Who was that?" he asked.

"Harpal, just told him I'd lunch with him," she said looking puzzled. "I was half asleep, shall I cancel?"

He smiled at her.

"I really mean it, I was hoping we might spend the day together—just you and I, see Bombay. Now I've gone and accepted his damn lunch."

"There's nothing to see in Bombay. Go to lunch."

"Will you come?"

"Three's not a good number. Besides I don't go out on the streets. I stay in my room. Sometimes late at night I walk around that silly arch out there, otherwise I stay put."

"We never seem to get a chance to..." her voice drifted off. "Something's always interrupting."

"Don't make a big deal out of it," he said, going into his room to dress.

"I love you," she shouted after him.

He returned a few moments later. "Don't," he said. "I love you too, but it's no good. I'm no good. I told you that last night."

*   *   *

Numerous expensive cars were lined up outside the entrance to a structure that resembled some flying saucer perched on the edge of a cliff overlooking the Arabian Sea. A clutch of doormen saluted as Harpal, with Laura behind him, strode into an elegantly appointed lobby. The lunch hour was in full swing, and the lobby was alive with the hustle and bustle of discreet assignations. Fat Congress Party politicians in Gandhi hats and fine cotton dhotis waddled off, attended by handsome male secretaries in suits and ties, to rendezvous with young girls working their way through college—or more likely just working. A group of Arab princes from Kuwait talked quietly in one corner with Bombay customs officers. The officers twitched at the thought of the receptive female flesh the Arabs would produce for them in return for certain "favors." Some young Parsee dandies conversing in muted Oxford accents leered at Laura and waved grandly to Harpal.

"I suppose you own this place too?" Laura said as they entered an elevator marked private.

"We built it," Harpal answered absentmindedly. "I don't know whether we still own it or not."

"What is it exactly?" she asked.

"Oh, I guess you'd call it a luncheon club, cum hotel—private one. There's a condominium attached."

"You mean brothel."

"Not exactly. You have to be a member and own an apartment. All cooking is done in a central kitchen and sent up."

He gazed at her with his amazing dark eyes. "I brought you here because we won't be interrupted. At the Taj my office may call, that's where they always look for me when I escape them. No one knows of this place, at least no one who works for me."

The elevator door opened onto a large apartment overlooking the sea.

"Quite an engineering feat this was," he said, "cantilevering twenty stories out over a cliff. You like it?"

"It's very beautiful," Laura said, awed by the surf by the surf pounding on the rocks below.

"Why don't you move out of your hotel and come here?" he smiled, opening a bottle of iced champagne.

As he came towards her from behind the bar, she admired his lanky body. He was a different breed, arrogant, yet warm; masculine, yet with gestures that seemed almost womanish.

They sat down on a thick Chinese carpet. "To you," he said, toasting her, "and to our future."

"Our future?"

"I have asked you to come here for a reason," he said. "I want to marry you."

"What?"

"Five simple English words: I-want-to-marry-you." He replied, sipping champagne; gazing at her over the rim of his glass.

"Just came out of the jungle," she said lightly. "Don't think I've anything to wear."

"And now you are at the seaside," he said. "Please don't joke with me. I am serious. I want you. I want to marry you."

"But I..."

"You don't believe in love, but I will show you that it exists," he said, lowering his eyes. "I desire that you shall be the mother of my children. I want to give you everything. I am very rich, richer than you even." He took her hand. "And I am also very gentle, though you may have received other impressions that night in Delhi."

"Do your brothers get to marry me too?" Laura smiled.

"Only if I die," he said, "and only if you were living in India. But we will live in your country. I own a ranch in California, also properties in Hawaii. I'll become a cowboy. Why not? I've spent half my life on horses."

"Why America? You mean you would become an American citizen?"

"A Sikh like me can never really leave punjab wherever he may go. But it would be impossible for us. Our marriage would not be accepted. Our children would be Anglo-Indians, despised by everyone. The days when one could live life peaceably in India have drawn to a close. Whether you accept my proposal or not, all the younger members of my family intend to leave quite soon. We were swindled once by Nehru in '47, we will not make the mistake of being crushed again."

He pressed a small chamois bag into her hand. "I believe you call this an engagement present," he said. "For me it is a token of my love for you. The first of many, I hope."

"But Harpal, we barely know each other and now suddenly..."

"Suddenly, nothing," he interrupted. "Nothing is sudden in this world. It all happens right on time, you are just not keeping up with it. Besides," he said, a smile playing at the corners of his mouth, "we know each other in the most important way a man and woman can. When things happen, let them happen. Don't resist. I've been thinking of you too long —four months now." His eyes narrowed. "I want you. I must have you. If you won't marry me, then be my mistress. I am very selfish, I know it, but I am also filled with love for you. We can get married today. Immediately. Civil marriage right here in this room."

He sipped his drink silently. "Otherwise who is going to save you, tell me that?"

"Save me from what? From whom?" said Laura indignantly.

"From yourself, of course. From your own craziness. You are too lovely to be acting so crazy.''

"I'm trying to become detached,'' she said.

"And you're going to find yourself deranged if you aren't careful. You'll have plenty of time for that after you have become a mother. That is the only real test for a woman. She must go through it. Only then will you learn true detachment.''

"And what about men?'' she asked.

"For men it is the same. For us the real test is when we begin to lose our strength to our sons.'' He leaned over and kissed her tenderly. "You feel guilty about the way you turned out because you don't fit any of the molds. Who is going to relieve that guilt?''

"I have found a great guru.''

"That is fine,'' he answered. "I have no doubt that you have. Every wife and mother should sit at the feet of a great guru. Family and children must have a guru. But you don't have babies with him. Your guru can only advise you, after all you are a woman. That for us is guru in itself, ask him. He will tell you I am correct. We can even bring him to California if you like.''

Laura sighed. "I can see it now. You'll keep me pregnant on a ranch in California—ten years of pregnancy. I'll become a breeder while you, the stallion, are off roaming faraway fields.''

"You must breed. That is your function, your duty as a woman. You must nurture and bring forth plenty. Woman has this power. She must use it, keep it pure, otherwise the whole world will go mad.'' He shrugged. "Like now.''

She opened the chamois bag and drew out a black walnut-sized stone cut like a diamond.

"Put it to the light,'' Harpal said, "and you will see what it is.''

She held it up and saw that it wasn't black but deep blue.

"It is called a black sapphire. It is the largest in the world as far as we know. King Philip of Spain acquired one from the Portuguese which is now in the hands of some American, but that only is second largest.'' He grinned.

"This has belonged to us for generations. It was part of an ancient breastplate worn once a year by our forefathers. On that day the King had to walk through his capital naked except for the breastplate and with his penis erect to show the people that the fertility of the state was secure.''

"What happened when he couldn't get an erection anymore?''

"Then his eldest son became King.''

Laura held up the jewel. "You think you can get me with glitter?''

"It's only for show,'' he said. "I don't need that to get you and you know it.'' He kissed her hand.

Laura gave way. His touch was warm and affectionate. Strength and calm radiated from him. She remembered his long hair falling over her that night in Delhi. Was she hanging on Sundar's imaginary Himalayan cliff she wondered, and was Harpal trying to save her?

Standing up, he gathered her in his arms and carried her into a bedroom. Outside the sea thundered like some cosmic heartbeat. Slowly he undressed her, kissing her body as he removed her clothes. Then he undressed himself and removing his turban, his hair falling to his waist, lay down beside her.

"What you don't know is the secret of this body," he whispered, pressing close to hers. "These muscles, these breasts, this womb, this lingam, they are all sacred gifts—all paths to heaven."

He kissed her lips, letting his tongue play gently over the corners of her mouth. "They are gifts—always remember—not your body, not my body, but gifts to enjoy and take care of. The body is not to be abused nor misused, either from greed or from guilt about it. It is the palace of the spirit, the temple of the soul."

Slowly she felt him entering her and let her hands run down his long back to the firm buttocks.

"This pleasure is granted so that other holy bodies may be made for souls waiting to come in," he whispered. "Only when we make children, then is sex holy, the body not despised, nor the organs profaned or turned into objects of loathing."

His hair covered them like a tent. "Your body is perfect," he said. "There is a great temptation for you to misuse it unless you have a man who can satisfy you fully."

He moved rhythmically inside her. She felt as if she were a sand cliff and he the sea, and that she was caving in slowly, on some rising tide.

She opened her eyes, meeting his as she gave way, opening and closing on him in waves of desire and fulfillment. He lay perfectly still, holding back and letting go inside her, the warm sperm flowing out, filling her. She locked her legs around his waist as he paused to catch his breath, kissing her eyes, her neck and breasts. He wanted to go on forever connected with her, swimming inside. Her hands trembled on his thighs. He felt her going out of herself, her inner membranes vibrating uncontrollably, sucking at the root of his fecundity. A groan rose inside him and he began to cry out softly in Punjabi, his pelvis lapping against her, twisting and turning ecstatically until he overflowed again. Laughing and crying he kissed her breasts, rolled over and slid onto the floor, in a final fervent discharge.

A vast stillness engulfed Laura. Peace, she thought, peace, rolling off through the infinite spaces inside me.

Harpal fell asleep beside her. Dark ringlets of his hair festooned her body. Suddenly from a long way off she heard a voice calling her name. It was so real she raised herself up, half expecting to see someone on the shore below.

"Do not disturb the naked defender of the gurus," the voice said. "He is a very good man."

It was the voice of the old woman she had heard in the temple, speaking in broken English.

"We have made a compact, remember, yes? I begged you not to ask but you insisted. Now it cannot be broken. You must give back the jewel, do you understand? It is to me that you are giving. You have chosen to go out. How can you go out whilst you are busy making new bodies? You must give back the jewel. It is too late now for you to choose a path with him. You have already begun to cross over. . . . If you go with him now you will go mad."

She felt tears welling inside her.

"You asked to have your burdens taken from you. I did not ask it. I am only here to fulfill your most true wish. You are already in the crossing, it is too late now. Give back the jewel and forget him."

Stirring beside her, Harpal sudden came wide awake with a frightened look. "I was dreaming that someone came and took you. I was . . ." He pulled her onto his chest. "Promise that you will never leave me," he whispered. "Please say it. If you leave me I cannot live, do anything with me, take everything. It is enough for me only to satisfy you hour by hour, night and day. I will do anything you ask."

She was unable to speak.

"Will you come with me to see my teacher?" she asked after some time.

"That is quite out of the question," he said as if she had made a joke. "I have my own guru. We do not jump around from one to another. Really, you must go to the husband's guru before the wedding. Some day, no doubt, after we are married I will visit your Indra."

"You said you would do anything I ask."

"Of course I did, but now you are joking. Come, let me call a Justice and we will be married."

She sighed and turned her head away.

"What has come over you?" He turned her face toward him. "See, am I not good to look at? I am, I know it. Do you see any flaws? Am I not well endowed—more than enough to satisfy you and give you strong, healthy children?" He rose to his knees, stretching. "Fathers have offered fortunes in dowry for me. Even now my older brother is entertaining over two hundred proposals of marriage for me."

"Is that why you are in such a hurry?"

"Yes, of course. Night and day they are harassing me. Because the memory of you haunted me I put them off, but soon they will insist and I will have to yield and it will be too late."

He leaned over her, touching her body delicately and staring into her eyes. "I beg of you. Save me. As I will save you. Otherwise my life will be hopeless—a hopeless idiotic frustration is all I can see."

But when they were dressed and about to leave Laura handed him the sapphire. "I can't take it. The burden would be too much for either of us to bear."

"What are you saying?" Harpal cried.

"You must keep it for me, I might lose it."

"Are you saying 'no' then, is that it?" he said quietly.

"No, I'm not saying no."

"Then?"

"I want a month longer to think it over. Can you wait?"

"Yes, I suppose so."

"I may be leaving Bombay soon—perhaps tomorrow. I have to take a friend who has cancer to see my teacher. I hope he will cure him. It should take about a month."

"Most women would do anything to get this," he said, bouncing the chamois bag in the palm of his hand.

"I'm not most women."

*   *   *

That evening while she was resting the phone rang. Laura picked it up sleepily. A laugh crackled through from the other end and she woke up fast at the sound of Indra's voice. "Where are you?"

"At a phone in the village of Kalpura about five hundred miles south of you. Near the sea. I hope you gave the gem back to that Sikh fellow," he said.

She sighed. "I thought you might have been there."

"Yes and no, I tuned in and out. Your waves were very strong."

"Yes, I gave it back. But he's really a lovely person. He even wanted you to come live in California."

"Lovely until after the ceremony, then you would see what would happen."

"I heard the woman again, the voice at the temple, she..."

"I understand," he cut her off sharply. "But why did you call Delhi?"

"I must see you. Things are difficult here; I would like to bring Jeff and Stan." The connection had become weak. She found she was yelling. "Yes, the one with cancer. No, no, he didn't get cured there. May I, yes thank you. How soon? In ten days I think... Just go to that town? Yes, I can remember it. Yes, I'll call you there if there's any change of..." The receiver clicked at the other end.

"Jai Ho," she said to herself, and hung up.

221

Jeff came in. "Who were you yelling at?" he asked.

"It was Indra," she said. "He's in South India, not far from Goa I think. He says he's willing to see both you and Stan. How is Stan? Did he see the Surgeon General?"

"He recommended a specialist here who has his own hospital. He gives him six weeks to six months. Wants to do another biopsy. Stan won't let him."

*   *   *

They went down to Stan's. He looked better and was up walking around. Carlos sat anxiously on the bed.

"Guess I needed rest as much as anything," Stan said to Laura. "You look well I must say—I guess you needed a rest too!"

"I had a call from Indra, he said he would see you."

He looked sharply at her. "Laura, tell me honestly. Should I go to New York tomorrow or shall I go see your Indra?"

"You're hanging your fate around my neck."

He smiled. "Maybe."

"What do you say, Carlos?"

"New York."

Laura didn't really want to be involved in this decision. She didn't like Stan and felt he was more or less getting what was coming to him. But the idea of bringing him together with Indra fascinated her and she knew if he went, Jeff would come along.

"What will happen will happen," she heard herself say. "If it were me I'd stay here."

"And go to your man?"

"As you like."

"Then it's settled." He looked at Jeff and Carlos. "We'll go to Goa and see this Grey fellow, and then see Indra. Have you located him?"

"He's about a hundred miles south of Goa."

"Good," Stan said. "Then it's settled." He turned to Carlos. "Did you say there was a steamer to Goa?"

"Right."

"Then book passage for tomorrow and we'll start to pack."

*   *   *

Jeff sat on the first-class deck of the Goa steamer and looked out over the glittering sea. Dubai was out there somewhere, he thought, remembering that he had forgotten to call Hadji before they left. Laura was in her cabin doing some sort of meditation and had asked him to leave,

222

which had pissed him off. Her affair with this Sikh was bad enough, now all this guru business. What a downer India was. He felt stifled by it, wondered why he hadn't left with Hadji, and why he was stringing along with Laura and this idea that he should meet her yogi. Perhaps he wouldn't, but he couldn't let Carlos get hold of the acid. He was sure Carlos would try to pull something so Wasu would get it. Jeff drummed his knuckles on the railing.

The sound of music drifted up from somewhere below, and he ambled down to the third-class lounge, which was crowded with hippies dancing and smoking dope. Someone passed him a joint and a pretty dark-haired girl gave him a line of cocaine. It was crowded and dark; the vibes were comfortably Western. The girl spoke tough English with a throaty French accent, gave him another hit. He edged closer to her and let his hand go between her legs.

"Let's dance," she said and led him to the floor where they pressed against each other till he got hard.

"I'm too stoned to dance," she said. "Let's go outside."

They went out to a narrow passageway that served as the third-class deck. A number of Indians slumped against the steel walls.

"You have a cabin?" she asked.

"I'm sharing it," he replied.

"Shame to let the coke go to waste." She smiled.

"How about one of the lifeboats?" Jeff asked.

She rubbed against him. "Too hard," she said. "I like soft beds."

The music stopped.

"Maybe I'll see you in Goa. I'll be staying at Anjuna..." she whispered.

"Sure," Jeff said. "Hope so."

The girl drifted back to the gloom of the third-class lounge.

Jeff went above deck and tapped on the cabin door.

"Yes?"

"It's me, are you finished?"

"Yes."

He opened the door and went in. Moonlight filtered through the shuttered window and onto the bunk where Laura lay.

He took off his clothes and lighting a cigarette, sat down beside her.

"Beautiful night," he said, not looking at her.

"Jeff?" she said after some time.

"Yes?"

"It's all over between us, isn't it?"

"Seems to be." He turned to gaze at her, rubbing his cigarette out with his heel. "Either you're balling Sikhs or meditating. I suppose you'll be balling this Indra next."

223

She slapped his face.

Jeff didn't move. "I told you I'm no good," he said, "but I'm just warning you. Yoga is not for you. You should marry this Harpal fellow, take him back to America."

"You'll see," she said. "You'll meet him and you'll see."

"Meet who?"

"Indra."

"I know all about him. Sundar said he's a sorcerer. And you're fascinated. He's put you through some things that changed you . . . But you're getting in too deep. This stuff is for Indians, it's their thing, not ours." He paused. "He only wants your money anyhow."

Laura's palm landed on his jaw. "Stop talking like that," she ordered angrily.

Catching her wrist he pinned her down on the bunk. "Laura, we've known each other for a long time," he said leaning over her. "I tell you this business isn't for you. I feel responsible for bringing you to India. At least go back to New York and come back on your own, then I'll be clear."

Looking at her he wanted to go on, wondered whether he could arouse her. The coke was working, he wanted to fly with her.

"I don't even know you," he said softly. "I've lived with you all this time and you're still a mystery to me, a beautiful mystery." He let his hand rest on her thigh and stretched out on the bunk beside her. "It's like the first time with you every time." He slid his hand to her stomach, watching her relax. "Your Sikh is no good in bed," he whispered. "Admit it."

She sat bolt upright. "You monster," she shrieked, "get out of this bunk!"

Holding her by the waist, he put his head to her belly.

"You didn't hear me," she said, her voice shaking. "I said to get the hell out of this bunk." She dug her nails into his back.

He sat back on his knees.

"There's no comparison between you and Harpal," she said.

He looked at her hard.

"Yes, you heard me. He might not be as good as you in bed and he might be better, but at least he's not an animal."

She got up, wrapped a cloth around herself, and began pacing the darkened room. "You freak," she hissed, "at least he's normal, he wants to have babies, not like you."

"Why do you take the pill if you want to have babies so bad," he said. "Come on, let's have babies, who said I didn't want to have babies?"

"I stopped taking it three months ago."

"Then come on, let's make a baby."

She stopped pacing and looked at him. "You're ready to become a

224

father, I suppose? What have you to teach a child? Can you do anything except press buttons and make up scams to get money? Your father wrote music, did he teach you how?"

"That was a scam too. What he wrote wasn't music." Jeff looked away from her. "But look at your father."

"And my mother's a button pusher."

"Are you ready to be a mother?" he asked.

Laura sat down on the bunk again. "I don't know, I never had one to teach me how—all I remember were nannies and no-no's. But I'm tired of just having sex. It leaves me so empty inside. You don't feel empty afterwards?"

Jeff shook his head. "I only want more. Don't you know that's my problem?"

She lay back in bed. "You're in love with your own cock—that's your problem, and that's why I always feel empty afterwards with you. You give it and you take it back. For you it's like jerking off. Instead of using your hand you use women."

"So what can I do about it?"

"Get out of the whole thing," she replied.

"Whatever that means." He said getting up and putting on his shirt and pants. "I'm going out for a while."

"You can lie down here—do we have to fuck?"

He spun around. "God damn right we have to fuck. When I want to fuck I do it." He slipped on a pair of sandals. "And I'll have no trouble getting any here either, even on this goddamn boat."

Slamming the cabin door behind him he stumbled down the gangway to third class. It was later than he'd thought. The music had stopped. Except for the sound of snoring the lounge was dark and silent. He went back to the first-class deck, lit a cigarette, and stood watching the moon go down in the west. To hell with Laura he thought, to hell with Stan and Carlos too. As soon as they'd dumped the acid he'd call Hadji. The boat plowed steadily on while flying fish raced alongside, leaving phosphorescent trails in the black water.

*   *   *

The boat docked early in Panjim and they breakfasted on the terrace of a modern hotel overlooking the harbor. Goa looked more like Christianstadt or Montego than the dreary India Stan had come to expect. Morning sun splashed against trim white and pastel stucco walls of old colonial buildings. The citizens wore pants and the streets were clean.

After breakfast they went in search of Jeff's friend Grey. The taxi sped down shady palm-lined avenues where old plantations lay decaying behind

225

bright hedges of bougainvillea and hibiscus. Across rice paddies that looked like magnificent green meadows, whitewashed spires of Christian churches loomed above the coconut trees. Laura could have sworn she was in Mexico. Stan had started coughing again.

The car pulled up in front of a high wall with ornate plaster moldings and an elaborate iron gate. Some men were painting the grillwork. Jeff got out and spoke to them.

"This is it," he said, jumping back into the car.

Inside the walls a heap of stone and stucco, cast iron porches and shuttered balconies, had been rescued from a jungle of overgrown plantings and a platoon of workmen was just putting the finishing touches on what Stan concluded must have been an expensive restoration job. "The dope business must be awfully good," he said.

"Looks like it," Jeff agreed.

They got out of the car and were led by an old woman down a high-ceilinged corridor through teakwood doors into an octagonal room with old red- and blue-stained glass windows. In a far corner a young man, naked except for some bracelets, was seated on the floor facing a woman, also naked. They seemed to be doing some sort of yoga. The young man rose and walked toward them followed by the woman.

"Hi, good to see you, man," he said cheerily to Jeff, extending a hand with painted fingernails.

Red nails reminded him of Hassan. Jeff flinched and introduced Laura, Stan, and Carlos to Grey who introduced his friend Joy. Grey was fresh out of Princeton into dealing and Joy was fresh out of Santa Monica into Grey.

"Looks like you're planning to stay for a while," Jeff said gazing around.

"Not sure," Grey shrugged, ambling to his stereo where he put on a Bach chorale. "Just got here a few months ago. Bought this old place without thinking. Now we've fixed it up, looks like we might stay. Goa's a good place. Good Christian smugglers, not those Hindus. You can buy anything here: privacy, protection, immunity—you name it. It's a tradition or something."

After lunch they talked on the beach in front of the house, "Isn't it dangerous to show all this money?" Jeff asked, "all these expensive renovations, your house, these grounds?"

"Not here," replied Grey indifferently. "They're convinced we're all millionaires anyhow. It just makes them mad if we don't spend it. In Goa they love money. Don't care where it comes from as long as you spend on them."

"You paying off?" asked Jeff curiously.

"A little. We had a party the other night, had the head of the Goa CID here, Panjim police chief, some local ones too. Spiked their drinks with acid and got them laid by a platoon of chicks—our sex shock troopers. They had a groovy time. Never had Western women, never had acid. They thought it was the chicks. Now they want more. Little acid, little sex. They'll do anything we ask them to do after a while."

"I got a half-million hits to get rid of for my friend Stan," Jeff said. "Can you do it?"

Grey whistled. "I don't know, man, that's a whole lot to move. The season's almost over here, you know." He doodled in the smooth sand with one long red fingernail.

"I'm really desperate, man. I agreed to distribute this stuff for him but I'm fed up. Want to get outta this fuckin' country."

"Some people don't like it, I guess," Grey said. "This is as far as I've been in India."

"Don't go anyplace else."

"Lots of people go up to Kashmir and Kulu."

"He only wants his cost back," Jeff said, getting back to his subject. "There's a guy in Bombay willing to pay cash but Stan wants it in a check in his bank in Switzerland. I know you can do it."

"Who's the Bombay cat?"

"His name's Wasu."

Grey laughed.

"You know him then?"

"Sure, doesn't everyone? But he can pay in Switzerland, he's got dozens of Swiss accounts."

"He told Carlos he wanted to do it in cash."

"Then Carlos is lying or Wasu was after some fishy deal. Cash!" Grey snorted. "Probably all counterfeit—or else he planned to steal it back before you got out of town. What did you say your cost was?" he added.

"I didn't say, but it comes to about three rupees a hit," said Jeff.

"That's not bad, but it'll take some time." Grey looked up, smiling. "A few months, that sound cool?"

"You think Stan can rent a house here?" Jeff asked.

"Sure, easy. There's one down the road, some French cat's just leaving. Got a terrific electric kitchen: juicers, blenders, a freezer, the works—really far out for Goa."

Later in the afternoon Jeff had tea with Stan. Laura was swimming and Carlos had gone off to the local hippie hangout.

"It's all fixed with Grey if you say so," Jeff said. "He says it'll take a couple of months but he'll do it. Also gave me a piece of interesting information: Wasu could have paid in Switzerland, has plenty of accounts there. Grey seems to know all about him, says the cash deal was a scam."

Stan looked pleased that he hadn't been tricked.

"Grey's got a house lined up if you want it."

Stan's cough had worsened although he looked better and had told Laura at lunch that the sea air made him feel good. But the pressure was there in his chest as well as a pain in his left side each time he tried to breathe.

"When can we move in?" he whispered hoarsely.

"Tomorrow if you like. Don't you want to look at it?"

"Not especially. Let Grey keep the acid locked up here. I'd like to go and see Laura's yogi, he's only a hundred miles or so down the coast. We'll leave Carlos in the house. I guess it has a phone?"

Jeff nodded.

"Good. We can reach him then in case anything happens. I'll see what the yogi says, then ... Then I don't know what—what can I say?" He smiled defeatedly at Jeff. "I'm at death's door, I guess." Stan fidgeted with his tea, mopping his saucer with a paper napkin. Jeff noticed his small pink hands trembling. "Do you trust Grey? He looks pretty weird."

"He's just got his own style," Jeff said. "You know Princeton boys."

Stan nodded. "We won't tell Carlos what we know about Wasu. He's just to stay in the house and stand by. There seem to be enough chicks here for him to play with, that'll keep him busy." Stan sighed heavily. "You'll come along with us to the yogi, won't you? I'm not sure Laura could handle it alone with—well, with me. I might fall apart altogether along the way. Carlos wouldn't know how to act with a yogi and I'm sure the yogi wouldn't want to see him, otherwise I would suggest you stay here."

Grey appeared wearing a towel. "Hope the tea's O.K.," he said to Stan. "Jeff tells me you're sick."

"They say it's cancer," Stan replied.

"Not much to say about that," Grey murmured, with a nervous look as though Stan might possibly transmit the disease. "Guess we all have to go some way, eh? Anyhow, they say India's supposed to be some sort of a special place to die in." He managed a bland smile.

Stan ignored Grey's effort at conversation. "So you'll do the work for us," he said abruptly.

"Sure, I'll try anyhow."

"I'd like to rent that house and leave Carlos in it while Jeff and Laura and I go south to see someone. I'll leave the acid with you. Is that cool?"

"I guess you trust me," said Grey.

"Is there any reason why I shouldn't?" Stan smiled. "But please, lock it up in some closet or something and don't give the key to Carlos."

"I understand."

"The coke business must be thriving," Stan said, changing the subject. He gestured at the house and garden.

"Can't complain." Grey shrugged. "We don't bother with the States anymore, too tricky. Just South America, here, and Europe."

Laura appeared on her way from the beach.

"Come, have some tea," Stan called to her. "Grey's found a house for us just down the road. We'll move in tomorrow, then we'll go search for your yogi. Have you got the directions?"

"Where are you going?" asked Grey.

Laura repeated the directions Indra had given her.

"Well, you can get a reasonably good car to the Goa border, but then there's a river and a ferry and on the other side it's India again where I hear you have to take your chances with taxis."

"I was afraid you'd say that," said Stan, coughing. "The whole idea of traveling in this country is enough to make you forget about it."

"I dig what you mean," said Grey. "I use bikes and motorcycles. Otherwise, I don't go out much. Anyhow, one place in this world seems pretty much like another. I never was much for sightseeing."

XII

ALTHOUGH THE SUN had not yet risen, the first cock was crowing as Laura, standing apart from Jeff as they waited for Stan by the hired car, watched a group of pigs pursuing a fisherman to his morning ablutions.

Looking small and green, Stan emerged from the vastness of the two-story colonial house.

"Even at a distance he looks sick," Jeff muttered.

Laura sighed. "I never liked him. I don't know why I'm doing this. I'm afraid I want to test Indra. Isn't it awful, what does that mean? It's terrible of me."

"Just your practical side," Jeff smiled, "all those generations of Wasps."

Carlos came out with Stan's luggage, obviously relieved not to be going. Handing over the luggage to the driver, he helped Stan into a rickety back seat. Exasperated, Stan's face went red as he sank out of sight inside the sordid vehicle.

"Is this the best we could do?" he rasped, as the car made a screeching start down the quiet lane.

"The good ones don't like to get up early," Jeff explained from the front seat. "Nobody wants to make long hauls any more, there's no money in it. Gas too expensive here."

As they traveled through groves of palm and mango on narrow roads bordered by oleander and hibiscus, the cool morning gave way to blistering heat. Reaching the Goa border at noon they paid off the driver, who insisted on treating them to tea and cookies in a grubby, fly-infested restaurant with piles of dead fish drying in the yard. When the antique steam-driven ferry arrived, there was a mad rush for seats. Coolies threw luggage inside and pushed passengers in through the windows. The boat moved away from the pier just as Laura got in, dragging Stan behind her. Jeff had to jump.

Across the estuary, assaulted on all sides by beggars and food hawkers, they knew they were in Hindu India again. Several taxi operators converged on them, yelling place names even Laura couldn't understand.

Then Stan got sick and began vomiting, which calmed things down

230

long enough for Laura and Jeff to get him into a taxi. But once inside, the crowd converged again, faces pressed to the windows. It was Jeff's first experience out in the country.

"Try not to get uptight," Laura said quietly. "It only excites them and makes them more aggressive."

Continuing south along the Arabian Sea their discomfort increased. The taxi swerved from side to side, avoiding potholes. The sun heated the uninsulated roof of the car so that whenever they stopped, which was often, the heat and the blowing dust became unbearable.

Stan slumped out of sight, coughing now and then. He was frightened, it was obvious to him he was getting worse. Curled up like a fetus, he tried to sleep but couldn't. He was sure he'd die in India, maybe even in this taxi. What was it, he wondered, that kept telling him to stay?

His lessons in self-preservation had come early in life and left strong and lasting impressions. But now feelings of guilt began surfacing inside him, here in the dust-filled Indian heat, feelings he'd never bothered much about or had quickly relegated to a remote corner of his mind. His mind had always been his strong point, it was like a computer: reliable, programmable, emotionless. What had guilt to do with him? But there it was, he couldn't suppress it, some higher value unknown to him was making him feel small and guilty. Was he nearing the end? Was his life going to pass in review—his utterly meaningless, unnecessary life, sordid and maudlin, except for the few times when sudden generosity had overcome his better judgment? Better judgment: greed born out of—? He tried to get a handle on it. Born out of fear. Yes, fear was the basic program and that's what he felt guilty about. Throw his life into the laps of the gods, that's what this trip was all about. Were there really people who could change fate?

Sometime in the early evening Jeff handled a change of cabs with a minimum of fuss, and after more sleep, Stan became aware that it was cool, dark and silent and the car had stopped. Glancing out the window he saw a small group of bare-chested young men dressed in white dhotis, holding flickering tapers.

They helped him across a stone courtyard to a spotlessly clean cement building with small sparsely furnished guestrooms. The air was lush and fresh. From outside came the sound of rushing water and ringing bells. A young man who looked like a black version of John F. Kennedy entered.

"Oh, gentlemen," he said in clipped English, "it is the custom here to bathe in our river and come to the temple on arriving. We have very few foreigners as it is somewhat out of the way. You are most welcome." He bowed slightly, beaming.

"How do you come to speak such very good English?" Laura asked as several young men crowded into the room behind him, peeking around and over each other like children.

"I am the eldest son of the Chief Priest of this temple. From British times the eldest son must be able to speak English. But you must bathe now—it will be most rejuvenating for you."

"We don't have any bathing suits," Stan said politely.

"We do not wear bathing suits, oh gentlemen," said the young man. "We have these." He produced some folded white cloths with red borders. "My sister will come for the lady. Here the gentlemen and ladies do not bathe together."

With the aid of several torches, Stan and Jeff found themselves awkwardly descending a flight of stone stairs toward the sound of bubbling water. Stan detested bathing in anything but a bath or shower.

"Remove the clothes and jump in," said the young man, waving his torch over the water.

"Is there anything in there?" Jeff asked.

"Only a few fish," the young man giggled. "They may nip at you but they are not dangerous—go ahead."

A crowd of men had gathered to watch the submersion. They tittered decorously as Stan and Jeff removed their lunghis and stepped timidly in. Surprisingly the water was warm, almost body temperature, and had a certain texture to it. Submerging himself over and over like a sea lion, Stan felt at once cleansed and stimulated, and almost enjoyed the quiet laughter and applause of the watchers on shore.

"Is this the sacrificial bath?" Jeff said as they paddled together out of earshot of their hosts. "I hear they still sacrifice strangers to their idols in these out of the way places, and bathe you before they do it."

Stan found himself regaining his sense of humor.

Back in the room they dried themselves and put on dhotis, which Stan showed Jeff how to tie. Laura came in dressed in a white sari. She seemed considerably cheered by the bath.

"Ah, they want you to wear dhotis," she said.

"Feels like a dress." Jeff fidgeted with the folds. "Do we really have to go to their temple?"

"He thinks they're going to sacrifice him—eat him for dinner," Stan said.

Laura laughed. "It's important to honor the local gods, rather like a toll fee. Come on, bring five hundred rupees and we'll go to the temple. I'm afraid it's something you'll have to go through with." She glanced at Jeff. "Really, they won't eat you! And they know Indra's out in the jungle somewhere. Unless we spend some money they won't tell us where he is."

The torches, the glint of the bronze and gold idols, the jewels, the beat of drums and music, gave Stan the feeling he'd been here before, and passing through a gate sculptured in a writhing frenzy of gods and goddesses that rose out of sight into the night, they entered a courtyard in

232

which hundreds of worshippers lay prostrate on the pavement.

The son of the Chief Priest came over to them. "The first puja is almost over. There will be another in a few minutes. You would like to do puja?" He cast an eye at Laura, sensing she understood his meaning.

"Yes, of course," Laura answered. "We will do Maha Puja."

"Maha Puja!" The young man's eyes bulged. "That is five hundred rupees, ma'm."

Laura drew him aside and let him see the five hundred rupee notes Jeff had given her. "I understand you might be able to tell me the whereabouts of a yogi called Indra," she said. "Maybe you call him Indrajit here?"

The young man did a double-take.

"You are a friend of his?" he asked, looking frightened.

"Yes," murmured Laura, fondling the hundred-rupee notes.

"I can take you to him in the morning." The young man smiled, his eyes on the money and his hand ready to take it.

"Then I think we will do the Maha Puja in the morning before going to see him. At the five-thirty puja. I think it is too late for us now, my friends are very tired and it takes some time for you to prepare for Maha Puja, I know."

"Yes, yes, of course," said the young man. His eyes followed her hands as she slipped the money back into her sari blouse, and he realized at once that Laura knew more about India than he'd come to expect from foreigners. For even if she gave him the five hundred rupees now it was too late to perform the expensive puja, which took many coconuts, kilos of ghee, and special herbal mixtures. She also seemed to know that once he got her money, he would most likely forget to get up so early in the morning. His almond eyes narrowed.

"Yes, of course, as you wish. We will perform Maha Puja at five-thirty tomorrow morning. Then I will take you to see the yogi of whom you speak. You must be hungry now," he said, smiling. "Will you take food in the dining hall or in your rooms?"

"In our rooms," replied Laura, trying to sound like a memsahib. It was a delicate situation. She could tell these were very elegant Brahmins even though they lived in the jungle. "And we are extremely hungry so you won't forget us, will you?"

At three-thirty the following morning Stan was awakened by a big bell clanging in the temple, and lay in bed listening to the delicious sound of water in the river below. Shortly after, the light was suddenly switched on, and Prakash, as he was called, stood at the door. Furious, Jeff dove under the blankets.

"It is time for snana," Prakash announced, grinning. "This morning you will snana at the main bathing ghat. Come, it is time. Otherwise, the Maha Puja will not be able to begin on time."

"Snana? Chris sake, what is this, some sort of a Cub Scout camp?" Jeff moaned.

"Not for Christ's sake, oh gentlemen," Prakash answered, "for Goddess' sake. We do not worship the Christ here, we are Hindus."

"Snana is bath, I presume," said Stan.

"The bath here is most healing, the water is filled with minerals and herbal tinctures. It is the jungle which is everywhere around us. If you worship here for forty days, all sickness goes."

"You think I look sick?" Stan asked.

"I think you have come from a long distance to get healed. You do not look too sick, but there is something inside, yes?" Prakash smiled.

*   *   *

Cursing under his breath Jeff followed Stan and the young priest down a red clay road from the temple to the bathing ghat. Mist hung in ancient banyans and pepul trees so large that twenty men could embrace their circumference.

"This place is very old," explained Prakash as they walked with dozens of other whiteclad worshippers headed for the snana. "It is recorded as having been an auspicious spot at the time of the Buddha. And even before that, back in the forgotten past, people have come here seeking immortal wisdom and healing."

The bathing ghat was a wide turning of the river that formed a deep clear pool about one hundred yards in diameter. Rocks jutted out over it, orchids bloomed in trees, and the scent of wild jasmine was so strong it seemed artificial. Naked yogis and mendicants sat performing their morning prayers, as a group of widows with shaved heads and red saris immersed themselves, repeating mantras.

"Some scene, eh?" Jeff muttered to Stan as they stood at the edge. "What now?"

"Do get in, it is not cold," Prakash said.

"Do we go in with our dhotis on or off?" asked Stan.

"If you are wearing something underneath, then you may take off, otherwise leave on."

"Well as long as we're in our jockey shorts," Jeff said, throwing off his dhoti, "we might as well have a swim."

Much to the astonishment of the onlookers who bathed but never swam in the water, Jeff and Stan swam to the opposite shore and back.

"Oh, gentlemen, you are excellent swimmers," a grinning Prakash said when they returned. "I have heard that in your countries peoples swim but I have never seen. We are much impressed. It is good, very good."

Laura had been bathing as Indra advised her, up the stream and out of

234

sight. She was giggling as she approached them.

"What's so funny?" muttered Jeff.

"You two. The jockey shorts in the middle of all this. They look so strange."

"You'd better put your dhotis on now, it is almost five-thirty," advised Prakash.

"Over these wet things?" Stan asked.

"It is the custom here to go directly from the bath to the puja. It is good if you are wet, then the Goddess is sure you are clean."

Jeff looked at Prakash as if he were mad.

Laura reached into her sari blouse and silently handed him the five hundred rupees she had promised.

Stan felt exhilarated; as though superior forces were pushing out poisons inside him. The feeling wasn't exactly pleasant, but he was glad something was about to happen to him at last.

The deep bass sounds of the temple drums echoed through the hills, summoning pilgrims to the sunrise puja. From every direction white-, red-, and saffron-clothed worshippers converged on the temple bearing offerings: coconuts, bananas, garlands of flowers on brass trays, mounds of rice and betel nuts. As they passed under the ancient gate the scent of burning ghee and wood sent Laura's mind hurtling back to the burning grounds. Priests wearing scarlet loin cloths darted in and out of the crowd, herding their devotees into corners for special pujas. Every imaginable form of devotion was going on simultaneously.

"Noisy, aren't they?" Jeff commented.

"No, just free," said Laura. "Each person is doing his own thing. They don't have group worship."

"Looks like a three ring circus to me," muttered Jeff.

"Don't you dig idol worship?" joked Stan.

At a sudden clanging of bells and a burst of drumming they were propelled by Prakash through a door into an inner temple.

Flaming tapers and oil lamps illuminated the priests and worshippers. On the stone steps of the shrine, coconuts were being cracked open and lights waved in front of a many-armed, big-breasted goddess astride a golden tiger. Prakash pushed them forward until they were directly in front of the idol, which was covered with garlands of walnut-sized rubies and diamonds. Laura watched Jeff with amusement as his mouth dropped open at the sight of the gems.

*   *   *

"Was that the Maha Puja?" asked Stan as they breakfasted later on. "It all went so fast and so much was happening, I didn't quite understand.''

"I suppose those stones are real," Jeff grumbled.

"Prakash told me they'd been stolen several times," Stan replied, "says they've always returned though and the thieves die horrible deaths.''

"Good thing Grey doesn't know of this place," Jeff said. "He'd figure out some way to rip them off.''

Prakash came into the room. "When you are finished eating we should go. He is up on the mountain.'' Prakash pointed to a peak that rose like a vast green pyramind, ringed with clouds. "It is a good climb for us, over five thousand feet. I have arranged for coolies to carry your luggage. There are other temples there and a place you can stay in. Himself, he is in a cave on the face of a cliff. It is covered by clouds, otherwise I could show you.''

At the last minute Stan realized it would be impossible to drive even part of the distance to the top and complained to Prakash.

"Oh, gentlemen," Prakash said, "the radiator of your car would boil over. It is not made to climb such a mountain, it would surely blow up. The road is for jeeps only.''

"If a car can't make it, how can we?" persisted Stan. "What about a jeep?''

"There are no jeeps. Only the forest guards have a jeep and they are out of station. The walk will give you a lift," he said, slapping Stan on the back. "You will see.''

Stan started coughing and choking.

"You must really look after that cough," Prakash commented, laughing. "You might be coming down with the grippe.''

Jeff and Laura exchanged glances.

*   *   *

Leaving the village behind them, they skirted rice paddies, and plunged into the jungle. About a half mile out, a forty-five degree incline started abruptly. Prakash strode ahead, an English athletic director on a Boy Scout hike, yelling mercilessly at the skinny undernourished coolies who ran barefoot ahead of him with hundred pound loads on their heads.

The pace was too fast for Stan. "Why must they go so fast and why do we have to keep up with them? Can't we just have a nice leisurely walk? Let them go on, I'm sitting down for a rest.''

Seeing Stan sit down, Prakash dashed back. "Oh, gentleman, you must not sit down. You will get more tired that way, and we will also miss our lunch if we do not get to the top by one o'clock. It is not far now," he said. "Come!''

Stan got up and started climbing again. Half an hour later the trail leveled out and they were on a high plateau of sparse jungle that lay shimmering and parched by the summer heat.

Stan turned to Laura. "I'm sitting down right now. Here. How much further?" he gasped, mopping his brow.

Prakash pointed to a small speck at the top of the green pyramid that loomed above them, shimmering in the haze.

"Look here," Stan said to Jeff. "You don't expect me to go there? He says *that's* where we're going."

Jeff stood panting. Sweat poured down his face.

"It's really only a few furlongs more, gentlemens," said Prakash. "Come, we must not delay or we will not get the lunch."

Stan could see it was useless to argue with a man preoccupied by food.

Thanks to the trials of the past four months, Laura realized she was in much better shape than either Jeff or Stan. "You go ahead, Prakash," she said. "Just leave one of the coolies with us and make sure he has water. We'll rest here for a while. Really, we're more interested in going slowly than we are in having lunch. You run ahead, we'll be alright."

"Then I will take my leave," Prakash agreed. "And this man is my own servant, not a coolie. He has a flask of drinking water."

After resting they set out and in a few minutes were in thick jungle again. Large stinging flies dive-bombed them, and when at last they came out of the undergrowth the path rose steeply in hairpin turns up an almost vertical cliff. Bits of rock gave way beneath Stan's feet and could be heard bouncing far below. His eyes blinded by sweat, Stan was sure he was going to die on the spot.

"Stop!" he yelled frantically, clinging to the burning rock of the cliff, "stop at once! This is crazy, I can't make it." The servant came and doused him with water and they began to climb again until finally the path, following the saddle of a broad ridge, leveled out once more.

At the higher altitude the air was miraculously cooler, and they could now see their destination, a group of temples nestled in one of the clefts of the mountain. Prakash and the coolies, white specks, were just arriving at the top.

On they pushed through groves of giant ferns, eucalyptus and palmetto. Small birds twittered in the tops of the teak and cinnamon trees. Suddenly the forest opened onto a broad meadow that sloped around the side of the mountain in a crescent of green waving grass, and just as they stopped to catch their breath, they were amazed to see an Arabian stallion bearing down on them at full gallop. Before they had time to think, the rider, a naked man with hair to his waist, swooped down on them, bent over and with one graceful movement caught Laura under the arm and lifted her onto the horse.

"Who was that?" cried Stan in astonishment. "He's really terrific!"

Jeff shook his head in disbelief.

"Far out," said Stan, as the horse jumped some bushes at the end of the meadow and scrambled up the side of a cliff. "Whoever he is, he can certainly ride!"

Jeff, who had always imagined himself a better than average rider, could see that he had been out-classed. "Rides like a stunt man," he admitted grudgingly. "Pretty cool!"

For a moment the horse and riders stood motionless, silhouetted against the sky. Then they turned, cantered across the field, and came to a stop in front of Stan and Jeff.

"This is Indra," Laura said breathlessly. Grinning, Indra shook his long hair free. And with a wild yell raised his left arm, twirled a rope in the air, and lassoed Stan around the shoulders.

Laura dismounted. Indra walked the horse across the meadow followed by Stan, who, roped like a steer, half walked, half ran out of sight into the jungle.

His mouth agape, Jeff watched in disbelief.

"What the hell is happening around here?" he said, eyeing Laura mistrustfully.

Once out of the meadow, Indra slowed his horse down. Even so, it was too fast for the exhausted Stan, who had to trot to keep up along the treacherous jungle path. He had no time to notice through the towering trees the splendid view of the valley below, nor did he pay much attention to the white-clad pilgrims who stood grinning, their eyes sparkling with delight and curiosity as this foreign captive was pulled along the path toward Indra's cave.

"What indignities I've suffered at the hands of these people," Stan was thinking. "A bug in a spider's web being hauled inexorably to its doom. Me, Stanley, one of the best brains in the West!" He thought of Sundaram and Kamala, of Ananda Baba and the despicable Saladin, and now a hooligan on horseback, and realized he was desperate to live at any price.

Soon the path ended and they arrived at the side of a sheer cliff where a clear stream of water gushed out of the rock into a pool before dropping a thousand feet into the jungle below. Indra dismounted and removed the rope.

"You are tired, no doubt," Indra said calmly. "Sit down here and after you're rested, take a dip in this pool. I'll bring you a towel and some fresh clothes." As Indra disappeared on a footpath over the face of the cliff, Stan had his first chance to observe closely this person whom he'd heard so much about, this huge brown man with his henna hair and boyish appearance. The sight of him now struck fear at some deep level of consciousness, as if the mere existence of such a creature invalidated everything he had hitherto known or believed in.

238

"If I were a dog," Stan thought, "every hair on my back would be standing on end!"

About a half hour later, Indra returned with a towel, soap, and cloth. "Here," he said, lighting a small brown cigarette, "smoke one."

"Is that tobacco? I never smoke tobacco." Stan replied hesitantly.

"Take it," Indra commanded.

Stan obeyed.

"When you have bathed, come and sit with me. The sun will just be setting, from there you get quite a view. But mind the path, it gets narrow and the wind can be treacherous."

Bathing in the small pool, Stan listened to the water which sounded like a chorus of voices singing inside the mountain. Now that he'd finally stopped moving he found he could relax, splashed around in the soft water, and wondered what would happen next. Washing and drying himself thoroughly, he put on the lunghi Indra had left and made his way timidly and carefully along the path. Rounding a corner he started back in fright. Over a precipice yawned a drop of at least two thousand feet. Vultures and kites glided ominously in space, floating on updrafts. From where he was standing he could see Indra's camp, nestled in a fissure of rock midway on the face of the cliff. Indra was sitting in front of a fire playing an instrument and singing, his body covered with ash. Fifty yards of narrow path remained.

"Are you all right?" Indra shouted across the chasm. "Don't think about it, just walk across. Nothing will happen to you."

Stan's knees went weak. Blasts of wind buffeted him. Not daring to look out or down, he kept his eyes glued to the almost non-existent path, clutched the face of the rock where he could, put one foot in front of the other, and, crouching, clambered across the last few feet.

"You looked like an old monkey, a lecherous old monkey coming to rape me," Indra leered, fluttering his eyelids and brushing back his long matted hair with a gesture that reminded Stan of Joan Crawford. "Welcome, welcome to the cave of the mad witch."

"Who?" gulped Stan.

"Me," said Indra. "Yes, it is true, I can tell by your face—you were seeing me as a woman just now, a female, eh? Yes, ah ha, that is most auspicious . . . most auspicious." He picked up a drum and rattled it wildly. "Ho! Ho! Ha! Ha! Oay!" he yelled out toward the setting sun. "I smell the blood of an Englishman. Yes! Is it not true?"

"I'm not English, I'm a Jew."

"Don't be self-centered," snapped Indra. "It wasn't your blood I smelled. What is 'Jew'? I'm not sure I know. . . . You mean like Moses in the Bible?"

"It's a Western tribal group."

239

"Has had many troubles?"

"Yes—always has been on the move," Stan explained. "Specializes in communications: money, writing, newspapers, radio, now TV. But mostly money—maybe we even invented it."

"Ah," said Indra, "that carries very difficult karma. We have tribes like that here, two or three separate ones."

"Yes?" said Stan, interested.

"They are called Marwaris and Jains and Parsees. The Parsees are the Pharasees of the Bible, the Marwaris are big moneylenders, the Jains are merchants and puritanical reformers—Gandhi was a Jain."

Indra put down his drum. "As I was saying, I smell the blood of an Englishman, did some Englishman come with you? A rather young, handsome, ah—I see him, yes, he is with Laura. Very upset he is. Called Jeff, is he not?"

Stan felt a tremendous force pulling at him and realized that Indra's words were a screen for something else he was doing, some mental exercise so strong Stan had to look away to avoid being turned inside out.

"You are a very guilty man," said Indra, shaking his head from side to side. Stan was surprised to find himself nodding in assent.

"You need not nod," he said. "There is no need for you to agree with me. But understand that I find you guilty."

"Of what?"

"You have a mother, I believe?"

Stan hesitated.

"Answer me," Indra said sternly.

"Yes."

"And she is your responsibility." Indra frowned.

Stan felt himself begin to shudder.

"Yet I see her in an institution of some sort. Very bad place. Very dirty—ah, I see. She is very unhappy about it, eh?"

"I put her in a very nice institution because she is getting old and she went crazy."

"She is not crazy," Indra snapped. "It is you who are crazy."

"That's not true!" yelled Stan.

"It is!" Indra yelled back at him. "She told you the truth about yourself and you couldn't take it so you had her put away!"

Stan felt a great rush of energy flowing into him.

Indra pointed dramatically to the setting sun. "You spend all this money on your desires and whims and on sex—don't deny it—and your poor old mother is locked up in a cheap old age home." Indra laughed uproariously.

Stan felt a chill envelop him as the red sun disappeared below the horizon.

"And you have come here," Indra went on, "because Laura has told

240

you I can heal what they call your cancer."

Indra leaned over the fire and with his long forefinger beckoned Stan nearer. "You know what I should do with you?" he whispered over the smoke and flames.

Stan trembled and leaned toward the naked giant, gray with ash, who whispered spookily at him through the smoke. "What should you do?" he asked hoarsely.

"Kill you," said Indra. "Right here on this spot. So easy." He gestured to the precipice showing all his teeth in a skeletal grin.

Stan felt tears well up inside him and made no attempt to stop them. Soon he was sobbing openly.

Indra retreated into a corner of the cave and returned after a while with a cup of hot tea. "Drink and cry—it is good for you," he said and picked up his instrument and began to sing.

Stan realized that he was in a situation over which he had absolutely no control. He couldn't stop his own convulsive crying, nor could he halt the flow of bitter memories of every sort that now flooded his mind. The man seated across the fire from him seemed to change from one moment to the next behind the smoke. For a time Stan thought he could make out a beautiful girl—or was it a boy? Then when a gust of wind blew the smoke aside the youth became a haggard old woman, an ancient sphinx-like creature, barely human. At each change he noticed that a fresh set of memories would parade through his consciousness.

Should he confess his guilt?

The question made him feel ridiculous, uneasy, and he glanced at the path wondering whether he should try getting back across the cliff while there was still some light.

"Don't think about escaping from me," said Indra, pausing in his song. "You will fall off if you go back now. I have waited a long time for you," he added ominously. "Now you are here, you shan't escape me. I owe it to your mother . . . to my Mother."

Stan fidgeted with his cup, unable to meet Indra's gaze.

"Do you want to confess everything to me here and now?" Indra said smiling.

"I can't," Stan mumbled and burst into tears again, spilling his tea. "I can't. I want to but I don't know how."

There was a long silence. The fire crackled. From far away came the sound of water rushing out of the mountain.

Indra stood up. "Get up, rodent. Come with me." He muttered.

Stan felt too weak to move.

"Come, get up at once," said Indra, prodding him with the tip of his chimtah.

Feeling weak in the knees, Stan struggled to his feet and fiddled nervously with the lunghi around his waist.

241

"What are you doing?"

"I'm afraid this will fall down. I mean, I'm not used to wearing..."

"Let it!" Indra said sharply. "Why are you all of a sudden so modest—you who pay for bodies, for flesh! Ha! Do you think I care what you are wearing or what you look like? I have seen everything under the sun. Yes, for centuries. Whether your cloth falls or not is nothing to me—here!" He reached forward and ripped the lunghi from Stan's waist. "Now you won't have to worry about that. You won't need it where you're going anyhow."

Indra grinned at the absurd figure of Stan standing in his jockey shorts. "What bumpy knees you Western fellows have," he laughed. "Come, follow me."

In a dark corner of the cave was a small opening, just big enough to squeeze into. "We go up through here," Indra said, "observe how I do it and follow where you see my feet go."

Stan struggled behind. After a few yards of vertical ascent, the shaft opened into a small horizontal passage where there was room to stand. Then there was Indra's strong warm hand pulling him up. "Follow me." Indra said and walked deftly along the passage.

Stan felt as though he were going toward the center of the world. It was warm and he could hear water splashing somewhere ahead. They came to a large underground chamber, warm and slippery. Indra clicked on a flashlight.

"Look there—the water is bubbling up out of the center of the mountain into this lake. A lake inside the top of the mountain—is it not marvelous?"

The light shone over a good-sized pool fed by water splashing over a rock at one end. It was difficult to judge the scale of the place.

"Come," said Indra, "we'll go behind the water now."

There were footholds cut into a small cliff. The size of the cavern now became apparent.

"A whole herd of sheep could go behind this waterfall," said Indra, waving the light at it.

The rock was damp and slippery where mosses grew under the spray. Then they were above it, climbing steadily up steep steps cut in another fissure. Indra paused, feeling the wall of rock. They seemed to have reached a dead end. "Ah," he said suddenly, "yes, it is just here." He pressed his back against the rock. Slowly a whole section slid to one side and Stan could see a pale light. "Now, up through this opening," Indra said. "We have reached our destination."

Stan struggled through the opening and climbed onto what seemed to be the stone floor of a room. "Stand up!" commanded Indra.

Stan stood up, but a strong wind sent him back on his knees. Looking around he saw a four-armed dancing male figure, silhouetted by the pale light from a crescent moon. They were in a small temple of arched openings. "Are we on the top of the mountain?" he asked.

Indra sat down in front of the huge stone figure and was lighting a fire from a supply of wood stacked in a corner. "Look for yourself," he gestured.

Stan walked around peering through the arches. He was subject to attacks of vertigo and, with sheer cliffs falling away on every side, began to feel very uncomfortable. He was also cold.

Indra gestured at the stone figure, whose four outstretched arms grasped battle gear and drums. Stone snakes writhed in its hair and around its neck. "This is Shiva," he said and, grinding something between two rocks, mixed it with oil and poured it onto the fire. "He is destroying everything. See how he is stamping down on the body beneath his foot. See his necklace of human skulls!"

Stan moved closer. Flickering over the polished black stone, the flames infused life into the frozen dance of annihilation.

"He is Shiva Bhirava, we call him Kalabirava—the destroyer," Indra said. "Now lean closer." Placing his outspread hand over Stan's head and skull, he dug his thumb into Stan's forehead, held him motionless for some time and released him.

"Now I must go," he said, standing up. "You will remain."

Pointing to a large black stone beneath the dancing figure, phallic in shape and highly polished, he indicated a red mark at the tip. "Do you see this dot?"

Stan examined the stone.

"You will stay here and stare at that," said Indra. "Remain seated—it's too windy to walk about and if your eyes become tired from staring, close them and just listen to your own breathing." He started down through the opening.

"Is that all?" Stan said.

"Isn't that enough?" asked Indra.

"But it's cold here, I haven't anything on, not even my cloth."

"Don't worry, you won't freeze."

"You bring me up here and now you're going to leave me just like that?" said Stan furious. "I'm very sorry, I can't stay. I can't spare the time...I..."

Indra burst out laughing. "You had better spare it if you want to go on living."

"But..." In all the craziness of the past two hours Stan had actually forgotten about the cancer eating away at him.

"No buts!" Indra bellowed, starting down through the aperture in the floor. "I'm leaving. Come down if you like—if you can! Why should I care about you, rodent! I am only helping you because your friend Laura asked me to. As far as you are concerned, I care nothing. You are trash to me.''

A wind howled around the lonely rock pinnacle, gusting through the arches. The flames licked fitfully at the base of the statue. Alone, Stan sat down in front of the fire. His first thought was of keeping warm and he glanced at the wood supply, but knowing nothing about fires he had no idea how long it would last.

He wondered how best to spend the night. After a closer inspection he saw that there was one corner that seemed to be less windy and, cautiously moving the fire into it, he edged himself onto the floor, curled up and fell into a fitful sleep.

Soon he began to dream vividly about his childhood. There was his mother, beautiful and loving, her face luminous. Then she was scrubbing floors and doing menial work for neighbors, her face and body growing older before his very eyes. He fought to kill off her progressively grotesque form, but could not.

Suddenly he woke up, terrified, wondering where he was. The fire was out, and he was cold. Outside the stars glittered in the black sky. "Are we nothing then?" he wondered. "Just specks in a vast chaos of equally meaningless specks?" He began reviewing his life. It had never occurred to him to do this but now it was happening automatically, the events of his life rushing by one after another. He'd never really considered dying. His life had been so filled with action, machines, and money, that he had come to think of himself as an object to be repaired and rebuilt indefinitely, provided one could afford it.

And now as he approached the end, what had it all meant? Was there any meaning? Why was he sitting here in front of this image of destruction, the dance of death itself, in a strange land—while inside him a microscopic community of organisms multiplied out of control.

Shivering uncontrollably, he realized he was cold, colder than he'd ever been, and crawled to the paving stone which covered the passageway. If only he could get down there, he might be warmer. But claw as he would and push and shove nothing moved, and he realized there was no escape. Yes, he could jump—and end it all. But would that really be the end? Something inside him was unfinished, incomplete, and cried out that he was not ready to die, not ready to give up.

Convulsed by spasms of crying and shaking, waves of self-pity engulfed him and he fell to the floor realizing he was a coward who didn't even have enough guts to bring the fiasco of his life to an end.

Suddenly his thoughts were interrupted by a series of loud crashes, one after another, like stones falling on the roof, and looking up, he saw sizeable rocks hurtling through the open arches onto the floor.

Several stones landed near enough to send chips biting into his legs. Fear swept him, and he cowered like a frightened rat in his corner. It wasn't possible! It couldn't be possible! He clenched his fists and pounded the wall. How was it possible for rocks to come flying through the air like this on top of a five-thousand foot mountain?

Just then a rock the size of a tennis ball hit the wall beside him and bounced into his lap. It was smooth and black, not unlike the rock Ananda Baba had brought up out of his mouth. Somewhere Stan had read of stones that fall in the night. They were supposed to be the work of poltergeists, but what were they? Now they were coming from all directions, big and small, pelting the roof of the temple like hail. He became numb with fright, his supply of adrenalin had been depleted by the "thing" growing inside him. His brain was too rattled to think clearly. A wailing assailed his ears until he realized it was himself, jabbering incoherently.

Then some deep instinct commanded him to follow Indra's directions. He listened to it as one attends a far off call. "I must sit up and do it," his conscious self said. "As stupid as it seems in a situation like this, I must." What else, after all, was there to do? And maybe the rocks would stop.

Dragging himself into the place Indra had shown him, he sat rigid, his face pale with fear, staring at the red mark on the stone thrusting up from the floor. As he stared he became aware that his breathing was shallow and irregular. He tried to regularize it, directing what energy he could still summon, counting so many seconds in and so many seconds out, so many in, so many out, in, out . . .

As one trained to observe changes in phenomena, he noted that the more regularly he breathed, the warmer he became. But the feeling of reassurance that this gave him was soon shattered. While staring at the dot on the stone, he could see on the edge of his vision a halo of fire around the head of the idol. If he looked directly at it, it disappeared, but when he observed it with his peripheral vision, the manifestation appeared again. He grabbed a stick and held it to the halo of flame without looking. When he withdrew the stick, it was blackened and smoking.

"So what?" he said, looking at it angrily.

But before his very eyes, dancing ponderously to the rhythm of many drums, the statue came to life. It was a frighteningly beautiful figure. Stan heard himself laugh, then yell, and heard his own breathing as though through an amplifier. Never in his imagination had he seen or thought of such a being.

Its skin was dark and taut over firm young flesh, its penis erect and hair a mass of curls with snakes slithering down across almost female breasts. The full lips were frozen in a sadistic tantalizing grin, dark eyes glittered between lashless lids.

Stan fell back on the floor as the figure advanced. "Who are you?" he

245

stammered. "Get out! Get out!"

The figure's eyes opened wide as if in rage. A great roar, then yelps and screams filled the air.

Oblivious of whether he was hot or cold or breathing or not, Stan started coughing. Large globs of phlegm were coming up, pieces of tissue and blood.

Enraged, he beat the floor with his fists, demanding the statue stop its dancing, hurled the stones that had fallen from the sky, hoping to demolish it and somehow be set free. But the statue danced on and finally, his mind past reasoning, his body exhausted, cut, and filthy, he lost sense entirely and rolled on the floor, screaming and crying and clawing at the place where he imagined the entrance stone should have been.

*   *   *

The eastern sky had turned pink. Low clouds, moving in from the sea, scuttled across the horizon, when Indra, asleep in the cleft of rock near his fire, was awakened by a shout.

"Hello, are you there? Hoy!"

Opening one eye, he saw Laura, followed by a young man, about to traverse the treacherous cliff path.

"On and on it goes," Indra thought to himself. Pretending to be asleep, he watched through almost closed eyes as the two began their crossing. "The American is coming," he thought, "so cunning, so unwashed, why do I smell blood when he is near?"

"You will please remove your shoes before stepping into this space," he said, opening his eyes as the two reached the edge of the cleft.

Jeff stopped to remove the special hiking boots he'd had made in London. Suddenly one slipped from his hand, tumbled down the precipice and caught in a bush fifty yards below.

"Don't go after it," Indra said, sounding like an English nanny. "If you do, you won't be able to wear it." He laughed as he always did when something got lost or stolen.

"They were new," said Jeff irritably, holding the other shoe.

"Throw the other one overboard too," said Indra sternly. "I don't think you're going to need them." He pointed to his solar plexis. "It has bad feelings about leather."

"Sorry if I've offended you," Jeff replied coldly, seating himself to one side of the fire.

It was a stand-off between them.

Laura knelt and touched Indra's feet in the Indian manner. Placing his hand on her head, he let it rest there a moment and gazed at Jeff.

"Quite a place you've got yourself here," said Jeff, trying to make conversation.

246

"I am smelling blood," Indra said, looking at him closely. "Why is it I am smelling blood when you are near me?" He released Laura's head and she sat up and stared at Jeff.

"Where is Stan?" said Jeff, not wanting to look at Indra.

"Green eyes," Indra muttered. "Very bad. Pathan. Very bad."

"What was that?" asked Jeff uneasily.

"Green eyes, very bad," Indra repeated. "It is the rule, it is not my idea. It is the old teaching."

"I don't see Stan," Jeff said to Laura, trying to ignore Indra's comment. "Didn't he come out here with you?" He looked at Indra. "Didn't . . ."

"Blood and green eyes," said Indra.

"What have you done with Stan?" Jeff asked loudly. "If something's happened to him, I'm here to . . ."

"Jeff!" whispered Laura reproachfully.

"You are here to *what*, me lad?"

"To find him!" Jeff shouted. "Where is he?"

"I pushed him off," said Indra quietly, gesturing at the edge of the cliff.

"You *what*?"

"Pushed him off," Indra repeated. "I couldn't stand him. I can see why the Ananda Baba wouldn't heal him—all the lying, the craftiness, like a weasel, and breaking wind constantly. Why prolong suffering like that?"

"Why prolong it!" yelled Jeff. "Why prolong it? Because he could've been with the best doctors in the world right now. . . . You have no right to push anyone anywhere."

"But I have pushed him," sighed Indra in his grandest English accent. "You forget this is India. Even you could disappear here at this very moment and no one would come looking." He frowned at Jeff. "It doesn't matter," he went on. "He went to the place he would have gone to sooner or later."

"You had no right!" Jeff repeated.

Indra gazed at him with fiery eyes. "When a man throws himself in my lap, I must decide the cure. It was best, believe me!"

"Let's get out of here," Jeff said, glancing at Laura. He stood up and brushed off his clothes.

"You're not going anywhere, young man," Indra said. "Sit down." Jeff sat down heavily.

"I see I have to give you a lesson." Indra put his hand into a pile of cloths and books near him and withdrew a revolver.

He uncocked it professionally to show Jeff and Laura it was empty except for one bullet. Then he snapped it shut and tossed it to Jeff.

Jeff caught it adroitly in midair.

"Now," said Indra, "point it to your head, twirl the cartridge chamber and pull the trigger."

"But that's Russian Roulette," said Jeff, his voice faltering slightly. "After you," he said, tossing the gun back to Indra.

"No! No! No!" screamed Laura hysterically.

Indra spun the chamber, put the pistol to his head and squeezed the trigger. Click!

"Your turn now," he said. Gazing coolly at Jeff, he tossed the gun to him again.

"I can't stand it," Laura burst out. "If you don't stop—both of you—I'm . . . I'm going to jump."

"Jump then," Indra said casually. "Jump if you like. It doesn't make the slightest bit of difference. You'll understand that some day. Go ahead."

Laura closed her eyes weakly. Jeff picked up the pistol, put it to his temple, and twirled the bullet chamber. But he couldn't bring himself to squeeze the trigger. "Why should I play this game with you," he said, putting the gun on the ground. "I came here to find Stan."

"It would cure you," said Indra.

"What!" Jeff laughed bitterly. "You mean finish me off—like Stan."

"Ah," said Indra smiling, "do you really care about him? After all I know he is not really your friend. Neither he nor you has any friends, except her maybe—and she has brought you here to test me." He looked reproachfully at Laura. "Give me the gun then," he said wearily.

"Perhaps I should keep it a while," Jeff said coldly, pointing the gun at Indra.

"Jeff!" cried Laura. "Put that gun down." She grabbed for it but he jerked it out of reach.

"No, no, let him keep it," Indra said calmly. He got a box of bullets from his bag and tossed them across the fire to Jeff. "Examine them, please, and fill the other chambers up—five more bullets."

Jeff hesitated.

"Do as I say!" Indra roared.

With trembling hands Jeff examined the bullets, dropped them into place, and closed the chamber.

"Now," Indra hissed softly, "aim the gun at my chest and empty it."

Jeff lifted the revolver and pointed it directly at Indra's heart. The smoke of the fire drifted between them as Indra went into his peculiar slump.

"Jeff, Jeff, no!" wailed Laura. "You don't understand, you don't know. Put that thing down, put it down!"

"Shut up," muttered Indra. "Pull the trigger. I pushed your friend Stan off the cliff. Eye for an eye. Pull the trigger!"

Jeff was angrier than he'd ever been. All the frustrations, all the doubts and contradictions of his life compressed into this moment.

"Shoot!" Indra ordered.

Jeff squeezed the trigger three times. The shots echoed out over the cliff.

"Again! Pump em all out, boy!" yelled Indra.

Again Jeff squeezed, this time until the chamber was empty. In the split second that it happened Laura thought she saw the bullets enter Indra's flesh and the flesh close behind them. Indra sat, slumped, veiled by the smoke of the fire.

"You see, it does not affect me," he sighed, holding out both arms grinning boyishly at them.

"It's some sort of trick," said Jeff, looking sideways at Laura.

"Yes, Indian rope trick." Indra laughed. "If it is a trick then reload and point it at yourself—or at her." He nodded at Laura.

Jeff realized his limits had been defined.

"You see," Indra went on, "what you do not understand is that some beings are different. Your society does not allow you to believe that men are not all equal, or that souls and bodies can be made immortal."

"Go ahead—fill the chamber and empty it into your body if you think it is a trick. If you want to compete with me, then you must now do as I say."

"I came here to find Stan, not to compete with you," said Jeff.

"You came here to find yourself but you are failing," replied Indra. "As I told you, I pushed him overboard. He was a very bad case. Absolutely no hope for him to continue in that body."

"You gave him another body then," said Jeff cynically.

"He will have," said Indra matter-of-factly, "if I choose. Perhaps I'll let him seek his own natural level." He laughed wildly. "Some pig or goat, perhaps."

"You'd think you were God or something," said Jeff. "Are you a god?"

"No, just empty." Indra pointed to his forehead. "Here—feel," he said, extending his arm across the fire to Jeff. "Flesh and blood."

Jeff touched the large muscular arm pulsing with energy and warmth, then grasped the hand that Indra offered across the fire. A familiar feeling, like an acid high, came through into his body.

"Have you taken LSD?" Jeff asked, holding Indra's hand.

"Several times. It has been given to me by your countrymen. It does not affect me."

"You think it is useless then?"

"It is not useless. It is equal to ten years of meditation practice. Think of it—ten years—in twenty minutes." Indra cocked his head, smiling. "It is most dangerous to give people the result of ten years' practice in twenty minutes. It is like opening Pandora's box—you know Pandora's box? Very dangerous for the social fabric. Not everyone is ready for power, for knowledge. It will destroy many. Not everyone can get out at once, some must stay. That is a Christian mistake, saying everyone can be saved. It was a political ploy—simplification for the masses. Rome had mass media, the prize was Rome in those days.''

He dropped Jeff's hand. "But I see you do not even follow the teachings of your Christ. If you had his faith, you could pick up the pistol and aim it at yourself."

"Without his training?"

"Believe me, my dear boy," Indra said patiently, "training is not at all necessary. Salvation comes in one moment. You can get there by training too, but people get sidetracked by too much training."

"Did Stan tell you about his project?" Jeff asked.

"He did not have time before I pushed," laughed Indra. "But I know it all anyhow. You are engaged in smuggling this drug. You must stop—it will do you no good."

He gazed at Jeff thoughtfully. "You could be a good sadhu," he said. "Come stay with me—I invite you. I will train you. You reek of garbage and sex craziness but that can be normalized. If you return to the smuggling business you might as well blow your brains out right now."

"But I'm not smuggling!"

"I know you call it distribution but you smuggled it into this country and our people think of it as that. They cannot believe anyone would ever sell for a loss." He paused. "Besides India does not need this drug. It is just another Western misunderstanding, thinking we need to be awakened. It is your country that is asleep and wishes to put the rest of the world to sleep with computers and other time-saving machines. Yes," he added softly, "I know everything that is going on."

"We in India must give up outside drugs, medicines. Let epidemics rage, let our armies go back to horses and elephants. Let our warriors attack naked with spears. Let our widows jump onto funeral fires and widowers walk naked into the jungle. That is the way to save India. We would become impregnable. Out of fear, no one would attack us."

"I'm leaving," Jeff said to Laura. He got up and threw the gun across the fire to Indra.

"You're *what?*" said Laura.

"I'm leaving. If you want to come then come now, or I'll probably be at the guest house until tomorrow morning. If you want to stay, then stay. I have to get back to Goa. There's all that acid. With Stan gone, Carlos will try to sell it to Wasu."

"Let him have it," pleaded Laura.

"No."

"You're thinking of a couple of million bucks, right?" said Indra in

250

American slang.

"You shut up," Jeff yelled.

"Jeff!" exclaimed Laura. "How can you talk that way after what you've seen?"

"I've seen nothing," said Jeff. "Just a few tricks. Your problem is that you believe all this—this bullshit. Houdini could do the same thing." He got up and brushed off his pants with a show of unconcern, but Laura could see he was disturbed and frightened.

"What will you do about Carlos?" she asked. "Will you tell him about Stan?"

"No," he replied, shifting his weight fretfully and looking hard at Laura. "Well—are you coming? At least if you have to get involved with these bla—" He caught himself about to say blacks. "If you must get involved with Indians, then marry that Sikh. He's certainly better than this one."

"Jeff, you don't know what you're saying." Laura felt waves of rage coming from Indra and was afraid for Jeff's life. "Please leave."

"He wants killing," Indra muttered.

"What?" said Jeff.

"Killing," said Indra aloud, tossing the pistol back to him. "You may need this where you are headed. Not for your friend Carlos. There is another, a woman—very dangerous."

Jeff was unnerved. How could he know? It was impossible. "You mean Kamala?" he said incredulously.

Indra smiled, nodding.

Laura looked surprised. "Who's Kamala?"

"He knows," Jeff faltered. "Ask him."

"Yes, Kamala. You know what Kamala means?"

Jeff shook his head.

"It means desire. Desire with the big D as you say. Take the gun," he said. "You may need it."

"But who *is* she?" said Laura.

"A friend of Sundaram's," Jeff snapped. "Why should I be afraid of her?" he asked Indra.

"Because she is the mirror. Your own actions, bouncing back, will catch you up." Gazing at the fire, Indra tapped a log lightly with his chimtah, and looked suddenly old, like a very old woman. "There are certain people who should never come to India and you are one of them." He paused, frowning at Jeff. "I can see that you do not believe me."

"What if I kill her with this?" Jeff said, bouncing the gun in his hand.

"Yes, you can try it," Indra answered, "but she is your mirror. I think you will not be successful. It does not balance out."

"We'll see," said Jeff and slipped the revolver into his belt. "Maybe

251

I'll see you later?" he added to Laura; and, crawling across the ledge disappeared into the morning mist that had enveloped the mountain.

His eyes closed and his face full of pain, Indra sat motionless at the fire.

"Why did you try to do anything at all with him?" Laura asked.

"For the same reason I took away the tumor of that ridiculous Elizabeth. It's my duty. But your Jeff isn't ready, can't begin to get out this time, and now he will go backwards. Anyhow, I tried. It's my duty to try to help anyone who comes to this fire. That's the rule. I'm not to go out, not to proselytize in any way. But I cannot turn anyone away."

"Even a 'low-caste rascal'?"

"Even an outcaste," Indra replied. "The caste business is all my immersion in this particular life—I was born in a high-caste body. But for us sanyasins there is really no caste, just as there is no world." He laughed. "Simple, isn't it?"

"Should I go with him?"

"No!" said Indra emphatically. "You cannot help him. He is far more powerful than you. He would destroy your soul—what you have built up so far."

"Who is this Kamala?"

"She is his *fate*. He has come all the way to India to meet his fate. See the play—is it not wonderful to watch?" He leveled his eyes at her. "Don't get mixed up in his fate. You have more important work."

"Shall I stay here?"

Indra gazed at her and sighed. "Relax. Stop thinking you're doing anything. We will do morning prayers. Then I will prepare food."

Standing up, he stretched, and gazed out to where the sea shone like a silver blue ribbon on the western horizon. "You can almost see the breakers rolling in on the beach. It makes me want to go," he said.

A warm breeze brought the scent of wild flowers from the jungle. They watched a leopard crouched on the cliff below, its tail twitching, waiting to attack something.

"How beautiful this place is," Laura said.

"Nothing is beautiful," Indra replied. "It only seems that way. It is neither beautiful nor ugly. The sea appears beautiful from here, but if you drink it you will die and in a storm it may drown you. The smell of the flower seems lovely, but it goes away. The flower will die, you might get asthma from it or a rash. The leopard is watching the monkey. It is hungry. When you call something beautiful, it is a function of your own desire." He paused, gazing at her. "Now do you understand? It is the same desire which is catching up now with your friend in the form of a high-class Malawa prostitute." Indra laughed. "She has even been given the name Kamala!" He laughed again. "If he knew Sanskrit, he would be warned."

After morning prayers Indra prepared a breakfast of tea and hot bread made in the fire.

"Did you really push Stan off?" Laura asked while they were eating.

"No," he said, "but I'm going to have to do it. It's the only way. There's no time for him to learn. And it's important for us that he be cured." He chewed his bread thoughtfully.

Was she to take him literally or figuratively, Laura asked herself, the way he lived, it was impossible to separate the two. For her, his very being was a commingling of impossible opposites.

"He's too bright," Indra said. "He's a genius, a siddha—a man of power—like me. All your Western scientists—your Einstein, your Oppenheimer, your Max Planck—they are all siddhas. But because they do not follow the rules, because they are impure, because they use their powers, or worse, hire themselves out to politicians ... Because of these things, they are the worst devils. We call them asuras. Asura is a greatly gifted siddha who has gone wrong. Like your Satan. They are the black magicians of our time. Especially that Oppenheimer, he should have known better, he knew the rules. He had received plenty of training from us. Unfortunately, his guru, one of us, did not know how to persuade him, to make him understand. He used words. You have to know how to make magic shows, to frighten them to their senses." Indra sighed. "Otherwise, no one will believe."

"How can I stop desiring then?" asked Laura.

"By worshipping," he said.

"Worshipping what?"

"Anything. Everything. Different things have different results, take you on different routes. But they all lead to the same place. *It* shines through everything—diamond, mud, rich, poor, animal, vegetable—you just have to see the many faces of *It*. They are neither good nor bad nor beautiful nor ugly.

"And remember that the world which you imagine is so real, is created by your own desire—the desire to keep this." Indra grabbed at his flesh, then yawned. "You must go now, but do not leave the mountain, and return to me in forty-eight hours."

She looked at him quizzically.

"Sit back and watch the play, dear Uma, sit back and watch the play. You are not to become involved. Your path is in another direction."

*   *   *

Laura made her way back across the cliff. Indra fiddled with his fire and was glad to be alone again. Westerners with their endless questions exhausted him—always so serious, no sense of humor or feeling. And now that animal Stan, he should be about ready.

Reaching the head of the passageway under the temple, Indra lifted the stone a crack so that he could observe his patient unseen. Two motionless columns of flesh were all he could see—two white hairy legs and two pinched feet. The sight disgusted him. "Leave this animal to his own fate. Why should I intercede?" he thought. But he knew that it was not his doing, what he had to do he did. The voices of his guru and his guru's guru backwards in time were directing him. They had trained him to watch the signs. The signs told him. His training was correct, the best since the age of six. Everything at the proper time, from the most secret and highest. His mother had seen to that. It was not his desire to save anyone. As a matter of fact, he preferred cultivating roses. But his duty was kindliness, even when kindliness might take a drastic form. The man had come to be cured. He would cure him.

"Are you all right?" Indra asked, pushing up the rock. "You have had 'a rough night' as they say, eh?"

Moaning, Stan collapsed at Indra's feet. "I've had a terrible night. Terrible!"

"So, you have seen what a hopeless animal you are, yes? You have seen it?"

Stan looked up.

Indra could tell he was ready. "You want to confess to me," he said, "like they do in that Roman Church. It's not necessary for you to do that. I already know."

"But my life," Stan said grimacing, "what I call my life. This series of stupid mistakes . . . I have seen it and more, I . . ."

Indra raised his hand. "I know it, all of it. I know all your life, you needn't tell me. You need not explain to me."

Recognizing for the first time that this barefoot, naked man might be his equal and more, Stan smiled weakly. "This world—is it all nothing then?"

"It is all nothing," replied Indra. "No Thing."

"Then why can't I end it here and now?"

"You can," said Indra casually.

"But I can't, I'm too cowardly. I wanted to last night. It would be suicide, though. Isn't that wrong?"

"You cannot end it because you are attached to it. Suicide is a relative notion. You are afraid because you believe it is something. You believe your desires.

"You Western people always oversimplify. Your teachers lost touch with the real thing centuries ago. They were made to lose touch with it by bigots like Aristotle."

"Is that so?" said Stan, realizing the implication.

"Yes, it is so. The secrets were too final for them, too final for the suppressed masses of the time. Aristotle even sent spies to watch his pupil

Alexander when he came here—to see that he didn't get it."

"Get what?"

"The truth."

"You mean our science doesn't give us Truth?"

"No."

"What is it then?"

"A Pandora's box of cosmic dimensions," sighed Indra. "You people are just wizards of a new order, manifesting illusion and more illusion by different means. You have the secret of mathematics but that's a cul de sac."

"And our instruments and all the inventions?"

"All mirrors—they do what they are designed to do, that's all."

"But what about this?" Stan pointed to his body.

"An instrument too—*the instrument* of instruments. Did you not see last night how it can be tuned, how it can receive?"

Stan nodded, unable to meet Indra's glance.

"You people who go by the name scientist are all second-class sorcerers. You need tools to perform your manifestations, exterior aids. Mind you, there is nothing wrong in it. What is wrong is that you have power and none of the training that *must* go with its use. And that you can learn only from a teacher of the first class." He laughed. "You only get it through tapas."

"What is that?"

"Austerities."

"What do they do?"

"Was your last night not somewhat austere?" Indra smiled.

"Yes."

"Austerities reveal the truth and lead to kindliness. No man should be empowered until he is kindly. That is one thing that separates first class from second. For us it is a prerequisite. For you that element of the teaching was lost centuries ago."

"And so?"

"See what is happening: Hiroshima—and birth control. Extremes, explosions, destruction of balance."

Stan looked up. "Can nothing be done?"

"Nothing!" replied Indra emphatically. "It has already been written."

Lying there in his jockey shorts, Stan was suddenly revolted by his scratched and dirty body. He could smell the poisons discharging from all its openings. "I wish I could jump," he said, gesturing outside.

"You can," said Indra simply. "Why not?"

"I told you, I have no courage."

"I will give you the courage," Indra said. "Nothing will happen to you because I am here. That is why you have come to me."

Stan felt something pour into him and fill him up—a sort of happiness and energy he had never known before. Trembling, he reached for Indra's hand. "Will you take me to the edge?" he asked.

Indra gripped Stan's cold and perspiring hand and pulled him to his feet.

"Do not be afraid," he said. "I am with you."

"Then I am going," Stan said flooded with energy. With a smile he released Indra's hand, went to one of the arches, and looked out over the precipice.

"Go ahead," said Indra, his smile like that of a mother watching a son's first steps. "You're not going anywhere. Go ahead, jump."

Stan paused, gazing at Indra, felt his whole system shift into a kind of super clarity, and jumped into space.

*   *   *

Indra bounded across the parapet in time to see Stan hit the rocks about three hundred feet below. He sighed. Why had he allowed himself to become involved with these people? It was all the trick of that old Tibetan witch, Dorje's aunt. Why had he let her complicate things with this girl and let the girl bring him two more. He knew why he had to, yet he felt vexed and put upon. And now, so much work, a work he had performed once as a young man with his first guru. He had been given explicit instructions in it again by his second teacher, the old woman, but he had only done it once more since her going. It would be a gamble and a fight.

Quickly making his way down inside the mountain, he squeezed through an opening in the cliff and started climbing down a steep path leading to the place where Stan had landed. A vulture had already spied Stan's body and was circling. Indra shouted it away. A great hornbill, like a giant bat, interested in the possibility of a meal, soared nearby. There was no time to lose—a tricky business this, especially in the south, with the heat. Usually it was possible only in cool climates, where the cells didn't rapidly decompose.

In moments he had reached the crumpled form. The fall had been broken by a bush halfway up the cliff and so there was no blood, which was good. After finding no pulse he examined the body thoroughly, recalling all the knowledge at his command: multiple concussions, compound fractures, etc.

Then he lifted the body onto his back—(what a stench—these meat eaters, he thought, disgusting practice)—quickly scrambled up the face of the cliff to his cave and placed Stan on his own sitting place. Removing Stan's jockey shorts, he washed the entire body carefully, prepared a place opposite his own and covered Stan's body with ash.

Sitting down in front of the fire, following the ancient practice until the energy flow inside him reached an effective level, he built up his fire and made offerings to it. Noting the angle of the sun, he judged not more than one hour had passed. There was still time. Another hour and although he might still bring him back, the memory would be gone.

Taking up his small two-sided drum, Indra stripped naked, moved around the body as he'd been trained, and after about ten minutes, jumped on it with both feet, and pressing gently at first, let himself go until he was dancing with full force on the limbs and torso. After a few minutes he could feel the breath coming back. Through his feet he could feel the slow rhythm as the body began to breathe again, and color returned. Now was the crucial moment. The head was his biggest worry because there had been concussions.

Kneeling beside the newly breathing body, he grasped the head between his large hands, charged now with a superhuman energy, and pressed the skull lightly with his palms. After about an hour, the mouth began to twitch, working its way into a smile.

Then the eyes opened.

"Are you all right?" Indra said into the eyes that stared at him as if from another place.

"Ah, ah, I, I ..." Stan's voice faltered. "I ... Ah ... Where am I?" A look of disbelief spread over his face. "I ... you ..."

"Yes, is it not as I said it would be?"

"But I'm here," Stan whispered. "Didn't I ... I did jump, didn't I?"

"Get up," said Indra gruffly. "I want to see if my work is finished."

Stan got up at once but his legs crumpled. Indra caught and held him. "Do you have much pain?" he asked.

Stan shook his head. "Only numbness and pins and needles in the arms and legs."

"Good," said Indra. Letting Stan down gently he covered him with a blanket, and threw a cloth around himself. "Do not try to move just now. You must remain perfectly still here with me for thirty-six hours. Then you will be all right. You may have more aches and pains, we will see."

"Am I dead?" Stan whispered.

"In a manner of speaking," said Indra coolly, smiling at Stan's radiant face. "You were an extreme case. I had to use extreme measures. And ..." He paused, looking at Stan. "There are certain conditions that are now imposed upon you."

Stan nodded.

"First of all, your cancer is gone. Your body is new again. Although you may be only dimly aware of it, you've been blown clean of all the old things, but ..."

"But ...?"

"You are wedded to me."

"Wedded?"

"Or welded," Indra said smiling. "Whatever you like. But you are in my power—totally. That is not a boast or a threat, it is simply a fact. It is what happens."

"It's the price I pay?"

"If that's the way you want to think of it." Indra sighed. "But you must understand, otherwise..."

"Otherwise?"

"I'll snuff you out."

Stan nodded. "And what are the other conditions?" he asked.

"Second, and just as important, you must never *never* reveal to anyone the details of what has happened here, even if you manage to piece them together. This is not for the average person to know; if you reveal anything your cancer will return. I will now be able to teach you how to do what has been done through me.

"Third, you will return to your own country. You will dispose of your wealth anonymously in some trust arrangement to be used to better the lot of aged women—direct gifts."

"Like my mother you mean?"

"Correct."

"And then..."

"Aha, and then my friend you will change your name and get a job—male nurse, I think they call it—in the cancer ward of a big hospital. You will work as a male nurse for some time." He paused, tapping the fire with his chimtah. "These things you will do. I will be in touch with you later with further instructions. You are being led now toward liberation."

"And will I see you again?"

"Yes."

"Do you know when that will be?"

"Yes."

"Can you tell me?"

"When the time comes I will be in touch with you."

Stan was filled with awe, exhilarated by a clarity and happiness he had never known. Everything he looked at seemed to sparkle and shine.

"Why did you save me?" he asked. "Because Laura Weatherall asked you to?"

"We are given our directions in strange ways," Indra answered. "But I didn't save you. I'm only an agent. You are saved it is true, and more than you know. You became fearless, that is half of it. Perhaps you were saved so that there will be someone of your kind, some 'scientist,' who understands, who has crossed over and come back.

"There is another point I have forgotten." He looked at Stan. "Before,

258

you had no feelings—not that you were neutral—you just had no feelings at all. You were outside of everything. Now, in order to cross over you must go through your feelings. And so I am requesting—in fact I insist—that you marry and have children.''

Stan gulped.

"Yes, yes, you must learn that attachment and go through it.'' Indra grinned. "Am I too hard on you?''

"Is that all?''

Indra looked thoughtful. "There is still time to save that animal, the one you caused to come here.''

"Jeff?''

"Yes. It is my personal wish that you destroy the LSD you brought. It gives too much perception without preparation, too much empowerment without tapas. It will only harm. And if you intercept Jeff in time, you might be able to save him.''

"You want him back here?''

"Yes. No. Yes, no. I am undecided. It is not clear to me at this point.''

"One other question,'' Stan said. "Can I be killed now?''

"Just now it would be quite easy. In a few days, next to impossible—except, of course, by me.'' Indra smiled.

XIII

CARLOS PACED THE HOUSE like a caged lion trying to figure out where they could have stashed the acid. He was sure they'd all gone crazy and hated them. So much money; so stupid about it, especially Jeff with his superstar complex. And now Stan was going to die. So stupid, always busy with some project. Now the project was cancer. Whew! He, Carlos, would need money and here was the chance—all that acid in three suitcases. But where?

Then it dawned on him. "Ah, Carlos, you are being very stupid. Of course, it's at Grey's." Sitting down on the veranda he lit a joint and stared out at the sea. He remembered seeing the bags loaded. Then he didn't see them again. When they stopped at Grey's house, what had happened? Nothing. That meant Jeff had left them in the car until he could talk to Grey. But how to find them. Grey was a dealer, a smuggler; if only Wasu would come to Goa before they got back . . . then everything would work just fine.

That afternoon Carlos saw Grey on the beach.

"They weren't so crazy as to take that acid with them, were they?" he asked casually.

Grey, busy making out with a chick, flashed his rings in the sun. "Don't worry, it's safe at my place," he said over his shoulder.

His guess confirmed, Carlos went for a swim, ambled back naked to the house enjoying the looks he got, sat down at the phone and booked a call to Bombay. As he finished his shower the phone rang. He lit a cigarette and answered.

"Hello, Wasu," he said into the phone. "Carlos, yeah man."

"Yeah, Carlos, yeah, it is me."

"How are you? Yeah, I'm in Goa, yeah . . . I think I can sell you that stuff. Yes, you want to come? You were just getting ready to come? Coincidence, eh? Bringing who? A female friend, yes. O.K., tomorrow. Jeff? No, he isn't here. No. Gone south with Stan, but he's coming back. Yeah, O.K. See you soon."

Carlos hung up the phone. When he saw Wasu Grey would shit. He would have to give up the acid. Otherwise anything might happen to

260

him—he was too vulnerable. Wasu could just take it and Grey would owe Stan a lot of bread. Carlos sat smoking, his hand still on the phone, weighing the possibilities of a showdown with Grey.

*   *   *

Two days later Wasu, Kamala, and Wasu's two bodyguards arrived in a big Mercedes with tinted windows. Kamala was feeling ragged. The drive from Bombay had been tiring. Though she knew him well, she had never thought she would find herself traveling with Wasu, a thoroughly disgusting person. Such noises he was always making, so much spitting and stopping to piss all the time drove her mad.

"Goa always depresses me," she said out loud. "All these pigs, everywhere you look, dirty pigs eating shit!"

Half-asleep, Wasu grunted.

"Wasu, creep of creeps," Kamala whispered under her breath. She had recently learned the word creep from Sundar and found the sound of it to her liking. It exactly fitted many of the men she had been forced to deal with in her life. This one was the worst. Creep of Creeps: it was a good title.

Wasu batted flies from his nose.

Kamala frowned and thought of her twin motives for making this horrible trip: the first to revenge herself on Jeff, the second to get some or all of Mr. Stanley's drug for the Baba. She must make them work together so that both ends were achieved. It was not her style to plan. She willed things and they happened. She thought of Jeff's body which still held a strong attraction for her. "But he is too filled with pride," she reflected. "No one will ever be able to harness that wild horse; something not nice is going to happen to him, I think."

She had told Wasu that Ananda Baba attached great importance to her mission, trusting that he would get the point. The Baba was the only person in the world Wasu feared: when the Baba prayed for him things went well, if the Baba was displeased with him bad luck came. On this fear depended the negotiations she would have to make over Baba's share of the acid. She had been trained to act on the moment—then let the moments come! She hoped it wouldn't be a long stay.

The car stopped in front of a large pink villa. Wasu woke up, the two bodyguards got out and opened the doors. Just as they were hoisting Wasu out of the car, Carlos came out, bare-chested and wearing a bright green lunghi.

"Hello Carlos," Wasu said, embracing him like a woman. "This is Kamala," he added over his shoulder.

Carlos saw at once that Kamala was miffed, broke away from Wasu and bowed formally to her. "Great piece of ass," he thought. "Wasu has

261

pretty good taste. It is a big house," he said to her warmly, "I have prepared a special room for you." He looked deep into Kamala's eyes before turning back to Wasu. "You'll be on this side of the house—there is a separate suite." He motioned the bodyguards ahead with Wasu's luggage. "You follow them—I'll just show Kamala to her room."

Kamala admired his lithe walk as he took her up the stairway of the central hall and along a corridor to an old-fashioned room with polished teakwood floors, campaign chests, and a brass four-poster bed with a canopy.

"I hope this will satisfy your needs," he said, smiling graciously at her. He strode into the bathroom. "You might like to freshen yourself after such a long trip—I will start the bath." He scanned her body. "Is there anything more I can do for you?"

"So you are Mr. Stanley's friend," Kamala said. "And how is Mr. Stanley?"

"Oh, he is not too good." Carlos tried to sound stupid. "He is very sick, you know."

"Yes, I know, I was with him at Ananda Baba's."

"I will see you later," he said, leaving the room hastily before she could ask him any more questions.

Having bathed, Wasu sprawled out comfortably on a big bed. The bodyguards had replaced their city clothes with lunghis and one was massaging the dark robust flesh of Wasu who, puffing a long Havana cigar, grunted appreciatively.

Carlos came in and sat down. Wasu picked up a newspaper which he pretended to read. Carlos compared himself with Wasu. "How could this stupid man have learned to read," he wondered, "while I, Carlos, have been unable!"

"So where's the stuff?" said Wasu all of a sudden, hoping to get the truth that way.

"I have it, don't worry." Carlos smiled blandly. He wanted to talk to Grey first. "But who is this Kamala?" he asked, to take Wasu's mind off the stash.

"A most high-class bitch," Wasu whispered. "Very, very expensive—famous in all Hindustan. She is devotee of Ananda Baba. I am also Ananda Baba devotee. He brings Wasu plenty good luck. I give him plenty money."

"But why she is coming?" Carlos asked.

"To see your Jeff—I think something she has against him. Also, the Baba wished to possess some of this LSD. Your Mr. Stanley, he is giving to Baba. Baba has tried and he likes, he is sending this Kamala to me."

"She's a beautiful chick."

"I don't like her," Wasu muttered. "She is too smart for a woman, she is like a witch. She treats Wasu not very good, like her dog." He paused, studying Carlos. "You like to make friendship with her, eh? Well you can try. She is too stuck-up, one very hard to get lady, very expensive. She might do with you for fun though, I do not know. Me, I won't pay her price. Anyhow, she don't want me—I'm too low-caste for her, too dark."

As soon as he could, Carlos left Wasu and found Grey lounging on his front porch. "How ya doin' Carlos," Grey said as Carlos sat down.

"Not too well. It is so hot and now a friend has come with a woman and two servants and I will have to feed them. Do you know someone who can cook?"

"I saw the car," said Grey. "Who is your friend?"

"His name is Wasu, he is from Bombay."

Grey's face changed color.

"You know him?" asked Carlos.

"Yeah," said Grey, "if anyone can really know him. You mean *the* Wasu, big Bombay rackets?"

Carlos nodded. "He is very interested to buy the acid. I think you are keeping it for Mr. Stanley. If you will just give it to me then the deal will be finished and I won't have to feed them. He eats a lot. Did you say you knew a cook?"

Grey remembered Stan's warning about letting Carlos have the stash. He had to play for time.

"I'd like to see him," he said, getting up. "Come on, let's go see Wasu."

Carlos remained cool. "Sure," he replied.

While one of the bodyguards prepared food for him on a small camp stove, Wasu amused himself with a copy of *Oui*.

"You are cooking for yourself?" Carlos said as he and Grey came in.

"I am always cooking for myself. It is an old habit. You can't trust people's food, too many poisons. He has to eat everything he cooks in front of me, from my plate—Ha!" He smiled at Grey. "My friend Grey, how are you? Come and sit beside me." Grey sprawled over the edge of the bed. "I have not seen you for a year. Why you not see Wasu when in Bombay, eh?" He slapped Grey's leg. "How's the cocaine business?"

"Slow right now—end of season," Grey replied, fishing in a pocket of his pants. "But I have something for you." He extended an ornate silver box toward Wasu. "Here."

Wasu took the box and opened it. It contained an ounce of pure cocaine.

"Tank you, tank you wary much," said Wasu, obviously impressed. "Carlos, see," he said rolling his eyes with pleasure, "tonight you bring me two, three, these hippy girls, see? Eh, Grey? You tell em big Bombay smuggler, big cock, with two big bodyguards, he got good cocaine, wants freakie time, give good money too."

Carlos was annoyed. He wanted to finish the deal quickly in case Stan

263

returned earlier than expected. Wasu had agreed to a price forty percent above what Stan expected. It would not do for them to meet.

Grey looked pleased. "There are some far-out chicks here," he said. "I'll put out the word for them to meet Carlos at my house, he can bring them over." Grey's gamble had worked, he'd got another day. He'd have to hand the acid over if Wasu started demanding it. It wasn't cool to go against him. Anyhow, the cocaine would buy some time.

*   *   *

Of the six girls who showed up at Grey's Carlos picked three, dropped some acid on them and took them over to Wasu. All night long grunts and groans, curses and sighs floated through the fragrant jasmine-scented gardens that surround the house.

The next day Wasu was completely knocked out and Grey, who had expected some sort of showdown with Carlos, was relieved when night fell and no word had come from the house next door.

The following morning one of Wasu's bodyguards arrived at Grey's with the message that Wasu was waiting for him.

"Very good coke," said Wasu with a wink, extending the empty silver box to Grey. "You got more?"

"Sure. Guess you had a good time, eh?"

Wasu didn't answer. "I had deal with Mr. Stanley," he said, leveling his eyes at Grey, "for some of the drug he is distributing. Now Mr. Stanley is away and Carlos says you are keeping it for him?"

"Me?" Grey said. "No, I don't have it. Carlos, what gave you the idea I have it? It must be in this house."

"I have searched this house," Carlos said menacingly.

"I thought Stan was here for some cure. I don't really know him—Jeff is my friend. You say you had a deal with Stan?"

"He's lying!" snarled Carlos.

"Now, come on Carlos, do me a favor and drop dead, eh?" Grey got up. "I got enough hassles without you laying trips on me. I don't keep track of other people's luggage. You're sure they didn't leave it in Panjim?"

"I saw the luggage come here," Carlos said emphatically. "It is a big house and I have searched, nothing is locked up, the bags are not here. You even told me they were with you."

"I did?" Grey said blankly.

"Yes."

"I must have been stoned."

"Don't fight," grunted Wasu. "It's too hot. Grey?"

"Yes?"

"Get more coke, eh? I have so many friends here. My friend Gonzales,

Chief of Police—you know him?''

"Yeah," said Grey, "he comes around the house sometimes."

"I have called him," Wasu went on. "He is coming tonight with two of his men. I need more coke and six girls—you can do?"

"O.K." Grey nodded. "How about some nice French ones?"

"Anything you say." Wasu leered. "I like anything!"

After he left Wasu, Grey began to get nervous. Wasu could blow the whole scene if he didn't get what he wanted. The bags would have to be gotten out of the house, but how? It wouldn't be that easy. For sure, the house was being watched.

Carlos had decided to share his profit with Grey and caught up with him outside. "Listen man, Mr. Stanley is going to die," Carlos whispered confidentially. "He may never come back from this trip—spitting and coughing so much blood when he left! Wasu has too much cash—dollars, can't get it out of the country now, but this way he can turn it into rupees. Our part would be twenty percent. It is something to think about, no?" He grabbed Grey's arm. "If Wasu gets mad he'll juss come to your house and take it. You'll see. Then nobody wins, eh? He is very strong with police here, good friends. They are always the biggest crooks, right? We should look out for ourselves."

*   *   *

As Jeff hurried over the mountain path, stones cut at his feet and the bandsaw fronds of the cane plants ripped at his shirt. Despite his agility, he hadn't gone barefoot in years. A warm mist rose from the steaming jungle and the gnarled trunks and limbs of the stunted oaks, green with moss and vines, seemed frozen in some crazy dance meant to scare him.

"So you have been out to see the guru and so early in the morning, too?" shouted Prakash from a pool near one of the temples, where he was saying his morning prayers. "That is good, very good to see the guru first thing in the morning." He rolled his eyes. "And in the bare feet too, very good. That way you get the shakti."

"My boots went over the cliff," Jeff replied.

"Oh ho," smiled Prakash, "that is the shakti also. She took them away from you. What a pity. I noticed them, they were very expensive I think. But of course on this mountaintop, as it is holy ground, leather is not worn here."

"Ho hum," muttered Jeff under his breath, not interested in Prakash's preaching, and headed for the room he'd been given in an old stable.

"And where are you going now?" called Prakash. "Come, they are going to serve breakfast. It is time to eat."

"I'm leaving, I'm going," Jeff said over his shoulder.

"So soon?" Prakash's eyebrows shot up.

265

"It's important I go back to Goa—I have some business there to take care of."

Prakash's face took on a conspiratorial look. "Oho, gentleman," he whispered, "I think you must be a big smuggler then. I like the smugglers—they give the large donation for the temple. Then the goddess She gives plenty good luck. They bring good foreign wash-and-wear cloth for the first-class pant. I wear the pant when I go to visit my cousins in Bombay," he said proudly.

"My business is real estate," said Jeff coolly, not wanting to get involved in Prakash's inner movie.

"Oh, what a pity," Prakash said sadly. "But you must not go now. First eat. You can't go without eating. I will go also after taking the meal."

Jeff wasn't exactly hungry. He was running, he had to keep going.

"I'd like to start before it gets too hot," he said. "I'm planning to leave immediately." He went to his room and gathered his things together as Prakash watched from the doorway.

"You must give these people a few rupees each," he said, realizing Jeff wouldn't understand that he, Prakash, was also supposed to receive a good sum for his services. But he could collect double from the red-haired woman. "So, my friend, have a good walk down, perhaps I'll see you at the bottom." He waved cheerfully and disappeared.

Once on the path Jeff soon realized it was going to be harder getting down than going up. While he stumbled along behind the coolie he'd hired to carry his bag, the coolie bounced ahead from rock to rock. To make matters worse leeches, dormant in the dry season, had been awakened by recent showers and, hungry for blood, attached themselves in numbers to his legs and feet. As he descended the heat increased, and he began to sweat and had to fend off huge tropical hornets and ticks that dropped from the trees and burrowed into his skin. After about four hours he reached a red dirt path where the coolie, having arrived much earlier, lay asleep in the shade of a giant fern.

By the time Jeff arrived in Kalpura the evening had come on even hotter and more breathless than the day. Inquiring about onward transportation he learned that there were no more buses until morning. A taxi, however, had brought some pilgrims in from the coast. They would be leaving after the evening puja, which was in progress. The driver asked Jeff his destination.

"Goa," replied Jeff. The driver rolled his eyes as if Goa were the moon, but after Jeff reached into his pocket and extracted a ten-rupee note, the driver decided to take him.

"It will be past ten when we reach the coast," the driver warned. "No cars will be traveling north from there—too many dacoits these days."

By the time they reached the coastal town taxis had stopped running and the drivers were asleep in their back seats. He would have to go to a hotel, the driver said, and took him to a dirty Victorian affair overlooking the sea, a relic of a bygone era when people with money had once traveled in India. Now it was a brothel of sorts for local politicians, army and police officers, and various traveling businessmen, who sat stolidly drinking whiskey under bare bulbs, in a green dining room with peeling paint. Simple-minded fat girls, trying to act fancy, waited to be taken into the rooms.

A waiter in a soiled white uniform brought some fried fish and rice covered with hot curry sauce the color and consistency of vomit. Jeff went to his room without eating. The cement walls smelled dank and there were cigarette burns and water marks on the furniture. The wooden doors separating the rooms had peep holes that had been filled up and painted over. The bed was a slab of wood with a soiled foam rubber mattress. He took a bath from a bucket, spread a lunghi over the mattress, and lay down under a creaking ceiling fan. Through the thin walls he could hear the squeals of the girls as they pursued their vocations.

Here in the south the woman was the aggressor and was supposed to jump around on top of the man to excite him until he humped her like a sow as quickly as possible. Immediately following this performance the girl would be treated to a big dinner, sometimes her only payment.

As the racket of love-making subsided, Jeff fell asleep, only to be awakened by a horde of bedbugs. After throwing the mattress onto the floor he lay down on the board and drifted into a dream. He was riding somewhere on an elephant. The elephant was going at breakneck speed and he, Laura, and Carlos seemed to be tied onto the animal. Like pieces of baggage they were wrapped up in sheets and blankets and tied so they couldn't move. He remembered thinking later how odd it was that Carlos was along—Carlos whom he so disliked, a fellow passenger on that great lumbering beast careening across India.

At cockcrow he was awake, muscles aching. Hating the fact that his body had been attacked, he washed and examined his various bites and cuts, dressed, paid his bill to a sleepy boy at the counter, and carried his bag a few blocks to the center of town. The taxi drivers were just rolling out of their cabs to piss in the stinking open sewers and stumbled into tea shops. Jeff had some tea and sat in an old taxi while the driver waited for more passengers. After nine more people were stuffed in, they started. The sun beat mercilessly down. As he stared out over the sea, Jeff made his plan: he would pick up his luggage and the acid at Goa, throw some of it into the sea, and get on a plane for Dubai. If there was enough bread in it and if Hadji wasn't too crazy, he might even get married there—who could tell?

* * *

When he arrived late the next morning he wasn't surprised to see Kamala having drinks with Wasu and Carlos on the porch of the pink villa. Though Jeff had disliked Indra, he hadn't been so stupid as to be blind to his power. He remembered the warning and was prepared for—whatever. When Carlos saw Jeff, he realized with resentment that his plan would have to be changed.

"Ah," said Wasu, standing up and extending a beefy hand, "the Big Man has arrived."

"Long trip, I'm bushed." Jeff said with a faint smile and a glance at Kamala. "Let me just clean up a bit, I'll be right down."

"He doesn't want to talk," grunted Wasu after Jeff had gone into the house.

"Leave him to me," put in Kamala wisely, "there is something between us. Have no fear, Wasu, I will see that we get what we have come for."

Wasu rolled his eyes and smiled broadly. "I see. That is good. You make him understand, eh? You tell him Wasu's offer is benefit to everyone, is fair offer. That he should agree. Otherwise..." He spat noisily into the sand.

"We will see," answered Kamala vaguely.

Carlos realized Kamala intended to cut him out. She would do business directly through Jeff. Now he had to get on her side so she would give him something when she was finished. And after all, wasn't Wasu his friend.

Jeff showered, smoked a joint in his room, and when he returned an hour later wearing only a cotton lunghi, looked cool and relaxed.

"Have a cold drink before lunch," Wasu invited. "Your friend Grey, he is asking us to lunch at his house."

"How's Stan?" Carlos asked.

"He's there with Laura, sitting on top of a mountain. I think the yogi might cure him—he's seeing him now. We'll know any day. Laura said she'd phone."

Carlos was sure Jeff was lying, that something else had happened. "How come you didn't stay?" he asked.

"Not my scene," replied Jeff. "I didn't get along with the guru, it was just a waste of time there for me." He gestured at the glittering sea. "Much better to sit here ... nice beach, good company ..."

"Too many pigs," muttered Kamala.

Wasu stretched his big body and got up grunting. "Then we go to lunch—you will come?" He poked Jeff.

"Think I'll go up and rest, I'm beat," Jeff yawned. "I'll see you later in the afternoon, O.K.?" He looked directly at Kamala.

A pang of jealousy struck Carlos and put him in a black rage. Why did Jeff get all the women while he, Carlos, did all the work?

*   *   *

In the quiet of the late Indian afternoon Kamala scratched at Jeff's door and found him awake, lying in bed.

"So you've come for your revenge," he whispered, taking her hand. "You look more beautiful than ever, if that's possible."

She sat on the edge of the bed and gazed at him. "You know I could have you killed for what you did," she said after a while. "I still have the marks."

"I suppose," he said, excited by her anger. No woman had ever been able to stay angry with him for long. He played gently with her sari until her breasts were exposed.

"You still have the feeling for Kamala, yes?" she said, letting herself relax against his body. He took her hand and guided it onto his erection, then drew her up to him, stroking her soft skin.

"Why were you so bad to me? It was not nice of you. See, there is still a scar," she murmured, displaying her voluptuous buttocks. He let his hand go across it, turning her slightly so the tip of his penis rubbed against her.

"You are too big for me," she said, holding him back. "You will hurt me again when you get excited."

"Suck it then," he said softly.

"Don't be crazy," she retorted, staring at him. "How could I get it in my mouth? If only I had some of that, what you call it—that acid, it relaxes me."

"You've taken acid?" Jeff was curious.

"It is a long story." She smiled. "Don't you have some? The Baba, he would like to have a large amount of it."

"Whew!" Jeff thought. "So she was after it too." He didn't want to talk business now. "Stan stashed it somewhere after we got here," he sighed. "I think Carlos knows where it is."

"Carlos has told us you know where it is," she said, fingering his nipples.

"Carlos is lying," Jeff said, pulling her close to him.

Kamala straightened up. "I must go, it is time for my nap."

He caught her by the waist, thrust his hand between her thighs.

"No, no," she said, getting up and pulling her sari about her. "Do not try to force me—if you get rough again you'll regret it."

She stood by the bed, looking down at him. "I find you so sexy, it's too bad you are so stubborn. Perhaps you can refresh your memory about where Mr. Stanley put the drug. This Wasu is a terrible man and he's getting impatient."

After he was sure no one would see him, Jeff slipped quietly out of the

269

house, went to Grey's and found him alone in the kitchen feeding vegetables into a juicer.

"Looks like they're after it," said Grey, handing him a glass of juice. "Can't you get it out, or can't you let Carlos sell it to Wasu?"

"And never see any of the bread ourselves?" Jeff planned to appeal to Grey's greed and not to reveal that he intended to throw most of the acid into the Arabian Sea. "They're watching me like hawks."

"They're watching this place too," Grey said, frowning. "Wasu could have me searched at any time. He's tied into the police. All he has to do is give the word. If they find it here, there's a big hassle, then I get kicked out of Goa and the cops give Wasu the acid for less than Carlos would charge him. I think you should make a deal with Carlos."

"Carlos is a shit," Jeff replied. "Don't worry, I'll have it out soon."

"But how?"

"It's full moon isn't it, or almost?"

"Day after tomorrow."

"Yes."

"Then have a big party. Invite all the cops, Wasu, Kamala, Carlos. Get everybody stoned, have lots of girls. Put the Chief of Police and Wasu in a room with five or six girls, plenty of booze and coke, and douse the whole place with acid." He paused, then continued thoughtfully. "There'll be so much coming and going, cars driving in and out that no one will notice me leave. But someone must watch Kamala. That sound O.K.?"

Grey nodded. "It should work."

*   *   *

Sounds of amplifiers being tested at Grey's house floated through the palms on the sultry late afternoon breeze.

Jeff could hear the twanging in his shuttered room where he lay in bed going over his plan. He'd packed his bag and Grey had given him the key to the closet in the servants' quarters where the acid was hidden. It was time for him to go down to the beach and engage one of the drivers that hung out at the bar there. The man had to be reliable and fast. He stretched, thinking about Kamala who hadn't spoken to him in two days although he had seen her twice. He thought of Indra's warning and fingered the butt of the pistol the yogi had given him. She might have plans for him, he didn't trust her. But he had his own plans, and if he let himself worry he would lose out, he knew it. The party would be a cinch. He could drop the bags out the low window of the servants' quarter and walk a short distance to the service yard. There, all sorts of crazy people would be coming and going. He'd hardly be noticed, especially if the driver parked his car with the trunk toward the house. He would have to find one that spoke good

English.

The air was heavy and still, sweet with the odor of jasmine and incense. As the full moon rose over the palms, the sound of the surf pounding on the far off reefs blended with the music belting out of the big amplifiers on the beach, calling all who could hear to come and boogie at Grey's, where the amenities of a brothel had been coupled with the perverse delights of a madhouse.

Grey stood in what he called the study: restored Spanish Victorian with a heavy dose of Tibetan thrown in. There were furs on black tile floors and expensive tankas on the walls. In one corner a massive Chinese screen enclosed a bar.

Grey was hoping Jeff would get the stash out of the house before Wasu blew the whole scene with a search. For himself, he had hidden his coke supply in an Ajax can in the refrigerator. That was what he cared about: it was pure crystal and worth a fortune. His whole lifestyle depended on that coke. But the scene was cool: himself, his friend Mike, and six girls. The cops would be cooled out on acid and chicks. Three of the girls were delegated to watch Kamala and three to watch the refrigerator.

People were coming now, wandering across the courtyard to the study. He saw Wasu followed by Kamala, sparkling with rubies, playing the aristocrat among the strung-out hippy girls in their made-up outfits. Wasu's two bodyguards brought up the rear, eyeing the chicks hungrily. With them came the local Chief of Police, Gonzales, in a tight leather jacket, shades, and high leather boots. He dug the Western chicks Grey always had for him. He liked zooming off with them on his bike, taking them to out of the way places he knew where he could struggle with them in the warm sand.

The girls Grey had ordered for Wasu and Gonzales arrived.

"Hey Gonzales," roared Wasu jovially, "how you are liking these Western smugglers, eh?" He slapped Grey on the back. "I think I come here, live near Grey. He got good women."

Grey produced a silver box filled with coke and gave Wasu a straw.

"I don't take through the nose, I rub into the gums," Wasu said, taking a liberal pinch with his big fingers. "It works better on the gums—don't destroy the smelling."

Grey turned to offer Kamala some but she waved him away smiling. She was admiring him; he was the first Western man that puzzled her. She had never seen a Western man with painted nails. Yet if he wasn't a hedjara*, what was he?

*hedjara=queer. Kamala would use it in that sense. Hedjara refers to homosexual young men, really transvestites, who form a sub-caste in India, live apart in their own communities and do charitable and social work—also male prostitutes.

271

"Can I give you some punch," he said politely.

"Water," Kamala replied, "I can get it." She was certain that something was going to happen tonight. Instinct told her she might have to think fast and she had been well trained to take only water on such occasions. She saw Gonzales take a healthy snort of coke but noticed that Wasu's bodyguards didn't.

As soon as Grey was out of earshot, she spoke to Wasu quickly in Hindi. "Have your bodyguards leave one by one—stand at opposite corners of the house so that each can see two sides. Do not let them be seen, have them hide in the bushes. If anyone asks, say you have sent them home, that you see there is no need for them here. Do you understand my meaning?" Wasu nodded slightly. "Tell them to apprehend anyone attempting to leave with luggage."

After a while, Wasu called the two young men one at a time, instructing them as Kamala had ordered. The guards disappeared casually.

"Now we will see what happens," she murmured.

Jeff walked into the room wearing white flannels and a cream colored silk kurta. He knelt beside Kamala. "Thanks for a wonderful night last night," he whispered.

She frowned.

"In my dreams you came to me. We made love all night long."

She looked into his eyes: so beautiful—so devilish! "And such stupid pride," she thought. "I could give him everything if he would let me."

"Why do you not return with me to Ananda Baba's," she asked suddenly. "He would like you. I cannot remain here much longer. We could slip away together, you and I."

He smiled at her.

"You are in danger here," she continued. "That Carlos and Wasu—they want what you've got. If they do not get it, something not nice might happen." She looked around the crowded room. "You are all foreigners for them, sitting ducks as you say." She gazed at him seriously. "With me you will be safe. What do you say?"

Jeff looked at her searchingly. It was a proposition he hadn't expected. Indra had warned him. Was she warning him too?

"I can't stay in India," he said with a shrug. "It's not my cup of tea."

"You are leaving soon then?" she asked.

"As soon as Stan gets back," he lied. "Shouldn't be much longer."

"I see," said Kamala, sensing the lie. "He will never listen to anyone or surrender to anyone," she thought. "How sad, how troublesome—what a pity!"

The evening wore on: Wasu and Gonzales got high and went off into a bedroom with some girls. The electric strings whooped and twanged, whipping the dancers into a frenzy of self-expression. Carlos came in and sat near Kamala. Jeff could see that he was high on coke and thought it was

272

a good time to leave. He began talking to one of Grey's girls and after a while asked her to dance, smiling and nodding at Kamala as he left the room.

As soon as they were out of sight, the girl split to the dance floor. Jeff made his way unseen to the servants' quarters at the opposite end of the house, where he unlocked the closet and removed the bags containing the acid. He peered cautiously out the window he had opened earlier. It was quiet. About fifty feet away he could see the car he'd engaged. Letting the bags drop into the shadows, he climbed out the window, jumped to the ground, picked up two of the bags and had started for the car when a sharp blow landed on his neck and his legs buckled under him.

*   *   *

Carlos sat staring at Kamala. Couldn't she see he wanted her.

"Where has Wasu gone?" he asked.

"Off in some room, I think," she said coolly.

"You are going to sit here all night?"

"You think I should go out and boogie?" she said, making the word sound ridiculous.

"You come—I show you," said Carlos. "Is not hard." He wanted to move with her, feel her big tits and her belly rubbing against him.

One of the bodyguards came into the room. "We have him," he said quietly to Kamala in Hindi.

"And the bags?" Kamala yawned.

"Yes."

"Lock them in the trunk of Wasu's car."

"What do we do with the fellow? He is unconscious now but he's got a gun."

"Drag him to the other house. Strip him and leave the clothes there. Then throw him in the ocean. If he wakes up and gives trouble, shoot him," she said coldly. "Then return the gun to my room and wait for me there."

The bodyguard nodded and left.

Kamala sighed and turned to Carlos. "That Wasu is becoming so difficult, now he wants *me* to come to him! I will not. He wants more cocaine. Ugh." She gazed at him listlessly.

"You want to boogie?" he asked eagerly.

"No, no, you go boogie," she answered disdainfully and yawned again. "I may go back to the house shortly, I am feeling rather tired, the heat you know."

Grey had come back to the study with two local police officers, big tough Goan boys. He was introducing them to his girls, the ones who had been watching Kamala. He'd just been to the servants' quarters, and was

273

relieved to find the stash was gone. He offered some cocaine around to everyone. When he came to Kamala she held up her hand.

"No thanks," she sighed lazily, "I think I will go home. The sea air, you know—it makes me too sleepy."

Grey's eyes traveled her body. She caught the look. "I see you are a very interesting man, Mr. Grey," she said, smiling seductively as she got up. "I would like to see you again sometime. Perhaps you should come see me. I am at Ananda Baba's ashram these days."

Carlos got up too and stood beside her. "Do sit down, Carlos," she said. "Enjoy yourself. I am quite able to get to the house myself. It is a short walk. Good night, Mr. Grey, it was a fine party. We will meet again, I think."

Grey nodded, watching her disappear across the courtyard in the moonlight. Carlos was pissed. He wanted her. "Everybody is having her, why not me?" he thought. He ambled outside where he boogied himself across the dance floor and disappeared under the palms. He wanted one more try at Kamala, one more; if that failed he'd see what Wasu was up to. He was high and felt like fucking. The night was bright. As he neared the house however he saw something that caused him to jump into the shadows.

Wasu's two bodyguards were hustling Jeff's naked body off the porch. Carlos stood staring, unable to believe his eyes. Almost automatically he began to follow them, darting from shadow to shadow the way he had learned as a child in the slums of Bogota. They crouched on the path to the beach like animals, trying not to be seen. He followed them to where the trees ended and watched while they pulled Jeff's body toward the glittering blue-white light of the sea. It was like an apparition. Suddenly, Jeff was up and struggling. Carlos heard a shot and saw Jeff fall. Forgetting himself, he ran forward onto the beach. The guards saw him and ran away, dragging Jeff's body along the beach. Carlos ran after them. Another shot rang out. The guards stopped. Carlos stopped too, staring, his mouth wide open. Jeff's body lay limp on the sand. Why had he let himself be sucked into this scene? "What the fuck am I doing here?" he thought. He didn't want it. He wanted Kamala, not this.

The two bodyguards started back toward him. Had they recognized him? To run would be suicide. He waited. "So you have got rid of that swine, yes?" he grinned, trying to fool them, afraid for his life now as they closed in on either side of him.

*   *   *

It was a long time since she'd had a really good meal. "I've got indigestion," she thought, listening to the rumbling in her stomach as she walked beside the sea. "But nowadays, my only real pleasure is in eating.

274

My desire is for food. I want food." She thought about all the milk her children drank, the ugly things, sucking her dry.

She'd heard that sometimes pigs eat their young by mistake. "Ha!" she thought, "it is probably no mistake." This had been her first litter. She hadn't known what she was getting into, she wanted to experience giving birth and didn't count on what came after. "If I have any more of them I might eat them by mistake, this baby business is terrible, always squealing and biting my tits."

Her social activities had been confined to the evening hours. Late at night after the little ones were asleep she would manage to escape. Then she would walk up the beach to enjoy the evening air and try to catch the tiny stalk-eyed phosphorescent crabs that darted in and out of holes at the edge of the sea. She was heading now toward the far end where the wild boars lived in the low deserted dunes. She wanted to get fucked roughly by the wild ones there in the moonlight. "So what if I have babies," she thought, "I'll eat them! There are too many pigs now anyway and not enough food."

She passed the rows of houses and shacks where the hippies lived. A few were still up, dancing, and she paused, listening to the music with one of her large hairy ears cocked forward.

At the deserted end of the beach she was surprised to see three men, two in suits and one wearing a lunghi. They were walking quickly. "They must be running away from something," she snorted instinctively after they passed her. "Maybe they've left something worth eating." She hurried further up the beach, following their scent, and came upon another human. He was lying on the beach moaning. The sand was all kicked up. She sniffed him, grunting with nervousness. She knew that he was bleeding because she could smell it. Her stomach jumped when she realized the human was watching her. His body trembling and his face covered with sweat, he tried to get away from her by rolling onto his side. She could see blood streaming from his back and felt sorry for him. But what could she do, she was only a pig. Sooner or later every creature goes dead. She'd seen many die, especially fish; they flopped around in the sand until finally they got very stiff with their eyes staring straight out at you. She had seen these humans kill pigs too, like herself, and she knew that someday she might be killed by them. She saw shit coming out of him and nuzzled between his legs for it. He kicked at her groaning but the smell so intoxicated her that she nuzzled him again. Just as she was nipping at him with her tiny sharp front teeth she heard loud grunts and the sound of hooves and then two of the wild ones arrived. They remembered her and knew she had come back for more but pushed her aside and grunting savagely, sniffed at the dying man. Then the biggest one lowered his head, caught the man with his tusks, and tossed him several yards away.

"My body, my body," she heard the man scream in a language she didn't know. "My body, get out . . . fuckin' pigs!"

She waddled to where the screaming man now lay crumpled and made gurgling noises. The wild ones were sniffing at her vagina, trying to lick it. Before she could stop him, one had mounted her and jammed his thing in all the way. She lifted her head snorting at him. She wanted to lick up some of the blood that was coming out of the man's back. Watching her across the man's body was the leader of the wild ones, the biggest in the herd. She stared into his dark brown eyes as he watched her getting fucked. Then he nuzzled his snout into the body and turning it onto its back, rooted between the legs and bit off the man's thing.

She was surprised when she saw him gulp it down. He must be really hungry she thought, eating something still alive, especially a man.

The man screamed, reached up and hit the wild one behind the ear with his fist. Blood was spouting from the place between his legs where his thing had been. The smell excited her. She dipped down, licking at him furtively. She had never before tasted hot blood but it was delicious. The one who had been on her got off and came around to see what she was up to, sniffing greedily at the blood. She snorted angrily and gave him a good nip on the snout. After all, there might not be enough.

Suddenly the human, who had been lying as if dead, opened his large green eyes wide, managed to stand up, and staggered away from her.

"Hadji! Hadji! Hadji!" she heard him scream as he reeled toward the sea, blood shooting out from between his legs. "Hadji! Hadji! Mama! Mama!" he yelled as his body sank and then, caught by the surf was sucked under and swept into the phosphorescent tide.

They ran to the edge of the water, watching for it hungrily. After some time a big wave came and washed the man back up again. His eyes were wide open now. He had the staring look of a dog she ate once after a car had hit it.

The wild ones ripped at the stomach with their snouts and gulped down large pieces of the warm flesh. They let her eat as much as she wanted. It was better than anything she had ever tasted. After they had finished she went with them behind the dunes where she let them all fuck her one by one while the others watched, licking their lips and gnawing on the bones that were left.

*   *   *

When they got down the beach, Carlos started casually in the direction of Grey's house and safety.

"No, no," one guard said, pushing him, "we go to other house."

"Wasu this way, Wasu at Grey's house," protested Carlos gesturing.

"No, no," they said in unison, "we go to other house—not Wasu."

He felt a gun in his ribs and obeyed. They reached the house and marched him into Kamala's bedroom, the room he had prepared so carefully for her. Kamala was lying on her bed in a sheer nightgown. "Tell these two goons to lay off," he said angrily, shaking the two men aside.

"He saw us killing the other one," they said in Hindi. "What to do?"

"Strangle him and throw him into the sea," replied Kamala. "Leave the room. Stand outside the door. When you hear me groaning you must come in and do it."

Carlos watched as they left the room, wondering what had been said. "Anyhow, it's good they have got that Jeff out of the way," he said. "Is no good man. Did you find the stuff on him?"

Kamala smiled, not answering. "How unfortunate for you to have seen all this," she murmured, gazing at him through half-closed eyes. "Come here, you must be so tired."

Carlos slumped on the bed, feeling more stoned than ever. He could see her big breasts, her creamy body beneath the chiffon nightgown. She pulled him close with one hand, lifted her gown and watched as he felt blindly for her breasts, masturbating himself with his free hand, while he buried his head between her legs. Opening her legs wide, she held down his head and groaned. One of the guards darted silently through the door, grinning and flexing his big bare hands.

She gave a sigh, and nodded. The guard leaped on Carlos, grabbed his neck and threw him onto the floor. Then he sat on him, squeezing his neck and beating his head on the floor until the body went limp.

"Now you'll have to get rid of this one," she said. "There is no time to lose. Do you think you can get him down to the sea without being seen?"

"There are many people wandering around," one guard said.

"It's pretty risky," said the other doubtfully.

"Well, you'll have to do it. One of you walk out and check to see the coast is clear. The other carry the body out quickly.

"After that," she said, smiling provocatively, "you may come back here."

They picked up the lifeless body and left. "What a lot of trouble tonight," Kamala thought. "Always so much trouble with these no-good Western people! Why don't they stay in their own countries?" She went to the window and watched the guards disappear beyond the trees. A few minutes later she saw them hurrying up the path and soon they presented themselves nervously outside her door.

"You can take showers if you like," she said pointing to the bathroom. "You must feel hot and dirty."

After they had bathed they came out in towels carrying their clothes. "We will go down to Wasu's room, we have fresh clothes there," they explained.

"Come here," she said to one of them. The guard stepped forward one pace. "Don't be afraid, I won't bite you. Come here! Sit down beside me." She let the other one stand. They were young Marathi wrestlers she guessed, and eager to please. She had to get them in her power to keep them quiet. It was something she was good at.

Running her hand over the heavy shoulders of the young man beside her she grasped his hair and pulled his face gently to her breasts while she motioned the other to come to her, and slid her hand under his towel to stroke his stiff penis. Then she groaned dramatically, lay back and closing her eyes, let them take turns fucking her until they both came.

Afterwards they got up smiling and took another shower. "Now," she said sternly, "one of you get Wasu. The other pack the car. We are leaving tonight." They made for the door. "And if you remain faithful to me, there will be other times." Kamala let her languid eyes follow them out of the room.

She got up, dressed, and packed rapidly. Soon she heard Wasu bellowing on the path from Grey's house. One of the guards appeared. "He is here, gone to his room."

"Take my bag then," she said. "I will go down and talk with him. We must hurry."

"Are you ready? We're leaving," said Kamala entering Wasu's room. She could see he was very high.

"Leave now?" he said, slumping into a chair. "What has happened?"

"I have the bags of LSD," she said. "They are locked in the trunk of your car. While you were having those girls, I was doing your work." She looked at him disdainfully. "Now get your things together and get in the car."

She stood on the porch in the dark. The moon had set and the first pale light of dawn shone in the east. Over at Grey's everything seemed quiet.

Wasu came out of the house, yelling impatiently at his bodyguards.

"Shhh," Kamala hissed. "Not so much noise, we must leave quietly!"

The guards opened the trunk of the car to put in the luggage.

Kamala motioned to Wasu. "See, here they are." She unzipped one bag and Wasu peered for a moment at the bottles of small orange pills before she closed the suitcase and signaled the guards to shut the trunk.

"So, we have it," said Wasu, grinning slyly.

"No help from you."

"How did you get it?"

"They caught that Jeff throwing the bags out a window. He had a gun. I had them take him up the beach and shoot him. Also your friend Carlos happened to see all this. Now they are both in the sea."

"Who has the gun now?" snapped Wasu.

"I do."

"But only Wasu will be suspected of murder when the bodies are discovered," he said, coming sharply awake and squinting at her.

"They will not be discovered," she said smiling. "This is Goa. If the tide does not take them out where the sharks are, then those bloody pigs will finish them off—they eat anything. Grey will think they have gone with us. And if by chance some trace of them is found, who will identify it? Don't be silly. After all, the Chief of Police is your friend."

Wasu looked relieved and slumped back in the seat. One of the guards backed the car slowly out of the drive. "Now where are we going?" he asked. "I must have breakfast."

"You will drive me to His Holiness," said Kamala, folding her slender hands and looking out the window.

"But that is two days' drive!" Wasu exclaimed.

Kamala's eyes blazed. "Is he not *your* guru?" she said angrily. "And you did nothing! If I left things in *your* hands we would still be there. The least you can do is drive me to the Baba's—after all, I have done this thing for him only."

*   *   *

Santa Cruz airport in Bombay was a mob scene. Several planes had been grounded and nervous passengers overflowed the waiting room. Stan sat with his briefcase on his lap. He had just called Sundaram in Delhi. There was no word of Jeff or Carlos.

After three days on the mountain with Indra, he had seen Laura briefly. She knew immediately that something had happened but as he was sworn to secrecy there was little to talk about. She told him Jeff had left before she could talk with him and that she was worried about him.

"I'm going to Goa immediately," said Stan. "Indra says he is in danger."

"I know," Laura said, "he told me that too. Then what will you do?"

"Destroy the LSD, leave India, give my fortune to charity, and disappear into an anonymous life." He smiled. "Funny, no?"

Laura smiled back. "You're lucky, the price is cheap."

Stan eyed her. "It wasn't all that easy."

She nodded. "So I may never see you again?"

"That's quite possible," he replied.

"Please try to send Jeff back," she said. "He might be difficult but Indra could handle him I'm sure."

Stan nodded. "I'll do my best."

Arriving in Goa to find the pink villa locked and apparently deserted, he had gone over to Grey's. The place was a mess and at noon no one was up except the servants. Grey had had a party—but where were Carlos and Jeff?

Not wanting to disturb anyone Stan walked down to the beach. The sea

279

sparkled, the water was clear and cool. Hot from the long journey, he took off his clothes and had a good swim. As he got out of the water he noticed something sparkling and picked it up.

It was Jeff's gold snake ring with the large emerald. "How lucky," Stan thought. "He'll be very pleased to learn that I've found it." He dressed and went back to Grey's.

Grey was in his modern kitchen. "Well! Did you just get here?" he said sleepily. "We had a full moon party last night—it lasted late. Too bad you missed it."

"My taxi had two breakdowns coming from the ferry," Stan said. "Otherwise I would've arrived yesterday afternoon. Where are Jeff and Carlos? The house is locked."

Grey was surprised. "So they all left?"

"Who?"

"Wasu," Grey explained. "He came here with a woman called Kamala—you know her, I think? Wasu was going to have this house searched but Jeff got the stuff out and disappeared. I'm afraid I gave him the key. Then I don't know what happened. You say the house is locked?"

"Yes."

"And there's no car?"

"No."

"Then Carlos must have taken off after Jeff with Wasu and Kamala."

He was too late then. He watched Grey making his breakfast, and knew he felt nervous about having given Jeff the key. A profound wave of boredom swept over Stan. He was out of it now. He had jumped out of it once and for all up there on the mountain. Grey's scene, all the scenes, all the actions of his own life, seemed remote and silly.

*   *   *

The feeling of unreality persisted and grew stronger. The world about him seemed mechanical and dead. He was able to look at people and know what they would do next and to his astonishment, if he looked long enough, he could know their past as well. At first he was disgusted and frightened by what he saw, but after a few days the disgust turned to sympathy, and he found himself wanting to help people if he saw they were about to lose something or to speak out to them when he saw through the mirror of their lives. But Indra had warned him about do-gooding. He was to keep to himself, not go out of his way to take action. If someone came to him, however, he could help.

At the Bombay airport his Paris flight was announced and there was a crush at the check-in counter. An Englishwoman with two children was just in front of him, accompanied by an American with a withered hand, dressed in the Indian fashion. They were arguing about a passport with the immigration officer.

"Her husband is sick," the American was saying. "He is being taken out on a stretcher."

The officer eyed the man suspiciously. "But where is he? I don't see him! The man must be with his passport or the passport with the man. Otherwise, how are we to know who is going or who is not?"

The American became frantic. "Look," he said, "her husband is a sick man. I am Dr. Loeb of Boston—his doctor. He is being taken out through another door.

Stan could see that Dr. Loeb of Boston was close to a nervous breakdown. "Can I help?" he said to the Englishwoman.

"Well I don't know," she said. She was on the verge of tears and her two children huddled against her. "What a terrible place this India is. What unfeeling people! My husband has been driven crazy here by one of their yogis. He's in a strait jacket going on first class. They're taking him out the side door. But this man won't let us through unless he is with us."

Stan drew his dark glasses out of his briefcase. He remembered Indra telling him Indians were afraid of glasses.

"Can't you just send one of your assistants with the passport to make sure it is the right man?" Stan whispered, sliding over the counter to the official a twenty-dollar bill folded in his own passport.

The officer looked at him and called one of his minions.

"Give this man your husband's passport," he said to the Englishwoman. "He will take care of it. You may pass."

"I can't thank you enough." The woman smiled at Stan after they'd gone through. "My name is Florence Long and this is my friend, Dr. Loeb from Boston. We've been waiting two days to get on this plane—this place is so chaotic, so inefficient!"

Just then a stretcher was rolled out toward the plane.

"There goes Reginald," the woman sighed.

"Is that Dad?" the boy said, looking disgusted.

"Yes, dear, it's your father."

The little girl started crying.

"It's all right, darling, don't cry. Daddy will be all right as soon as we get him home to England, you'll see." She glanced nervously at Stan. "This terrible country," she said shuddering. "I could tell you stories that would make your hair stand on end. The things that have happened to us—you wouldn't believe!"

Stan smiled. "Let me help you with your parcels, " he said. "It's time to board."

XIV

LAURA HAD STOOD ON the terrace of one of the Brahmins' houses watching Stan disappear down the mountain path. She hoped he might find Jeff and somehow talk him into coming back. But somewhere inside she knew it would never happen; Jeff had been too frightened and Indra too uptight. "What awful problems men have with each other," she thought and went to her room to collect her things. Indra had decided that when Stan left it would be better for her to come to him. She paid for her food and lodging and walked out to the cave.

It was a very grand place, two thousand feet above the jungle, five thousand above the sea to the west. During the day kites circling in the air gave dimension to the space beyond. It was like riding through the sky in a chariot, especially when clouds rolled in from the sea. At night the warm breeze blew salty and strong, whipping up the fire and blowing coals onto the floor. There were strange moanings in the rock and the delicious sound of water somewhere inside it.

"So now you have had your wish, Uma," Indra said. "I hope that will be the last time you test me. One has been cured, which I must now bear for a while." He sighed. "The other wasn't ready. It is a pity, the young strong men like him are almost never ready, unless there is a severe shock. For a man the training must begin at birth, otherwise it is most difficult to separate the inner one early in life without the proper training. The delights of the body are too strong."

"What is the proper training?"

"Austerities. By performing voluntary austerities you break your way into the control room."

"Where is that?"

"Not in this time and space." He smiled. "They say it is behind the sun, on the other side of the fire. What they mean is it exceeds the speed of light, is below most static things like rocks, beyond protons. It is called the black fire by some, the place where the intent of the universe is stored, behind the mouth of Ma Kali. The fire is her mouth, the gate . . . any fire anywhere."

"A cigarette?"

"Yes, of course, I said any fire."

"Do you mind my asking how you cured Stan? He seemed a new person."

"No, I don't mind," Indra said. There was a pause. "You may ask—but it is not for me to tell. Like all cures, he did it himself. I was only the catalyst."

Laura's mind wandered. She was aching for some flesh contact. Indra's translucent body seemed even more beautiful, more perfect than she remembered. She longed to touch him but was afraid, for he was sacred to her. She felt guilty about these feelings, trapped by skin. The man trap was her main trap, she thought.

"Why do I have this desire for touch, for skin? After all you have shown me I still have it." She gazed at him steadily.

"Because it is natural," he said. "It is what makes the world go. Kama is what moves nature. You should have had children long ago, at fifteen, fourteen, then desire is transmuted. Everything is energy. If you keep on satisfying your physical desire all the energy goes out, and if you suppress desire it will turn against you. It must be transmuted." He stared at her. "If I desire to make love to you and sublimate that energy, then I can use it to get in touch with your inner one and take you across. Not using energy uselessly, that's the gag."

"But shouldn't I go to Harpal and have babies—or is it, like the old woman said, too late?"

"By all means go, if that is what you want. Go to America with him. It is the greatest of tests for a woman and man to have children. I have had them in other lives," he said seriously. "One must teach children courage and selflessness, and finally one loses one's own attachments that way.

"But this Harpal—he cannot see, at least not this time. He is too busy satisfying himself, too greedy. He is into the skin thing very heavily, more than you. Once you have seen past the skin to the bones, then you begin to get out."

"Can't you show him?"

Indra sighed. "You don't know India. He is a Sikh and has too much pride. He wouldn't take advice from me. And it's too much to break that kind of pride. There is a different time for every soul. Chances don't come too often, and some keep missing them. When you miss a chance the body starts freezing up and getting old. You can see it in people. They get frozen into distorted shapes. The body passes up a chance for the soul to get out, the soul gets even by strangling the body. Then the body freezes and when the inner one is finished, everything freezes and disintegration takes place."

A cloud drifted across the cliff face below the cave. "It must be very warm down below," Laura said. "Here it's very pleasant though."

283

"Neither pleasant nor unpleasant," he murmured, smiling at her. "If we were down there it would be the same. We would be there where also it would be neither pleasant nor unpleasant."

"But aren't some places better than others for sitting?"

Indra shook his head. "There are certain places for certain practices, but no generalizations. Water and wood are required for certain practices where long isolation is necessary. To tune your instrument first you must learn to hear it, to use and read it. For that isolation is necessary. Sometimes we fast; sometimes we eat meat or fish, drink wine, and have women. For courage, dangerous elements are sought out: snakes, wild animals, precipices, diseased areas, rot, slime, fever, burning ghats, Piccadilly, Hollywood." He grinned. "The only proof of the success of the practice is in action: how well you manage to spar with this desire world until you can get out—even though you have 'seen' and know that it is all made up. 'Life is the stuff that dreams are made of and dreams are the stuff that life is made with.' Your Shakespeare, he was a great yogi, like Kalidasa . . . better.

"After seeing, some decide to stay out—become hermits, eccentrics, yogis like me. But it is equally possible to be involved in action as long as you remember it is all a play directed from elsewhere. When you can keep out—no matter what you are doing—then you go further beyond, you start going across. You begin to get the power to manipulate events. What you wish, that you will see becoming a reality. It can be frightening. You may only think something and it will happen even at great distances. These are signs of power. It is a dangerous period because it becomes easy to play around, healing this one and that one. But that is also desire and action."

"Is it wrong to use your power to heal then?"

"Healing the body can prepare the soul to get out. The paradox is that when the soul finds itself the body usually comes right on its own. Really there is no right or wrong. As long as you use power you will be linked to flesh through action. When you stop using it, one more cord gets cut."

"What's the goal?"

He shrugged and smiled, a far-off look in his eyes. "That is not for us to know. Wave strengthening mostly. All we do know is that there are worlds in which embodiment is no longer necessary for the soul."

"You mean spiritual?"

"That is another made-up thing. Spiritual and material. All made up. Spirit's matter and matter is spirit. They exist simultaneously. In certain practices we learn to slow down the rate of manifestation in the desire world so that we get into other worlds."

A fog had now enveloped the mountain and wisps of it floated through the cave. Below, the towering cinnamon and teak trees reached up damp and dripping. Far away a barking deer ran in the forest.

"See how fear traps us," Indra said. "The deer is so afraid of the leopard that when it catches his scent it becomes frightened and starts barking. Then the leopard knows exactly where to go. Fright always attracts the mortal enemy, it sets up a vibration in the other worlds which must be balanced. It commands the object of the fear to manifest itself through a series of events which usually seem accidental. That is how some doctors create disease in their patients if they themselves are frightened of disease. But fear can also be used to cure."

He looked at her. "You have more fear to get rid of. You need more training in that department. You need more wisdom teaching for a good rudder."

Laura knew it was a big decision. He was asking her to go further out and gave her a lopsided smile, revealing his perfect teeth. He looked like an eighteen-year old hustler with the eyes of the Mona Lisa.

"How long will it all take?" she asked.

"I dunno." He laughed. "It could take a few months, it could take a few years. You want to go on?" He looked slightly surprised.

She thought of Harpal and in her heart already knew what it would be like to spend her life with him. What she didn't know was the path Indra offered. The unknown. She realized she had always been looking for the unknown.

"Should I want more?" she asked the Mona Lisa.

There was no answer, just a smile.

"Then what must I do next?"

"You have decided?"

"I'll go on," she said. "To see what happens next. Once I danced on the tables of a nightclub in Rome just to see what would happen."

"What happened?"

"I got kicked out."

He chuckled.

"What must I do now?"

"Now I must send you away," he said. "I am getting too fond of you. If I am fond of you, how can I teach you? You can go to Nepal though if you like."

"Nepal!" she exclaimed, thinking of all the strung-out people she knew in Katmandu.

The barking of the deer had stopped. Indra turned his nose into the wind. "Leopard—what a stink. He's having a lovely feast now in the moonlight. Souls who torture animals or humans become cats later on—they go into those kinds of bodies."

"What will I do there?" Laura asked.

"Where?"

"In Nepal."

"Ah yes, Nepal." Indra slumped over and gazed into the fire for a long time, rattling his chimtah and rapping it on the logs as if knocking on a door somewhere inside the fire. "In Nepal there is a very old soul who is going to leave his body soon. Only one person looks after him. His disciples have all been sent away. But he will let you stay although it will be tough for you—it's a violent place."

"Cold?"

"Not cold, although the snow peaks are all around. It is warm but very rainy, a deep valley fourteen days east of Katmandu, south of a river called Arun."

"And what will I do there?"

"Help the servant. For three years he has been looking after the old man without assistance or relief. The old man is a genius. The servant is a simple soul, and very devoted. He doesn't understand the old man but he worships him like a god, so the real meanings come through to him.

"The old man is half there and half across. He is a siddha who never uses his powers, a great jiana yogi—that means philosopher, wise one. He is a siddha of wisdom. You need this grounding in the wisdom side. You don't need books, just contact him. It will all rub off on you."

"Can't you give me wisdom? Haven't you already?"

"It's not my cup of tea to teach that." He smiled. "You forget I threw all my books into the Ganga in '47. I know it, like I know the Hatha Yoga from birth, but neither wisdom nor Hatha Yoga will get you out. You must know them," he said, "but I can't teach them—it's too boring for me."

The wind had come up warm and soft. "You'd better get some sleep now," he said. "Tomorrow is Sunday. On Monday you must go."

"So soon?"

He gazed at her seriously, his lips full and pouting. "There is no time, always remember that," he said, leaning toward her across the fire, his muscular arms resting on his knees. He looked like a young Sioux warrior in the old photographs she had seen. "I could keep you with me, I would like that," he added. "But if you stayed I would find myself using your attachment—it can be used, I know how. After all, it is desire. Kama. I could use you like a battery charger. It would be fine for me, but you would be hopelessly trapped in your body."

Laura looked into her lap, not able to meet his eyes.

"Do not fret. We *will* be together again. Now it would only send you backwards. As long as you have the desire for this—" He stroked his shoulders and chest, puffing out his pectoral muscles. "As long as this interests you, your association with me would be fatal for your inner one. You need more power to be with me, more detachment. You have to shift into neutral. Then we can be together again.

"Staying with me or going to Harpal are both traps for you right now. If you can understand this you will save years in the crossing."

She had to admit she desired him. Physically he was the most perfect man she had ever known; his beauty, neither masculine nor feminine,

286

surpassed reality.

"Could I bear your children?" she asked hesitantly, feeling like she might be walking the plank.

"Ah Uma, how I would like that!" He smiled and reached across the fire to take her hand. "But it is too late for me—you must know that. I am neither here nor there. Do not think I am abandoning you or throwing you out. Trust me, I can see ahead. I know why you came and what will happen. For certain I can tell you that fate has not brought us together for nothing. We will be together. It may be sooner than we both imagine. You will come to me again as flesh and blood, but..." He gazed through her as if seeing something far beyond.

"But what?" she asked. "Is there more?"

"You will see when the time comes. Do not imagine we are separate. I will be with you always. There is a great work which we are to do together. I cannot say more. You know how to reach me, that I can be anywhere. All you need to do is practice."

He stirred the fire and put on two big logs. "That should see us through the night," he said. "Let us sleep now."

The next day it was drizzling. Clouds ringed the mountain and the whole world seemed damp and gray. During the afternoon he took her through the passage to the temple where Stan had been, and when he pushed up the floor stone, the sun was shining brightly.

"You see," he said with satisfaction, "we thought because there were clouds below that it was a gray day. To us the whole world was dull and gray. Now that we're on top, it's sunny." He helped her out of the passageway.

"This is a strange place," she said. "It feels very old."

"Ruins and ruins on ruins and more ruins. Hindus, Buddhist and Jain ruins, and before that, Egyptian. Everyone has fought over this mountain. From the sea it looks like a perfect pyramid. Yogis have been sitting here since forever." He sighed, pacing around the edge near the arches. "And now tourists come. We are lucky it is not the season. . . . Vat iss your name, lady?" he hissed, mimicking the schoolboy's questions. "Vat is your native place?"

They laughed together. "What trash! What trash they are teaching in these schools. I am too tired of it, I pray to be taken but She won't allow it." He gazed toward the horizon.

"Why not jump off?" Laura peered over the precipice.

"That would be *my* desire then and *my* action. It doesn't work that way. I would just go into another body again." He stared at her.

Suddenly the clouds below them parted and Indra pointed to a grassy meadow far below on the mountainside. "See there, near the stones?"

"You mean the monkeys?" Laura asked.

"Watch!"

287

An enormous spotted leopard was leaping after the monkeys. "As a boy I could have picked that one off from here in one shot. See how it moves." He shielded his eyes against the sun.

"You shot animals before?"

"I was a crack shot—my father had me trained. All that is wrong but I was too young to know. I'm paying for it now." He turned. "Shall we go?"

"Can't we wait to see the sunset?"

He grimaced. "Must we?" He sounded like a tired husband trying to be polite. "I worship the sunrise, not the sunset."

Laura got up to leave but he saw how much she wanted to stay. "Let me just do some small puja then," he said, sitting down. He lit some incense and mumbled under his breath as if talking with the dancing god. "Shiva, lord of yogis," he said aloud.

Then he pointed to one of the arms, which had been knocked off the statue and restored incorrectly. "A fellow called the Tipu Sultan did that," he said. "He was famous for destroying temples as he was a Moslem. He came from the east, the Deccan, and he got to here, but he got no further. The priests from the temple at Kolpura healed his ailing war elephant, restored its sight when it went blind. He had his cannon trained on the temple—he wanted the rubies and the diamonds. But when the elephant was healed he went away."

"What was his name?" asked Laura.

"The Tipu Sultan. He used to go out raiding, would catch the British officers, take their wives, and make the husbands jump off a cliff like this one. He lived on a mountain some two hundred miles east of here. Tipu's Jump they called it. When he was tired of the wives of the British officers, after he'd worn them out having intercourse with them day and night, he would force them to jump too." He paused and lit a small chillum. "Imagine the scene: Tipu raping and tantalizing the sex-starved blue-eyed girls who had come out to 'heathen' India to be with their husbands. And when finished with them he pushed them off—personally!" He laughed. "The British went crazy and sent out a young fellow called Wellesley who finished Tipu off in a bloody battle. After learning a few tricks in India, Wellesley went back, finished off Napoleon and became the Duke of Wellington." Indra paced around the small room, looking out impatiently at the setting sun.

"Oh Ma, oh ma, oh ma," he shouted, as the sun melted into the sea. The sound echoed down the mountain. "Oh Ma, ma, ma, ma, please please please take take take me me me . . ."

She was to leave at dawn. Getting down the mountain was a problem because of the jungle heat; every activity had to be finished by eleven in the morning.

At three-thirty he was shaking her awake. "Take a cold bath from the bucket and come to me at the fire," he whispered, stroking her forehead. At the fire he gave her ash which she dusted over her shaking body while he prepared bread and tea. Over tea he gave her instructions on how to find the old man. She was to go first to Benares and then to Katmandu, where a schoolmaster named Lal would help her.

Indra fussed over her like a grandmother—or a lover—as she prepared to leave. He gave her several amulets, a jewel, and a tin of dry food that he'd prepared. "Eat only this until you have reached the old man," he said. "It is very sustaining and will keep you from getting ill. If you eat the food served nowadays in these places they call hotels, you are likely to get very sick."

She touched his feet, then got up to leave. He looked sad and thoughtful on the way to the cliff path.

"Don't look back or you might fall off." He smiled. "Always remember, 'never look back.' Now go—I'll see you on the other side."

*   *   *

Arriving at the Delhi airport two days later, Laura recalled how exhausted she'd felt the last time she was there and suddenly realized how strong and alive she felt. But now it seemed as though she were moving through a world of dead machines and almost dead people, and the brightly lit sterility of cement, plastic, and steel made her uncomfortable. She had difficulty focusing on the simple business of the pushbutton phones recently installed at the airport. On both sides of her coins jangled, voices croaked and after two wrong numbers and one busy signal she finally reached Sundar.

"Is it really you?" his voice chattered on the other end. "Where are you?"

"I'm on my way to Benares and then to Nepal. Yes, Nepal!" she shouted. "I don't know exactly where Jeff is. If he gets in touch with you, will you have him write me through Poste Restante, Katmandu?"

"Yes, of course, dear girl, I will find him. But can't you at least spend a night here and rest up? There are always planes to Benares. I can get you on one anytime."

"I have to meet someone there," she lied, not wanting to see him and be barraged with questions about what she'd been doing. "One more thing," she added, "if you see Harpal or hear from him, tell him I will write. *Write.* To his apartment in Delhi. The same, yes, O.K."

"You will return in how many days?"

"A few weeks, maybe a month."

"Have no fear, A. K. Sundaram is here!" he yelled.

"Yes, of course, I will stay with you then." She heard her flight being called. "Yes, thanks. *Thank you.*"

Landing in Benares early in the morning, Laura took a taxi to the ghats on the Ganges, had the driver wait while she bathed in the holy water, and drove on to the bus depot, where she spread her cloth on the floor like everyone else and went to sleep. The next morning in the pink dawn she was on the bus rolling out of Benares toward Nepal. Flowers hung over pictures of the gods mounted in the front of the bus. The driver had done puja and incense floated out the window as they sped across the Ganges plain.

She felt solitary but not lonely. After her experiences with Indra it was hard for her to imagine that she would ever feel alone again. She fell asleep with her head propped against the half-open window and woke later to the gears grinding and cool air blowing in. They were in the foothills; the first monsoon rains had fallen, turning the dry jungle green. Mango trees were crimson tipped with new leaves and flame trees were in full bloom everywhere. By late afternoon they reached Daveghat, where the Buddha was supposed to have been born at the junction of the Kali Gandaki and Marsyandi rivers. Daveghat was a peaceful village more or less untouched by the jangling hustle of the plains. She got a room for the night in the house of a poor family. The next day, following Indra's directions, she took a rickshaw a few miles out of town. There in the jungle she found the ruins of a temple he had described and spent the day repeating a mantra. In the evening she returned to Daveghat and did puja in the temple. The next morning before sunrise the bus left for Katmandu. All morning long they crossed the Mahabharat mountains and by late afternoon the peaks of Annapurna loomed golden in the blue sky. The bus reached Katmandu after dark. The brightly lit streets and bazaars were thronged with tourists. Chinese soldiers brushed elbows with hippies and bank presidents from America. Drums sounded from Bodanath temple and from Swayambunath came the peal of bells.

She'd thought about spending some time in Katmandu but confronted with the tawdry tourist attraction it had become she found nothing much that interested her and was afraid if she stayed she would inevitably run into old friends who had settled there to pass their days in the inevitable fog of hashish and opium.

WE ACCEPT FIRST NATIONAL CITY BANK CREDIT CARDS the signs read everywhere. Laura wondered if any of the beggars pretending to be holy men could credit your account to First National City? She had a credit card and decided to use it at the most expensive hotel in town. At least there she would see no one and could have a last hot shower before going off to find the old man. Her destination was a remote area near a small village on a tributary of the Arun river. She was supposed to get a travel permit for this

290

section but Indra had advised her against trying; a man called Lal would smuggle her in if necessary. He turned out to be a very likeable schoolmaster in his forties. It was fortunate that she had come just then, he told her, because school was out and he would be able to take her himself, at least to the village nearest to where the old man was sitting. It would be a two week journey. The oddest thing to Laura was that he said he had never heard of Indra, although she showed him his own address written by Indra, a photo of him, and the directions to the village. He also had no information about the old man. Nevertheless, he was willing to go. He would hire three horses and two extra men, he said, one to cook and one to care for the animals. Laura protested that she could cook but Lal explained that she would be too exhausted after long days of riding or walking at high altitudes.

Three days later he came to the hotel to tell her that everything was arranged and that if she agreed they could start the next morning. The last night she took a long hot bath, finished packing, and wrote a letter to Harpal. It was a long letter; in it she told him that she loved him but that she had to have time and was going off treking for a month to think things over. Later she found she had put the letter into her bag but had forgotten to mail it.

*   *   *

They followed the great central valley eastward, keeping the white peaks of the Himalayas on their left, until the rim of the valley had narrowed to a deep gorge. Lal pointed out Everest and on the far horizon the great snow mountains on the border of Sikhim. Miles below, the valley's narrow floor appeared various shades of green threaded with silver ribbons of streams and rivers. Dark canyons of pine, oak, and deodar rose above them. The air was like fine crystal, the ancient caravan path paved with massive gray slabs. Flutes in the mountain meadows mingled with the sound of temple bells and the bells of cows and goats. Evenings the conch horns of holy men echoed across the valleys, saluting the gods and demons of the eternal snows. Everywhere they went they met smiling faces. Some offered milk or ghee, many offered a smoke on the chillum. Laura felt exhilarated and relieved to be away from the sullen plains of India, where it seemed that grace and good feeling among strangers was only a memory.

They crossed the Arun on a bridge, precariously suspended at least a quarter of a mile above the gorge, constructed of homemade rope and wood. On the other side they climbed a high mountain range and descended into a protected valley. Pine forest gave way to teak jungle, where hidden villages appeared, built on stone terraces. The sound of water was everywhere, the orchards ripe with lemons and apricots. Further

291

down the landscape was tropical: bananas flourished, bamboo and mahogany trees roofed out the sun.

Late in the afternoon on the fourteenth day they arrived at their destination, a village built around a hot spring, hot enough to boil an egg in, that bubbled out of a pale blue hole that looked like a morning glory. The people of the village were friendly and excited by the unexpected arrival of a foreign visitor. Soon Laura was taking a hot bath in the home of the village head man. Fresh hot water flowed from an ancient central system to every house in the village. The place was said to be two thousand years old, the air was sweet with flowers and the lazy smell of hay drying on the rooftops. Holy men mingled with bright-eyed children and townsfolk in a small stone temple complex near the spring. Inside there was a monolithic black stone with two gleaming mother-of-pearl eyes, a primitive statue representing the ancient guru whose descendants still lived in the village. Laura, bringing flowers, knelt before the statue to pay her respects. When she opened her eyes she had the feeling Indra was somewhere just behind her at the edge of her vision. She turned but the image had vanished.

The head man with whom Lal had arranged her lodging was a poor but robust Brahmin, about forty, who spent most of his time barefoot smoking chillums with cronies around the temple. His wife was a beautiful woman in her twenties, who prepared delicious food and smiled a toothless smile as she tended her fire and cared for numerous small children.

After a long conversation with their host, Lal informed Laura that the villagers held the old man in considerable awe. Although many of them had never seen him, there were all sorts of stories about what went on at his forest ashram, about seventy miles by foot up the deep gorge of a tributary of the Arun. Lal had to return to Katmandu and couldn't accompany her further, but he made arrangements with the head man, who would take her up the river and have her luggage and provisions carried by his servants.

The Brahmin, communicating in broken English, explained that it was a very difficult walk and that Laura ought to rest for a few days before they started. The path lay in the riverbed itself. It would be tough going, over boulders and rocks, and they might even have to spend one night on the way. He scrutinized Laura wondering, she knew, whether this foreign lady was aware of what she was getting into. Nevertheless, two days later after a hearty breakfast and a few last words to Lal, Laura found herself with the Brahmin and four servants climbing a high path cut in the wall of a cliff overlooking the gorge. After about a mile the path dipped precipitously over a series of steps and landings, and ended in a washout at the edge of the dried-up riverbed.

The Brahmin jumped onto a boulder, trying hard to find the semblance of a path up the gorge, which was closed in by sheer cliffs on either side covered with lush tropical foliage and alive with brightly colored birds and butterflies. When located, the river proved to be a small stream that wound along the floor of the gorge. In places water had collected in pools, where bright green snakes lay waiting to eat frogs, and scorpions backed away at their approach, seeking safety under boulders big as houses. After about five miles Laura was too exhausted to go on, and let her guide know that she wanted to make camp. He seemed delighted and sat down at once to smoke a chillum. After a few puffs he handed it to her and darted up the stream where he bathed, singing and making loud noises. Later he returned to cook a simple meal of rice and dal.

In the high-walled gorge evening came early. Laura climbed into her sleeping bag while the Brahmin and his servants took turns sitting up with an ancient rifle, to scare away the wild pigs and leopards who were the real owners of the place.

Next morning the Brahmin woke her just as the first shaft of light filtered through the jungle. The servants were already having their tea and after a bath and breakfast she was ready. A few hundred yards further on the gorge opened, and the heat was intense. About two miles further the valley broadened and the path ascended out of the riverbed, following a low bank bordered by a grassy meadow, beyond which lay the jungle. The Brahmin signaled his servants to put down their loads and remain there.

Laura started to speak but the Brahmin put his finger to his lips.

"Servants stay here," he whispered. "Old man he is not liking visitors. If he see you with luggage he send you away. Shhh." He beckoned Laura to follow as he made his way stealthily through the tall grass. There in a clearing carved out of the thick jungle were three mud huts with pointed thatch roofs, surrounded by a low bamboo stockade. A strange grinding noise, rddd rdd rddd, came from one of the huts.

They walked up to the fence and slipped in through a half-open gate. The strange sound continued, rddd rdd rddd. The Brahmin opened a rolled grass mat he had been carrying and motioned Laura to sit down on it next to him in front of the largest hut.

"A witches' lair," she thought as she looked around at the neatly kept gardens and the smoke curling up from the eaves of the hut. Above the cliff of the river gorge the tops of the snow peaks gleamed gold in the afternoon sun.

The noise stopped. Suddenly there were two voices arguing. They got louder and louder. Then a fat jolly looking young man, his arms raised against a barrage of objects being hurled at him from within, almost backed into Laura. Stumbling to one side, he stared at her in wide-eyed disbelief, his hand clamped over his mouth. He stood perfectly still until the noise began again, rdd rddd rdd. It went on and he was just tiptoeing to the front door when it again stopped and a squeaky old voice began cursing in a language Laura didn't recognize. "Tunzing," the voice inside said, "Tunzing!" There were more curses but the young man remained motionless.

After a few minutes a tiny fat man peeped out of the open door.

Laura gasped. It was the little old man she'd seen dancing in the fireplace in England, and again in India in a dream. He looked, as he had then, like a tiny brown version of Santa Claus. Masses of matted white hair and beard made his face seem like a seed in a ball of white cotton. Naked except for a mud colored rag tied around his waist, his fat little stomach stuck out like a pumpkin as he stood eyeing them, as surprised to see Laura as she was to see him. Walking a few wobbly steps to a nearby mat he sat down. Fiddling with his cloth he withdrew from somewhere a pair of thick glasses. Huge magnified brown eyes suddenly fastened on Laura.

"We are making butter today but the rope keeps breaking," he muttered in a cracked voice, looking at her like a college professor about to expel a truant student. Gesturing at the fat young man he said, "This fool forgot to bring rope on his last trip. Do you by chance have some?"

The Brahmin fell flat on his face in front of the old man and after receiving a perfunctory blessing, whispered something to him and went off in the direction of the baggage.

"And who might have sent you?" he said sternly to Laura after the Brahmin had returned with the rope. "There are instructions that no one is to come here, and no one stays here except Tunzing. I roam around out of my body most of the time." He smiled knowingly. "I'm making final preparations for leaving it altogether."

"Indra sent me," she said simply.

He removed his glasses and pushed the hair out of his eyes. "Young lady, please do not tease me in such a manner, it might be dangerous for you." He wiped his glasses and put them on again. "Do you by chance have a photo of this person you call Indra?"

"Yes, a photo and a note," Laura said, delivering the packet which Indra had prepared for her into the trembling hand of the little old man. He tore at it, trying vainly to open it.

"Tunzing," he muttered. "Please open this." His voice was barely audible. His eyes were slits in his old wizened face as Tunzing broke the seal and cut open the stitched-up cloth with a knife.

Then he handed the opened packet to his master who held it in his hand for some time before looking at the contents. After examining the photo of Indra and reading the note, the old man got up, grabbed a bamboo stick and waved it wildly in the air as if he might strike her. "Young lady," he said, "where and when did you get these things?" His voice was shaking with emotion.

"About three weeks ago on a mountain in south India," answered

Laura.

There was a slow-motion pause during which the old man let the stick descend and resumed his seat. Laura became aware that they were sitting beneath an ancient pepul tree. In the warm wind the leaves rustled like falling water. The old man sat looking at her through his lenses, and after a while a smile of satisfaction spread slowly across his face. Suddenly he sighed and began laughing in a high tee-hee-hee giggle.

"Tunzing," he blurted out, still laughing as he removed his glasses and wiped away the tears that streamed from his deep-set eyes, "Tunzing—bring me something to give this young lady! And my red bag ..."

Tunzing disappeared inside the hut and returned moments later with tea in a battered brass pot, four equally battered brass cups, and an old Benares sadhu bag. The old man fumbled in the bag, extracting bits of this and that—small newspaper packets yellow with age, a few gem stones, an old shriveled lemon.

"The twice born can read the book of Brahma ... does that mean anything to you?" he asked.

"You mean going backward and forward," Laura answered.

He smiled at her over the top of his glasses and held out a small tin box decorated with a crudely stamped picture of the Taj Mahal against a deep blue sky. In one corner a pink airplane was flying.

"Well, aren't you going to open it?" he spluttered. "Open it—what do you see?"

"Ash," she said smiling.

The old man grunted, put on his glasses, and looked at her again. She reached out to return the box. "No, no, it's yours. Keep it carefully," he said, stroking his forehead with the tips of his fingers, palm out, looking through her into another kind of space.

"I suppose you have come prepared to stay?" he grumbled good-naturedly.

"To be honest, this man's servants are waiting with provisions and luggage across the meadow," she replied.

"Yes, yes, yes," he said, pulling at his nose. "Tunzing, have them bring her luggage." He leaned forward, squinting. "Now tell me, young woman, where did you meet Indra and what were the circumstances?"

"At a cocktail party in Delhi about six months ago."

"At a what?"

Laura smiled. "At an evening party in Delhi."

"And what was he doing in Delhi?" The old man seemed irritated.

"He was staying in his old family house which was deserted and in ruins. When I first met him he was dressed in a suit and wearing a turban."

"He looked young then?" the old man inquired.

"Yes, quite young. The next day I went with him to the Himalayas. Later we went to a large burning ghat where he gave me an initiation, then to the top of a mountain overlooking the Arabian Sea."

"Hmmmmm," he sighed. "Did many people seem to know him?"

"A few. He was reputed to be a rather dangerous character."

"Tee-hee," the old man snickered, "I should think so."

The afternoon was turning into evening. "And where will you sleep tonight?" he asked.

"Just here, where I am sitting. Will that be all right?"

"It gets chilly late at night—do you have blankets? I think perhaps we have an extra one." He paused, his hands trembling slightly in his lap. "It is time for me to have a bath and retire," he said. "Tomorrow we will see about more permanent quarters for you. You are welcome to stay, but you must keep to yourself a good part of the time." He smiled. "I trust you are more or less used to this life by now. Of course you will have to do your own cooking."

*   *   *

For the next three days the old man decided to remain silent. He wrote out orders for Tunzing on a small slate and for the servants of the Brahmin, who stayed on and in record time built Laura a small hut of mud, bamboo, and thatch.

On the fourth day, Tunzing shook her awake. She glanced at her watch—three in the morning!

"He will see you now," Tunzing whispered. "You must have a splash from the bucket and I will take you to his hut."

Laura lay half-awake listening to Tunzing noisily performing his ablutions outside. He seemed to be carrying on a multiple conversation, taking various parts and changing his voice to fit each character, interspersing the lines with loud coughing, blowing, and spitting. She splashed herself from the bucket at the side of her hut, dried off, and put on a fresh cloth.

When they entered the old man's hut they found him sitting on a charpoy covered at one end with a thin torn cloth. Two candles on either side of him illuminated the hut, which was well constructed, paneled with large pieces of split bamboo, and lined with shelves containing many ancient-looking books and scrolls. There was also an altar containing a bronze statue of Kali and other objects.

"Do you not find that there is a materialist elite at work in the world today?" he asked when she had seated herself. He looked bright and scholarly. "And do you not find that they are generally pretty trashy people?"

Laura wasn't quite used to launching into heavy discussions first thing in the morning.

"I'm supposed to be one of them, I guess," she said.

"I know you think that, but you are not," exclaimed the old man emphatically.

"I'm not?"

"Of course not—otherwise, he wouldn't have sent you." There was a long silence. Laura felt as if she were on a precipice. Tipu's Jump maybe.

"Just now I have been meditating on the Katha Upanishad," he said suddenly. "Do you know it? I think out loud to myself every morning and Tunzing pretends to understand. I suppose you will also pretend to understand. But do not imagine that you can fool me. Words are all drivel. If *I* don't understand them after all these years, then how can you?" He chuckled. "You know the story of Natchiketas? Of how his father did sacrifice to the gods with all his old worn-out cattle? So many cattle he gave all the time because he had big herds, but never the good ones, always the old inferior ones. The gods became irritated and sent Yama the god of death to take his son Natchiketas to the realm of death where he was instructed in the secrets concerning immortality."

"I have read the translations," Laura said hesitantly, "but I never understood the instructions, just what it was that Yama was teaching."

"No one does," said the old man. "That's what I mean about words. Only the keys are given, not the details. It is like a secret shorthand for teachers; the jumping-off points are there, but all the details are left out. It is that way with most of the important texts, the words are just a reminder."

After three more days the Brahmin and his servants left for their village. One day began to melt into another. Each morning Laura would be awakened by Tunzing to sit with the old man. They sipped tea and ate hard biscuits until the sun came over the rim of the gorge. Then there would be puja and he would give her something to read which they would discuss the next morning. The old man had a vast storehouse of knowledge inside him, and seemed delighted that someone had come who was interested and could understand at least part of what he had to say.

Laura never knew what he did during the day. Late in the afternoon he would come out, take a bath, and sit. Sometimes he spoke to her, but more often he would remain silent in front of his hut, his eyes closed, his body erect and still. A great calmness seemed to radiate from wherever he was.

Tunzing taught her how to milk the cow and afternoons she would accompany him to the edge of the jungle where they would cut special vines, wild banana and dube grass that the cow liked. The weather was unusually dry, the rains almost a month late. The whole jungle seemed to be waiting for them to begin. At first Tunzing got on her nerves with his incessant speeches, his grunting, and compulsive body noises. She could understand why the old man threw pots at him from time to time. Slowly, however, as she watched his devotion to the old man—a devotion that never seemed to exhaust itself even though he might be awakened at any hour—she began to feel humble and inadequate by comparison.

"If you get tired cooking for and feeding that body you are burdened with," the old man said one day, "then just give it milk. That's all I'm taking. There is plenty of jungle fruit hereabout. We have lived on it for years. Milk and fruit are enough for this season. We have two kilos of milk a day, that is more than enough for all of us."

Laura was tired of cooking, she had to admit it. "It's these things that tie us to this world," he said, pointing to his teeth. "Teeth always want to chew." He grinned. "I have been trying to lose mine for years but they won't go. Perhaps we should file them into sharp points and send Tunzing out to catch some wild game: we could dine on delicious partridge or quail, deer and wild pig—I hear they are great delicacies in the West." He went off into peals of laughter.

"Would you do it?" Laura asked.

"If you cook me wild pig, I will eat it," he said, his eyes twinkling. "Would you do it?"

Laura pursed her lips.

"I thought so—too much chewing, isn't it?" he giggled.

Fond as he was of poking fun at her he was never sarcastic. She felt that in some weird way she had found the father she had always been looking for. "Maybe that's why Indra sent me here," she thought, and slowly she found herself looking after his needs until after a while she had relieved the harried Tunzing of part of the burden he had carried for so long. After the morning puja she would sit with Tunzing in his hut while he stirred his fire and prepared milky tea for her, grinding cardamom and other spices according to the mood of the day. He never spoke except to give directions although he knew English well—he had been taught some by the old man and had learned more listening to the English lessons broadcast in the evening on Radio Ceylon, which he just managed to pick up on his portable shortwave radio.

One day he asked her a question. It was something of an event. "Will you stay during the rainy season? It is coming soon, you know."

Laura smiled. "I am not supposed to plan," she said. "Would you like me to stay? Would *he* like me to stay?" She nodded toward the old man's hut.

"He has become most fond of you," Tunzing said with a grin. "It is very good for him, you being here."

"Are you sure?"

He nodded.

"Then I shall stay."

"It is very hard though," he said, looking at her seriously. "It rains three to four inches each day. We may all get sick. The old man may go this time. He almost go—went—last rainy season."

"I'm not afraid," Laura said, looking directly into his eyes for the first time.

"He is getting weaker. If he begins to go there are certain things I must do for him, certain instructions to be carried out. You could be of great service to me at that time although you will not understand just what is happening. You will have to follow directions carefully."

"What about supplies?" she asked. "Do we have enough sugar, candles, oil, rice, and so on?"

"One of us will have to go down the river to the village. In the past I have gone but now he is weaker, I don't like to leave him—I have to help sometimes with the bath and the bowel movement. Will you be afraid to spend one night out by yourself on the way down? If so, I will go. When the rains begin the river rises. There is no way to go then except over the mountain. That way is very dangerous with snakes and the wild pig and leopard and taking one week to go and one week to return. I shall give you a spear and there is a shallow cave midway where you can spend the night. If you keep your fire going you should have no trouble. If the animals come just build up your fire and sing. I had two small bears sitting with me all night once."

"Ah," Laura thought, "Tipu's Jump coming up!"

"When shall I go?" she asked.

"Tomorrow," Tunzing said hesitantly. "Is it too soon? The rain could begin anytime. You must go and come within four days."

*   *   *

The trip down the dry riverbed was easier than she had expected. Near evening she spotted the shallow cave exactly as Tunzing had described it, about twenty feet up a narrow path on the side of the gorge. Hauling up enough driftwood to last the night, she took a bath, leaned the spear against the opening, and fell asleep. During the night she woke; the fire was almost out. As she was putting on more wood she noticed, just out of range, two large glowing eyes. She had seen eyes like those before and recognized the smell. Remembering Tunzing's words, she continued to build up the fire, hummed a song she'd learned from Indra and tried to repeat a mantra he'd given her for just such an occasion. To her disgust she found her knees were wobbling with fright. Finally the fire blazed up and she could see the leopard, a large young female, lying on the path purring loudly. She was surprised at how much it resembled a big kitten. After what seemed an eternity it yawned, got up, and leapt into the riverbed.

When she tried to go to sleep again she was sure she saw Indra standing below. She didn't try to look directly—to focus on him—and the image lasted for some time. Finally it saluted her and vanished. When she woke she found that she had overslept. It was full morning and the sky was overcast, with thunderheads piled up in the eastern sky against the Himalayas. She would have to hurry now. She ate some of the dry food Tunzing had prepared, clambered down the cliff path to the river and headed downstream.

When she got to the village she bought provisions from the list the old man and Tunzing had made and hired coolies immediately, determined to set out the next morning. She met the Brahmin head man on the street and returned with him to his house while the orders were being filled and packed into bundles. He persuaded her to rest one day, all the time trying his best to dissuade her from returning.

"You are not knowing how much it rains," he kept saying. "You will not survive the damp climate. Send coolies back with supplies, you hurry Katmandu before rain is getting bad. You are foreign woman, not fit for rainy season."

She thought of Harpal but not like before. Living in the jungle with the old man and Tunzing was changing her. Things she once thought important were falling away. The old man was teaching it all to her now. How could she leave? It was a test. It was her chance to go through that door once and for all.

The next morning after a hot bath at the temple, she had breakfast with the Brahmin.

"You *must* not return, memsahib," he said, looking very serious and sad.

"But I am one stubborn foreign woman," she said with a smile. "You've delayed me one day now. The old man will worry—that's no good for him. I am leaving tomorrow."

*   *   *

It was spitting rain the following afternoon and she was still three miles downstream from the clearing. She was just debating whether to make camp and give the coolies a rest or to push on, when Tunzing appeared around a big boulder.

"The old man sent me," he puffed. "He said you were coming, that I should go get you. If you stay in riverbed this night you might get washed away. Come, we must hurry!"

"Is he all right?" Laura asked quietly as they hurried over the rocks. She could tell by the look on the young man's face that something had happened. "What is it, Tunzing?"

"He could not get up today. He did not recognize me for nearly half the day. Now he has told me he will not take food, he will fast until—until his body lets him leave. The time has come." He was fighting back tears. "Let me carry the spear," he said, taking it from her. "He understands everything. I will just run ahead and tell him you have returned. Take the flashlight—it is going to get dark fast." He started ahead and then turned, smiling warmly. "We were afraid you might have run away."

When they arrived the coolies put down their bundles and left immediately, afraid the rain would block the way and leave them stranded.

They watched the light of the coolies' torches disappearing downstream, then Tunzing turned toward the old man's hut. "Come in now," he said. "He is expecting you."

The old man was sitting up. He put on his glasses and spoke softly to her. "This body has had a partial stroke—you know stroke, of course?"

Laura nodded.

He fidgeted with some manuscripts that lay in front of him, then wrapped them in a scarlet cloth. "There is so much more I want to tell you, after all. I have been following you for quite a time now."

"Then it *was* you in the fireplace in England?" she said.

He smiled, nodding his head. "Even before that. That was only the first time you were able to see."

He lapsed into silence and gazed at her over his glasses. "Indra was right," he said, clearing his throat, "it is better and easier to leave this body *before* it starts to go. In any case, now that I have been given the sign I intend to leave this one within the next ninety days. It is time. You must carry on as usual." He smiled. "Your trip to the village was O.K.," he continued, using the American slang. "Did you see someone?" He tittered slyly.

"Who?" asked Laura, testing him.

"I see you are testing me—a Western failing," he sighed. "Oh well, that is your problem. Whom did you see? Indra, of course!"

"How did you know?"

"He appeared here too, and told me he would stop and see you in the cave. He..." the old man's voice drifted off. Then he looked at her sharply. "That box I gave you, the tin box..."

"With the ash?" Laura said.

He nodded. "I burned the body of the yogi you call Indra on this spot almost nine years ago. He insisted on leaving his body before it began to age. He fasted and I carried out his instructions for burning the body just as he was leaving it. That was nine—no twelve years ago, before Tunzing came here." He cleared his throat again, smiling and watching her intently. "Now you know a great secret. What do you say?"

"I say it is a work of great art," Laura said earnestly.

"Indeed it is," returned the old man. "A lost art. Many have been given the opportunity but few take advantage of it. The work is too simple and too hard. Few can comprehend it. Most reject it. They don't see the possibility."

"Is that your path now," she asked, "or have you already done it?"

He looked at her seriously. "It is a possibility, one of many. You flatter me—no, I have not done it before. You will help Tunzing?"

"Yes, of course."

Each morning about eleven the clouds would pile up against the great peaks visible above the river gorge and it would begin to rain. Fierce winds and electrical storms swept overhead, jumping the small valley which grew more humid every day. The river rose steadily. Tree frogs, crickets, and huge cicadas began to sing in the grasses. Orchids burst forth from leafy nests high in the trees and showered down sprays of white blossoms. The jungle was coming alive in a way Laura had never imagined possible. One morning she awoke to see a bright green snake, about eight feet long, draped over the center pole of her hut, eyeing her cautiously. Each day she led the cow to graze on the new shoots of grass which seemed to grow several inches every night. Tunzing taught her to make curd, and ghee and butter from the curd, and to mix the whey with spices into a delicious light drink. Cooled in the spring it was good for the stomach in rainy weather.

One day Tunzing asked her to help him. Together they dug a pit about four feet deep, two feet wide and six feet long. She wondered whose grave it was to be, but there was no indication from Tunzing and she didn't ask. After they had finished he removed all his clothing except for his loincloth and got into the hole, sitting full length as if in a bathtub, his head just above the surface of the surrounding earth.

"Now please, you will fill the mud in around me," he said. "Take the shovel and cover me—everything except the face."

As she filled he removed his loincloth so that he was naked. She noticed that he was facing North.

"You are wondering about this, no doubt." He grinned. "We do it as a protection against the diseases of the monsoon. You will have to take over my duties for twenty-four hours. Do you think you can manage?"

"Yes, of course," Laura said. "But hasn't the monsoon already begun? It's been raining every day."

Tunzing laughed merrily. "This! This is nothing," he said. "You have not seen the monsoon. When you see it you will understand."

The clouds were black overhead.

"What will you do when it rains?" she asked, worried.

"Nothing. Only my face will get wet, and that is supposed to happen."

That afternoon it began raining and rained a steady downpour all afternoon. She stayed in the old man's hut, tending his fire. In the evening she milked the cow, who had been moved to a shed attached to the hut. Then she boiled the milk and prepared tea and bread for herself over the old man's fire while he sat dozing. After eating she fell asleep.

About midnight the old man groaned and tried to speak but his tongue wouldn't work. She could tell he was having another stroke, she had seen her grandmother have one and knew the signs. His bowels had moved under the shock and she could see the fastidious little man was greatly upset.

She built up the fire under the large brass vessel containing the washing water, removed his cloth, bathed him front and back and put on a fresh cloth, then eased him onto the soft skins and got him to sip some lemon water. For the first time she realized what had been accomplished in her trip to the burning grounds with Indra. Everything was the same now. She had stopped discriminating between pleasant and unpleasant things. The desire world was going. Things she could never have imagined doing before now seemed easy. She was sloughing off being afraid.

After she had built up the fire she took the soiled cloths out into the rainsoaked night and by the light of her flashlight tucked under one arm, washed them downstream from the spring. The river had begun to sound like a freight train. She returned to the old man's hut just as a light gray appeared in the sky, but the downpour continued. The cow had to be fed and milked. She went into the lean-to and mixed the feed for the cow. The huge brown beast watched her with great limpid expressionless eyes. One ear was cocked back toward the wall where the old man was now snoring peacefully. The cow had been with the old man for over six years and was very fond of him. Laura had seen her kneel down before him and put her brownish pink wet nose on one of his bare feet as he sat playing his flute. She thought about the steaks she had eaten at Sardi's and decided that it must have been in some other life, not this.

After milking and boiling the milk she lay down, exhausted. What had she got herself into, she was thinking, when she remembered Indra's advice to her. "Don't think. What you call thinking will drive you crazy. Repeat your mantra and don't think. Everything will go right. You will be in tune when you've erased all your tapes."

It was against everything she had ever known but it was the only thing that really made sense to her, now that such an incomprehensible chain of events had led her to this particular place in space and time.

Hours later when she awoke the sun was out. The old man was awake, blinking at her. She got up.

"I must see to Tunzing," she said. "He is buried in a hole outside."

The old man managed a garbled tee-hee but he couldn't wipe his watering eyes. She wiped them gently and went outside.

Tunzing's eyes were shut but she doubted he was sleeping. She got the shovel and started removing the mud. "The old man has had another stroke," she whispered as he got up out of the hole. "His tongue and left side seem to be paralyzed."

Tunzing showed no emotion. He bathed with rainwater from one of the buckets, put on a fresh cloth and went to the spring with the old man's brass bucket which he filled with fresh, clear water. Inside the hut he poured out a cupful and holding it to the old man's lips massaged his shoulders and arms gently.

"Now I will be very busy," Tunzing said softly to her. "You must carry on with the chores but be available. There are times I may need help in turning him over and so on."

Laura went to her hut and lay down, but was too tired to sleep. In the evening out of habit she went to see the old man. He was seated in the lotus pose, propped up by a board which Tunzing had placed against the charpoy. His eyes were closed. Tunzing was seated to his left reading to him from some oblong manuscript. He asked her to bring more wood and build up the fire. When it was burning vigorously he offered large quantities of all the supplies into the fire, muttering in Sanskrit while he threw handfuls of rice, sugar, and ghee into the flames, and then the personal effects of the old man, his prayer bell and flute—finally even his glasses.

The old man sat straight as an arrow now without using the board for support. His legs were crossed flat on the floor. In his right hand he held his prayer beads. Tunzing took them and dropped them into the fire.

Later, after she had gone to bed, Tunzing called her to sit on the old man's right. All visible signs of breathing had stopped. After he had taken the old man's pulse Tunzing began to read aloud again from one of the texts, sitting close to him and reading in a low voice into his left ear.

The reading continued for five days. It rained almost the entire time, day and night. Neither Laura nor Tunzing ate; they drank spring water and took naps between Tunzing's readings at three-thirty and eleven-thirty in the morning, three-thirty in the afternoon, and again at eleven-thirty at night. By the end of the fifth day there was no sign of life in the body of the old man, no pulse, no breath. Yet there was no rigor mortis, the body remained erect, and no decomposition had occurred.

The readings continued for three more days, during which Tunzing used a small drum and silver bells to accompany himself. Laura's job was to keep the fire going, the cow milked, and the ghee lamps lit. On the eighth day Tunzing laid down the drum and bell carefully.

"Get the shovel," he said. "It is time now. We must dig out the fire to a depth of almost eleven feet. It will be very hard work."

"Has he left his body?" Laura asked.

"Partly," Tunzing replied. "The total separation will come during the next twenty-four hours. We must dig fast. We will take turns digging and piling the earth in the far corner of the hut. It is important that certain things happen at just the proper moment."

It was impossible for her to tell whether the old man was dead or alive. What was dead and what was alive, really? By three the following morning, they had finished the hole. Five bags of salt were emptied onto the bottom. Then they lowered the old man's body, still erect, using the long cloth on which he was seated. Tunzing began alternating layers of charcoal, ash, and salt, and just before the head was covered, asked Laura for the box of ash the old man had said was Indra's. Pouring half of it over the old man's white hair he returned the box to Laura. Outside the rain poured down, and the river rolled on like thunder. Tunzing went out and returned with a metal rod about as thick as a finger and two arms long.

"Please hold this carefully here, just where I am placing it," he said. Laura held the rod, which gleamed like gold. "Seven metals," Tunzing said, as he picked up a hammer and struck a swift blow on the top of it so that the rod was driven into the skull of the old man.

Laura started back.

"What are you doing?" she cried out.

Tunzing smiled calmly. "Oh, this is most important," he explained. "The last of his bodies, the subtlest, has gone into this rod which now is resonating with the vibration. It will continue to do so forever. There are ways you can get in touch with it if you know how. Now please hold the rod until I fill in the remaining space."

When the work was complete the rod stuck up about nine inches above the surface on which cut stones were laid. After nine days with hardly any sleep, Laura felt like bursting into tears, but what was there to cry about? After all, wasn't it a joyful occasion when someone got out of their body? Exhausted, she walked to her hut and lay down. Tunzing came in with some barley soup and dry wood for her fire.

"Sleep for a while now," he said gently. "The rain is over for a few days. Sleep until you are well rested and I will complete the work."

Her sleep was fitful. She dreamed of Harpal, Jeff, and Indra comingled with each other, and woke up feeling tired and stiff. Tunzing was digging something. Wondering how long she had slept, she got up, made tea, and swept out her hut. Her back ached and although the sun shone brightly, it was so humid she could hardly breathe. Perhaps the Brahmin had been right. Perhaps she was just a foreign memsahib!

When she went out she was surprised to find the old man's hut gone. Tunzing had removed the roof grass and piled it for the cow to eat. The poles were stacked neatly in a pile and he was leveling the mud walls to the ground. The bright sun made Laura feel dizzy. She caught hold of the corner of her hut to keep from collapsing and wondered if Indra had known what would happen. Less than two months and now the old man was gone. She was to have learned wisdom from him, philosophy, so much else. Indra had said it would be a rudder for her. Now the rudder was gone. She felt a great loss, which seemed out of proportion to the length of time she had known the old man. He'd been so touchy about questions she hadn't even been able to ask further about his appearance to her in the fire or in her dreams.

Tunzing caught sight of her and leaned on his shovel. He was making a platform about a foot high. In the center the rod protruded above the stones.

"Why burial?" she asked. "I thought the body was always burned."

"Burning or salt, it amounts to the same thing. Two different methods for two different kinds of going out, one movable, one fixed. In a matter of days the salt will dissolve everything."

Thunder was rolling now in the west. "How long did I sleep?" she asked.

"About thirty-six hours. How do you feel?"

"Weak." She smiled faintly.

"You need food now. I will prepare. Go back to your hut. You'd better get in more wood, it's going to start raining again."

On her way to gather wood she looked in on the cow, whose hut had been moved next to Tunzing's. The poor beast knew that the old man was gone—or was he? Was anyone ever really gone? She kept thinking she'd been sent to this place for a reason. What was the reason? To learn, he'd said. What had she learned? She tried to think again but her brain was dull. By the time Tunzing ducked into the low door of her hut it was raining again. He placed a large plate of food in front of her with a cup of tea and left immediately, as quietly as he had come. She had no appetite but forced herself to eat, thinking she needed energy. There were things she had to do to help Tunzing and she had to keep moving to keep up her strength, otherwise she felt as if she would rot or turn to fungus. Her menstrual period was very late. Was she pregnant with Harpal's child she wondered, or was it just the general weakness that seemed to have come over her with the onset of the rains.

"After hunger is satisfied," she could hear the old man's voice inside her, "people think up all sorts of useless ways to pass the time—war, sports, games, 'the arts'..."

She felt sickish and drank the tea. It made her feel worse. She remembered she had some milk of magnesia pills in her bag, fished them out, took three and drifted off to sleep beside the fire. In the dark of the night she woke out of a nightmare she couldn't remember. The night herons were screaming out in the rain and she became aware that she was lying in a pool of sweat. As soon as her eyes could focus she felt waves of nausea. Crawling to the hut door, she pushed back the gunnysack covering and began to vomit. Even when everything had come up she still wanted to vomit more. Finally, so weak she couldn't even crawl, she rolled back into the hut and under her blanket. The fire was almost out. It was raining too hard for Tunzing to hear if she called. She put wood on the fire and sat before it and for the first time considered escape, wondering whether she and Tunzing could make it over the mountain. But what about the cow? The tigers and jackals would eat her in no time.

The next morning Tunzing brought her a very bitter decoction of certain roots. She got up and gargled with spring water, scraping her tongue and blowing water out her nose. Then she took some stomach medicine Indra had given her and lay down thinking again about leaving. "When you've got bread, you can always run away from yourself," was one of Jeff's favorite expressions. Well, it had suddenly been made very difficult—perhaps impossible—for her to run. Maybe this was what she'd been sent here to learn.

Her period still hadn't come. "If I'm pregnant," she thought, "at least it will make me healthier to live through this weather."

After two days it began raining again. In the morning about eleven it would stop for about an hour, giving her just time to run out, do her laundry and pick up some wood. Then it would rain through the afternoon and all evening without letting up, harder than any rain she had ever seen. The river was full. What had been a broad roadway of rocks and sand was now a torrent of boiling churning water carrying everything before it.

As the days passed, Laura began to lose track of time. The fire was her main concern. Most of her energy went to hustling wet wood and stacking it around the fire to dry. She had broached the subject of escape to Tunzing but he seemed not to hear her and had muttered something about the impossibility of twenty miles of mountain trails. For him it was just another monsoon, she supposed, and of course he wouldn't think of abandoning the place where his master had left his body.

A few days later Tunzing came in and slumped down in front of her fire. His face was livid and he seemed hardly able to move his body. She felt his forehead and found it burning with fever.

"I think I have pretty bad jungle fever," he said softly, smiling. "Maybe I am going to follow the old man."

"Nonsense," Laura said, knowing it was not nonsense. "You stay here. I will get your bedding and whatever else you need. There is no sense keeping separate fires going until you feel better."

Adrenalin poured through her body. Her whole system now on alert, she began repeating the syllables Indra had given her at the cremation ground.

Tunzing told her what he needed and during a break in the rain she carried his belongings to her hut. By evening he was really sick. There was no time now to think, only to act: keep the fire going, keep things clean and boiled, milk the cow, collect firewood, nurse Tunzing. After a few days and nights he could barely move and began having diarrhea and violent sweats. In three hours he could drink an entire pail of water. She had to clean and dry him every four hours. The rain poured down; none of the cloths would dry and she began ripping up what few extra clothes she'd brought so that some dry rags would be available.

"How much longer will the heavy rain last?" she asked him one night when he seemed to have regained his senses.

"Two more months," he rasped. "For two months you cannot get out."

"What about the mountain? Shouldn't I try to make it across, get to the village, bring a doctor?"

"There is no doctor in that village," he said weakly. "Mountain path is most dangerous. Do not worry about me, I am not afraid. I am going to follow the old man. I can see that he is needing me. When I go, then you must take the path you wish. It may be very hard for you here all alone."

The next night he became delirious and woke up screaming for the old man to save him, repeating mantras and singing in a childish voice between cups of water. During one lucid moment he gazed at her. "It is the cholera," he whispered hoarsely and crawled to the hut opening and pointed to some bushes outside. "Chop plant, make stew, give to me," he said and rolled back onto his mat.

She dashed out into the rain and hacked at the bushes with a machete. Then she chopped them up and put them in a pot over the fire. The green mass gave off a bitter smell and tasted violently astringent. As soon as it was cool enough she spoon-fed it to him. His face was thin and haggard, his once plump body a dehydrated sack of bones. The decoction seemed to help him though, and he stopped needing water. For a few days he seemed to be getting better.

When he told her it was cholera Laura remembered that she had once had cholera immunization shots. She found her International Health card and looking on the page for cholera, discovered that her period of immunization had expired. She had heard that sometimes the immunization effect lasted longer. Nevertheless, she had to face squarely the possibility that she might get sick like Tunzing. For some reason the thought didn't upset her. She had the strange sensation of being outside of it all, that things were happening around her. Even her own body was out there, while she, the observer, was somewhere else. "Though I walk through the valley of the shadow of death, I shall not freak," she kept saying to herself. This was it: Tipu's Jump!

308

Tunzing died two days later. Somehow she managed to drag the body through the rain to his hut. "Poor man," she thought, "he has been so faithful."

The poles and other wood from the old man's hut lay stacked in the hut. One by one she brought them and piled them inside Tunzing's hut as she had seen it done. Then she dragged the body on top of the heap, piled all his belongings around him, and poured ghee over the whole thing hoping the hut would burn down.

Gathering coals from her fire for a fire she managed to get one going under Tunzing's body, but the wood was too damp. Everything was too damp. She couldn't get the bamboo poles to burn and the hut was filled with acrid smoke.

Returning to her own hut she lay crying for some time. When she returned to Tunzing's hut the fire had gone out completely. She knew she had to get rid of the body before it began to decompose. Shuddering, she dragged the cold stiff corpse a hundred yards from the hut to the edge of the jungle where she knew it would be eaten by jackals.

Returning to her hut she sat shivering in front of the fire. Having to abandon Tunzing's body—he who had been so bright with love and faith—filled her with anguish. She gazed down at her cracked and calloused hands, the once beautiful hands of Laura Weatherall, 610 Park Avenue, New York City, and knew that she ought to get more wood. But there was enough for the night, to hell with it. In the morning she would get more.

She never got around to it.

The next morning the fever hit her. It was worse than the Sirocco, the burning Sahara wind that scorches everything in its path. It knocked her over and her thirst was monstrous. Knowing she would soon be too weak to do anything, she placed a bucket under the eaves of her hut, just outside the door, to collect rainwater. Managing somehow to get to Tunzing's hut, she pulled the wood she'd piled there to her own place. There was always a chance someone might come or that she might ride out the sickness. Perhaps Harpal would get her letter and come to rescue her. In it she had given the name and directions to the village down the river. The letter! She had no memory of mailing it. Fumbling in her bag, she felt the crumpled envelope. She'd forgotten to renew her cholera shot and even to mail that letter. Certainly something was working to make her forget.

Feeling very alone she began asking herself final questions, summing up her life. First she tried recalling all the good times—all her satisfied desires. Had they been that important and where were they now? In her heart she knew that Desire was endless, an endless urge for action and

309

fulfillment. What seemed to stand out were the times she'd really extended herself, beyond her own desire into acts of human kindness.

Closing her eyes she began repeating the syllables Indra had given her. During the night, through the steady rain and thunder, she heard the whoops and screams of the jackals as they devoured Tunzing's body. The next day attacks of diarrhea alternated with jets of vomiting and soon she was too weak to move and could only lie by the fire feeding wood into it.

Off she would doze into strange dreams like bad acid trips accompanied by the quick time *thump thump thump* of hard rock music. Finally she lost all track of time and seemed to be drifting in an awful purgatory of boredom and terror.

One night she thought she heard Indra's voice and lay half asleep listening. "Are you all right?" it repeated quietly, over and over. She closed her eyes tightly. Tears poured down her cheeks, mingling with the cold sweat.

"You said you would be with me again," she whispered. "Where are you? I'm lost."

"I am here in the corner on your left."

She raised herself on one elbow, thinking he was there in the room with her.

"Do not look directly," the voice said. "Look into your fire."

She wiped her eyes and stared into the coals.

"Now, can you see me out of the corner of your eye?" the voice said. "Come—without looking directly—you must try. Try!"

Staring at the fire she could just make out on the periphery of her vision the flowing silhouette she knew so well, the unmistakable look of him that had first attracted her in Delhi.

"Yes, I can see you now."

"You must try to sit up then," his voice said. She came totally awake. His voice was in the room. It was not in her head, it was really in the room. Or was it?

Gathering her remaining strength she sat up.

"Now your strength is coming back. Get wood. You must build up the fire. After you get it blazing well remove all your clothing. Go outside in the rain, let the rain wash you off, cut the rope and let the cow go. Then burn all your soiled things in the fire."

She managed to crawl around the hut, throw the wood from Tunzing's hut into the fire and release the cow. Then she put her clothes in the flames and crawled out the door. Her body shook with cold. Shuddering she contrived somehow to stand up in the rain which never stopped. Her thighs and buttocks hung in wrinkles like an old woman's flesh. How long had she been lying there, she wondered.

After cleaning herself, she staggered back through the door. "Good," his voice said as she entered. "Can you sit up now? Sit up in front of the fire, let it dry you off. You can—go ahead."

She tried but fell backwards.

"Try," his voice said harshly. "Do some breathing and try again."

She breathed deeply in the special way he'd taught her and after a while was able to sit up.

"Now you must offer all the food you have into the fire—all of it!"

The new wood caught and the fire began to blaze up. Crawling to where the supplies were kept she began throwing handfuls of rice, wheat, and lentils into the flames. The fire hissed and crackled.

"Do not delay," he said urgently. "Throw the whole lot in. Have you any ghee?"

She nodded.

"After you have finished offering the food take the ghee and rub your body with it."

She turned toward his voice wanting to ask why.

"Do not look toward me, it is not time yet. You must only follow directions."

She rubbed the ghee over herself. Her skin felt like greased leather but she felt better, as if the fever might be leaving her. "Am I... are you?" she stammered, "is the fever leaving, am I...?"

"The fever is not leaving," he said firmly. "You are going to leave the fever. Have you got scissors somewhere, if not a cooking knife will do."

She reached for her bag. As she looked for the scissors, her travelers checks fell out with the letter to Harpal. She counted them and found seven thousand five hundred dollars. She laughed to herself. Now she understood Stan's frustration at having so much bread and getting cancer.

She could hear Indra laughing. "Throw that trash into the fire, throw it all! And toss the scissors to me."

She threw the checks, the letter, and the bag into the fire. Then she threw the scissors in the direction of his voice.

"Good," he said. "Now I am coming behind you and I am going to cut off your hair."

She felt warmth behind her and his hands gathering up her hair. In three snips it was done. She saw the hair go into the fire and burn.

"Terrible smell," he whispered into her ear.

"Now I want you to close your eyes. There are certain things that must be done. Close your eyes and repeat the syllables you learned before. Keep repeating until you see them with your inner eye. Do not open your eyes until I give the word."

She could hear more wood going onto the fire. The heat was intense.

"Did the old man make it?" she asked. "Is he with you?"

"Yes and no," Indra replied. "He got further but he didn't use the proper key although I told him. He didn't believe me. He is fixed, while I am movable.''

There was a pause during which she heard him wrestling the large bamboo poles into the fire and she began to see the syllables gleaming against the endless blue field, as she had at the cremation ground.

"But you have the guts," he laughed, "and I am the key."

Up to that moment she thought he had come to heal her, to rescue her. Now she realized it was going to be different, very different. For the first time she realized it was going to be the end. She was surprised to note how cool she felt about it.

"Where are you, really?" she whispered.

"Don't ask silly questions," his voice rang out. "Keep your eyes closed. There is not much time left. Are you seeing the syllables?"

"Yes."

"Good. Now you must repeat all three mantras I have given you simultaneously. Have you been practicing that?"

"Yes."

"Then begin now. Repeat them all together on three levels. Can you do it?"

"Yes."

"Good. Then we will begin. Remember: do not under any circumstances open your eyes until I tell you."

The sound of the rain and the fire began blending in her ears. She had a vision of a fountain of liquid fire, like a volcano erupting and obliterating everything. She had no trouble repeating the first, then the second, and finally the third set of syllables. They seemed to be working in tandem. She felt high and exhilarated. It was like tuning in three channels at once. She was so filled with their sounds that her exterior senses seemed to have stopped functioning.

Then, as if from far away, from some golden sundrenched island deep in her heart, she heard his voice calling her.

"Open now, open your eyes."

She opened her eyes.

The fire was blazing before her, an inferno that would soon burn down the hut, but she felt no heat. It was like watching a movie of fire and slowly even the sound of it faded. She was getting out. She kept repeating the three mantras and after a few moments Indra's naked form appeared across the flames. His body became palpable before her eyes as he extended his arms toward her through the fire.

"Do not be afraid. I am truly with you," he said.

"I'm not afraid any more," she answered calmly.

"Before I was in the room with you," he said smiling. He looked younger than she ever remembered seeing him. She wanted to go with him, to be with him. She burned with desire for him.

"Before I was in your old space, that world's space," he said. "Now I am on the other side. That is why the voice you are hearing sounds far away. Can you hear me?"

"Yes," she answered and stopped short. She could no longer hear herself speaking.

"You can hear me but you cannot hear your own voice—is that correct?"

She nodded.

"Or the fire or anything?"

She nodded again.

"Good, that is good." He grinned. "Then it is time. Now look at the point on my body where I have taught you to look, yes?"

"Right."

He reached toward her through the flames. "Concentrate on that place and follow directions. Feel yourself do as I say. Do not take your eyes from the point. Ready?"

"Ready."

"Are you all right?" he said.

She nodded, feeling deliriously happy. Homeward bound, she thought.

"You look wonderful," he said, his eyes sparkling. "Now squat in front of the fire. . . . Correct. Right. Very good.

"Ah ha!" he cried out and with a roar of laughter that filled her whole being leapt into the flames and crouched there, his arms extended. "I am going to catch you. Ready?"

"Yes!"

"Now—Jump! JUMP!"

Printed in the United States
31250LVS00001B/246